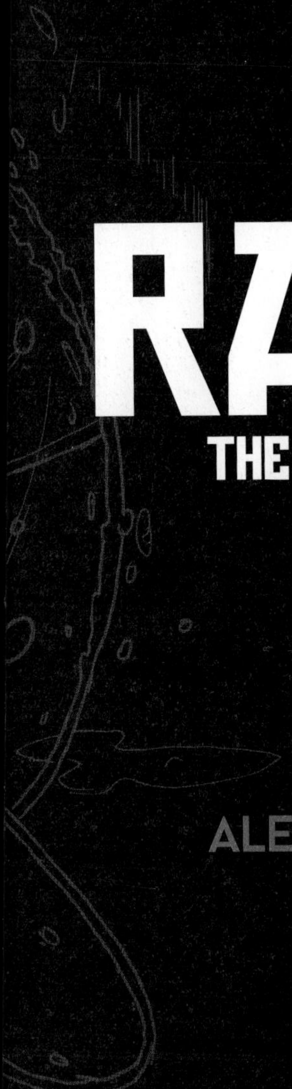

RASPUTIN™

THE ROAD TO THE WHITE HOUSE

CREATED BY

ALEX GRECIAN **&** RILEY ROSSMO

image

www.imagecomics.com

RASPUTIN, VOL. 2: THE ROAD TO THE WHITE HOUSE
ISBN: 978-1-63215-633-4
First Printing

For information regarding the CPSIA on this printed material call: 203-595-3636 and provide reference #RICH-660801.

For international rights, contact:
foreignlicensing@imagecomics.com.

RASPUTIN™

THE ROAD TO THE WHITE HOUSE

WRITER
ALEX GRECIAN

ARTIST
RILEY ROSSMO

COLORIST
IVAN PLASCENCIA

LETTERER
THOMAS MAUER

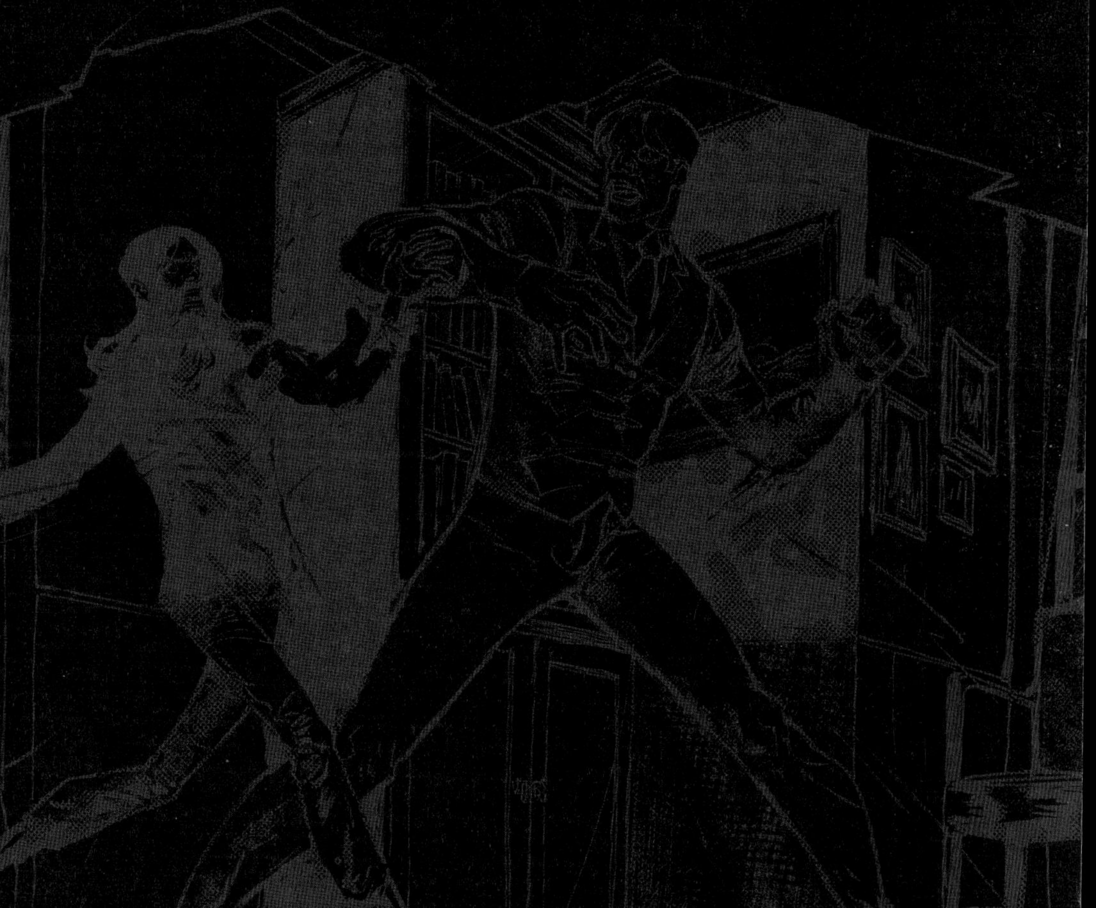

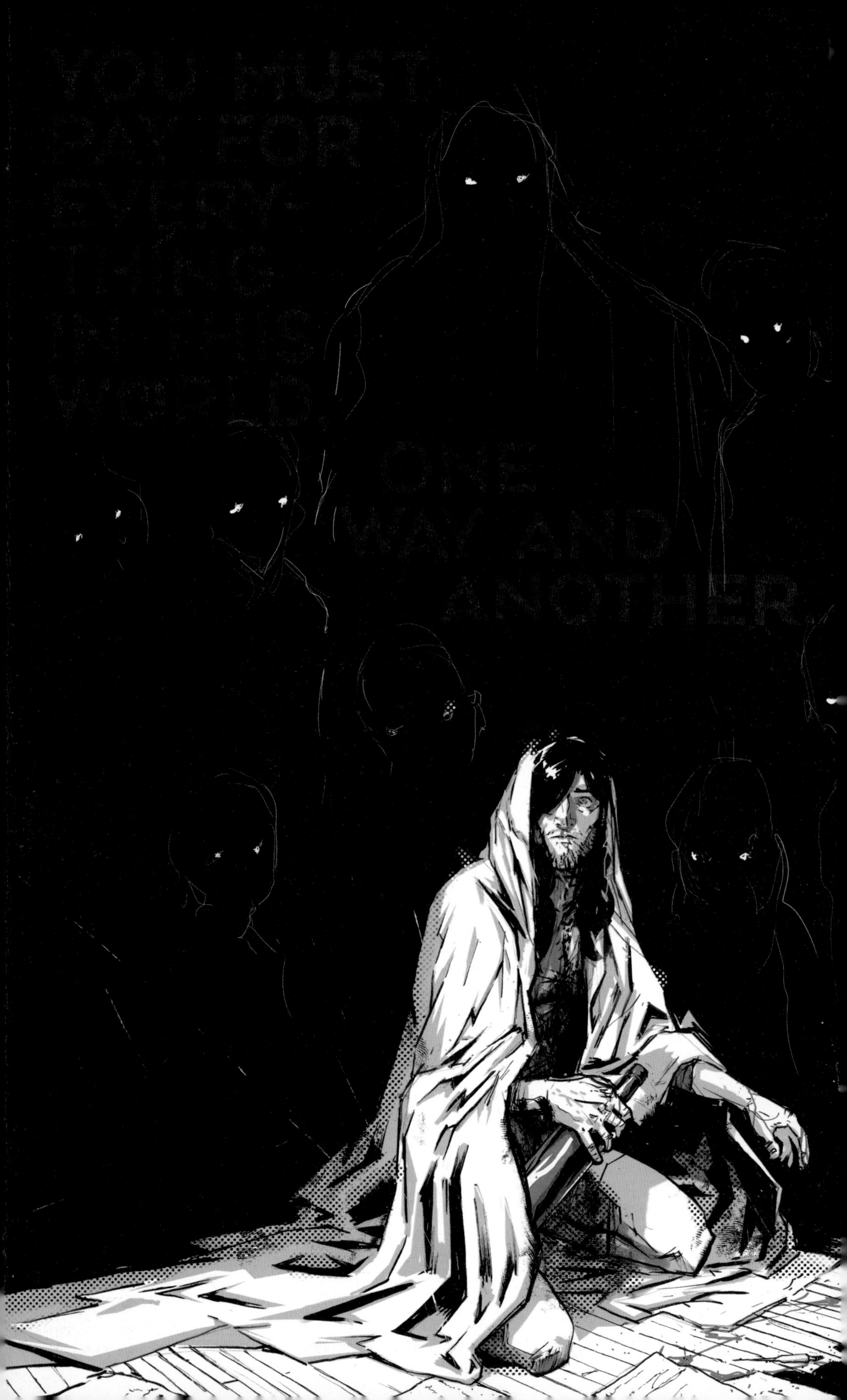
YOU MUST PAY FOR EVERY-THING IN THIS WORLD, ONE WAY AND ANOTHER.

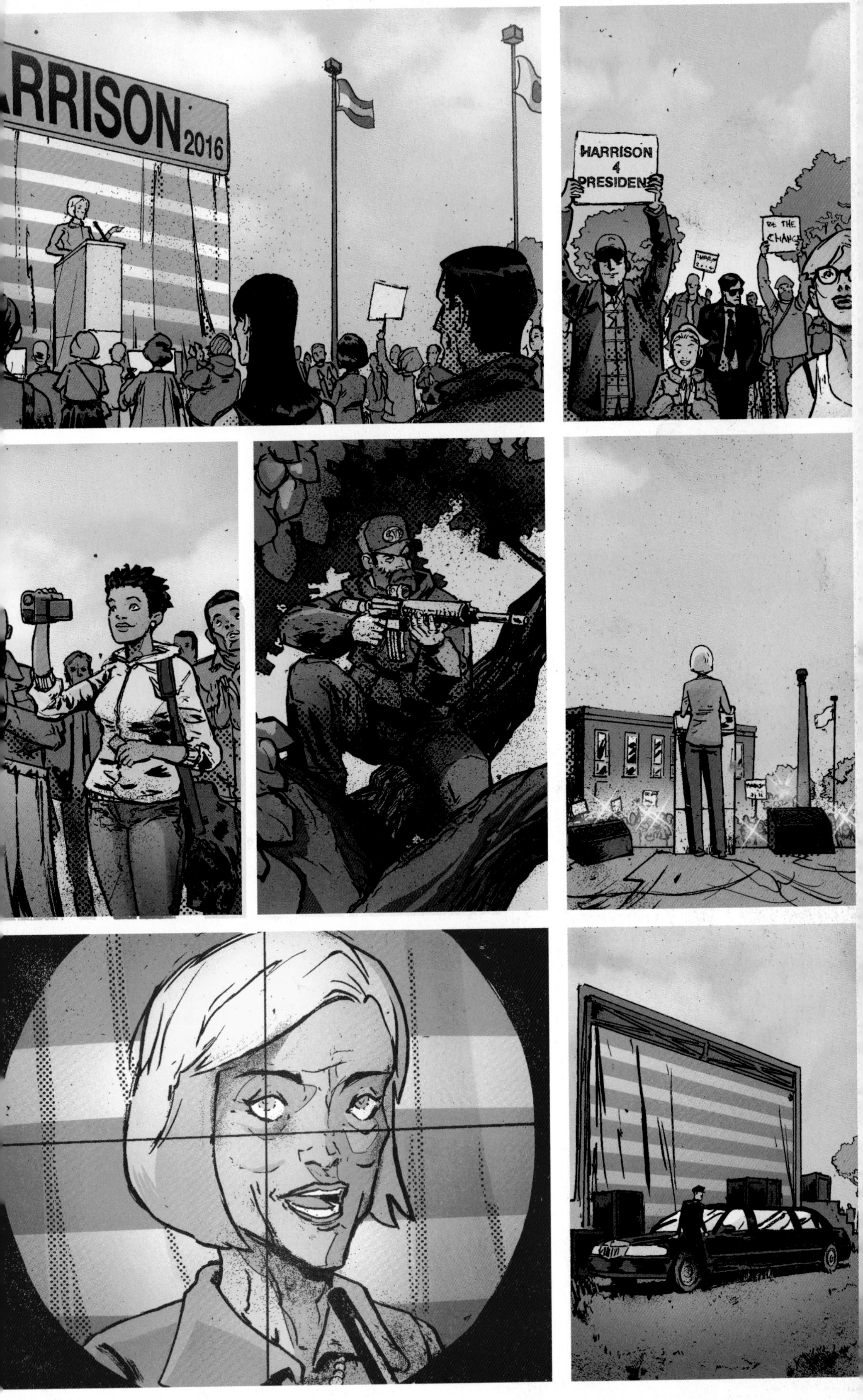
ARRISON 2016
HARRISON
4
PRESIDEN
BE THE
CHANG

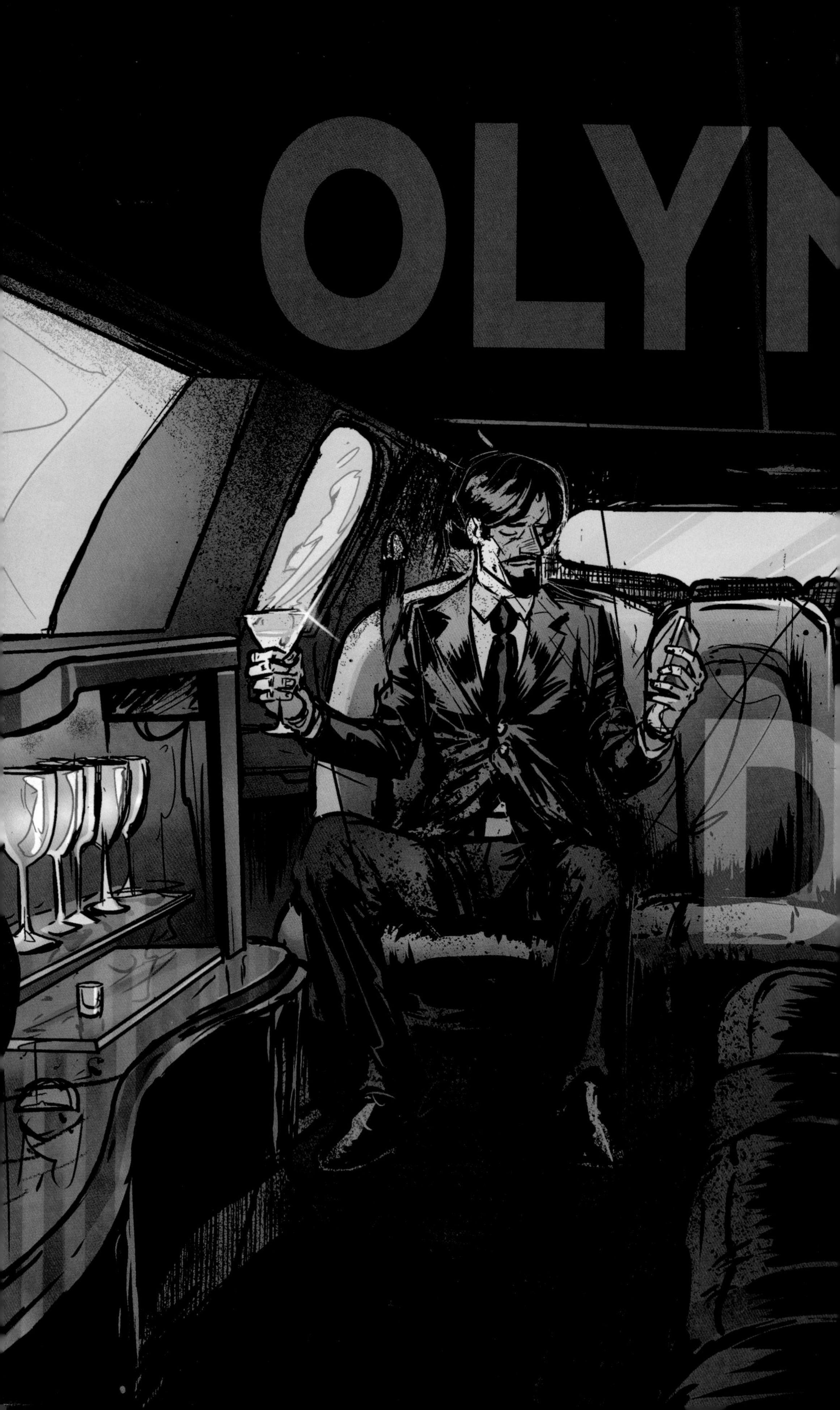

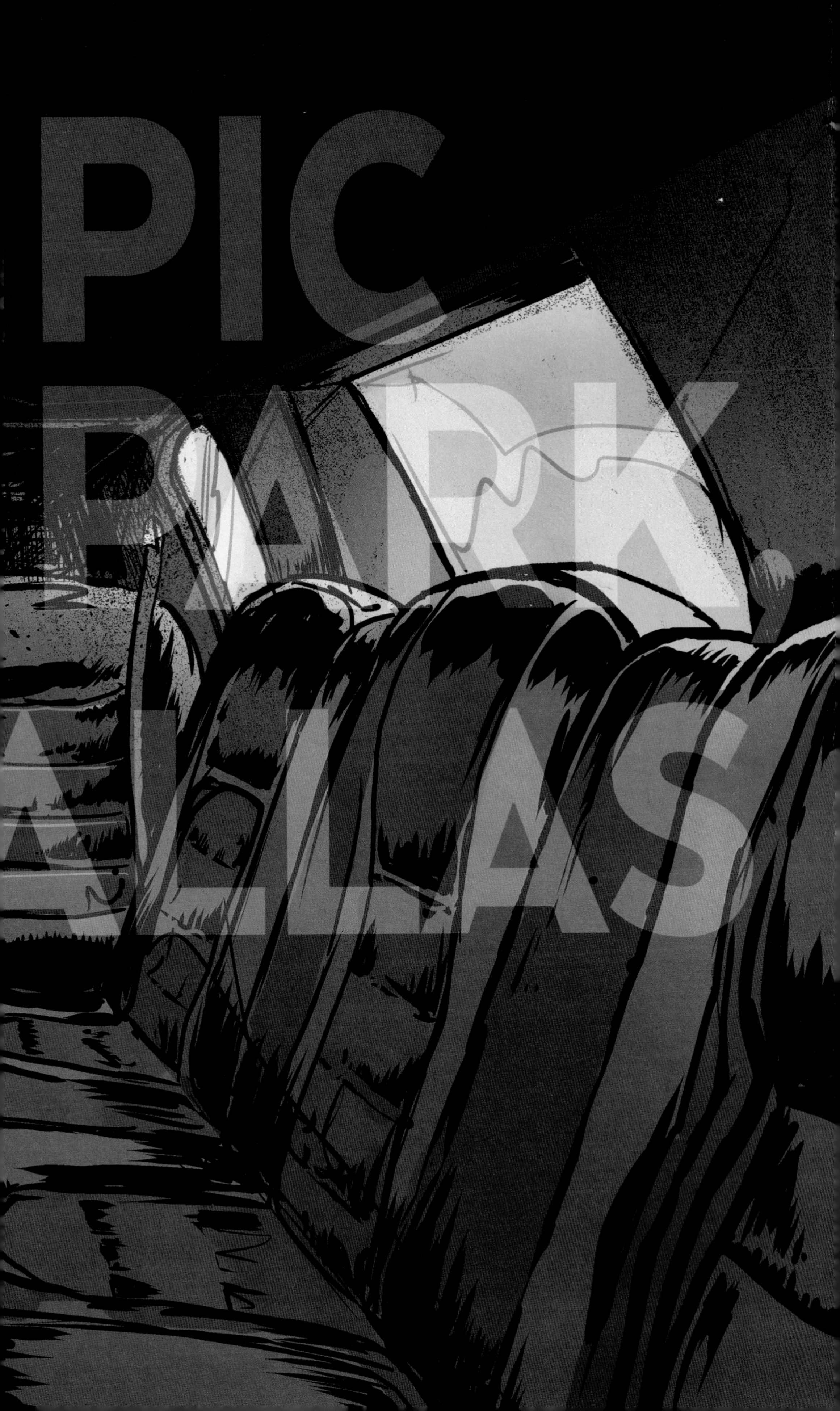
PIC
PARK.
ALLAS

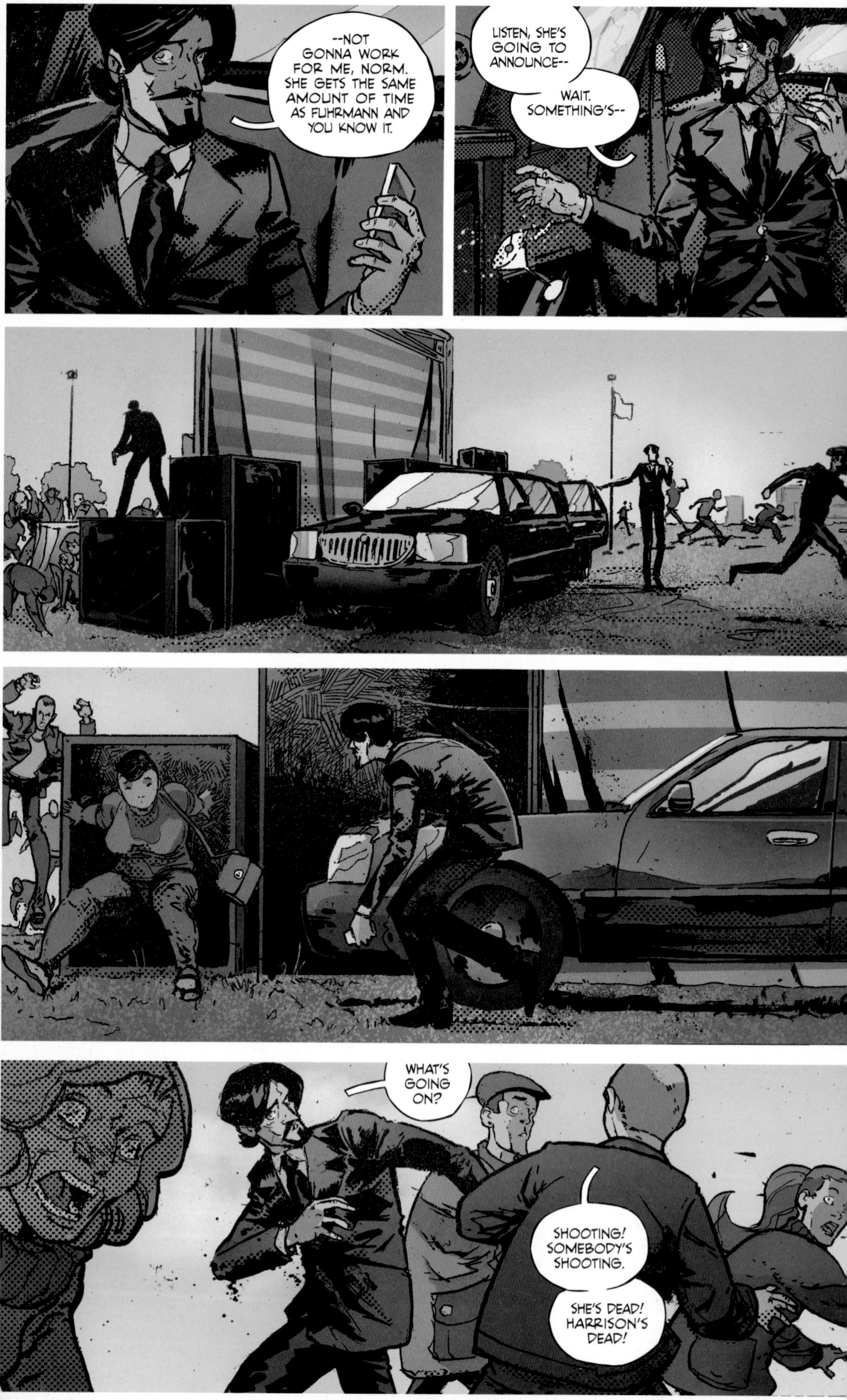
--NOT GONNA WORK FOR ME, NORM. SHE GETS THE SAME AMOUNT OF TIME AS FUHRMANN AND YOU KNOW IT.
LISTEN, SHE'S GOING TO ANNOUNCE--
WAIT. SOMETHING'S--
WHAT'S GOING ON?
SHOOTING! SOMEBODY'S SHOOTING.
SHE'S DEAD! HARRISON'S DEAD!

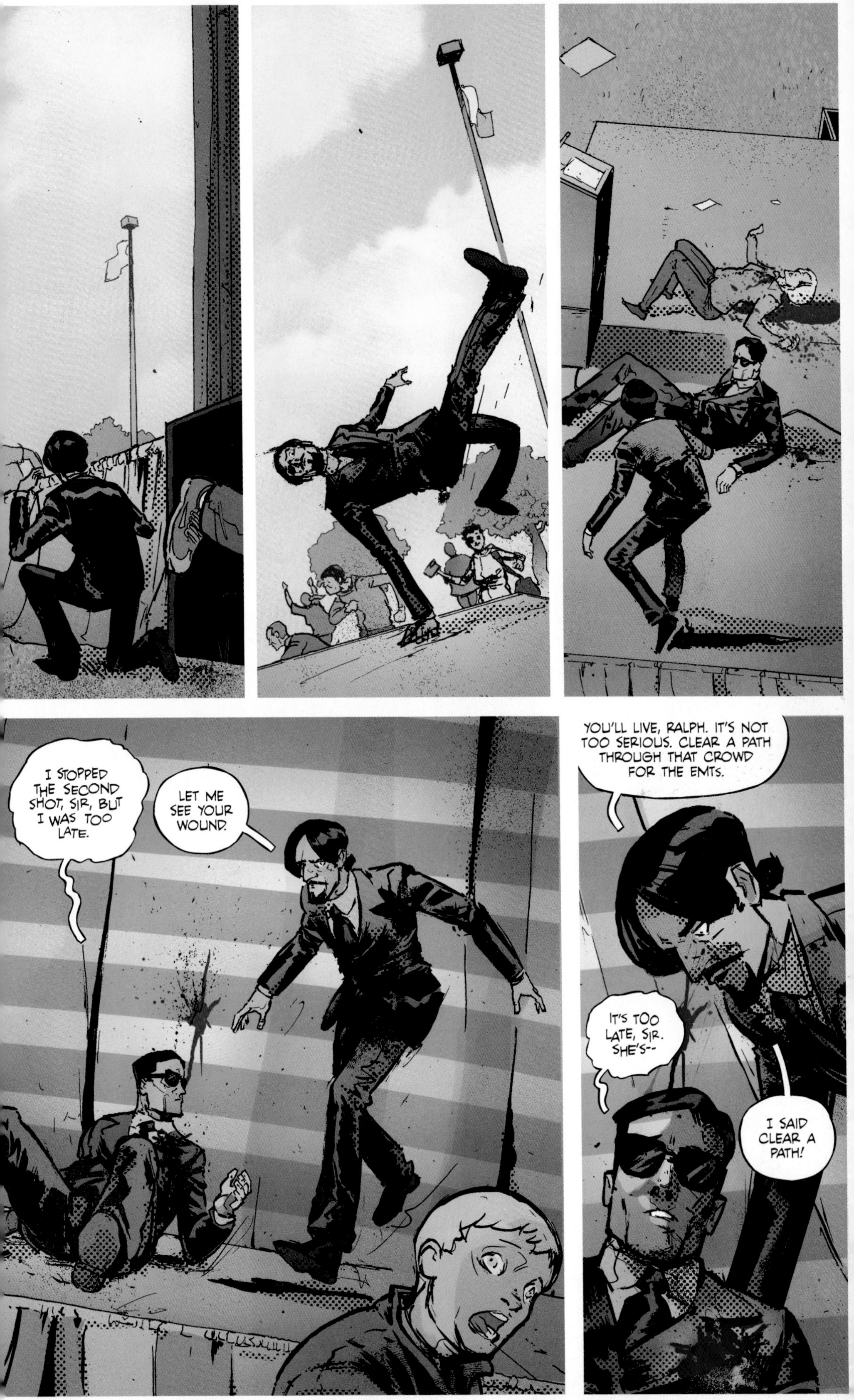
I STOPPED THE SECOND SHOT, SIR, BUT I WAS TOO LATE.
LET ME SEE YOUR WOUND.
YOU'LL LIVE, RALPH. IT'S NOT TOO SERIOUS. CLEAR A PATH THROUGH THAT CROWD FOR THE EMTs.
IT'S TOO LATE, SIR. SHE'S--
I SAID CLEAR A PATH!

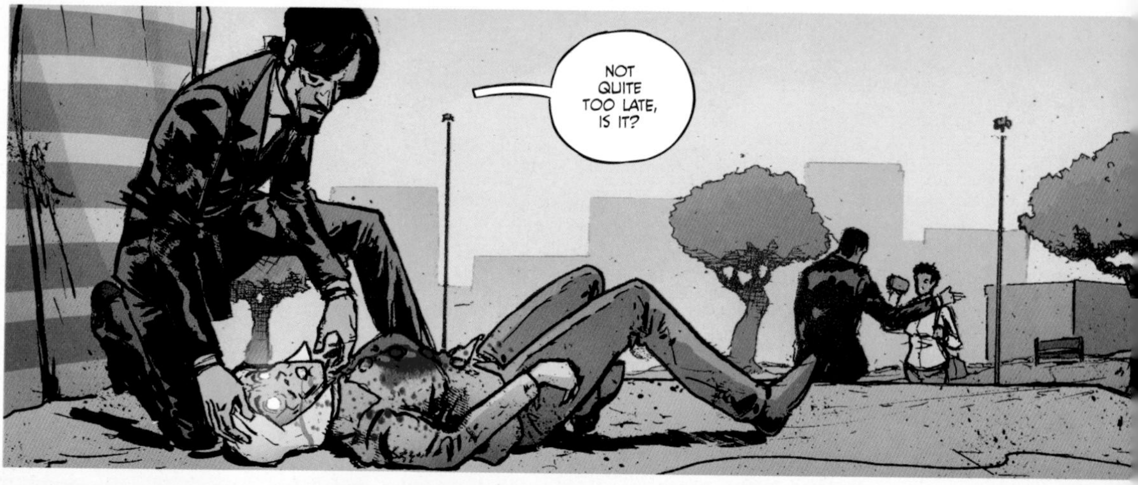
NOT QUITE TOO LATE, IS IT?
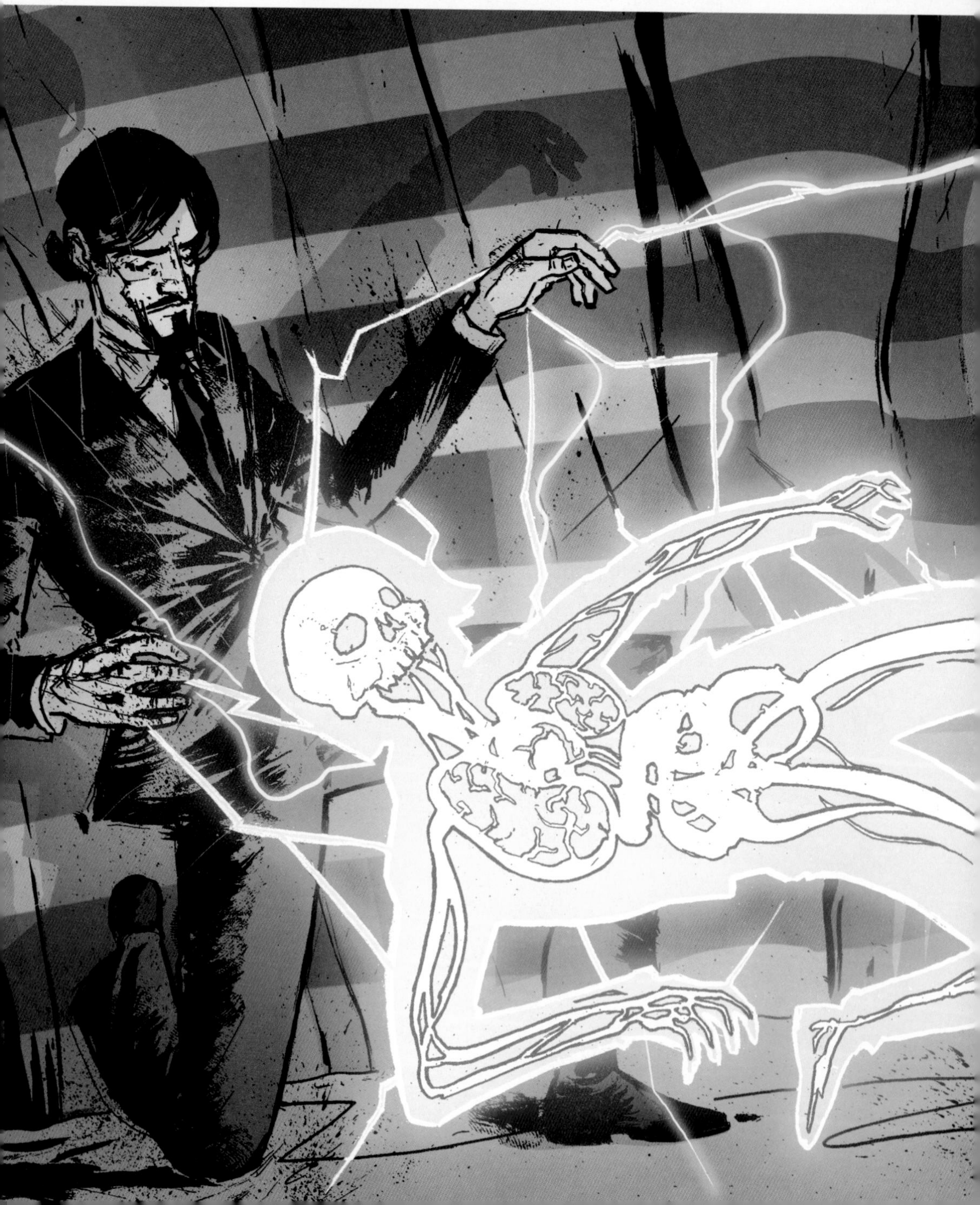

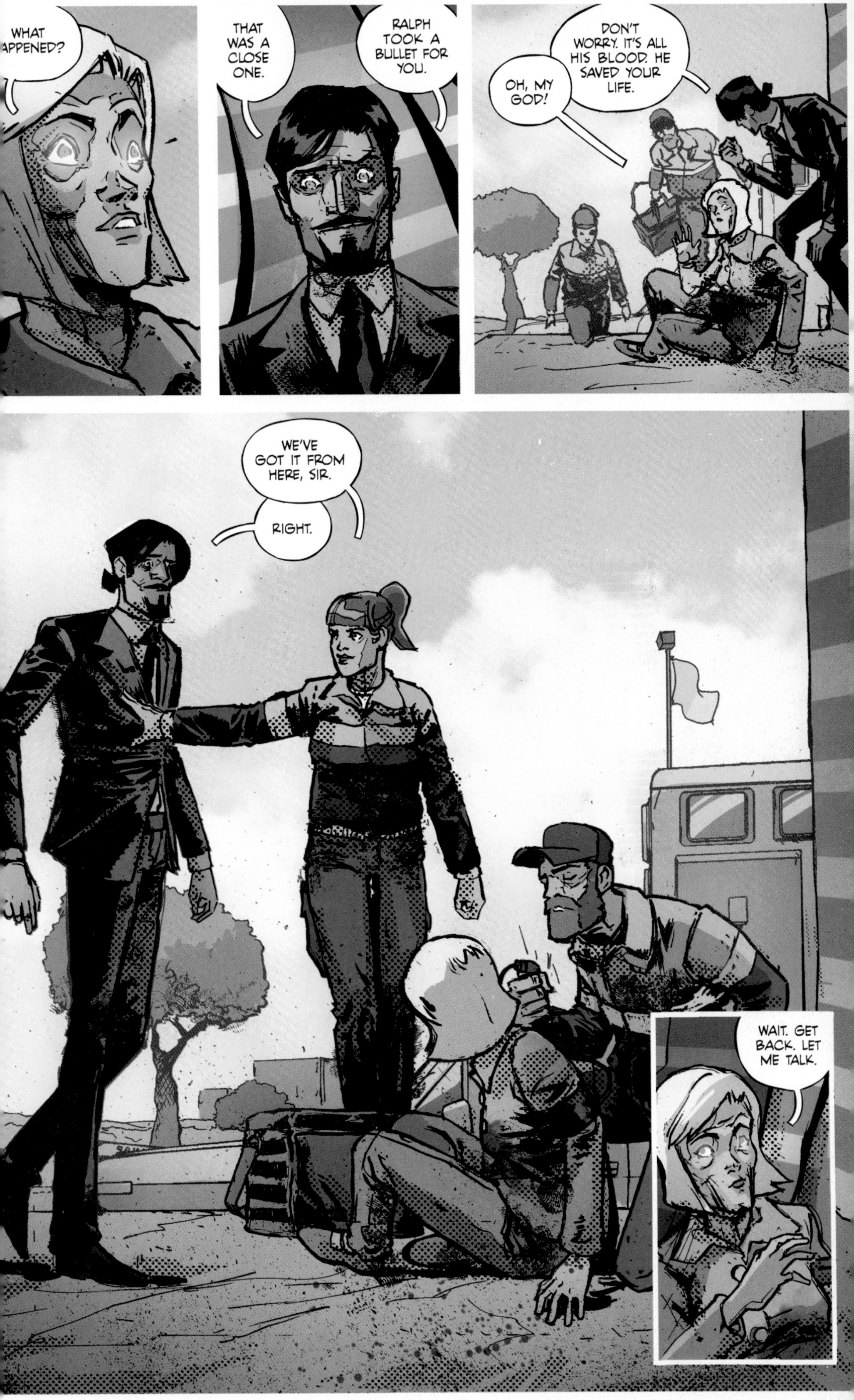
WHAT APPENED?
THAT WAS A CLOSE ONE.
RALPH TOOK A BULLET FOR YOU.
OH, MY GOD!
DON'T WORRY. IT'S ALL HIS BLOOD. HE SAVED YOUR LIFE.
WE'VE GOT IT FROM HERE, SIR.
RIGHT.
WAIT. GET BACK. LET ME TALK.

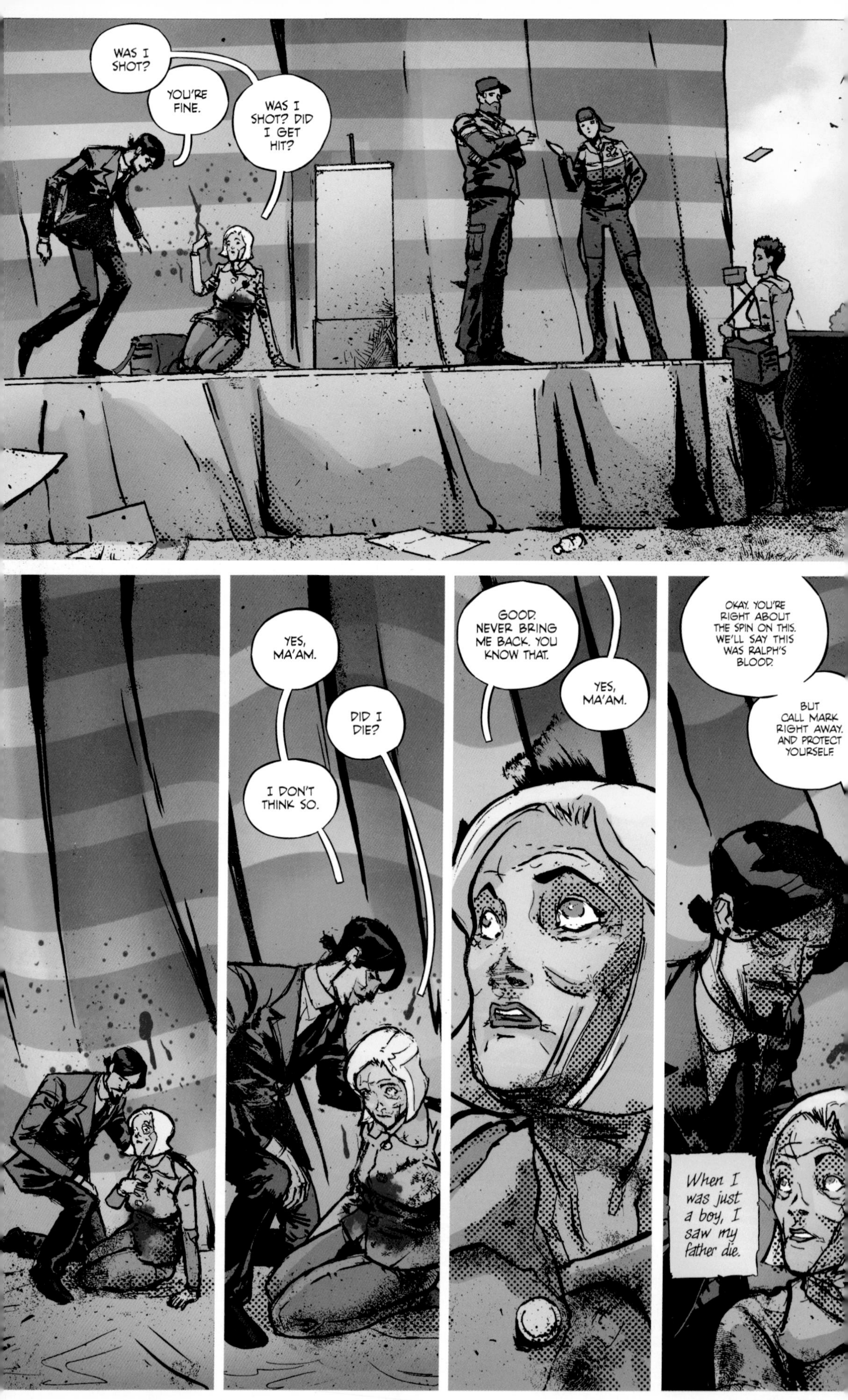
WAS I SHOT?
YOU'RE FINE.
WAS I SHOT? DID I GET HIT?
YES, MA'AM.
DID I DIE?
I DON'T THINK SO.
GOOD. NEVER BRING ME BACK. YOU KNOW THAT.
YES, MA'AM.
OKAY. YOU'RE RIGHT ABOUT THE SPIN ON THIS. WE'LL SAY THIS WAS RALPH'S BLOOD.
BUT CALL MARK RIGHT AWAY. AND PROTECT YOURSELF.
When I was just a boy, I saw my father die.

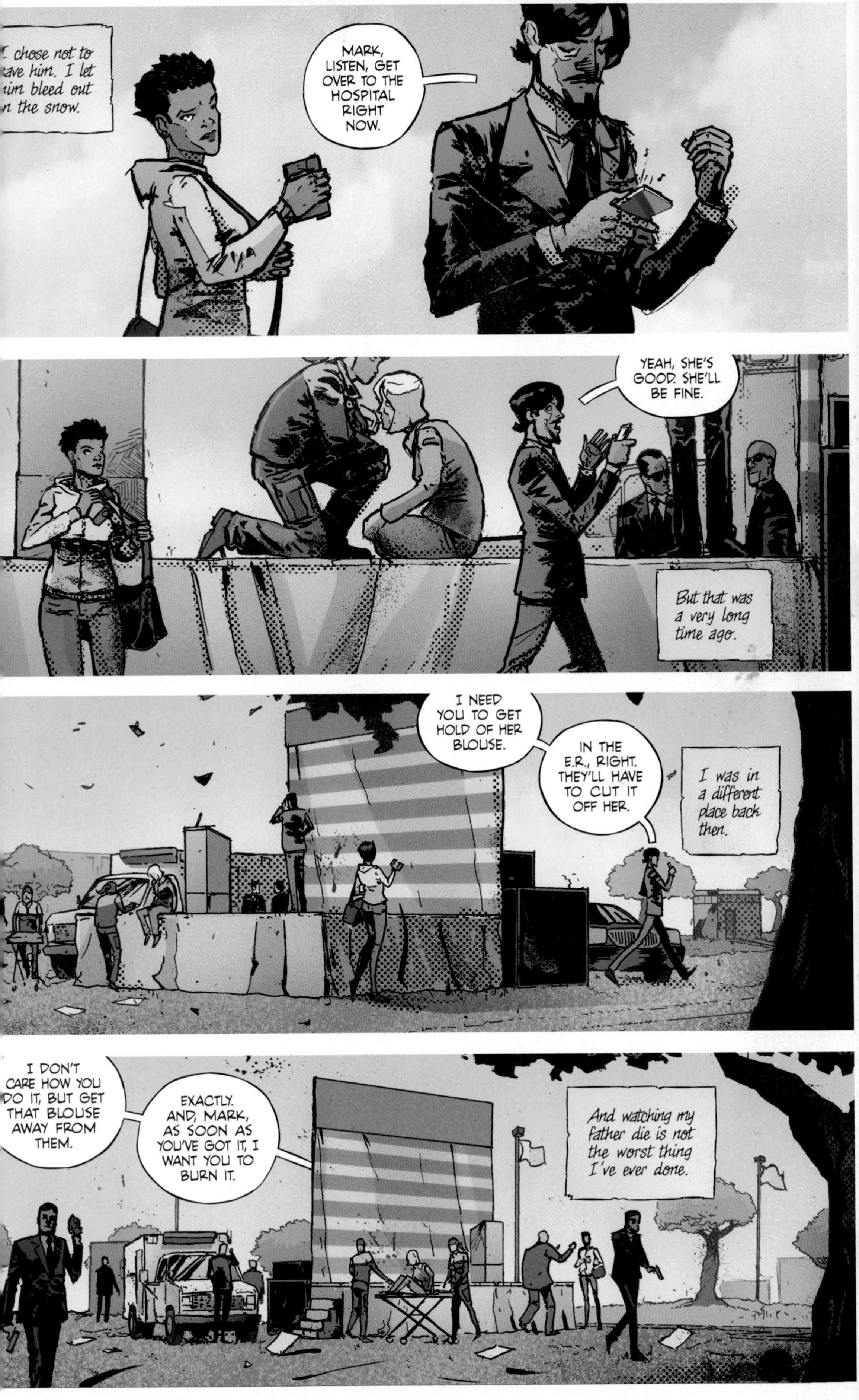

I chose not to save him. I let him bleed out in the snow.
MARK, LISTEN, GET OVER TO THE HOSPITAL RIGHT NOW.
YEAH, SHE'S GOOD. SHE'LL BE FINE.
But that was a very long time ago.
I NEED YOU TO GET HOLD OF HER BLOUSE.
IN THE E.R., RIGHT. THEY'LL HAVE TO CUT IT OFF HER.
I was in a different place back then.
I DON'T CARE HOW YOU DO IT, BUT GET THAT BLOUSE AWAY FROM THEM.
EXACTLY. AND, MARK, AS SOON AS YOU'VE GOT IT, I WANT YOU TO BURN IT.
And watching my father die is not the worst thing I've ever done.

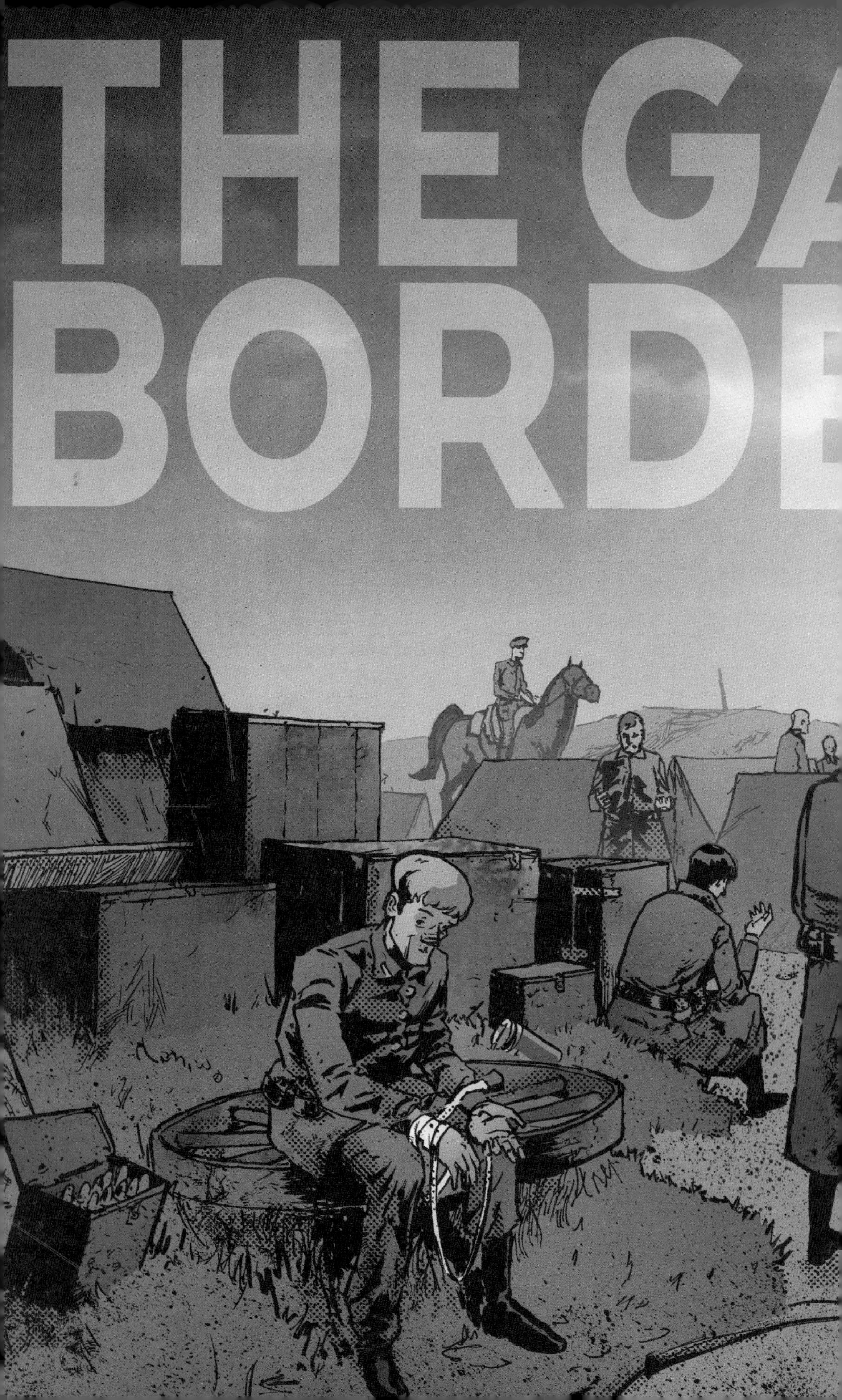
THE GA
BORDE

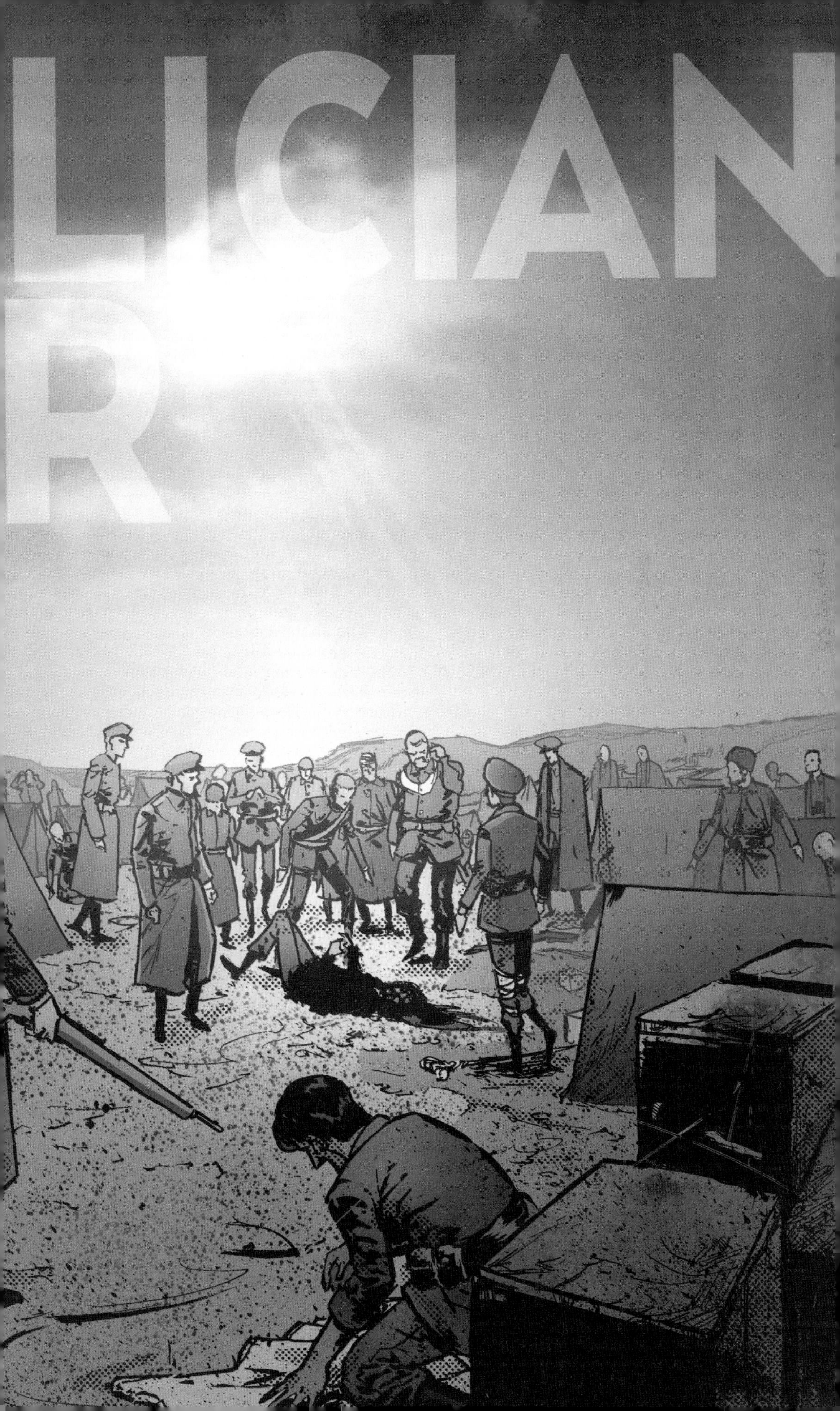
LICIAN
R

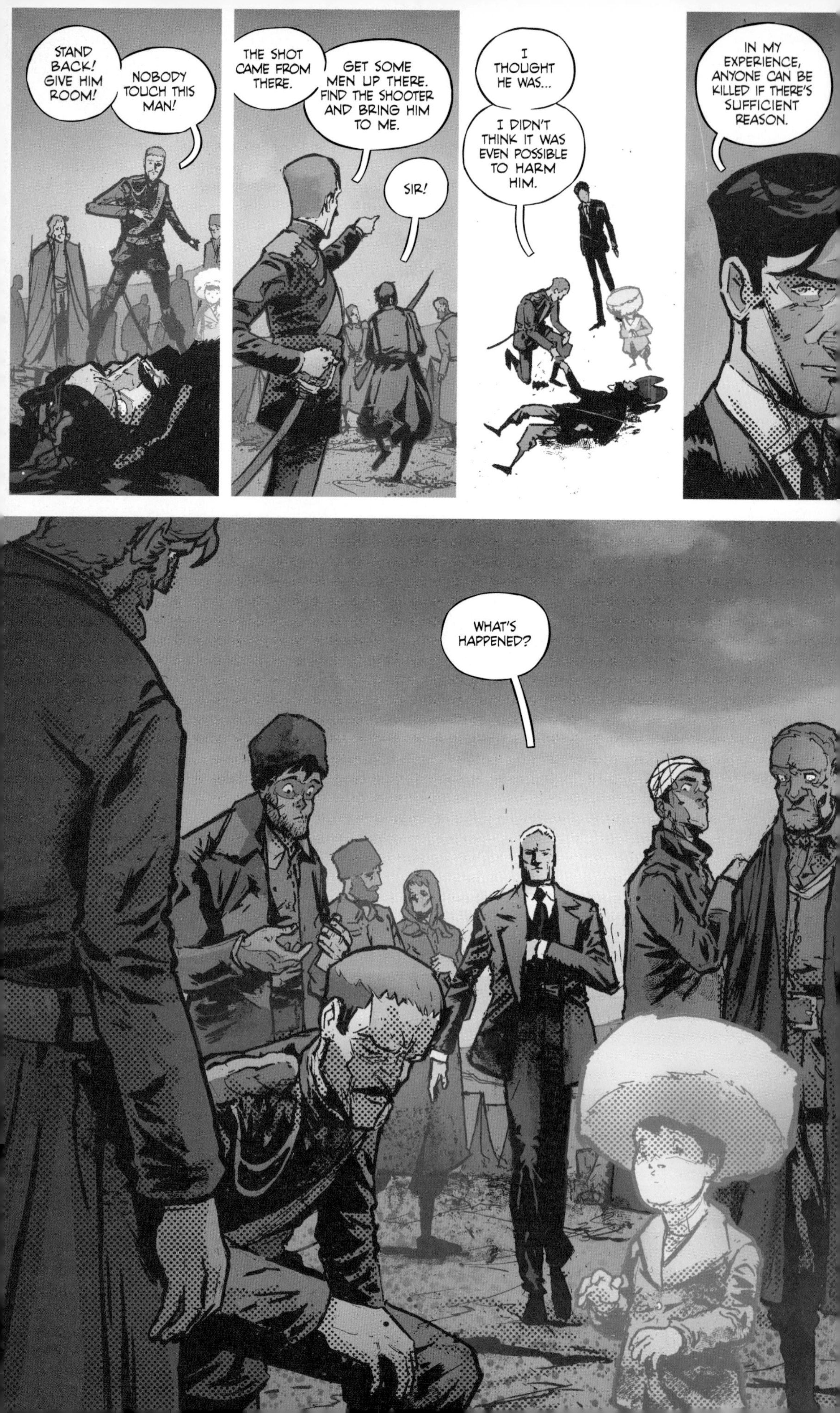
STAND BACK! GIVE HIM ROOM!
NOBODY TOUCH THIS MAN!
THE SHOT CAME FROM THERE.
GET SOME MEN UP THERE. FIND THE SHOOTER AND BRING HIM TO ME.
SIR!
I THOUGHT HE WAS...
I DIDN'T THINK IT WAS EVEN POSSIBLE TO HARM HIM.
IN MY EXPERIENCE, ANYONE CAN BE KILLED IF THERE'S SUFFICIENT REASON.
WHAT'S HAPPENED?

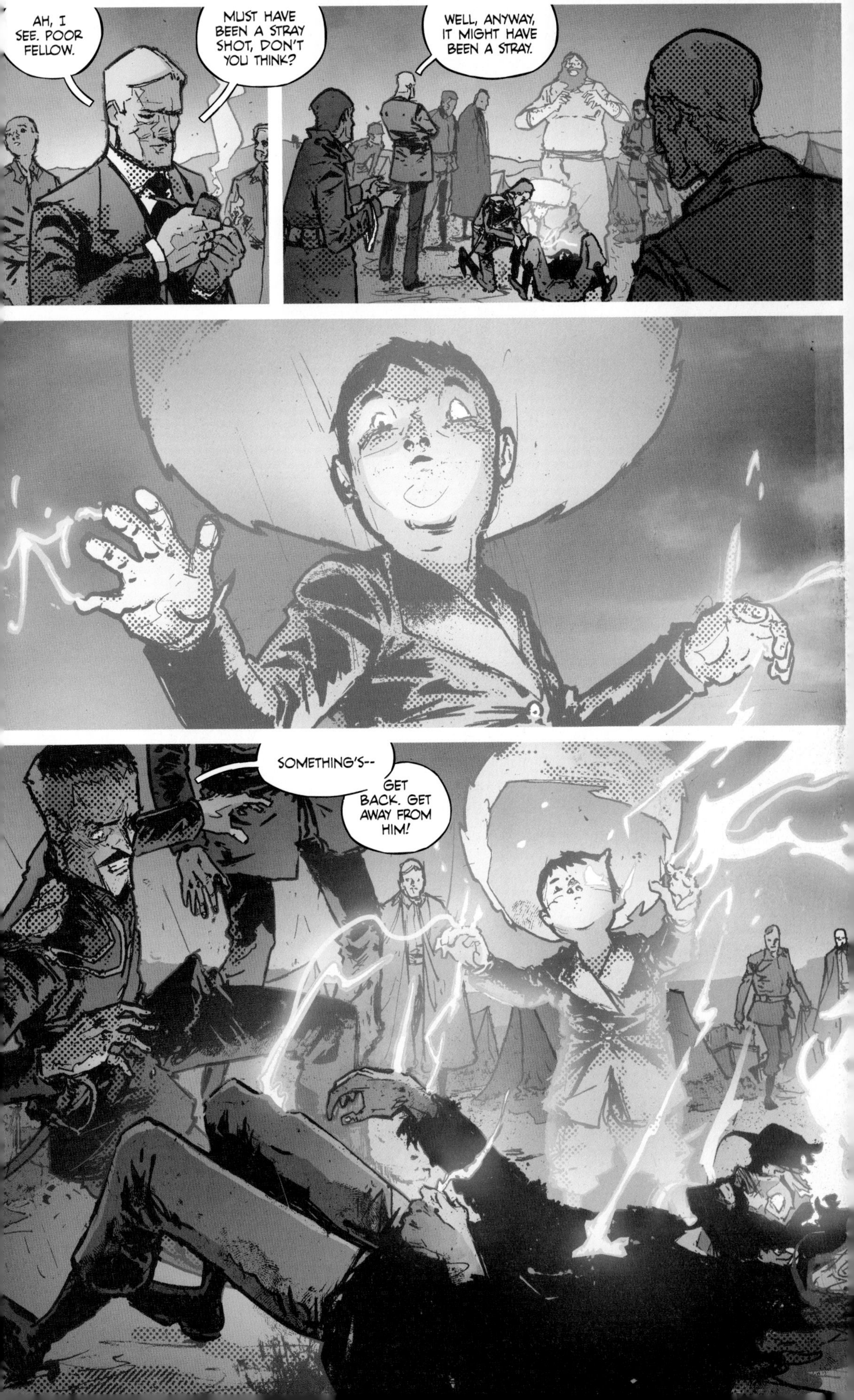
AH, I SEE. POOR FELLOW.
MUST HAVE BEEN A STRAY SHOT, DON'T YOU THINK?
WELL, ANYWAY, IT MIGHT HAVE BEEN A STRAY.
SOMETHING'S--
GET BACK. GET AWAY FROM HIM!

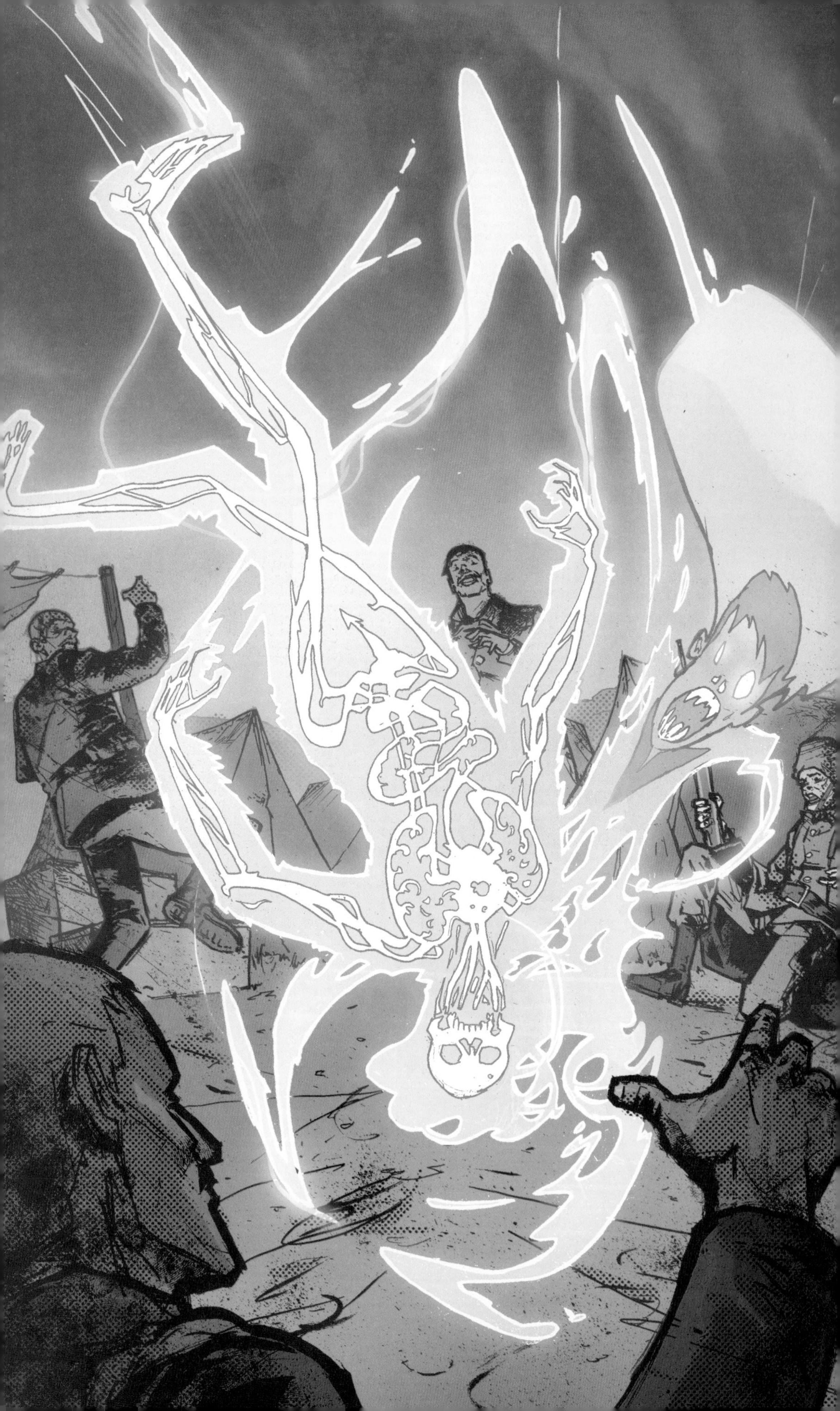

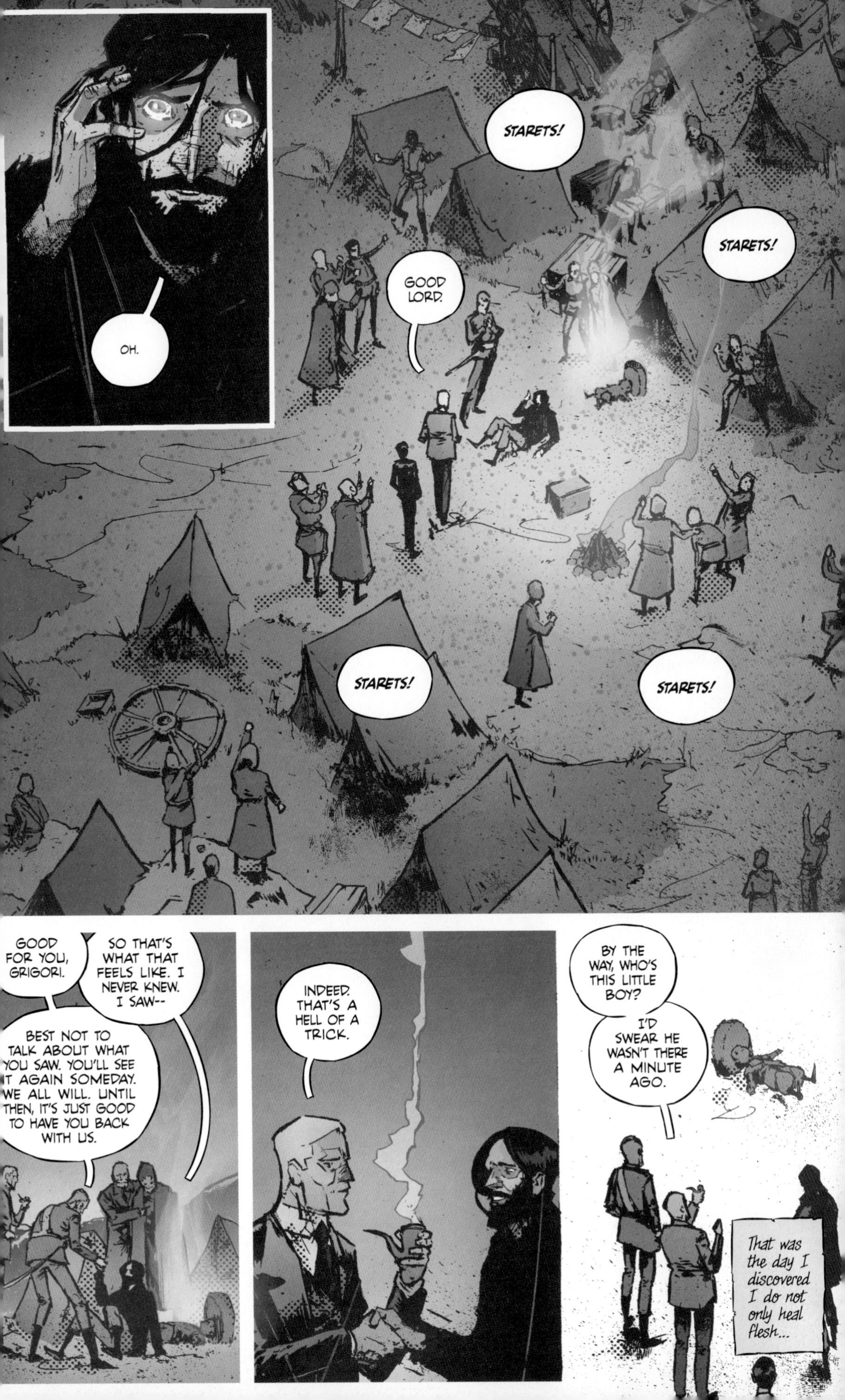
OH.
STARETS!
GOOD LORD.
STARETS!
STARETS!
STARETS!
GOOD FOR YOU, GRIGORI.
SO THAT'S WHAT THAT FEELS LIKE. I NEVER KNEW. I SAW--
BEST NOT TO TALK ABOUT WHAT YOU SAW. YOU'LL SEE IT AGAIN SOMEDAY. WE ALL WILL. UNTIL THEN, IT'S JUST GOOD TO HAVE YOU BACK WITH US.
INDEED. THAT'S A HELL OF A TRICK.
BY THE WAY, WHO'S THIS LITTLE BOY?
I'D SWEAR HE WASN'T THERE A MINUTE AGO.
That was the day I discovered I do not only heal flesh...

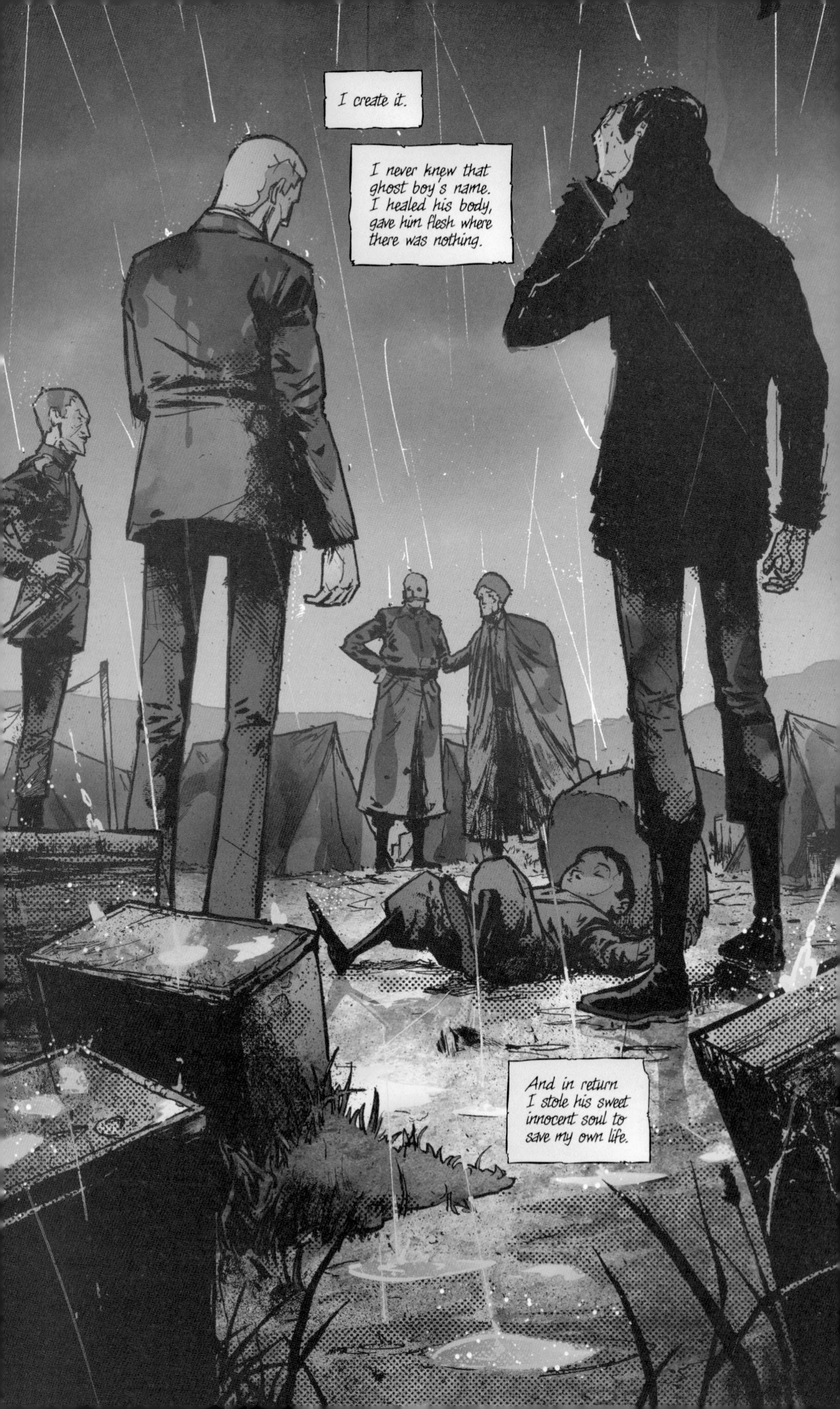
I create it.
I never knew that ghost boy's name. I healed his body, gave him flesh where there was nothing.
And in return I stole his sweet innocent soul to save my own life.

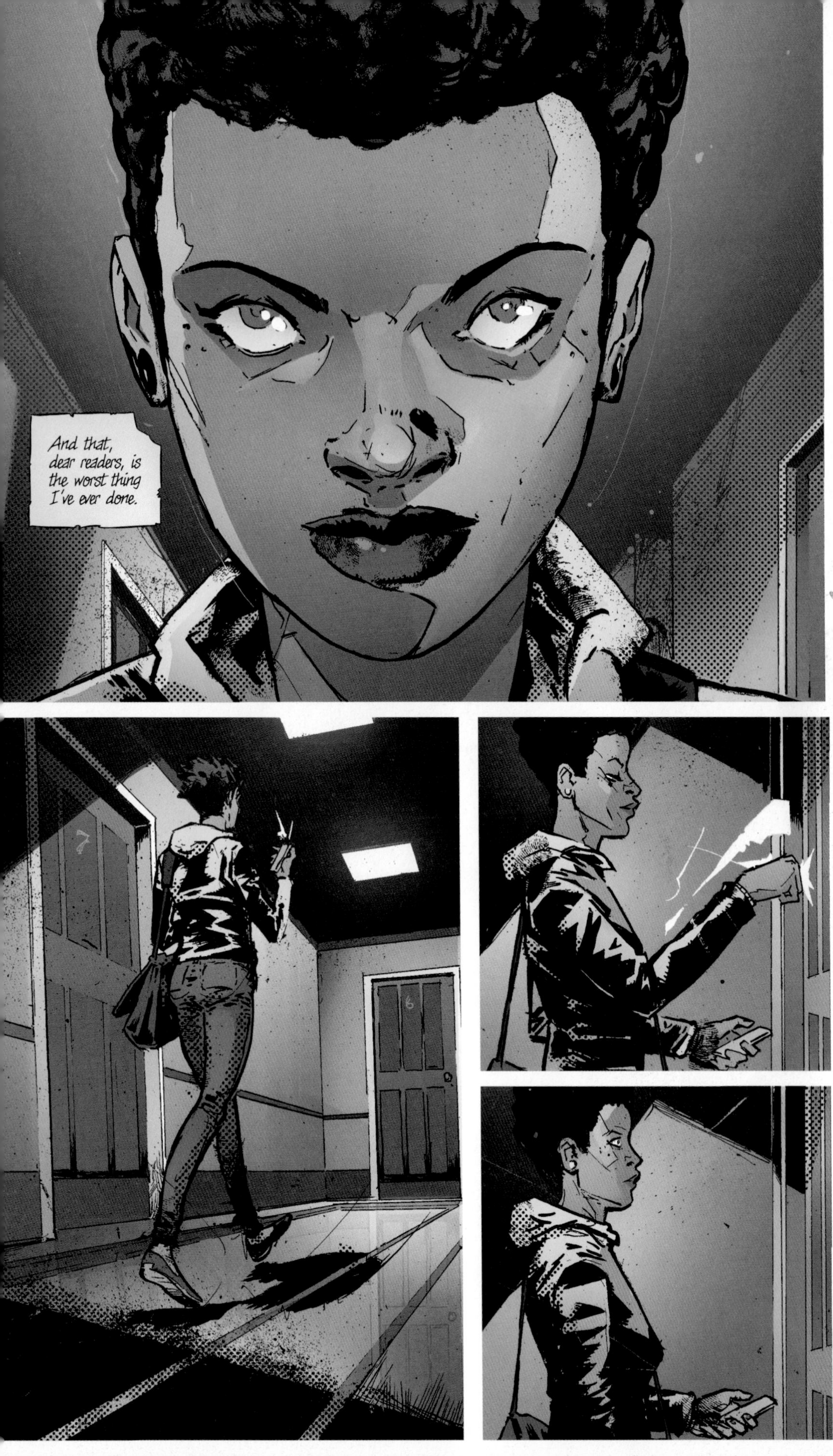
And that, dear readers, is the worst thing I've ever done.

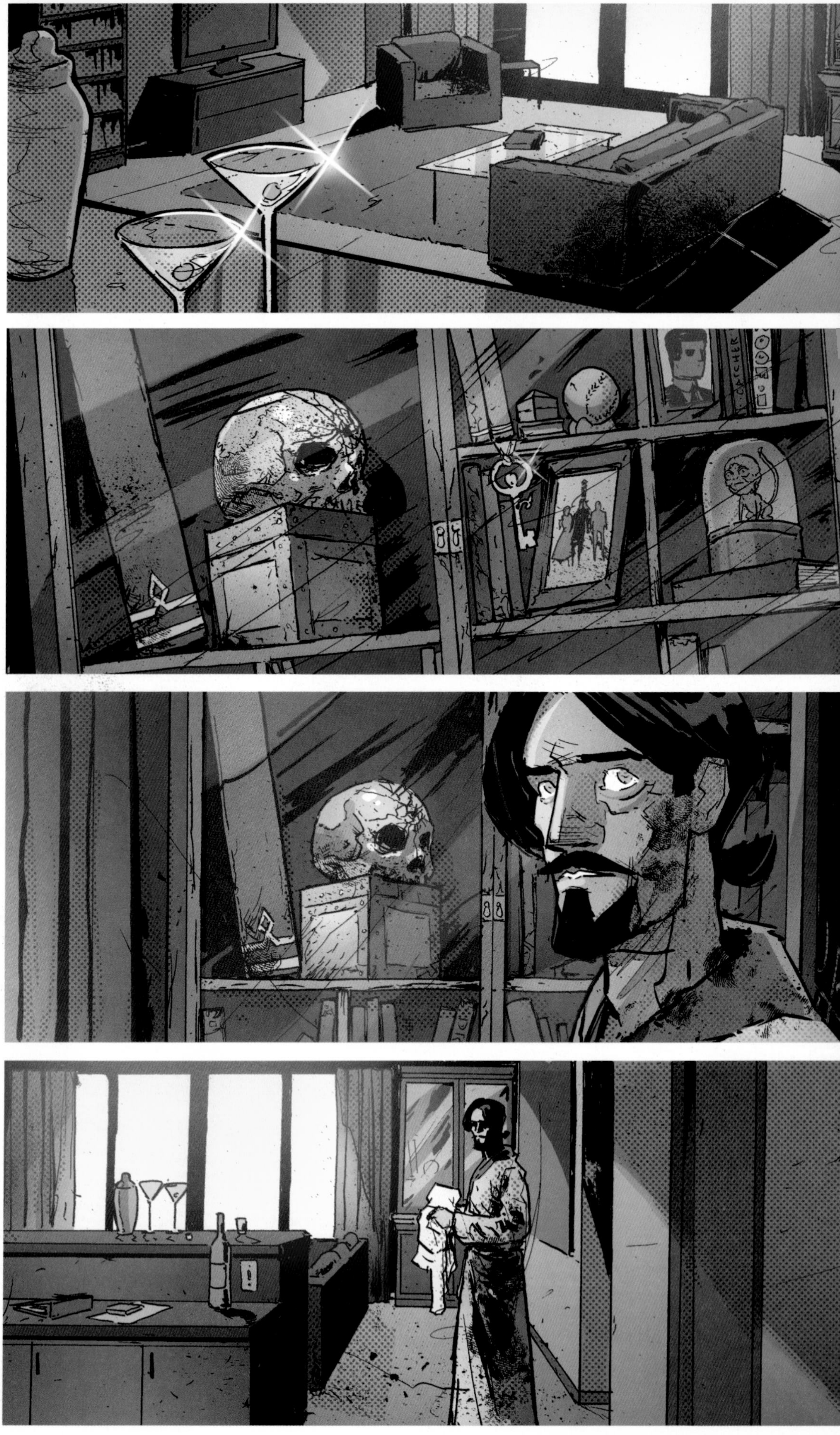
CATCHER

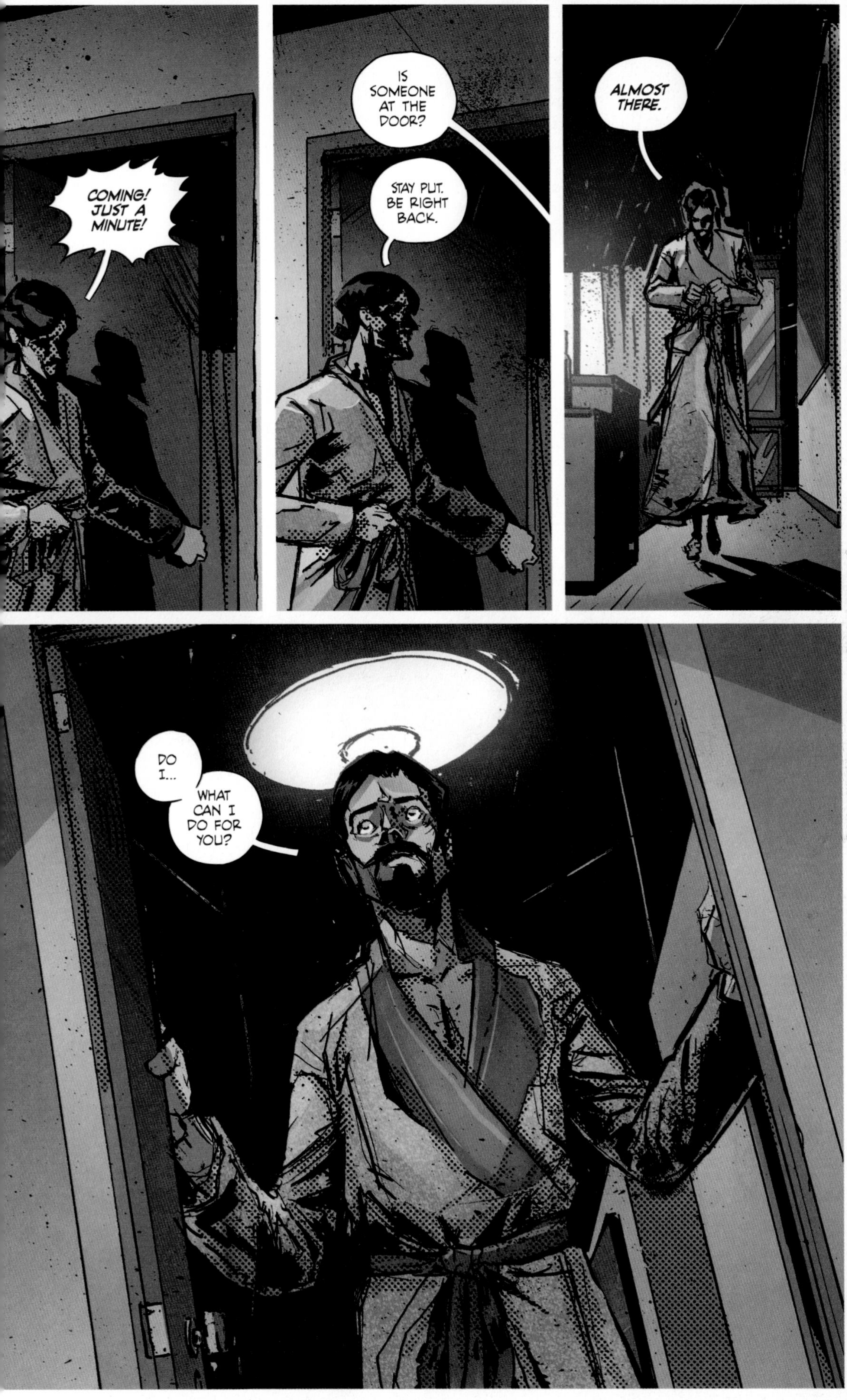
COMING! JUST A MINUTE!
IS SOMEONE AT THE DOOR?
STAY PUT. BE RIGHT BACK.
ALMOST THERE.
DO I...
WHAT CAN I DO FOR YOU?

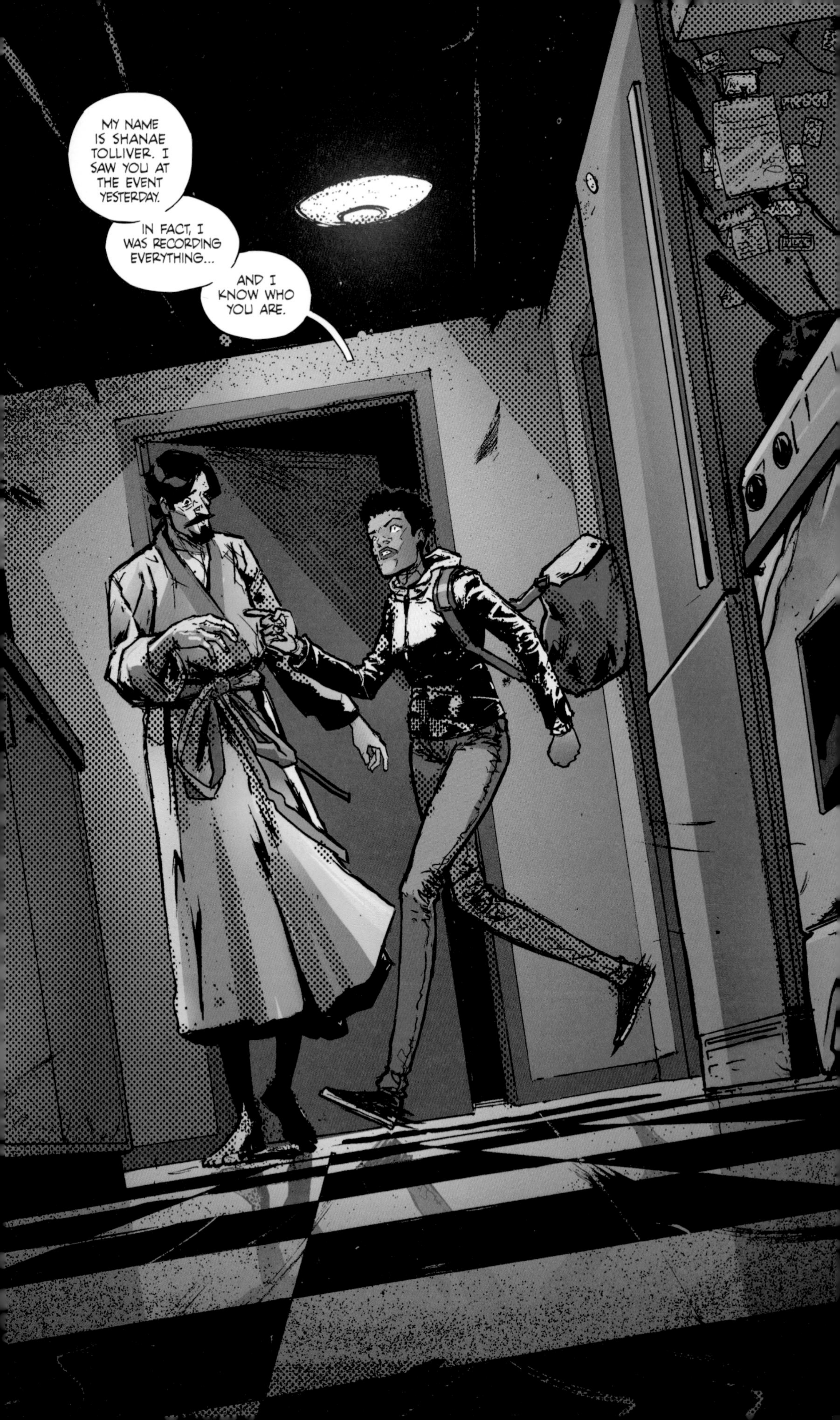
MY NAME IS SHANAE TOLLIVER. I SAW YOU AT THE EVENT YESTERDAY.
IN FACT, I WAS RECORDING EVERYTHING...
AND I KNOW WHO YOU ARE.

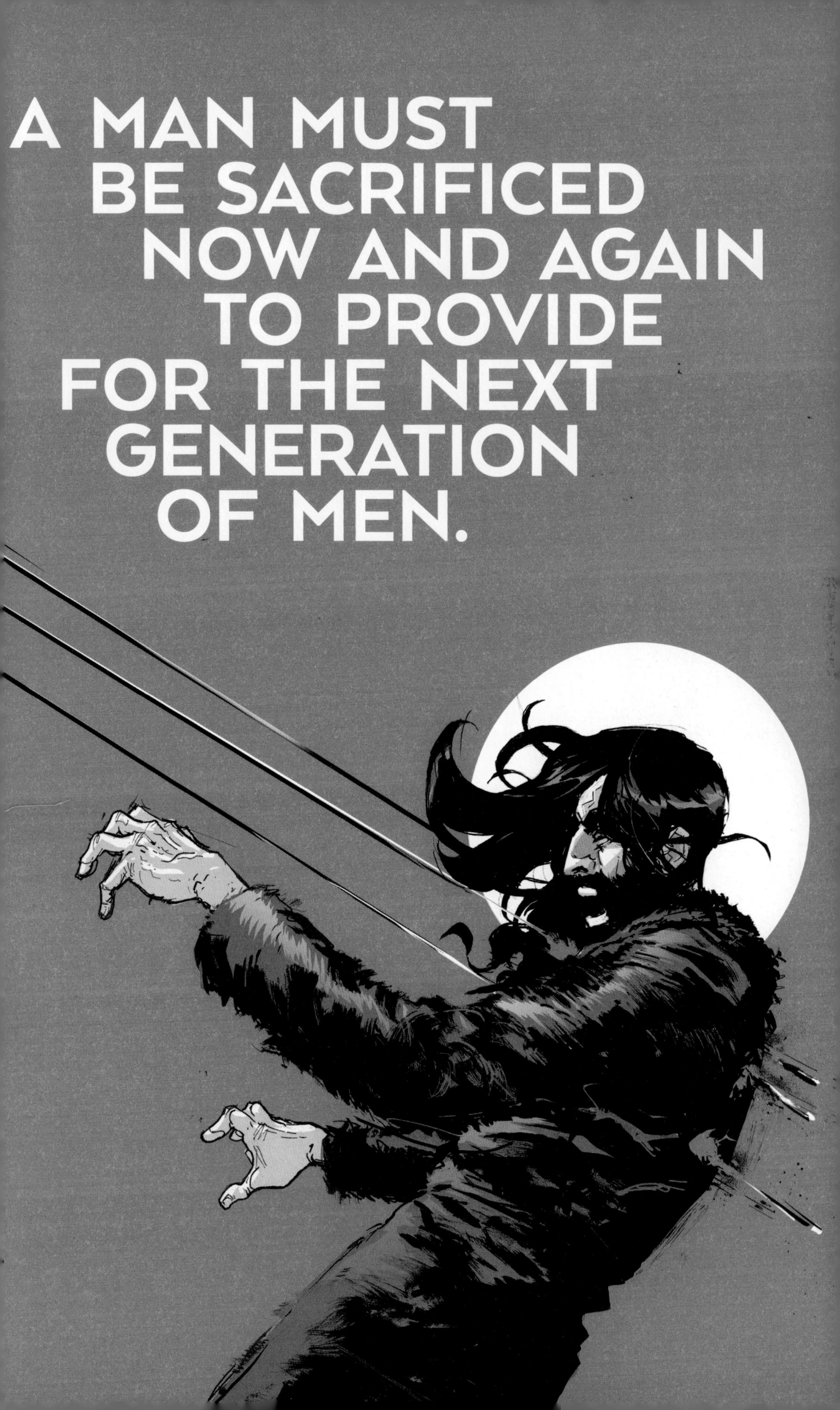
A MAN MUST BE SACRIFICED NOW AND AGAIN TO PROVIDE FOR THE NEXT GENERATION OF MEN.

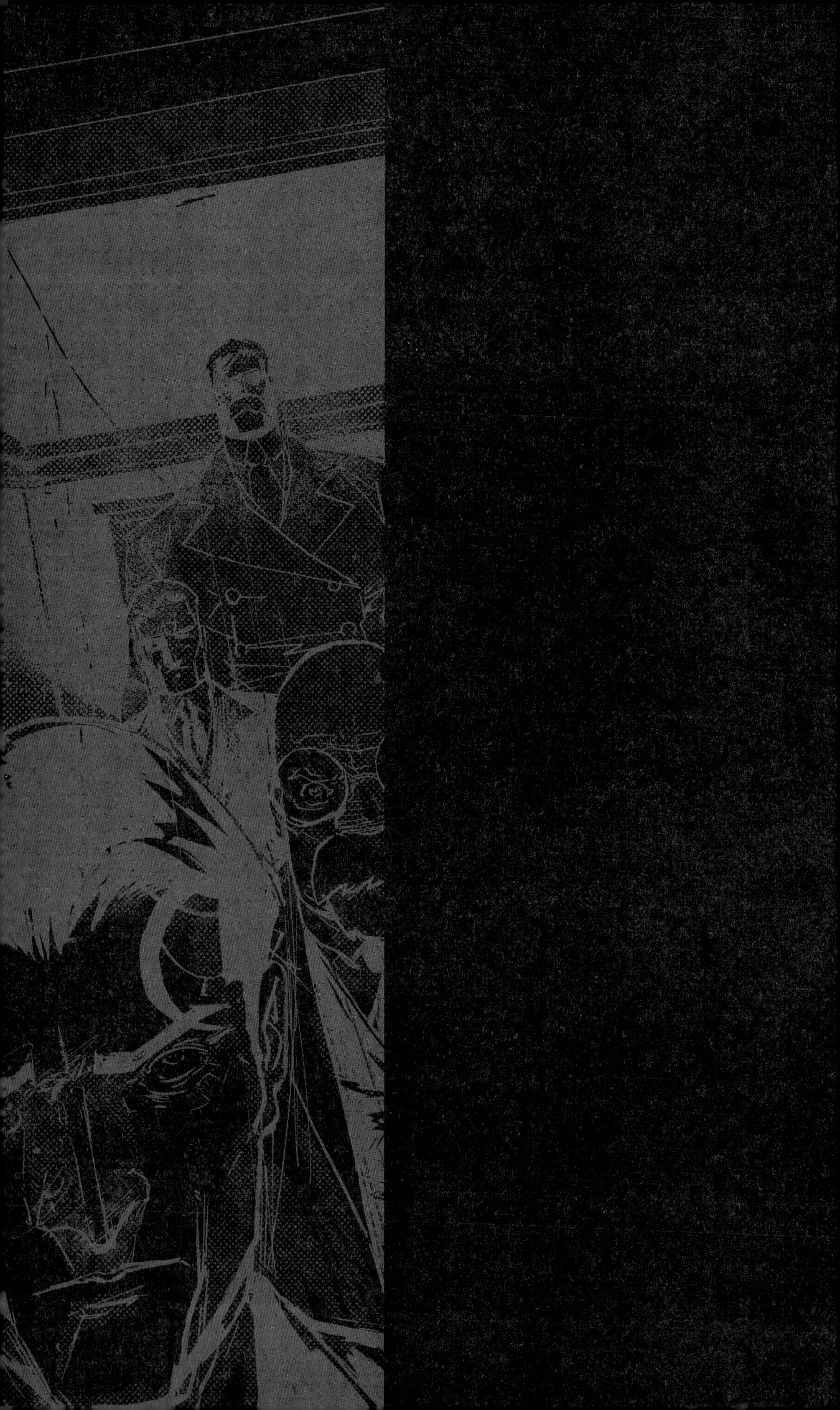

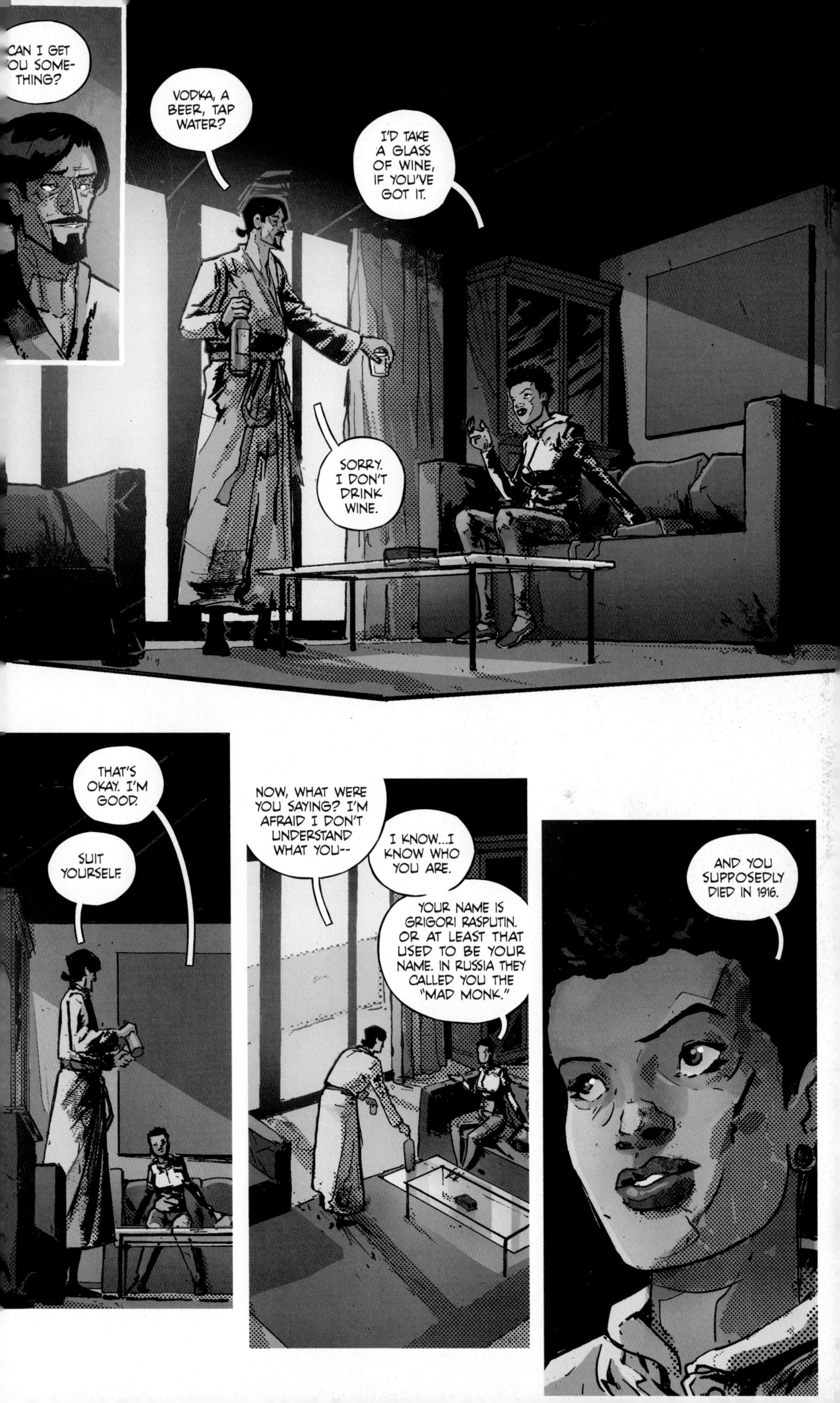
CAN I GET YOU SOME-THING?
VODKA, A BEER, TAP WATER?
I'D TAKE A GLASS OF WINE, IF YOU'VE GOT IT.
SORRY. I DON'T DRINK WINE.
THAT'S OKAY. I'M GOOD.
SUIT YOURSELF.
NOW, WHAT WERE YOU SAYING? I'M AFRAID I DON'T UNDERSTAND WHAT YOU--
I KNOW...I KNOW WHO YOU ARE.
YOUR NAME IS GRIGORI RASPUTIN. OR AT LEAST THAT USED TO BE YOUR NAME. IN RUSSIA THEY CALLED YOU THE "MAD MONK."
AND YOU SUPPOSEDLY DIED IN 1916.

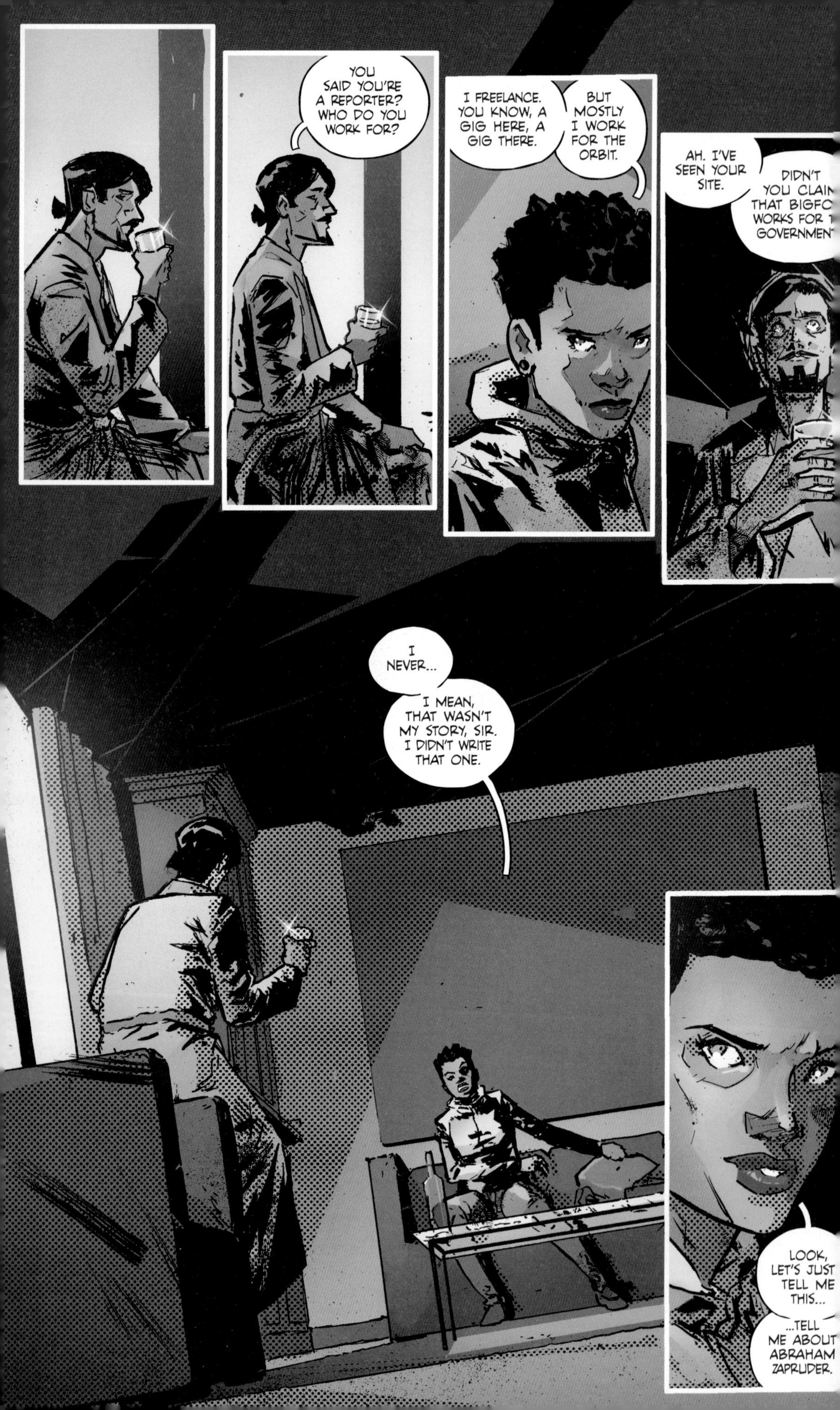
YOU SAID YOU'RE A REPORTER? WHO DO YOU WORK FOR?
I FREELANCE. YOU KNOW, A GIG HERE, A GIG THERE.
BUT MOSTLY I WORK FOR THE ORBIT.
AH. I'VE SEEN YOUR SITE.
DIDN'T YOU CLAI THAT BIGF WORKS FOR GOVERNMEN
I NEVER...
I MEAN, THAT WASN'T MY STORY, SIR. I DIDN'T WRITE THAT ONE.
LOOK, LET'S JUST TELL ME THIS...
...TELL ME ABOUT ABRAHAM ZAPRUDER.

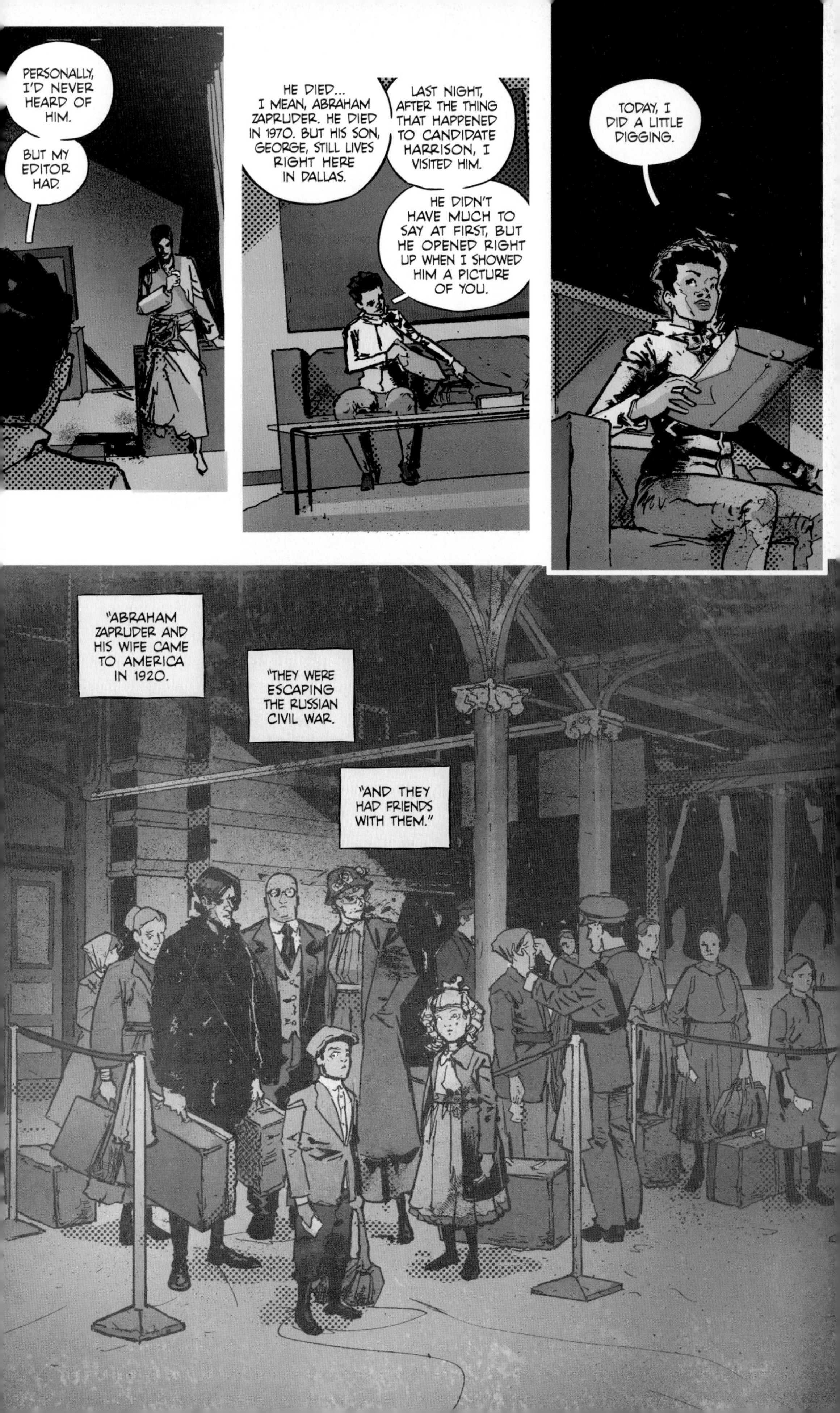
PERSONALLY, I'D NEVER HEARD OF HIM.
BUT MY EDITOR HAD.
HE DIED... I MEAN, ABRAHAM ZAPRUDER. HE DIED IN 1970. BUT HIS SON, GEORGE, STILL LIVES RIGHT HERE IN DALLAS.
LAST NIGHT, AFTER THE THING THAT HAPPENED TO CANDIDATE HARRISON, I VISITED HIM.
HE DIDN'T HAVE MUCH TO SAY AT FIRST, BUT HE OPENED RIGHT UP WHEN I SHOWED HIM A PICTURE OF YOU.
TODAY, I DID A LITTLE DIGGING.
"ABRAHAM ZAPRUDER AND HIS WIFE CAME TO AMERICA IN 1920.
"THEY WERE ESCAPING THE RUSSIAN CIVIL WAR.
"AND THEY HAD FRIENDS WITH THEM."

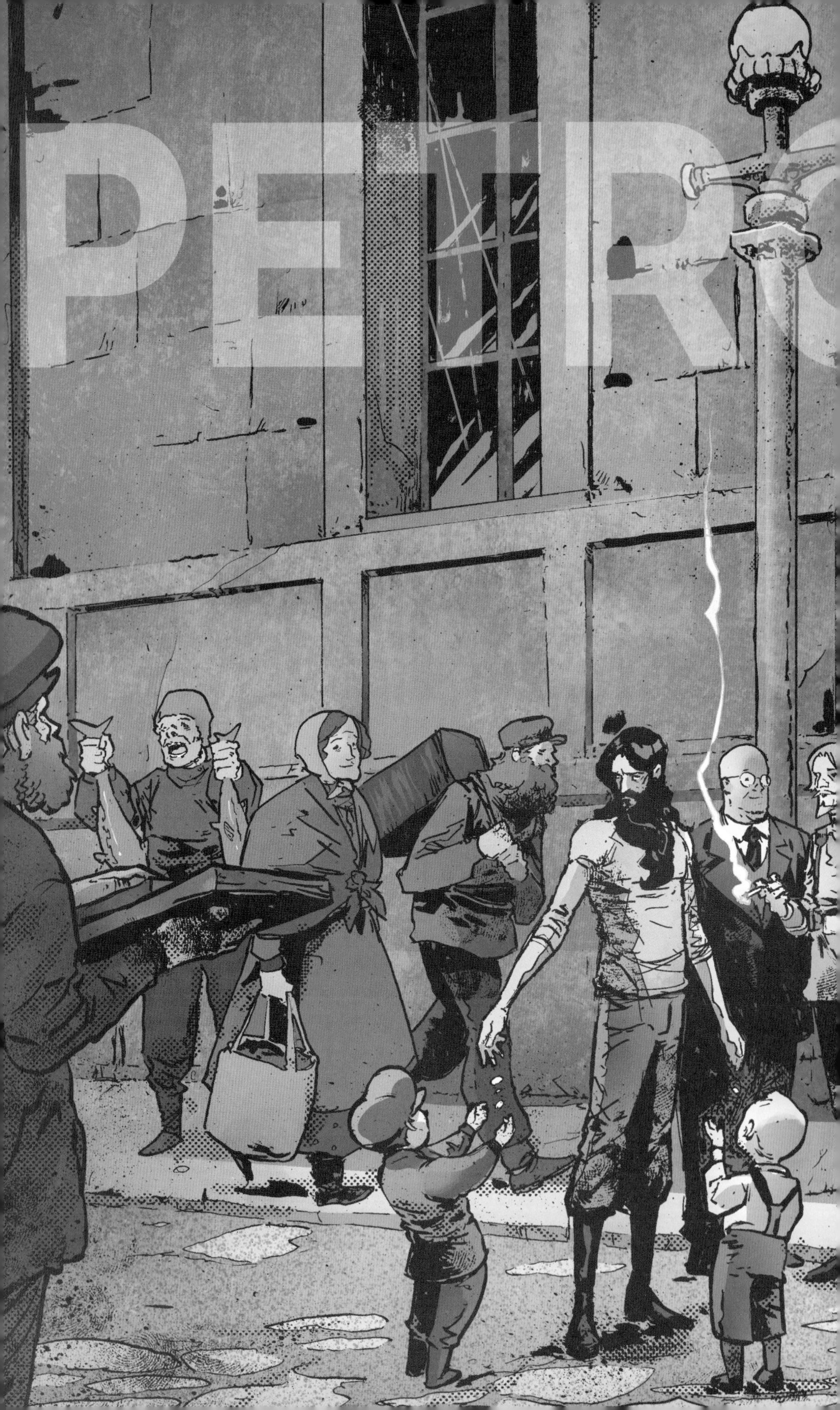
PETR

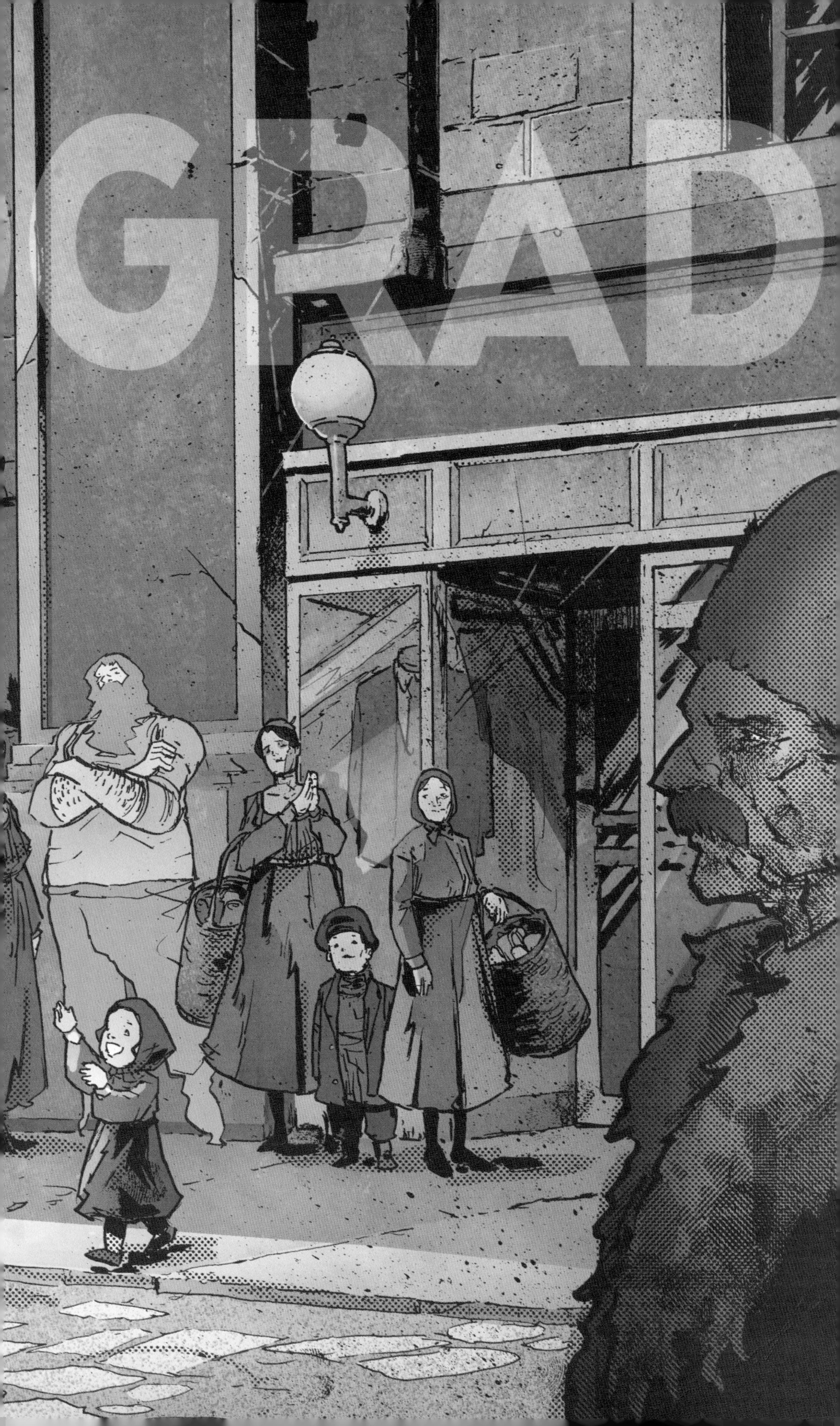
GRAD

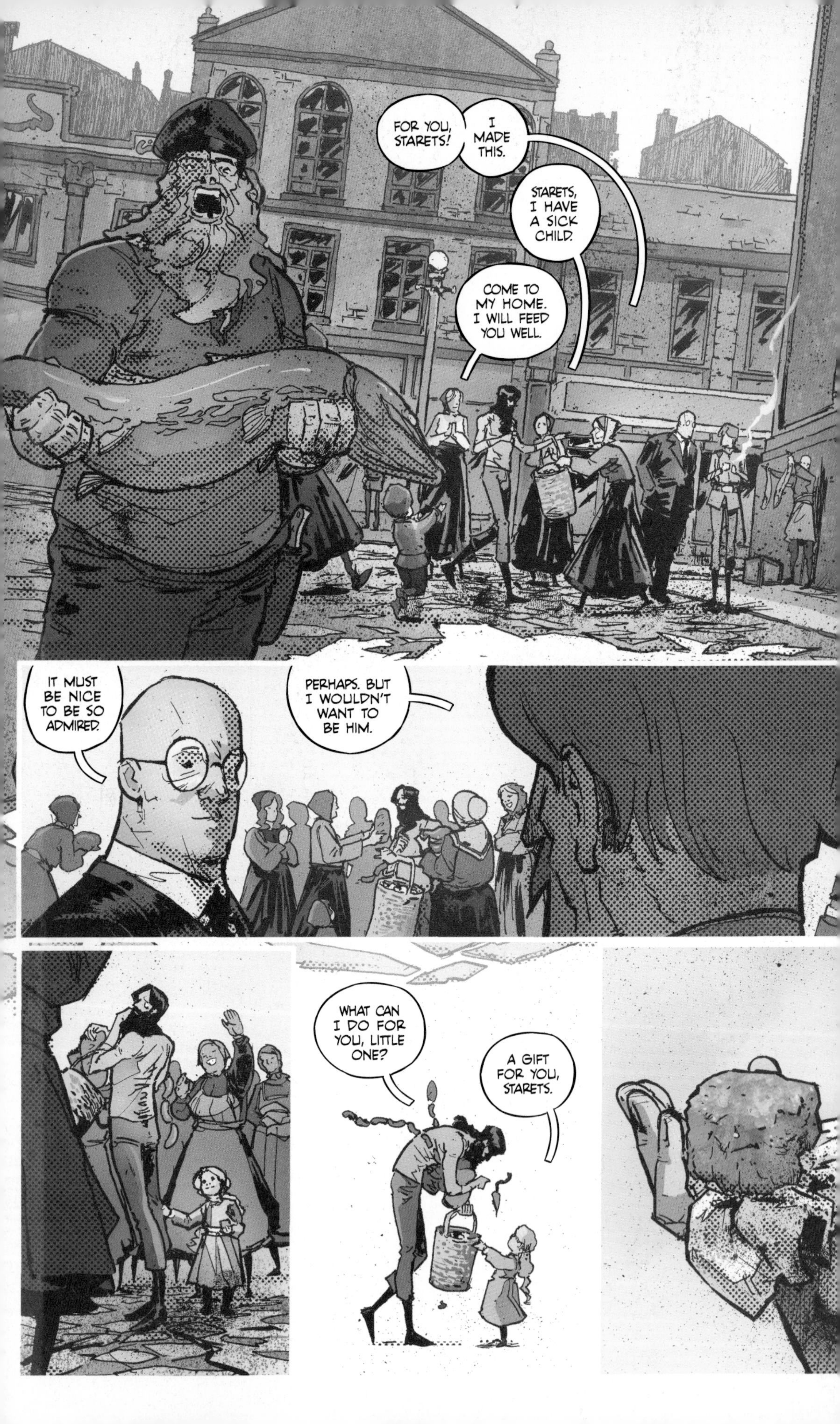
FOR YOU, STARETS!
I MADE THIS.
STARETS, I HAVE A SICK CHILD.
COME TO MY HOME. I WILL FEED YOU WELL.
IT MUST BE NICE TO BE SO ADMIRED.
PERHAPS. BUT I WOULDN'T WANT TO BE HIM.
WHAT CAN I DO FOR YOU, LITTLE ONE?
A GIFT FOR YOU, STARETS.

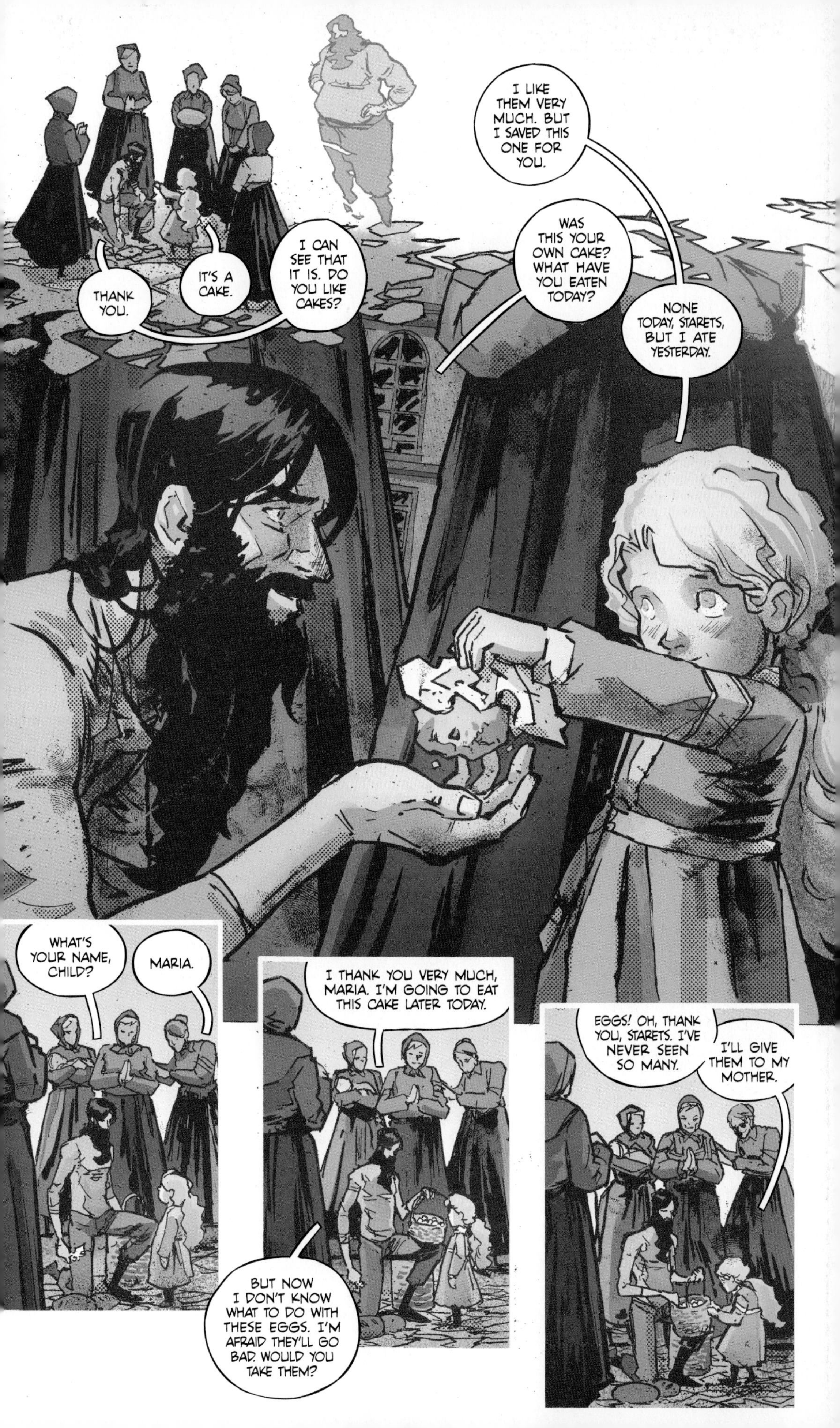
IT'S A CAKE.
THANK YOU.
I CAN SEE THAT IT IS. DO YOU LIKE CAKES?
I LIKE THEM VERY MUCH. BUT I SAVED THIS ONE FOR YOU.
WAS THIS YOUR OWN CAKE? WHAT HAVE YOU EATEN TODAY?
NONE TODAY, STARETS, BUT I ATE YESTERDAY.
WHAT'S YOUR NAME, CHILD?
MARIA.
I THANK YOU VERY MUCH, MARIA. I'M GOING TO EAT THIS CAKE LATER TODAY.
BUT NOW I DON'T KNOW WHAT TO DO WITH THESE EGGS. I'M AFRAID THEY'LL GO BAD. WOULD YOU TAKE THEM?
EGGS! OH, THANK YOU, STARETS. I'VE NEVER SEEN SO MANY.
I'LL GIVE THEM TO MY MOTHER.

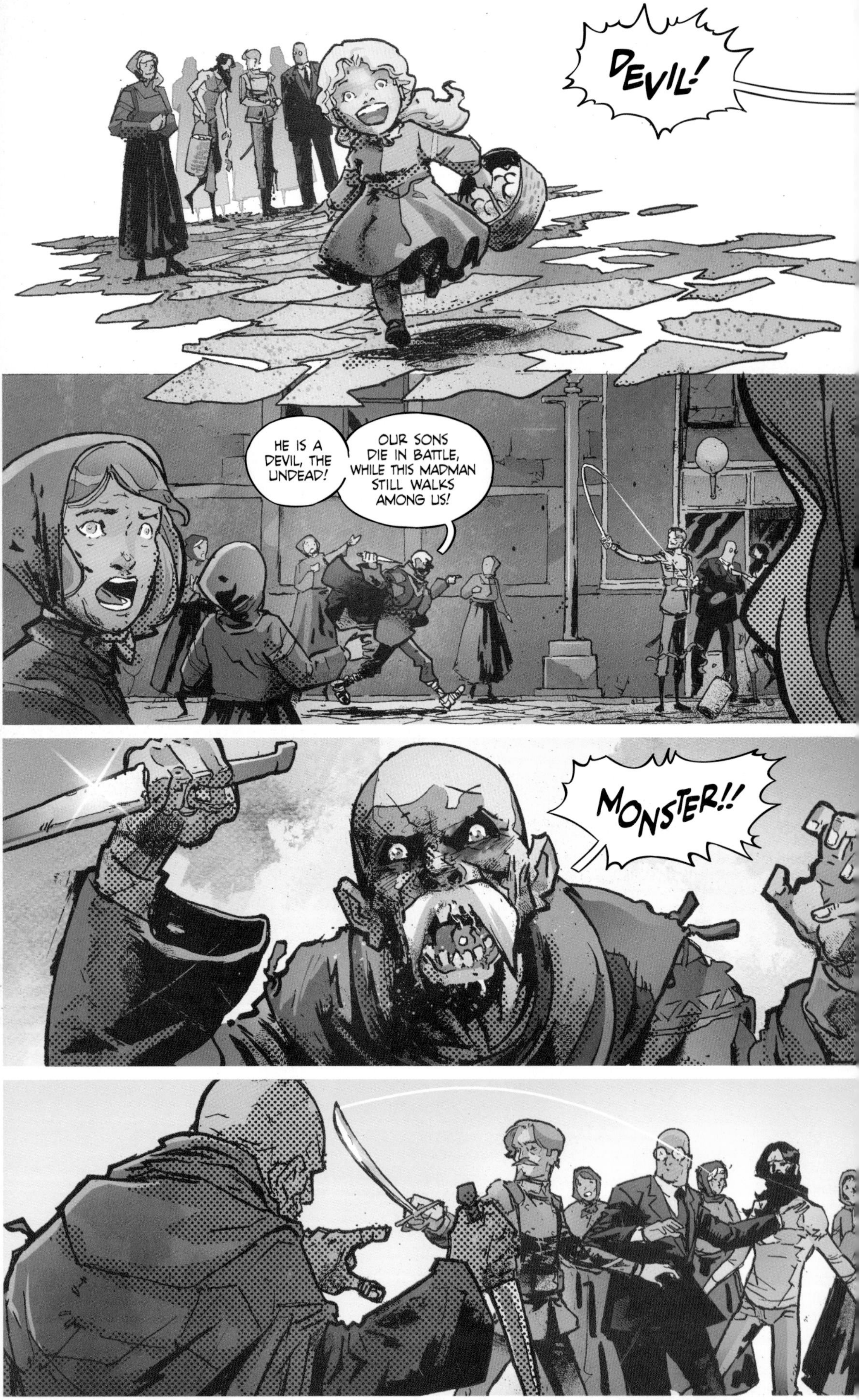
DEVIL!
HE IS A DEVIL, THE UNDEAD!
OUR SONS DIE IN BATTLE, WHILE THIS MADMAN STILL WALKS AMONG US!
MONSTER!!

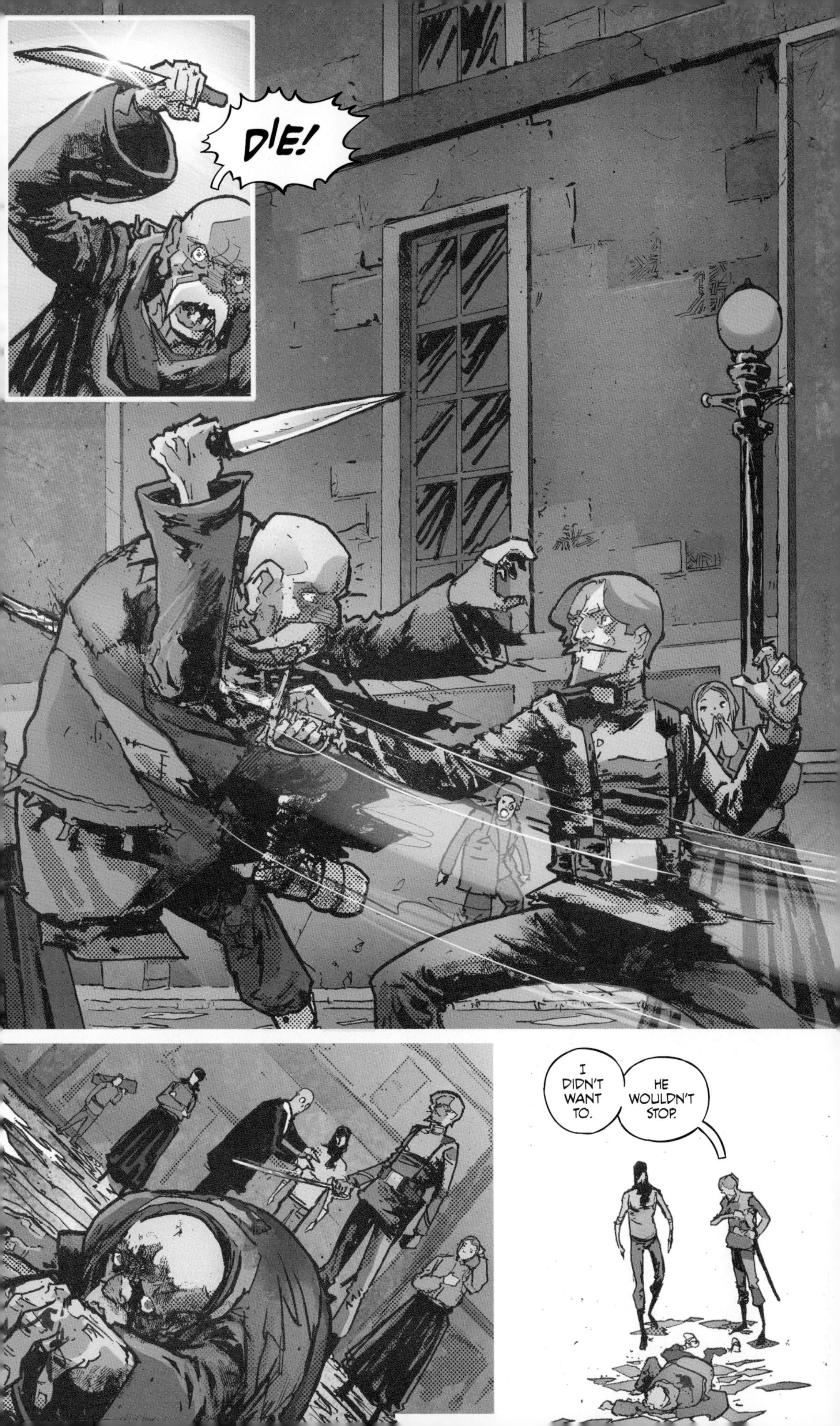
DIE!
I DIDN'T WANT TO.
HE WOULDN'T STOP.

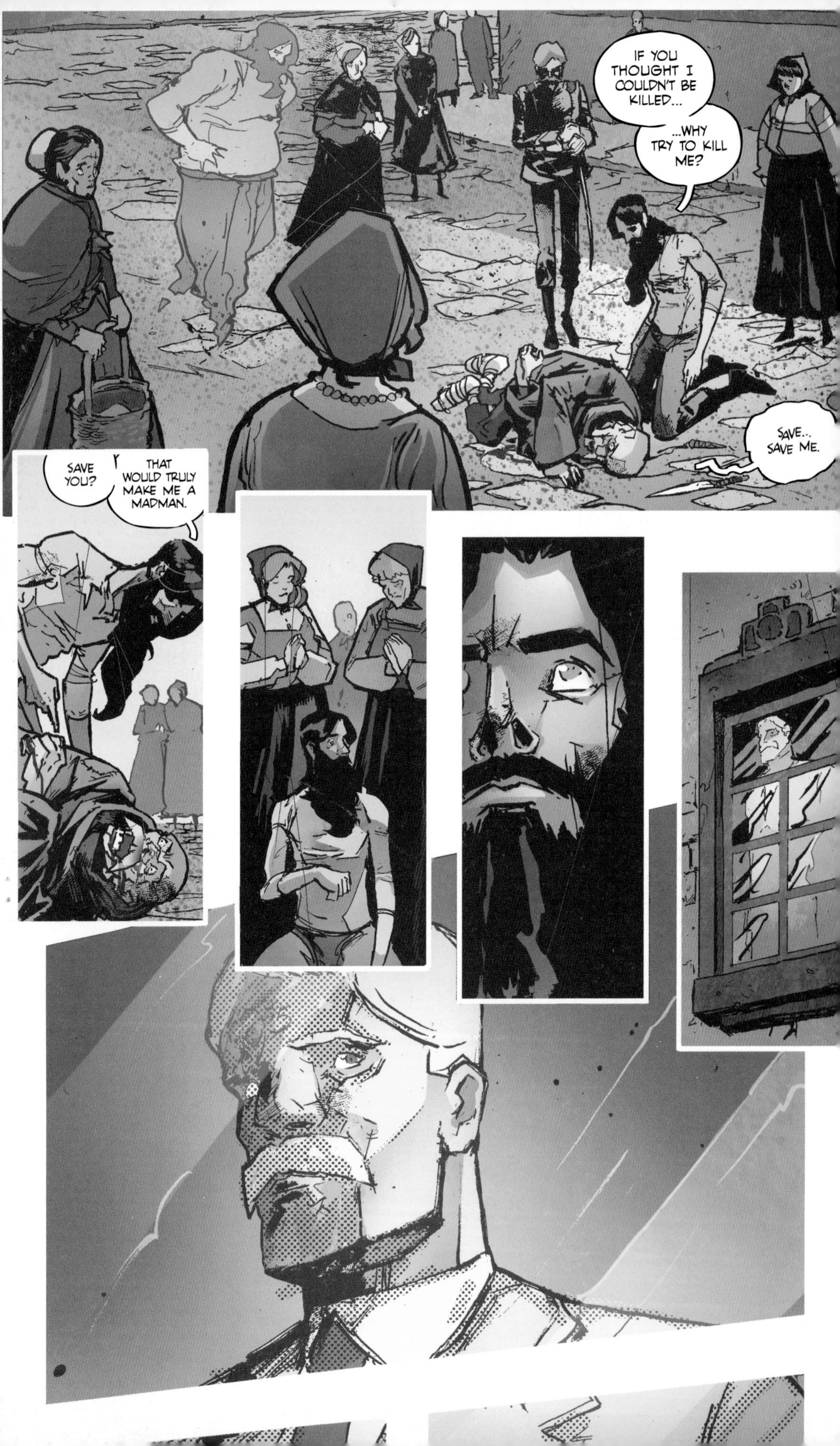
IF YOU THOUGHT I COULDN'T BE KILLED...
...WHY TRY TO KILL ME?
SAVE... SAVE ME.
SAVE YOU?
THAT WOULD TRULY MAKE ME A MADMAN.

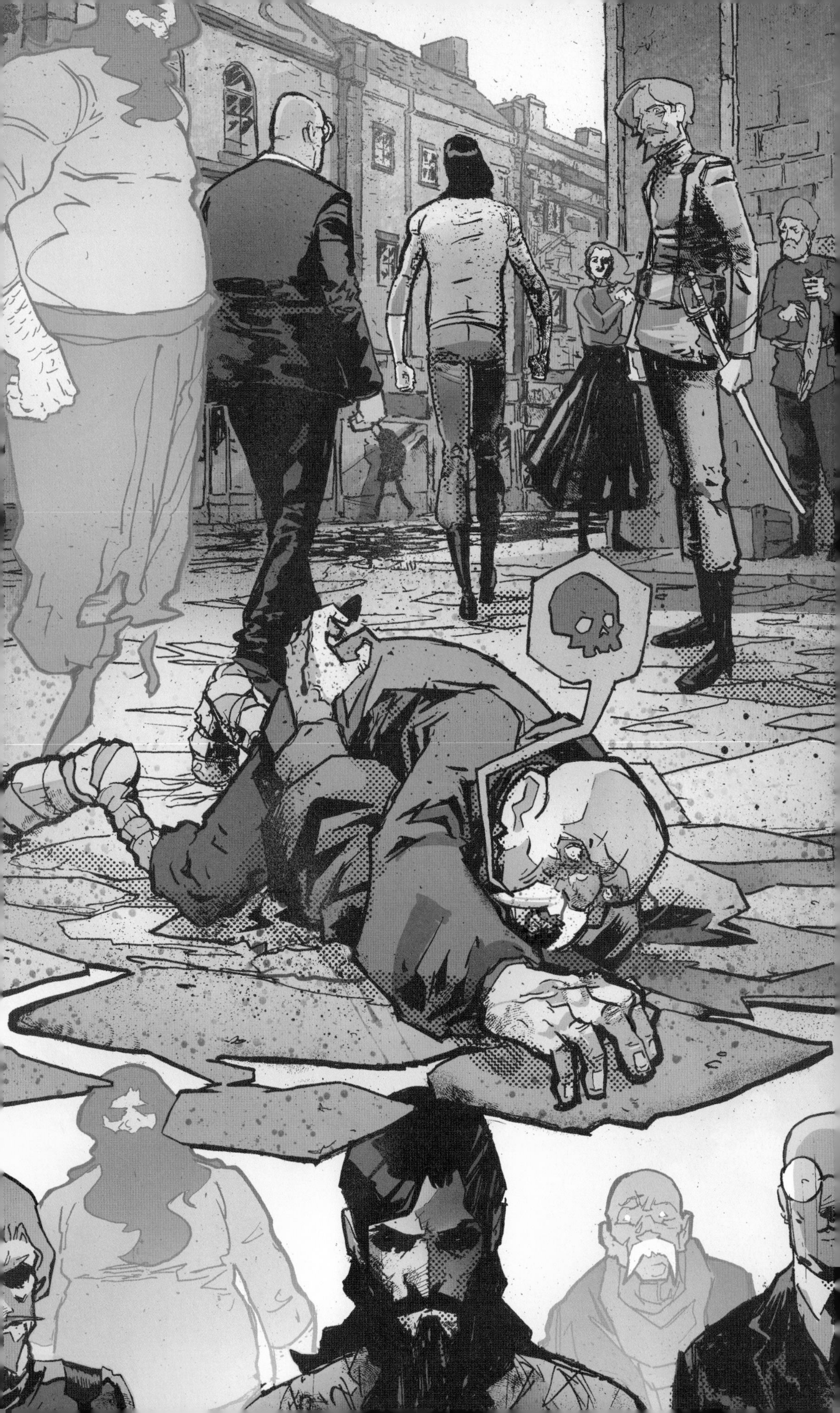

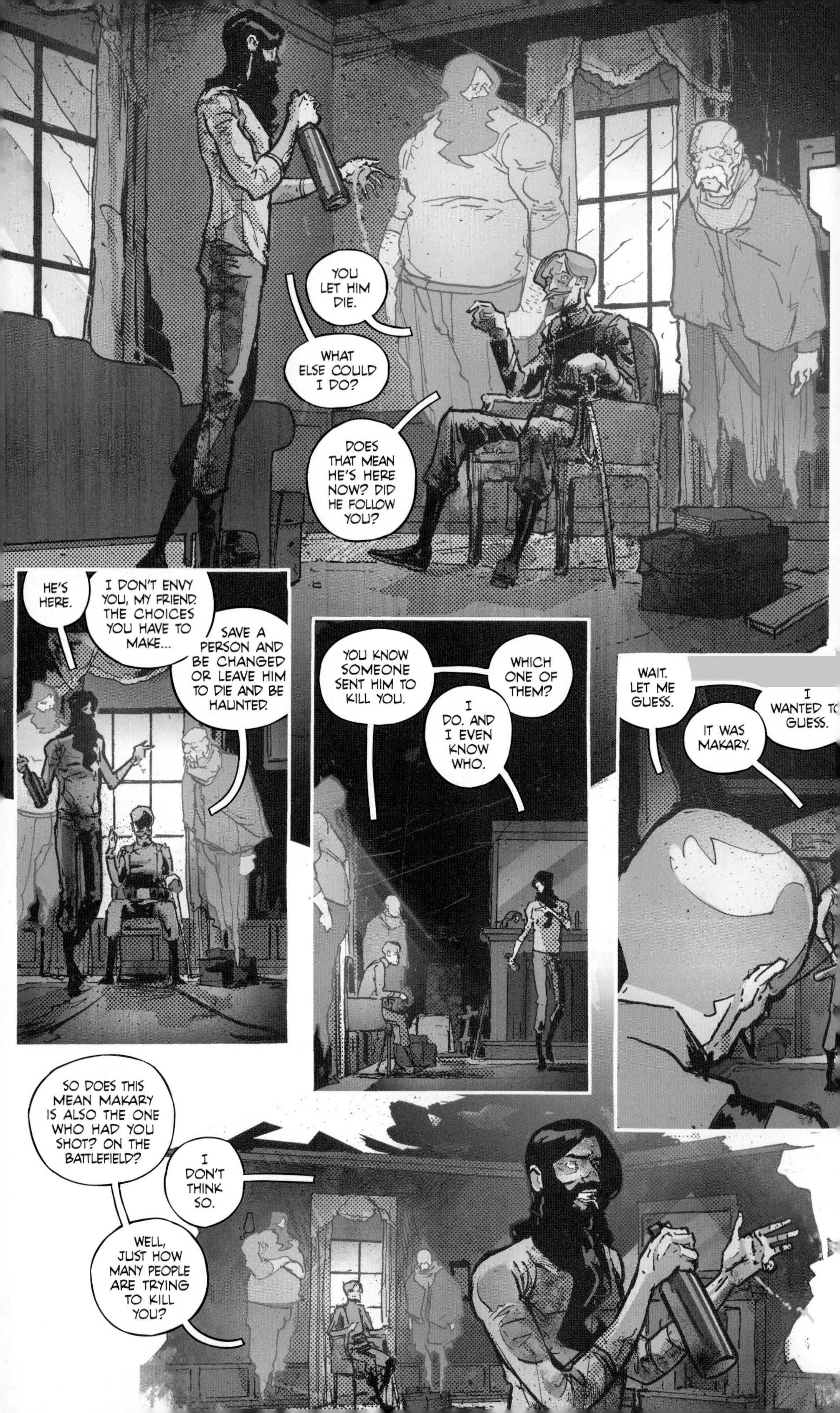
YOU LET HIM DIE.
WHAT ELSE COULD I DO?
DOES THAT MEAN HE'S HERE NOW? DID HE FOLLOW YOU?
HE'S HERE.
I DON'T ENVY YOU, MY FRIEND. THE CHOICES YOU HAVE TO MAKE...
SAVE A PERSON AND BE CHANGED OR LEAVE HIM TO DIE AND BE HAUNTED.
YOU KNOW SOMEONE SENT HIM TO KILL YOU.
WHICH ONE OF THEM?
I DO. AND I EVEN KNOW WHO.
WAIT. LET ME GUESS.
I WANTED TO GUESS.
IT WAS MAKARY.
SO DOES THIS MEAN MAKARY IS ALSO THE ONE WHO HAD YOU SHOT? ON THE BATTLEFIELD?
I DON'T THINK SO.
WELL, JUST HOW MANY PEOPLE ARE TRYING TO KILL YOU?

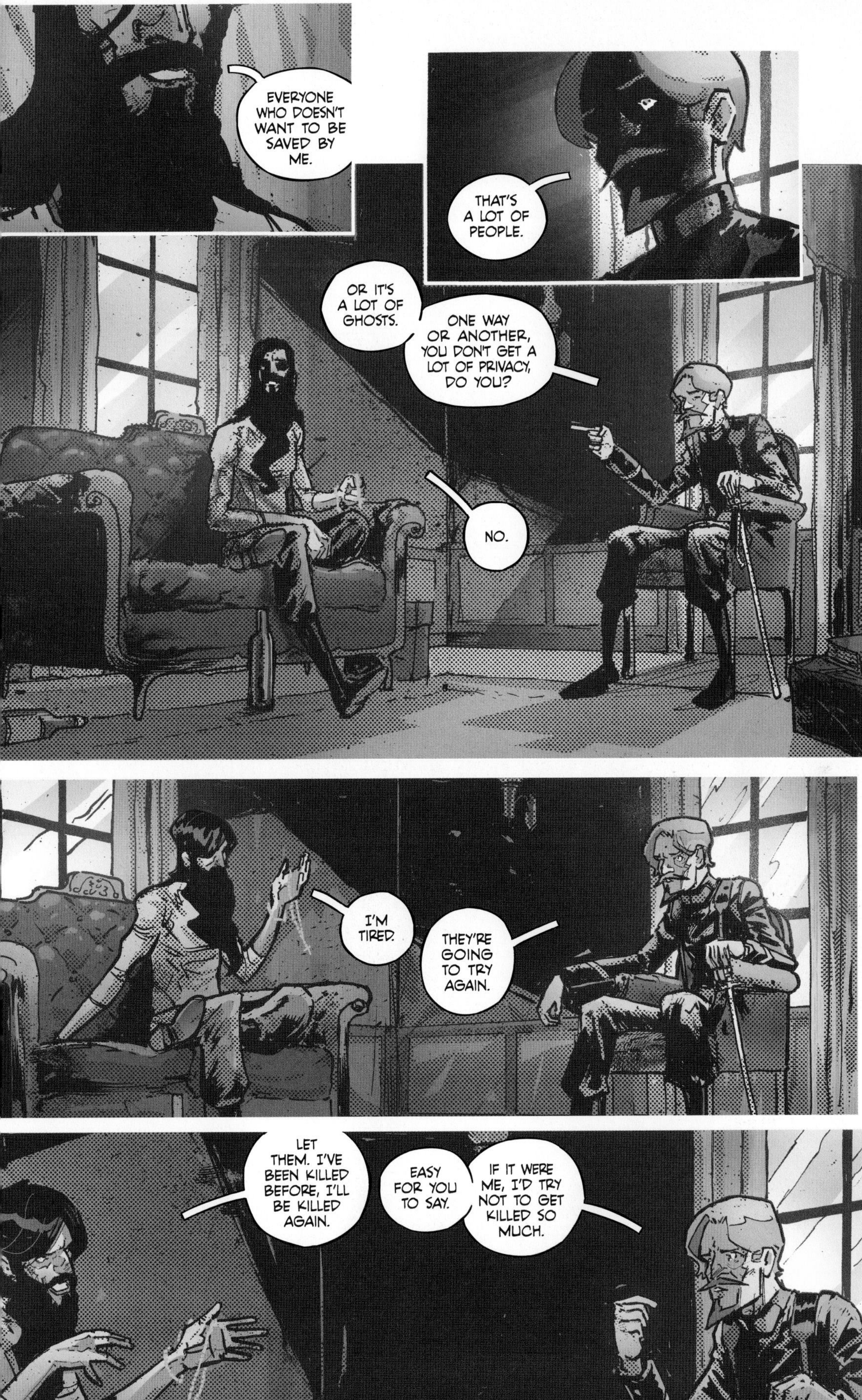
EVERYONE WHO DOESN'T WANT TO BE SAVED BY ME.
THAT'S A LOT OF PEOPLE.
OR IT'S A LOT OF GHOSTS.
ONE WAY OR ANOTHER, YOU DON'T GET A LOT OF PRIVACY, DO YOU?
NO.
I'M TIRED.
THEY'RE GOING TO TRY AGAIN.
LET THEM. I'VE BEEN KILLED BEFORE, I'LL BE KILLED AGAIN.
EASY FOR YOU TO SAY.
IF IT WERE ME, I'D TRY NOT TO GET KILLED SO MUCH.

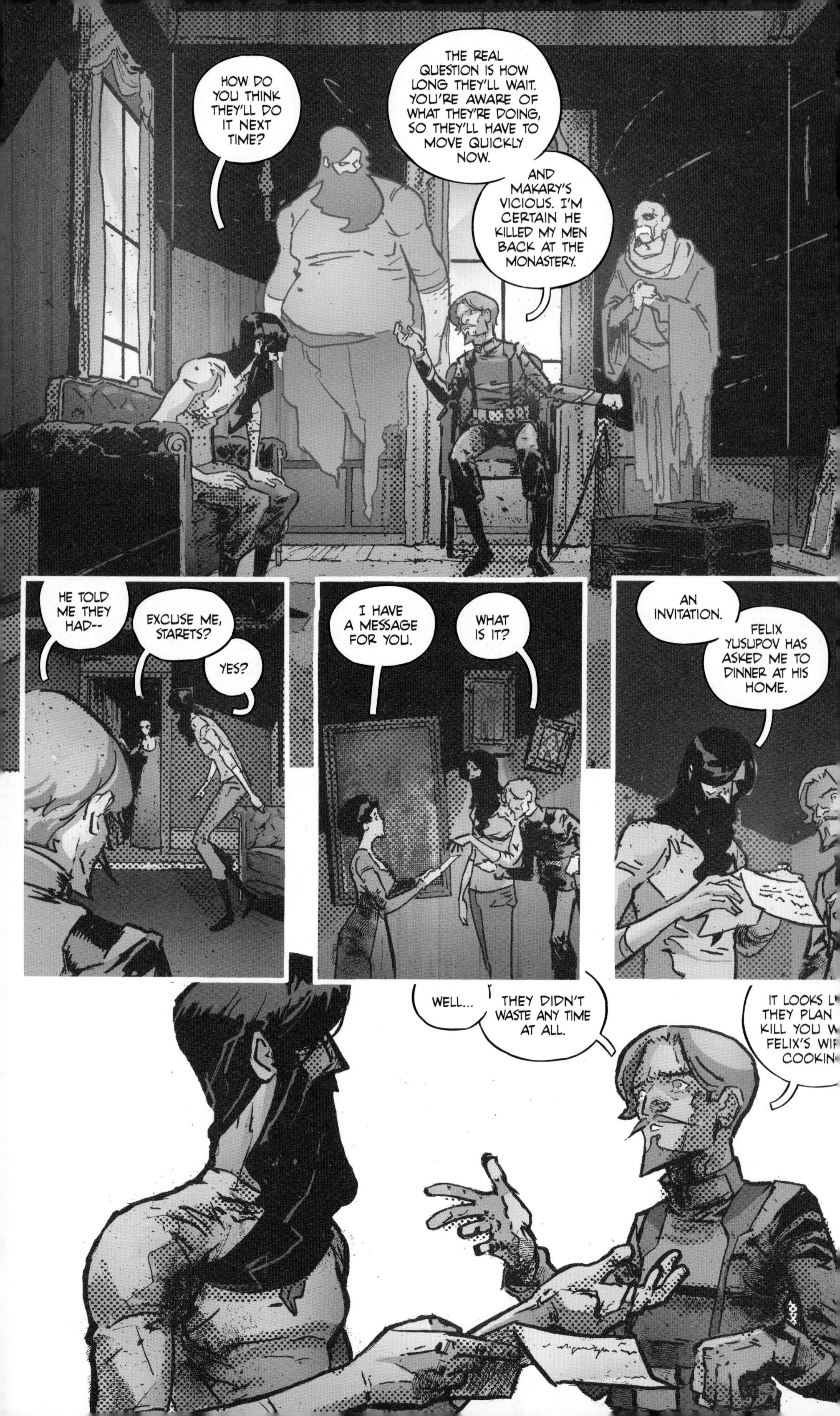
HOW DO YOU THINK THEY'LL DO IT NEXT TIME?
THE REAL QUESTION IS HOW LONG THEY'LL WAIT. YOU'RE AWARE OF WHAT THEY'RE DOING, SO THEY'LL HAVE TO MOVE QUICKLY NOW.
AND MAKARY'S VICIOUS. I'M CERTAIN HE KILLED MY MEN BACK AT THE MONASTERY.
HE TOLD ME THEY HAD--
EXCUSE ME, STARETS?
YES?
I HAVE A MESSAGE FOR YOU.
WHAT IS IT?
AN INVITATION.
FELIX YUSUPOV HAS ASKED ME TO DINNER AT HIS HOME.
WELL...
THEY DIDN'T WASTE ANY TIME AT ALL.

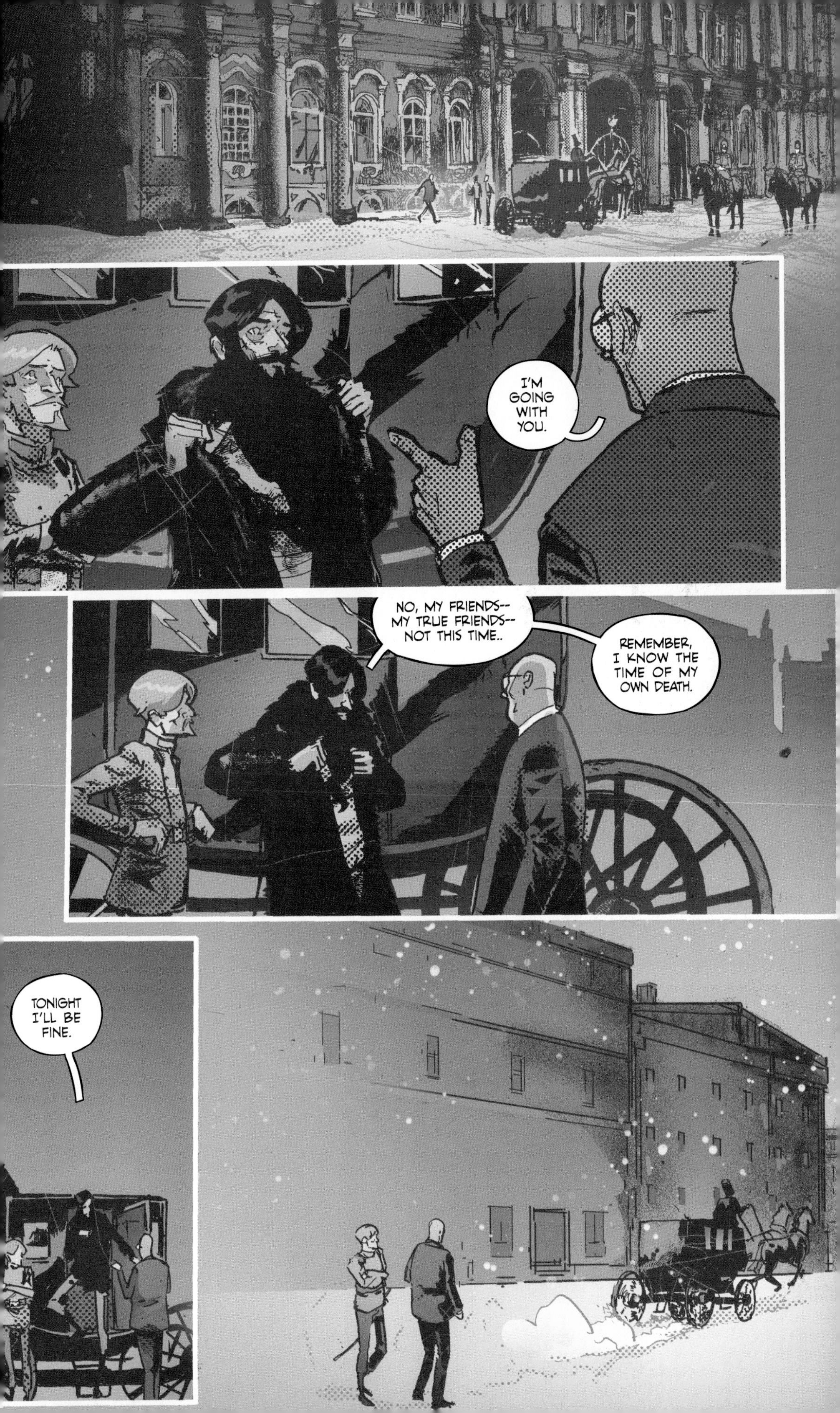
I'M GOING WITH YOU.
NO, MY FRIENDS-- MY TRUE FRIENDS-- NOT THIS TIME..
REMEMBER, I KNOW THE TIME OF MY OWN DEATH.
TONIGHT I'LL BE FINE.

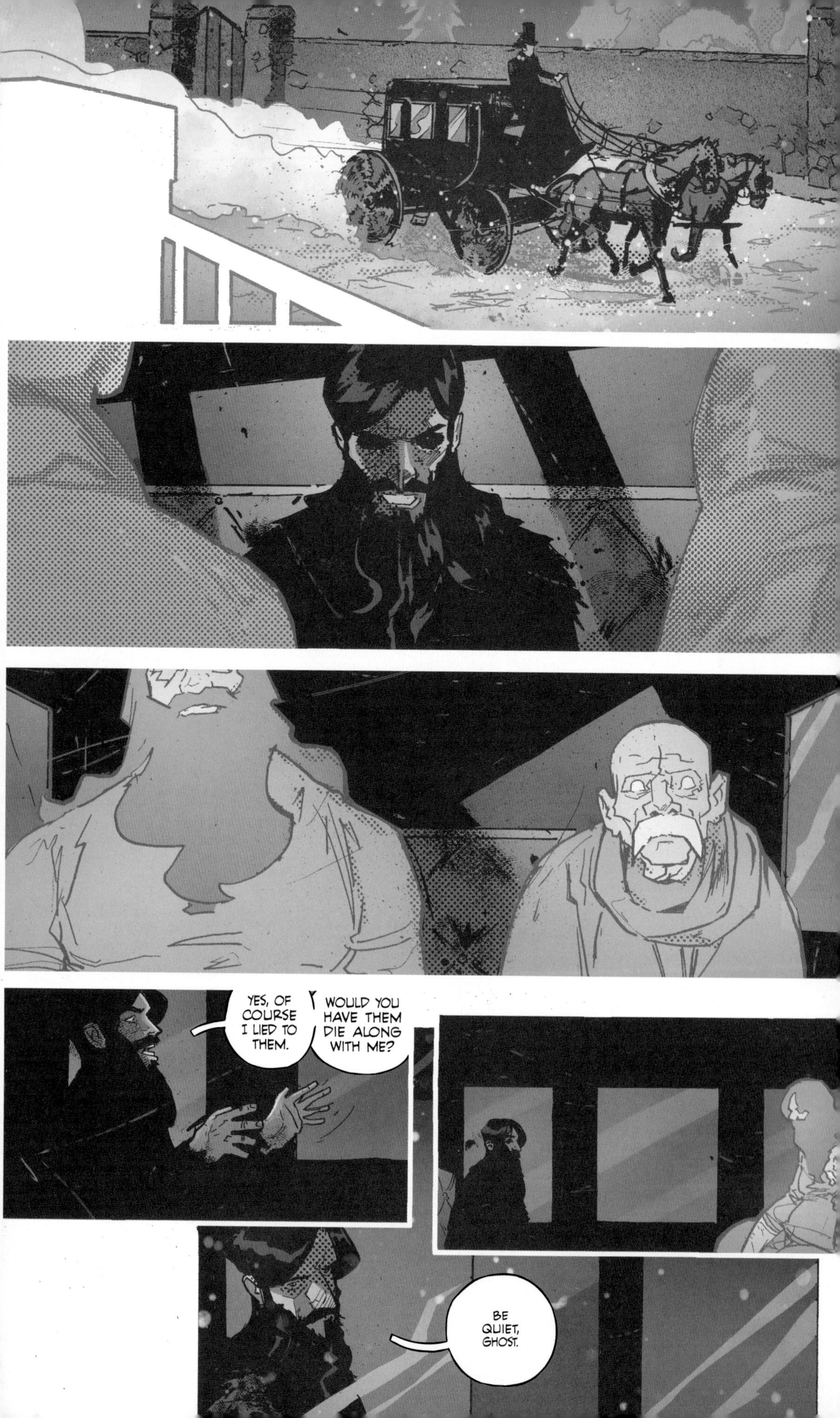
YES, OF COURSE I LIED TO THEM.
WOULD YOU HAVE THEM DIE ALONG WITH ME?
BE QUIET, GHOST.

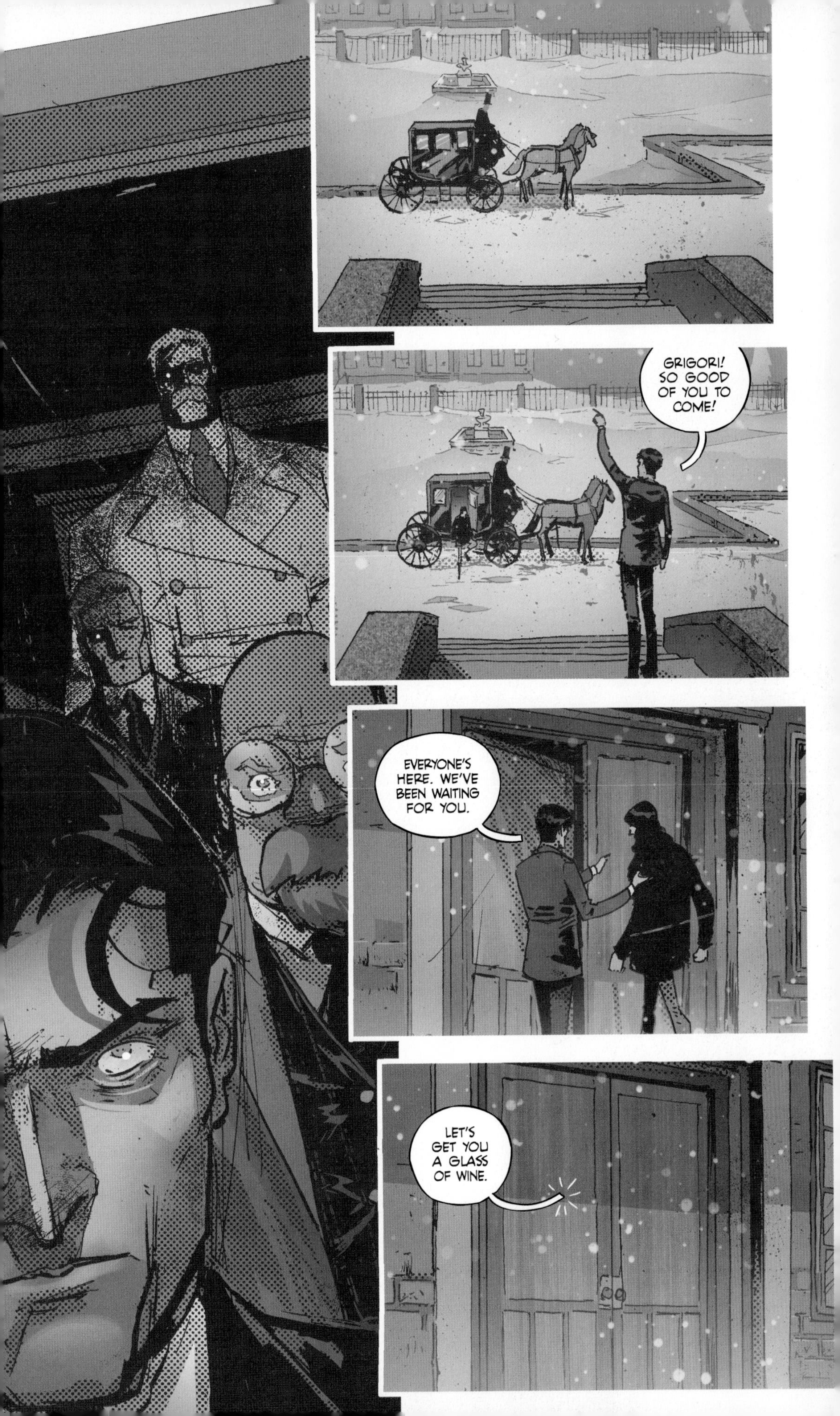
GRIGORI! SO GOOD OF YOU TO COME!
EVERYONE'S HERE. WE'VE BEEN WAITING FOR YOU.
LET'S GET YOU A GLASS OF WINE.

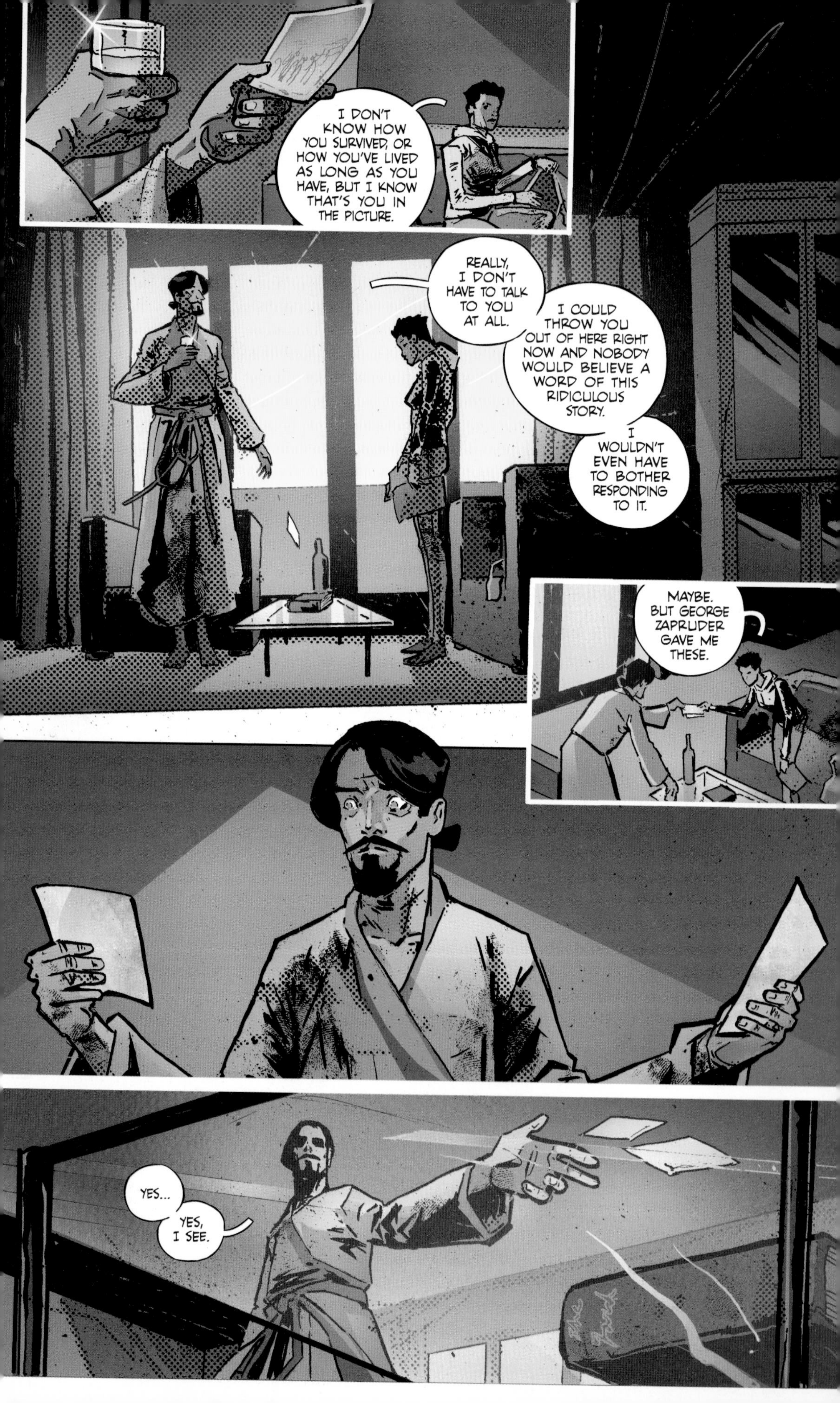
I DON'T KNOW HOW YOU SURVIVED, OR HOW YOU'VE LIVED AS LONG AS YOU HAVE, BUT I KNOW THAT'S YOU IN THE PICTURE.
REALLY, I DON'T HAVE TO TALK TO YOU AT ALL.
I COULD THROW YOU OUT OF HERE RIGHT NOW AND NOBODY WOULD BELIEVE A WORD OF THIS RIDICULOUS STORY.
I WOULDN'T EVEN HAVE TO BOTHER RESPONDING TO IT.
MAYBE. BUT GEORGE ZAPRUDER GAVE ME THESE.
YES...
YES, I SEE.

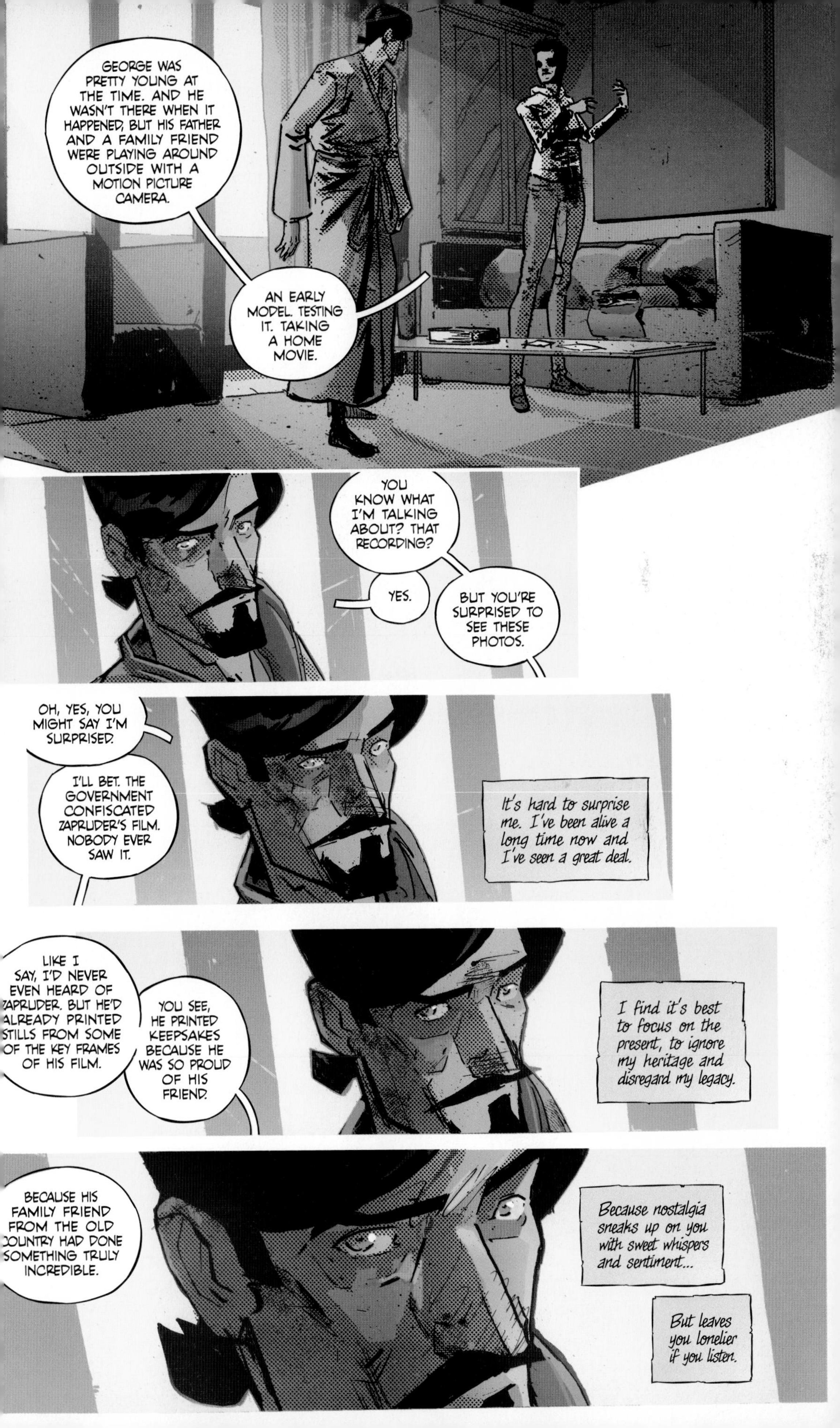
GEORGE WAS PRETTY YOUNG AT THE TIME. AND HE WASN'T THERE WHEN IT HAPPENED, BUT HIS FATHER AND A FAMILY FRIEND WERE PLAYING AROUND OUTSIDE WITH A MOTION PICTURE CAMERA.
AN EARLY MODEL. TESTING IT. TAKING A HOME MOVIE.
YOU KNOW WHAT I'M TALKING ABOUT? THAT RECORDING?
YES.
BUT YOU'RE SURPRISED TO SEE THESE PHOTOS.
OH, YES, YOU MIGHT SAY I'M SURPRISED.
I'LL BET. THE GOVERNMENT CONFISCATED ZAPRUDER'S FILM. NOBODY EVER SAW IT.
It's hard to surprise me. I've been alive a long time now and I've seen a great deal.
LIKE I SAY, I'D NEVER EVEN HEARD OF ZAPRUDER. BUT HE'D ALREADY PRINTED STILLS FROM SOME OF THE KEY FRAMES OF HIS FILM.
YOU SEE, HE PRINTED KEEPSAKES BECAUSE HE WAS SO PROUD OF HIS FRIEND.
I find it's best to focus on the present, to ignore my heritage and disregard my legacy.
BECAUSE HIS FAMILY FRIEND FROM THE OLD COUNTRY HAD DONE SOMETHING TRULY INCREDIBLE.
Because nostalgia sneaks up on you with sweet whispers and sentiment...
But leaves you lonelier if you listen.

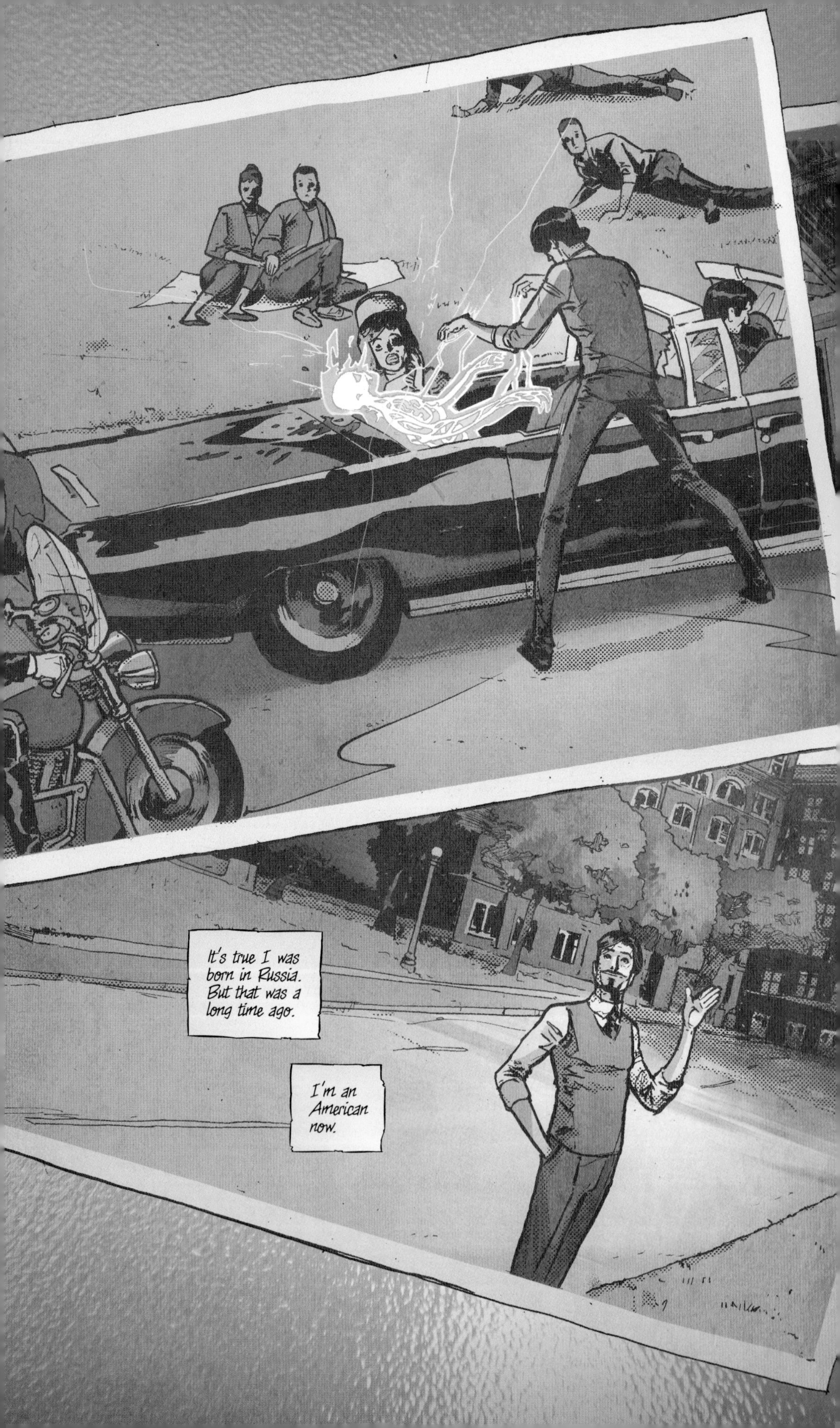
It's true I was born in Russia. But that was a long time ago.
I'm an American now.

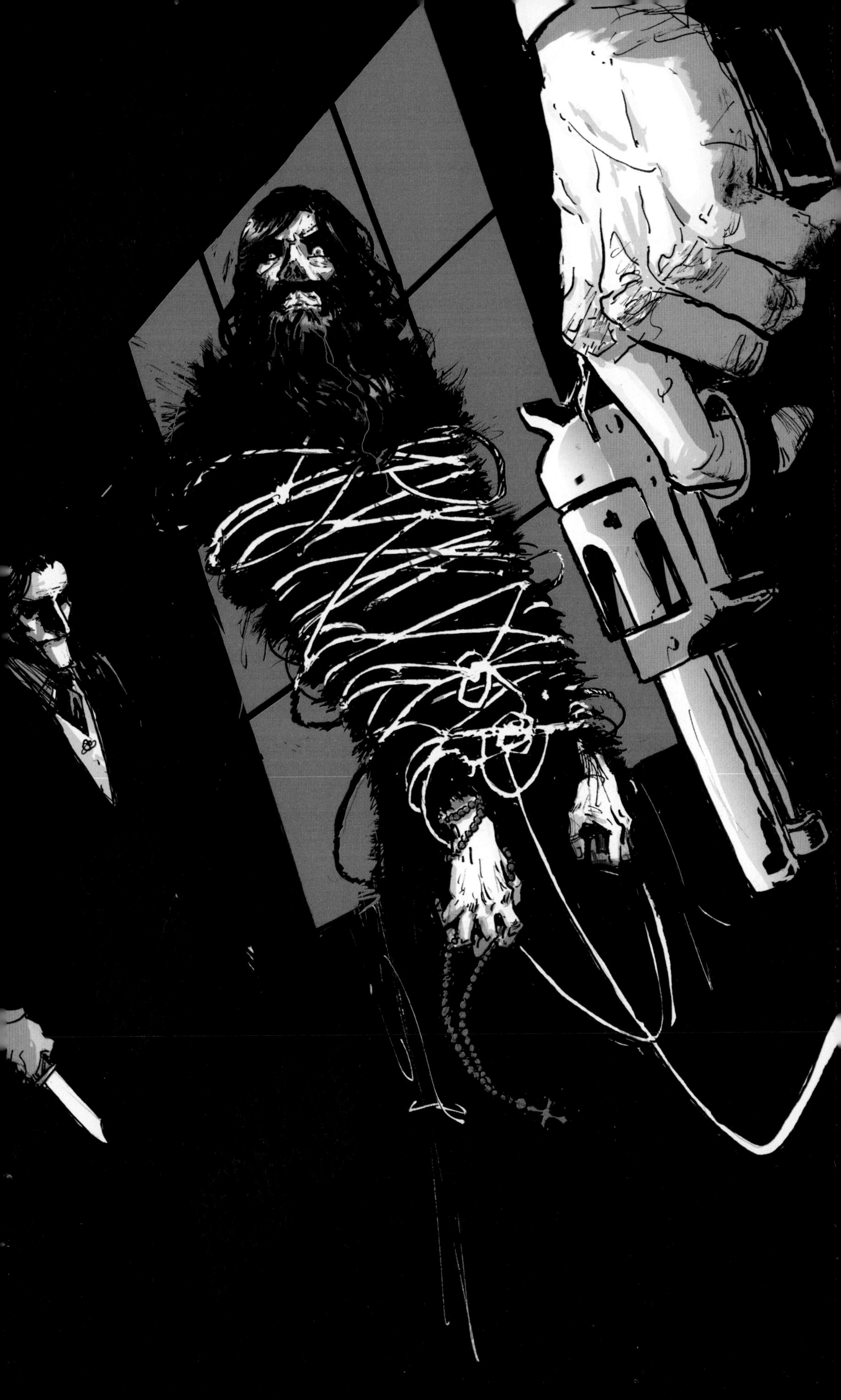

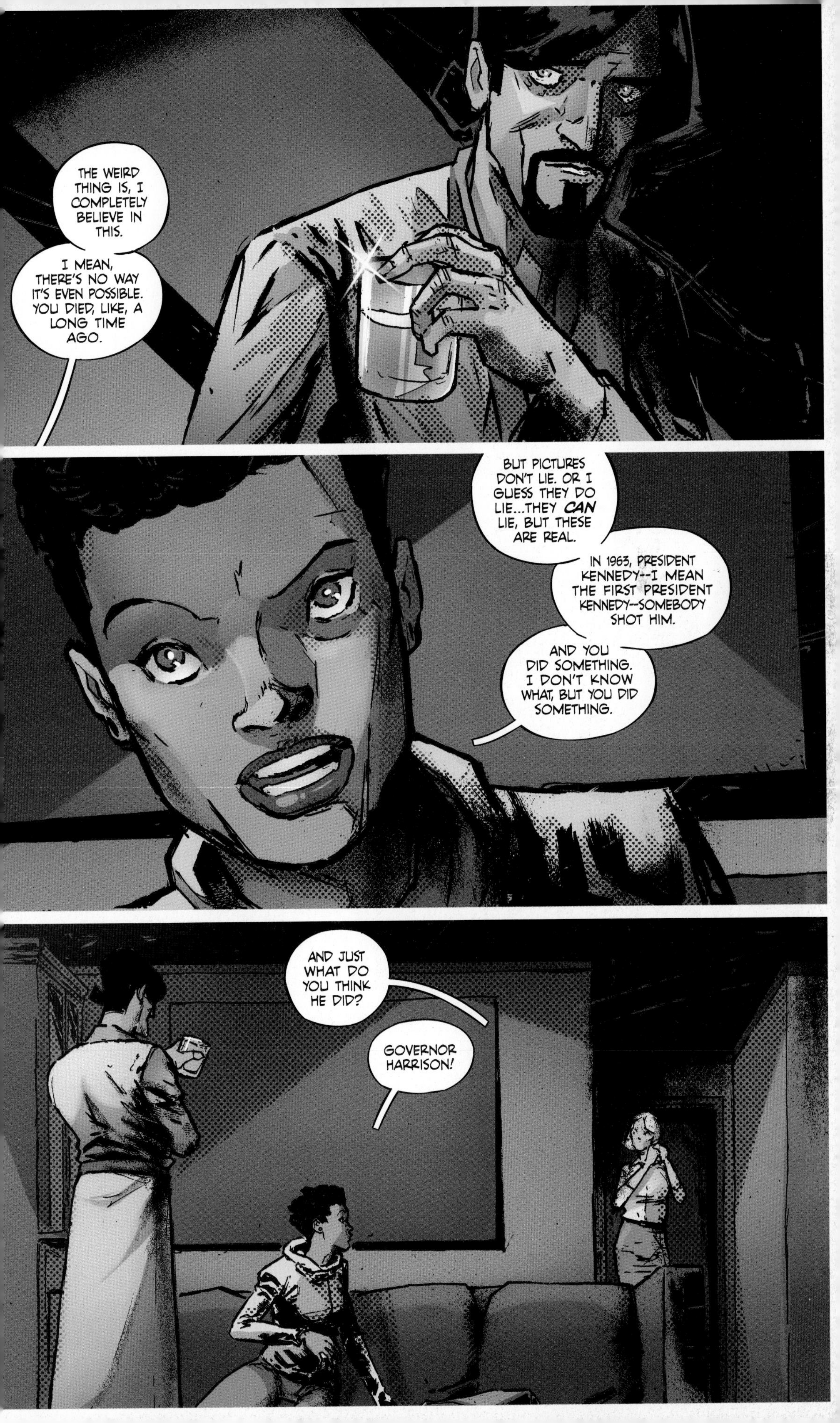
THE WEIRD THING IS, I COMPLETELY BELIEVE IN THIS.
I MEAN, THERE'S NO WAY IT'S EVEN POSSIBLE. YOU DIED, LIKE, A LONG TIME AGO.
BUT PICTURES DON'T LIE. OR I GUESS THEY DO LIE...THEY *CAN* LIE, BUT THESE ARE REAL.
IN 1963, PRESIDENT KENNEDY--I MEAN THE FIRST PRESIDENT KENNEDY--SOMEBODY SHOT HIM.
AND YOU DID SOMETHING. I DON'T KNOW WHAT, BUT YOU DID SOMETHING.
AND JUST WHAT DO YOU THINK HE DID?
GOVERNOR HARRISON!

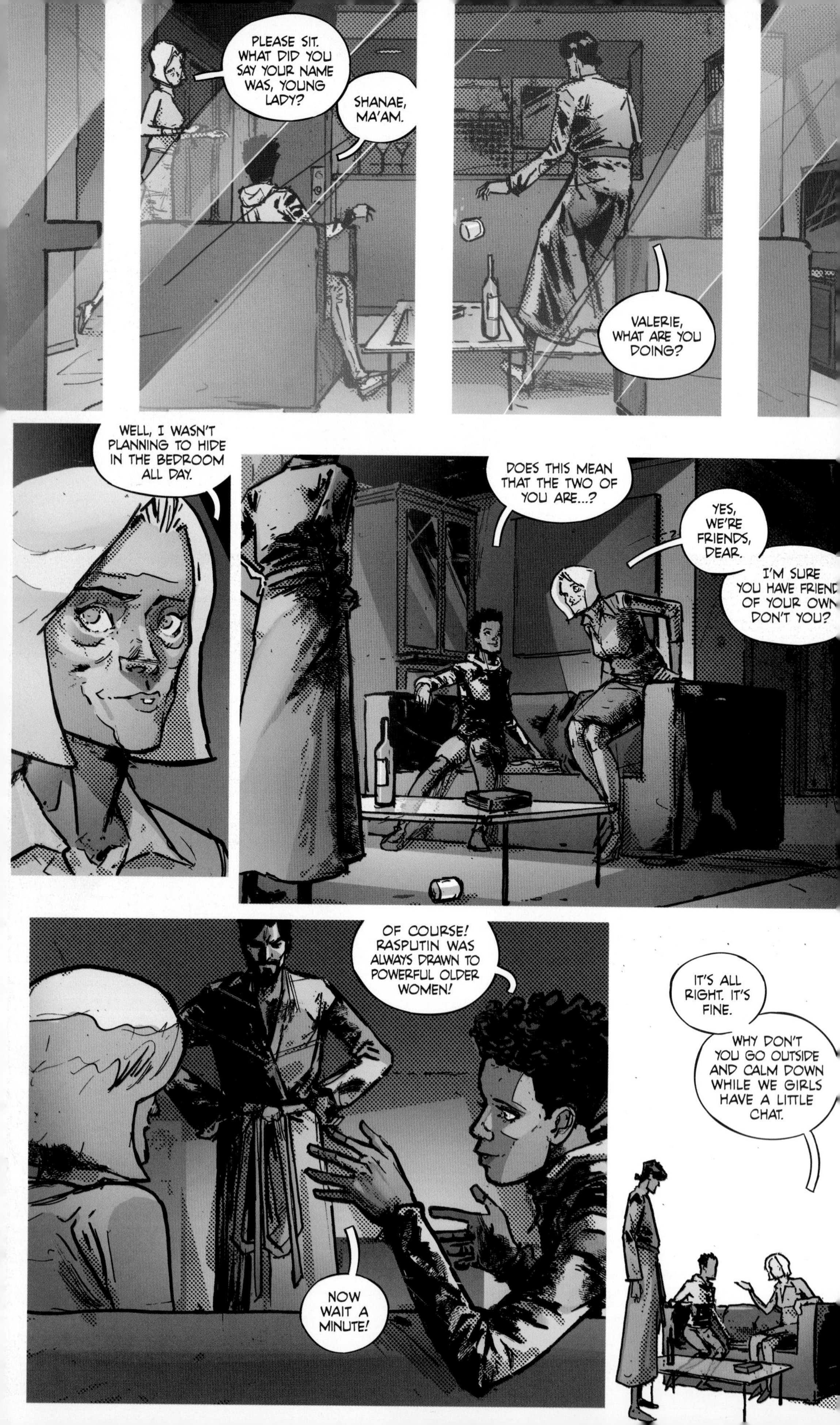
PLEASE SIT. WHAT DID YOU SAY YOUR NAME WAS, YOUNG LADY?
SHANAE, MA'AM.
VALERIE, WHAT ARE YOU DOING?
WELL, I WASN'T PLANNING TO HIDE IN THE BEDROOM ALL DAY.
DOES THIS MEAN THAT THE TWO OF YOU ARE...?
YES, WE'RE FRIENDS, DEAR.
I'M SURE YOU HAVE FRIEND OF YOUR OWN DON'T YOU?
OF COURSE! RASPUTIN WAS ALWAYS DRAWN TO POWERFUL OLDER WOMEN!
NOW WAIT A MINUTE!
IT'S ALL RIGHT. IT'S FINE.
WHY DON'T YOU GO OUTSIDE AND CALM DOWN WHILE WE GIRLS HAVE A LITTLE CHAT.

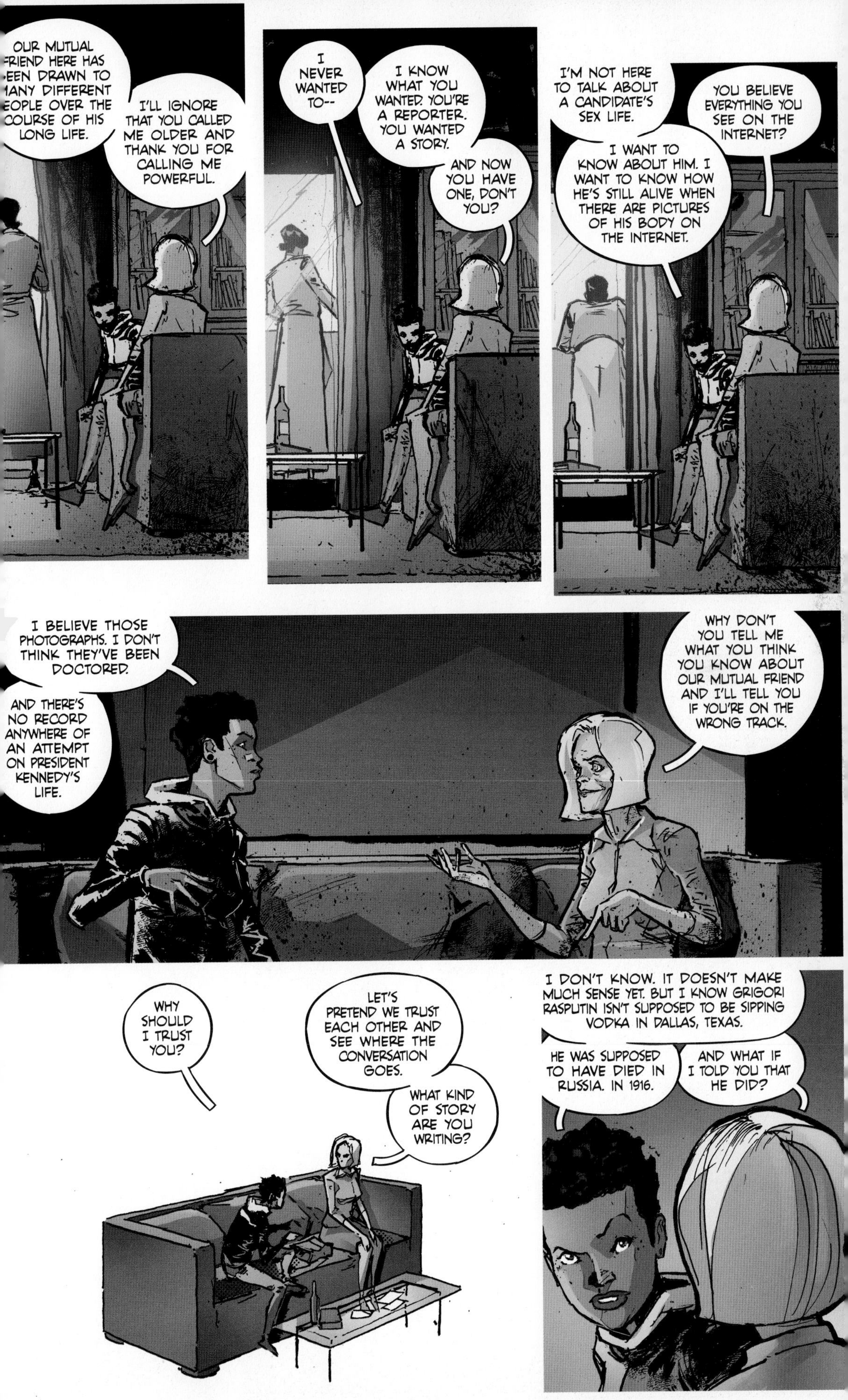
OUR MUTUAL FRIEND HERE HAS BEEN DRAWN TO MANY DIFFERENT PEOPLE OVER THE COURSE OF HIS LONG LIFE.
I'LL IGNORE THAT YOU CALLED ME OLDER AND THANK YOU FOR CALLING ME POWERFUL.
I NEVER WANTED TO--
I KNOW WHAT YOU WANTED. YOU'RE A REPORTER. YOU WANTED A STORY.
AND NOW YOU HAVE ONE, DON'T YOU?
I'M NOT HERE TO TALK ABOUT A CANDIDATE'S SEX LIFE.
I WANT TO KNOW ABOUT HIM. I WANT TO KNOW HOW HE'S STILL ALIVE WHEN THERE ARE PICTURES OF HIS BODY ON THE INTERNET.
YOU BELIEVE EVERYTHING YOU SEE ON THE INTERNET?
I BELIEVE THOSE PHOTOGRAPHS. I DON'T THINK THEY'VE BEEN DOCTORED.
AND THERE'S NO RECORD ANYWHERE OF AN ATTEMPT ON PRESIDENT KENNEDY'S LIFE.
WHY DON'T YOU TELL ME WHAT YOU THINK YOU KNOW ABOUT OUR MUTUAL FRIEND AND I'LL TELL YOU IF YOU'RE ON THE WRONG TRACK.
WHY SHOULD I TRUST YOU?
LET'S PRETEND WE TRUST EACH OTHER AND SEE WHERE THE CONVERSATION GOES.
WHAT KIND OF STORY ARE YOU WRITING?
I DON'T KNOW. IT DOESN'T MAKE MUCH SENSE YET. BUT I KNOW GRIGORI RASPUTIN ISN'T SUPPOSED TO BE SIPPING VODKA IN DALLAS, TEXAS.
HE WAS SUPPOSED TO HAVE DIED IN RUSSIA. IN 1916.
AND WHAT IF I TOLD YOU THAT HE DID?

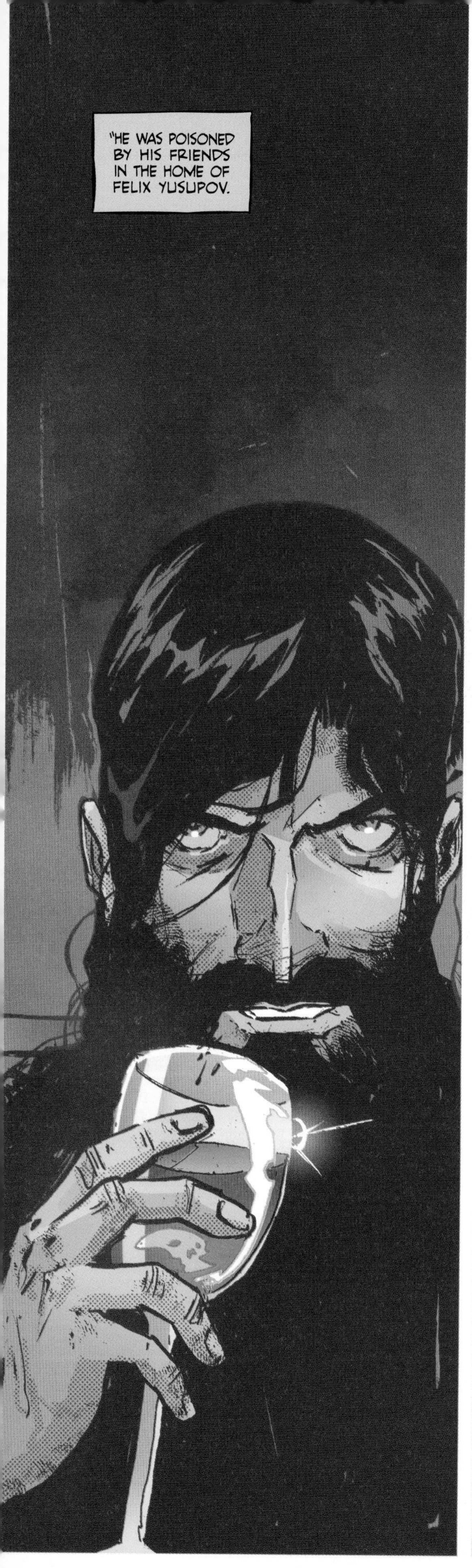
"HE WAS POISONED BY HIS FRIENDS IN THE HOME OF FELIX YUSUPOV.
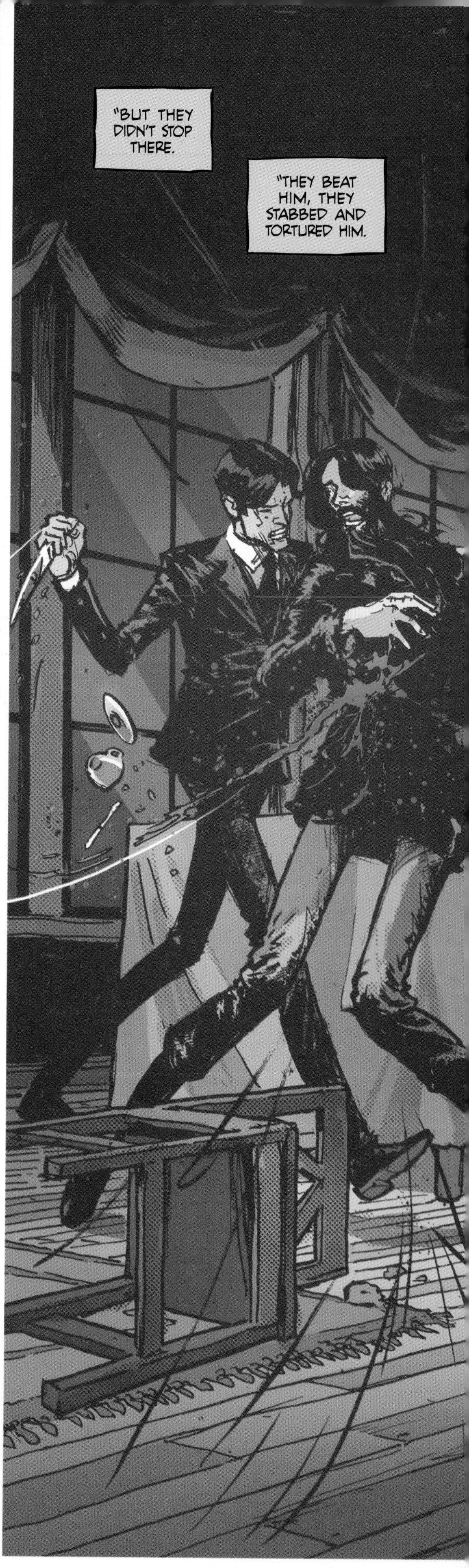
"BUT THEY DIDN'T STOP THERE.
"THEY BEAT HIM, THEY STABBED AND TORTURED HIM.

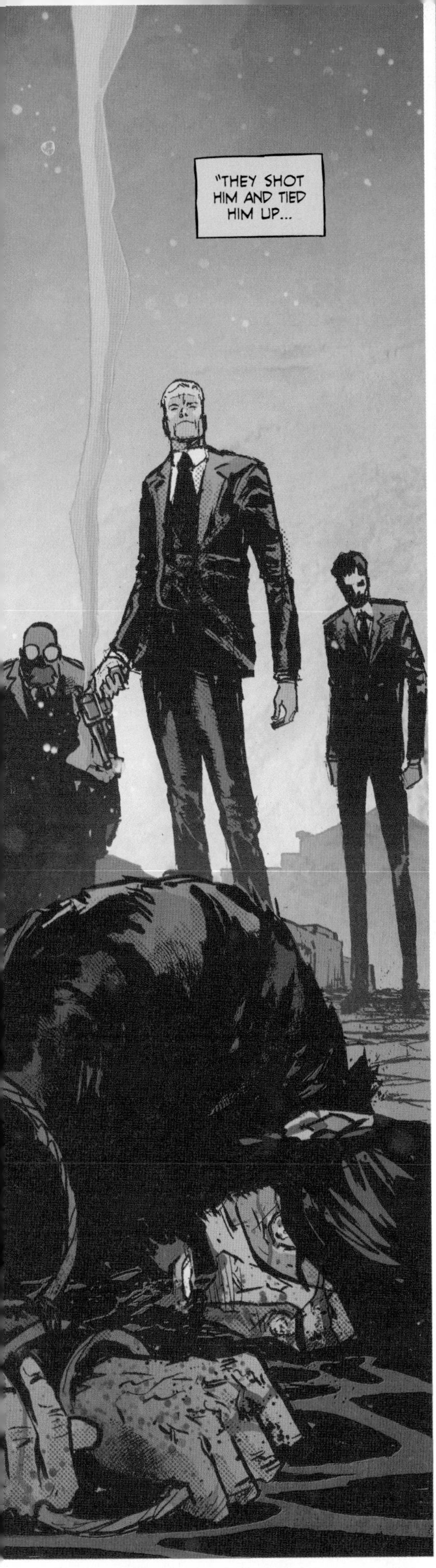
"THEY SHOT HIM AND TIED HIM UP...
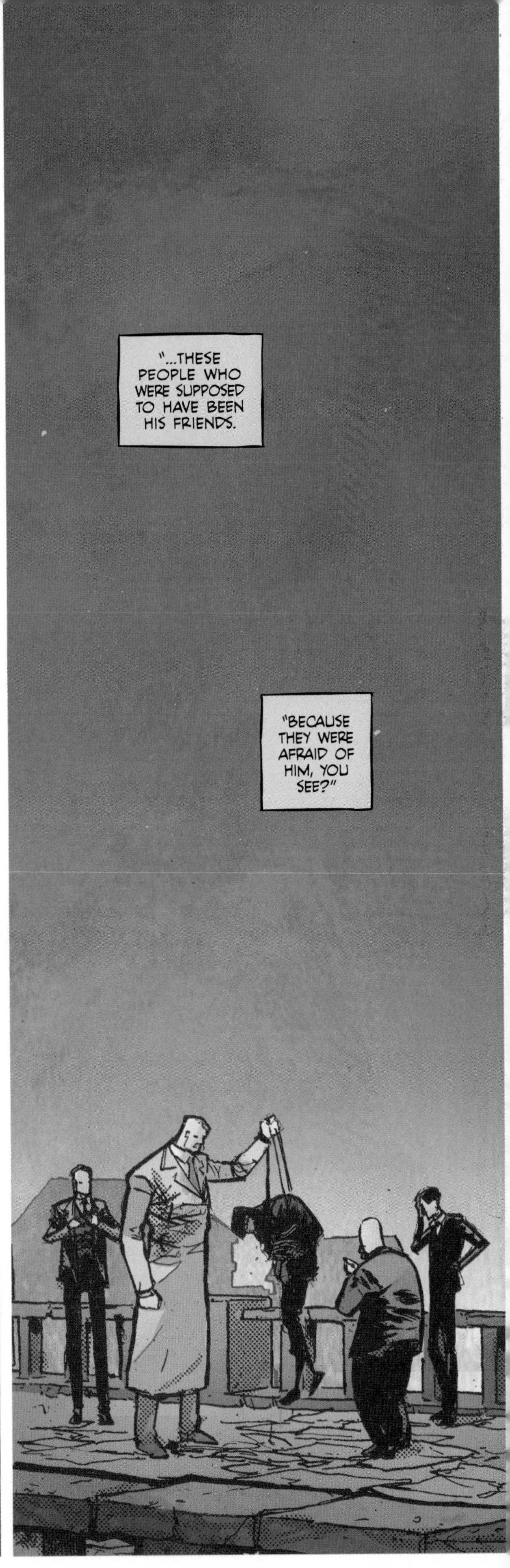
"...THESE PEOPLE WHO WERE SUPPOSED TO HAVE BEEN HIS FRIENDS.
"BECAUSE THEY WERE AFRAID OF HIM, YOU SEE?"

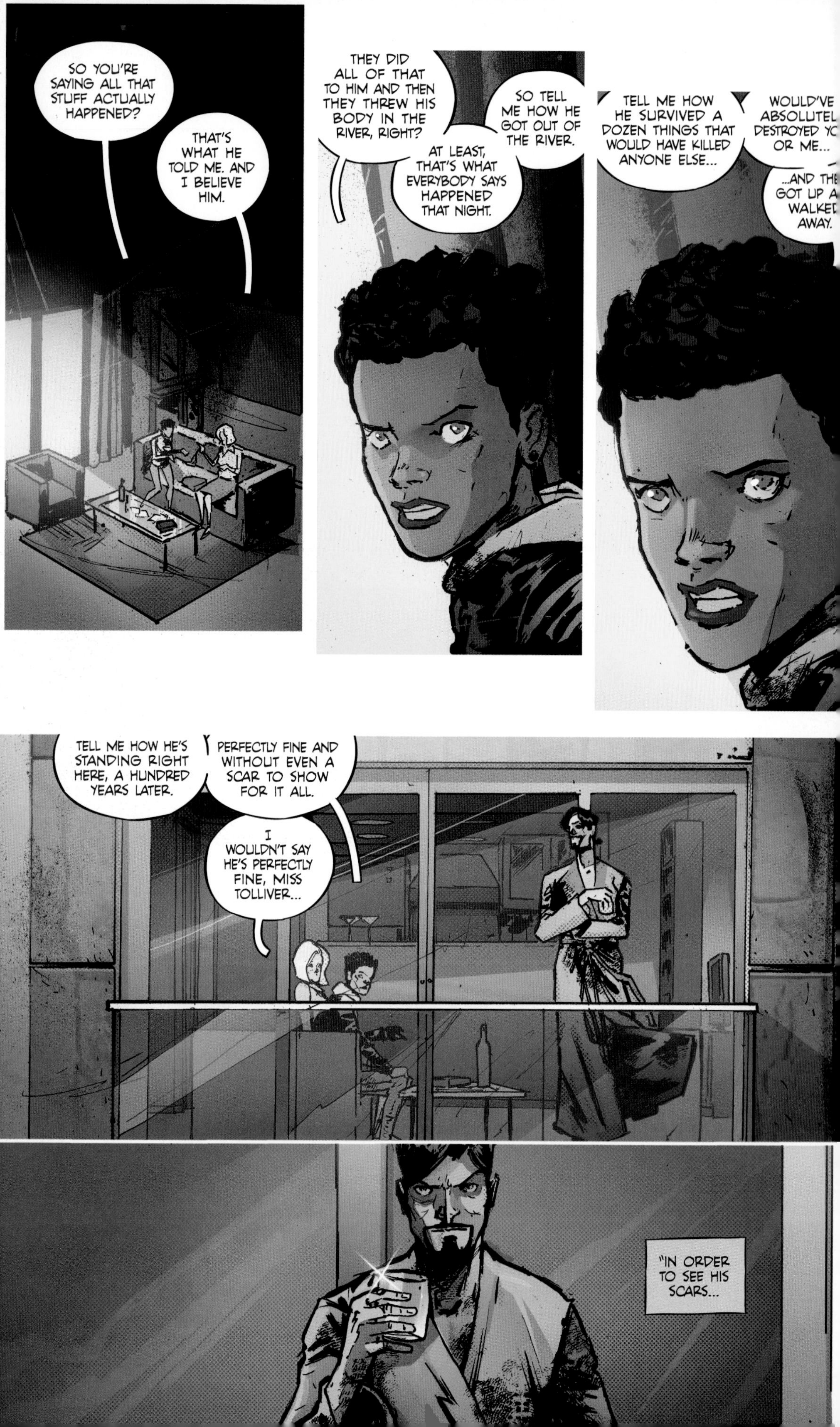
SO YOU'RE SAYING ALL THAT STUFF ACTUALLY HAPPENED?
THAT'S WHAT HE TOLD ME. AND I BELIEVE HIM.
THEY DID ALL OF THAT TO HIM AND THEN THEY THREW HIS BODY IN THE RIVER, RIGHT?
AT LEAST, THAT'S WHAT EVERYBODY SAYS HAPPENED THAT NIGHT.
SO TELL ME HOW HE GOT OUT OF THE RIVER.
TELL ME HOW HE SURVIVED A DOZEN THINGS THAT WOULD HAVE KILLED ANYONE ELSE...
WOULD'VE ABSOLUTEL DESTROYED YO OR ME...
...AND THE GOT UP A WALKE AWAY.
TELL ME HOW HE'S STANDING RIGHT HERE, A HUNDRED YEARS LATER.
PERFECTLY FINE AND WITHOUT EVEN A SCAR TO SHOW FOR IT ALL.
I WOULDN'T SAY HE'S PERFECTLY FINE, MISS TOLLIVER...
"IN ORDER TO SEE HIS SCARS...

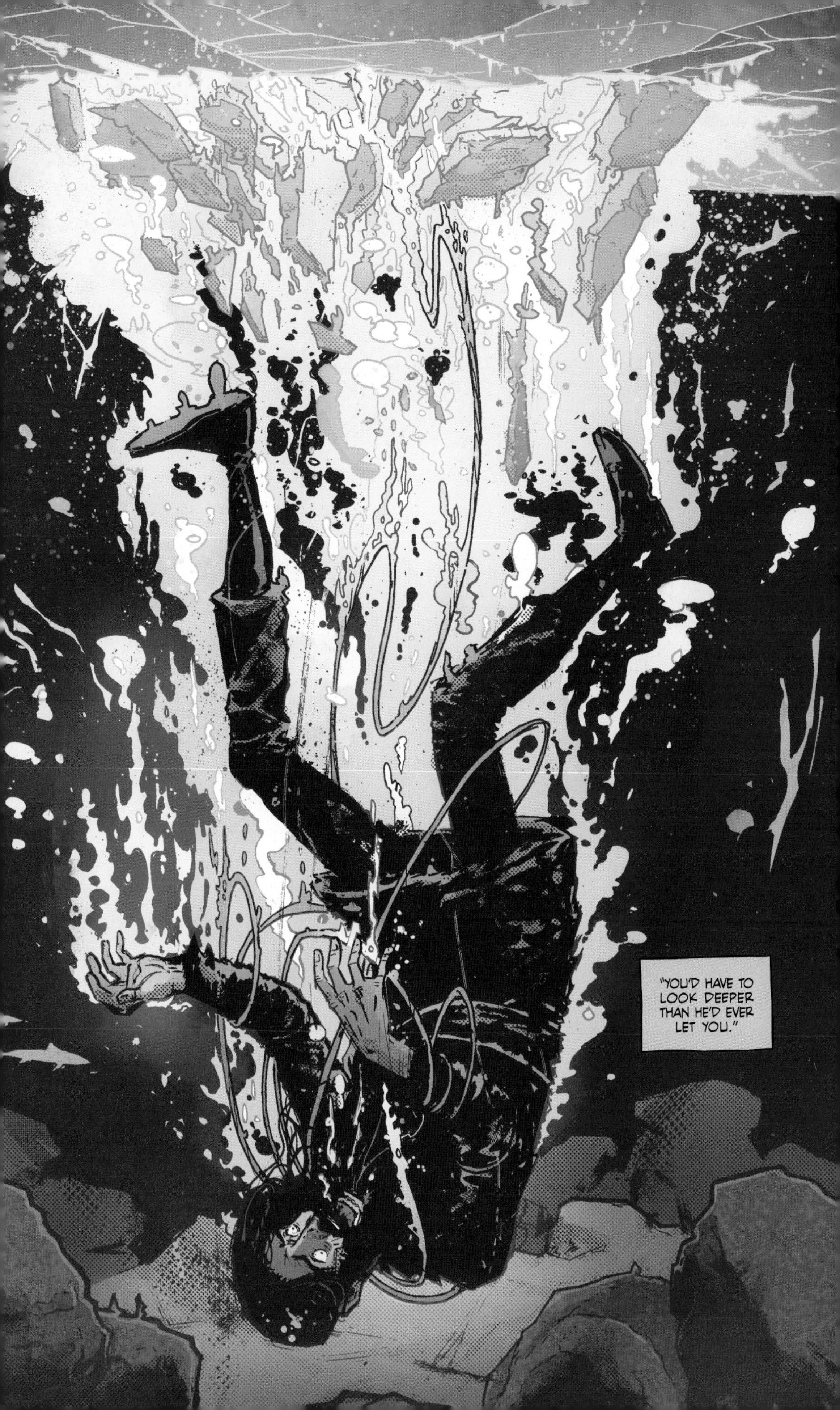
"YOU'D HAVE TO LOOK DEEPER THAN HE'D EVER LET YOU."

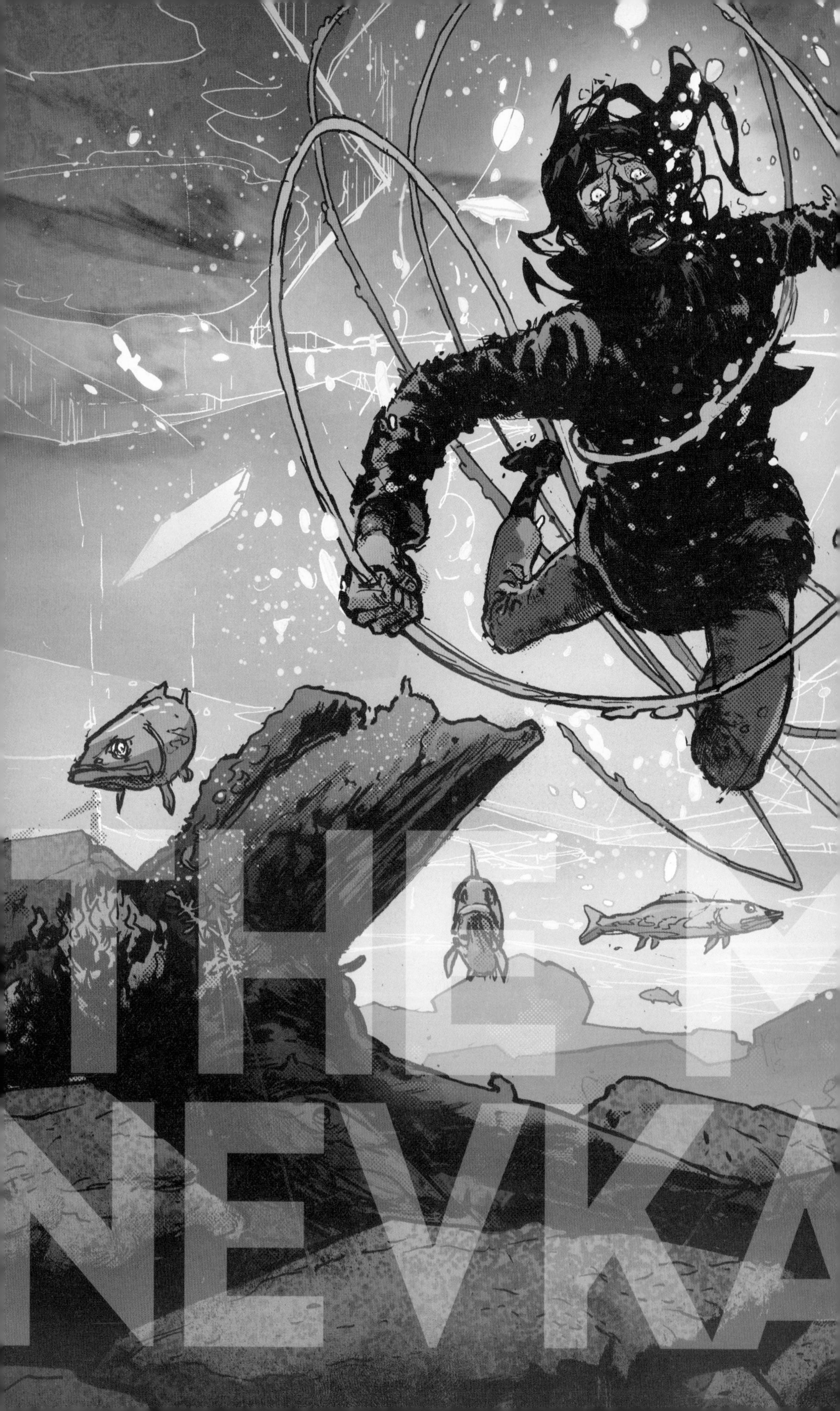
THE
NEVKA

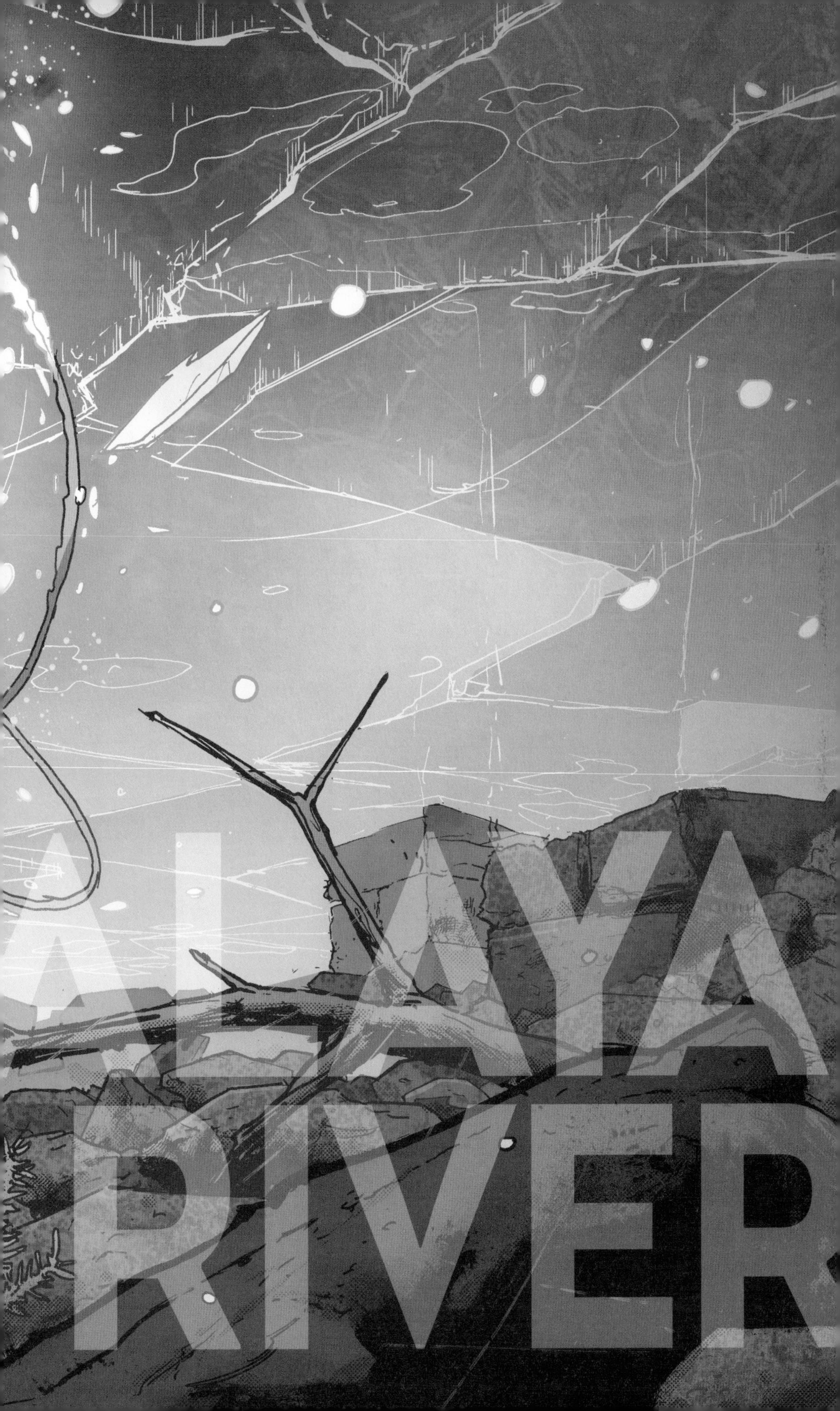
LAYA
RIVER

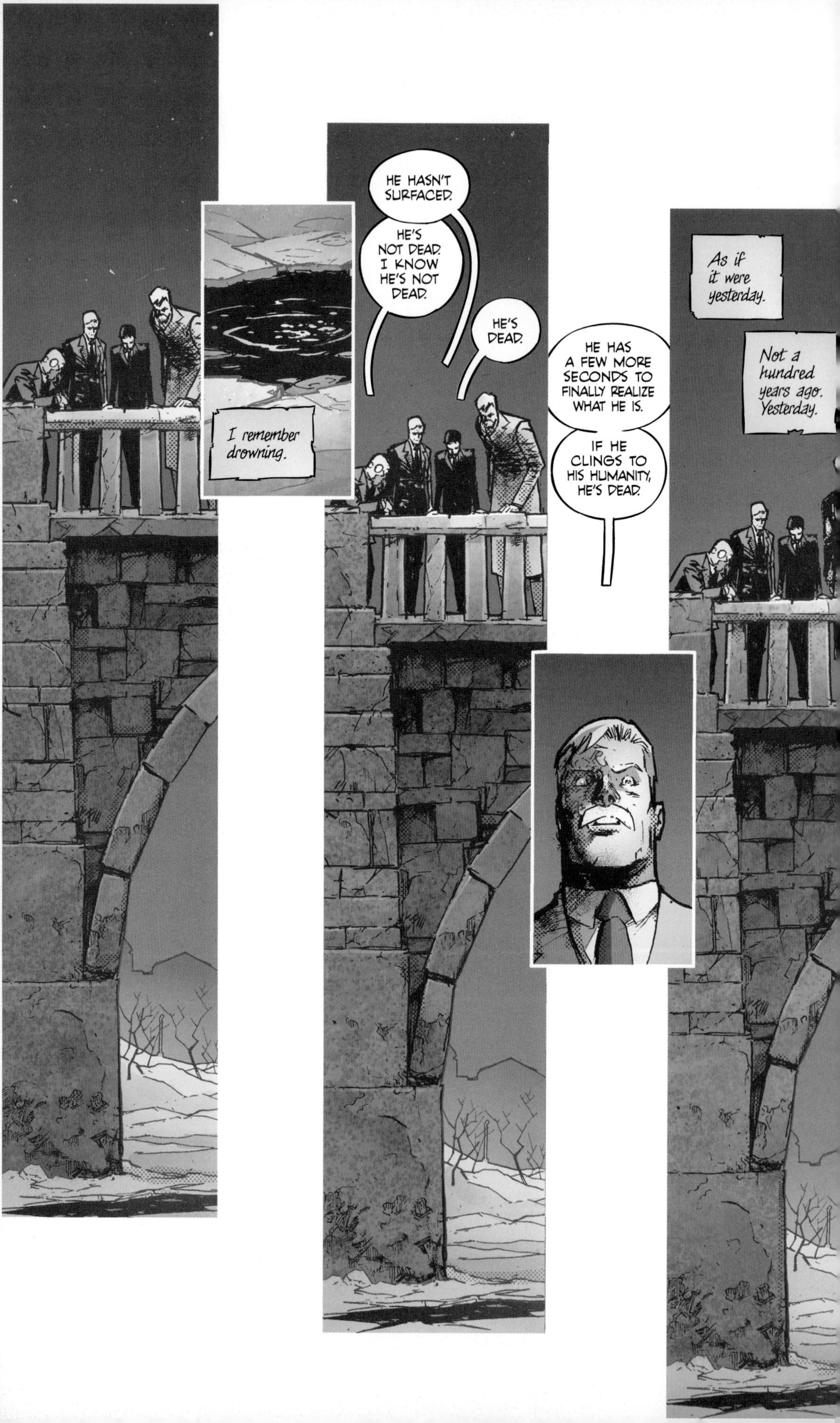
I remember drowning.
HE HASN'T SURFACED.
HE'S NOT DEAD. I KNOW HE'S NOT DEAD.
HE'S DEAD.
HE HAS A FEW MORE SECONDS TO FINALLY REALIZE WHAT HE IS.
IF HE CLINGS TO HIS HUMANITY, HE'S DEAD.
As if it were yesterday.
Not a hundred years ago. Yesterday.

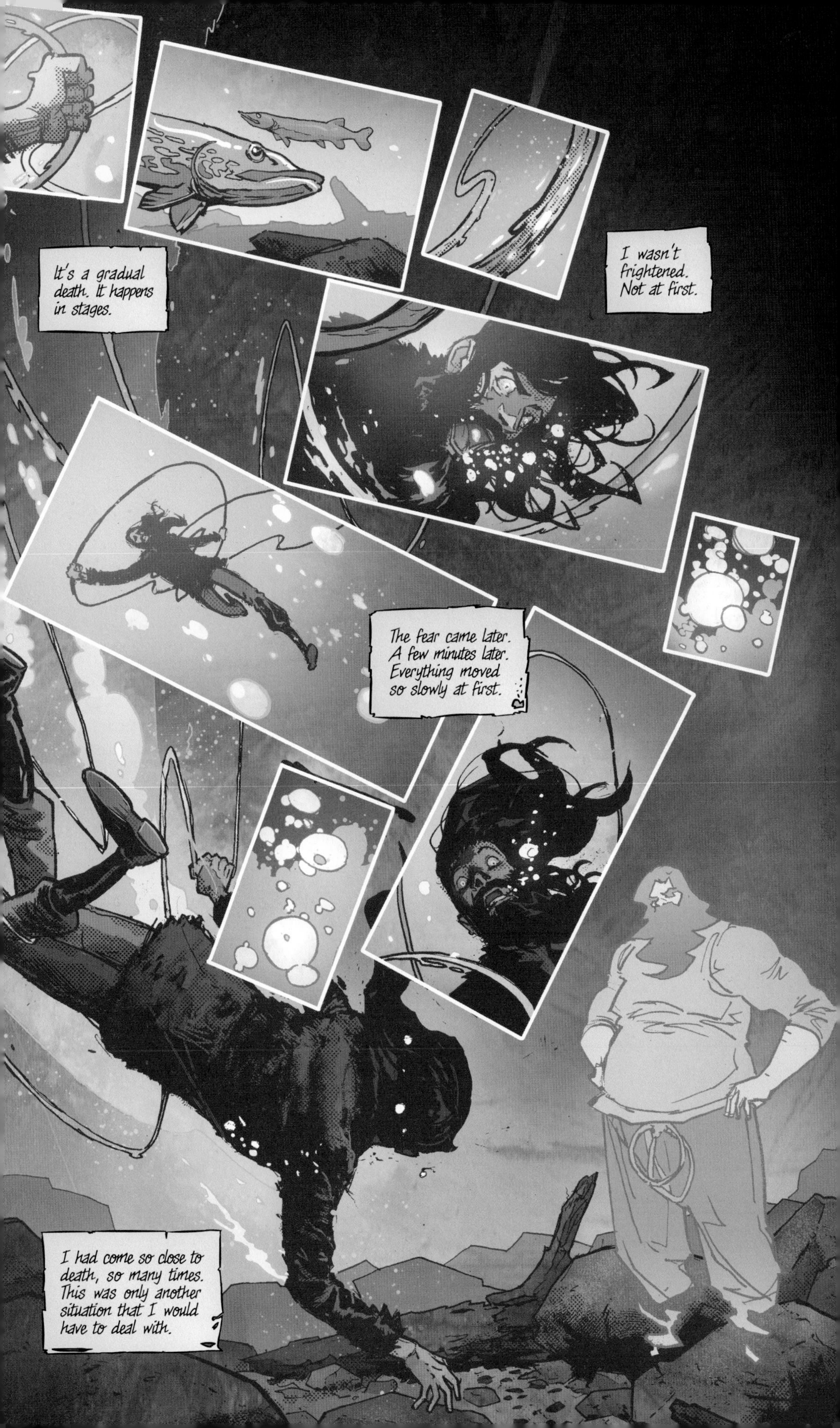
It's a gradual death. It happens in stages.
I wasn't frightened. Not at first.
The fear came later. A few minutes later. Everything moved so slowly at first.
I had come so close to death, so many times. This was only another situation that I would have to deal with.

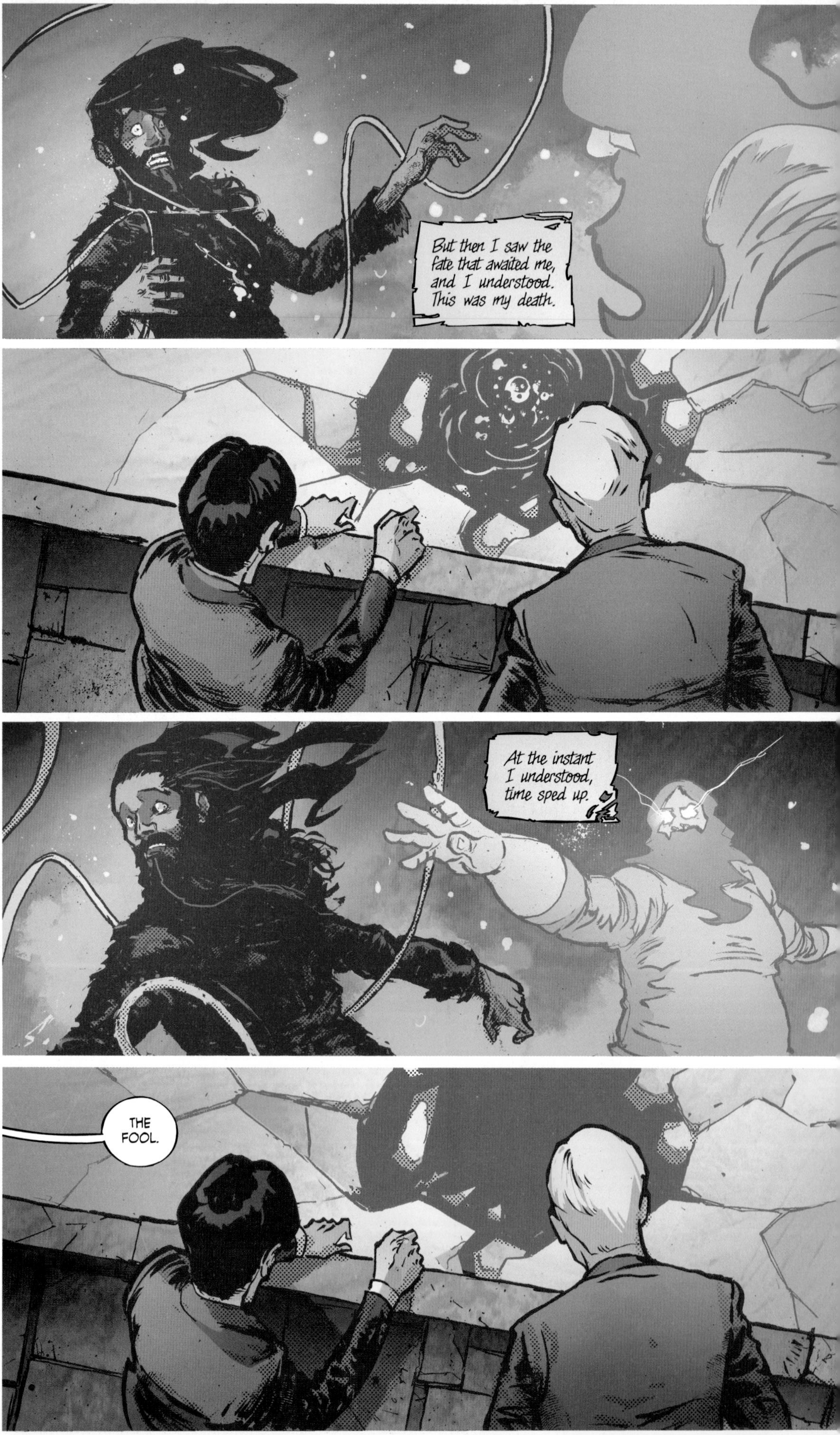
But then I saw the fate that awaited me, and I understood. This was my death.
At the instant I understood, time sped up.
THE FOOL.

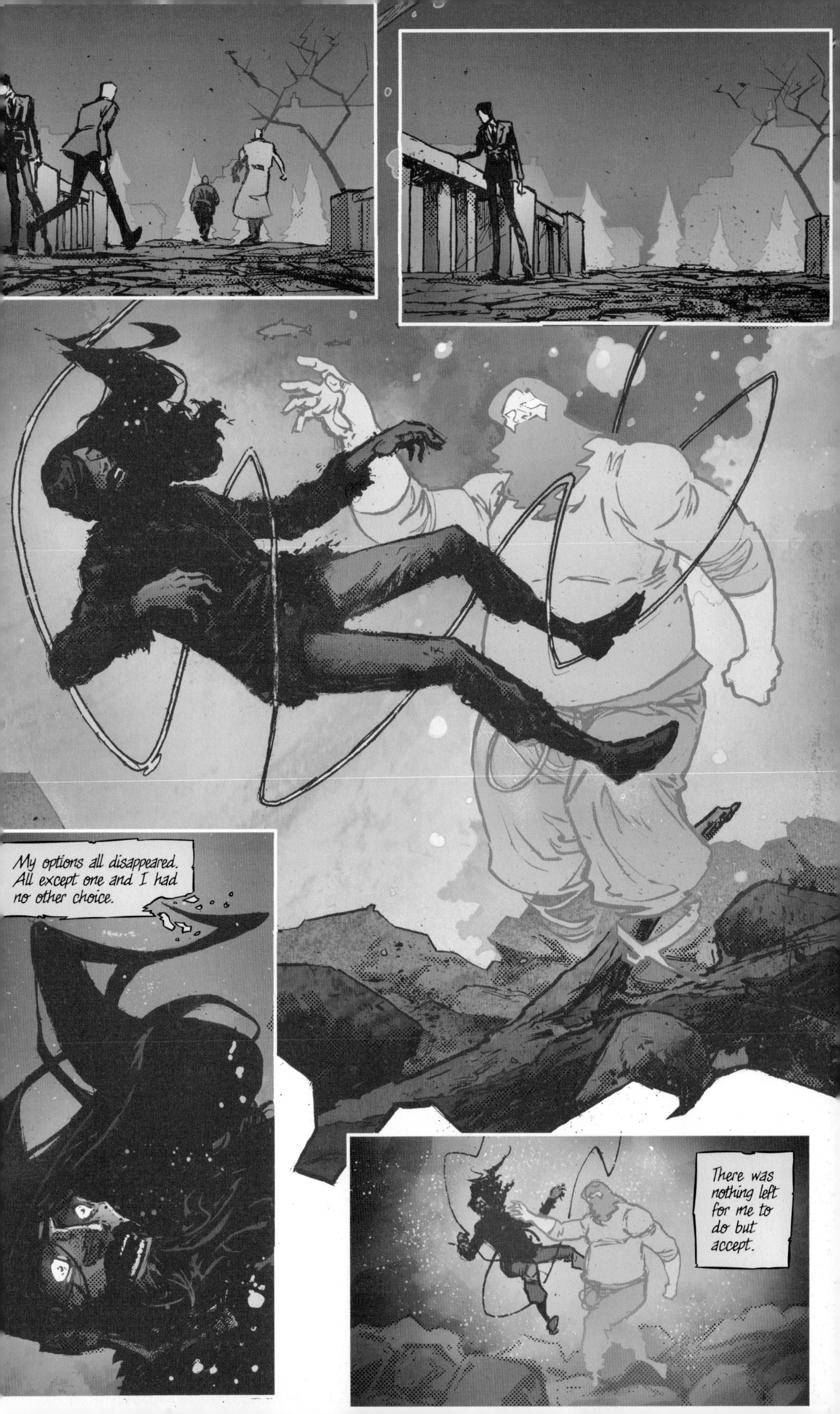
My options all disappeared. All except one and I had no other choice.
There was nothing left for me to do but accept.

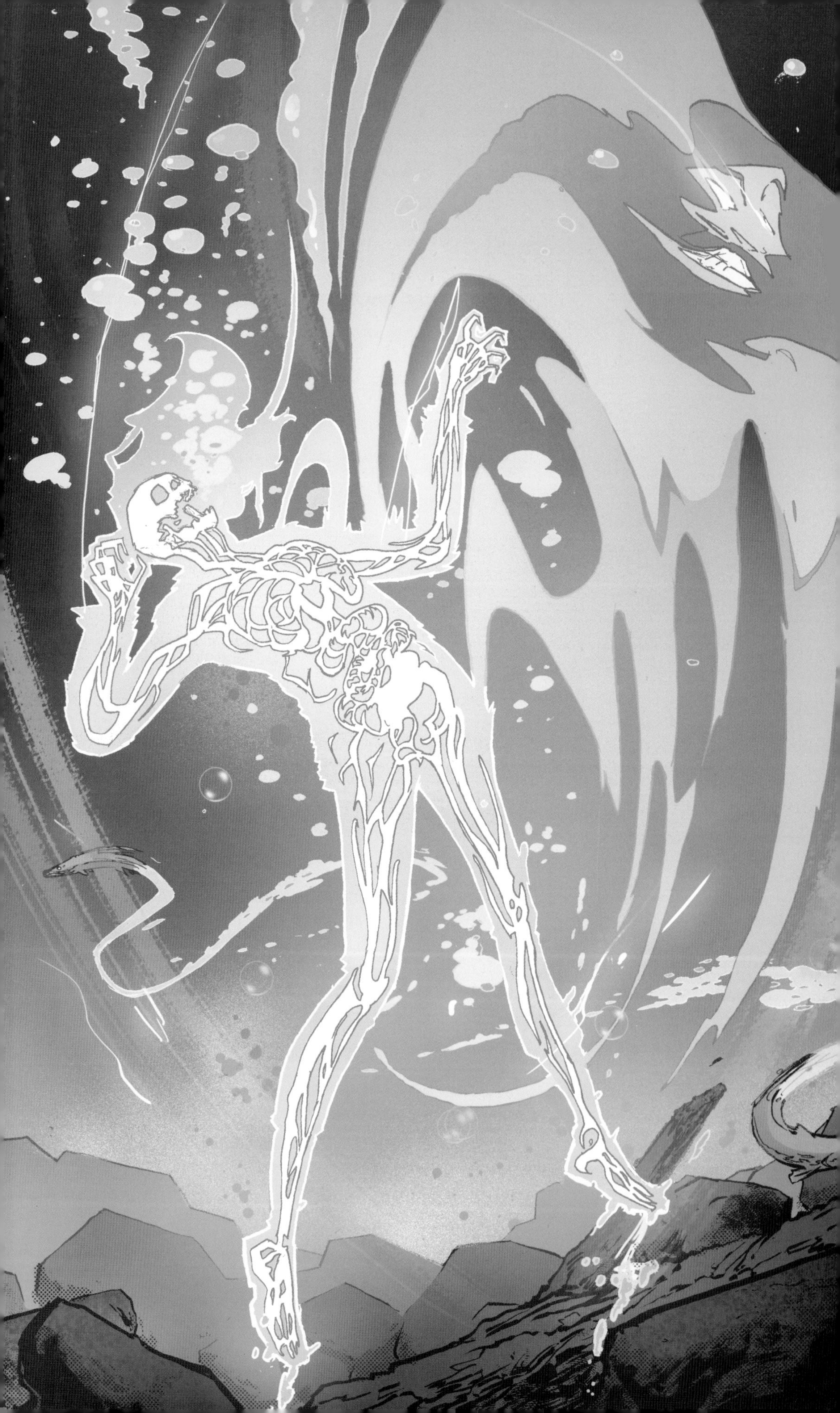

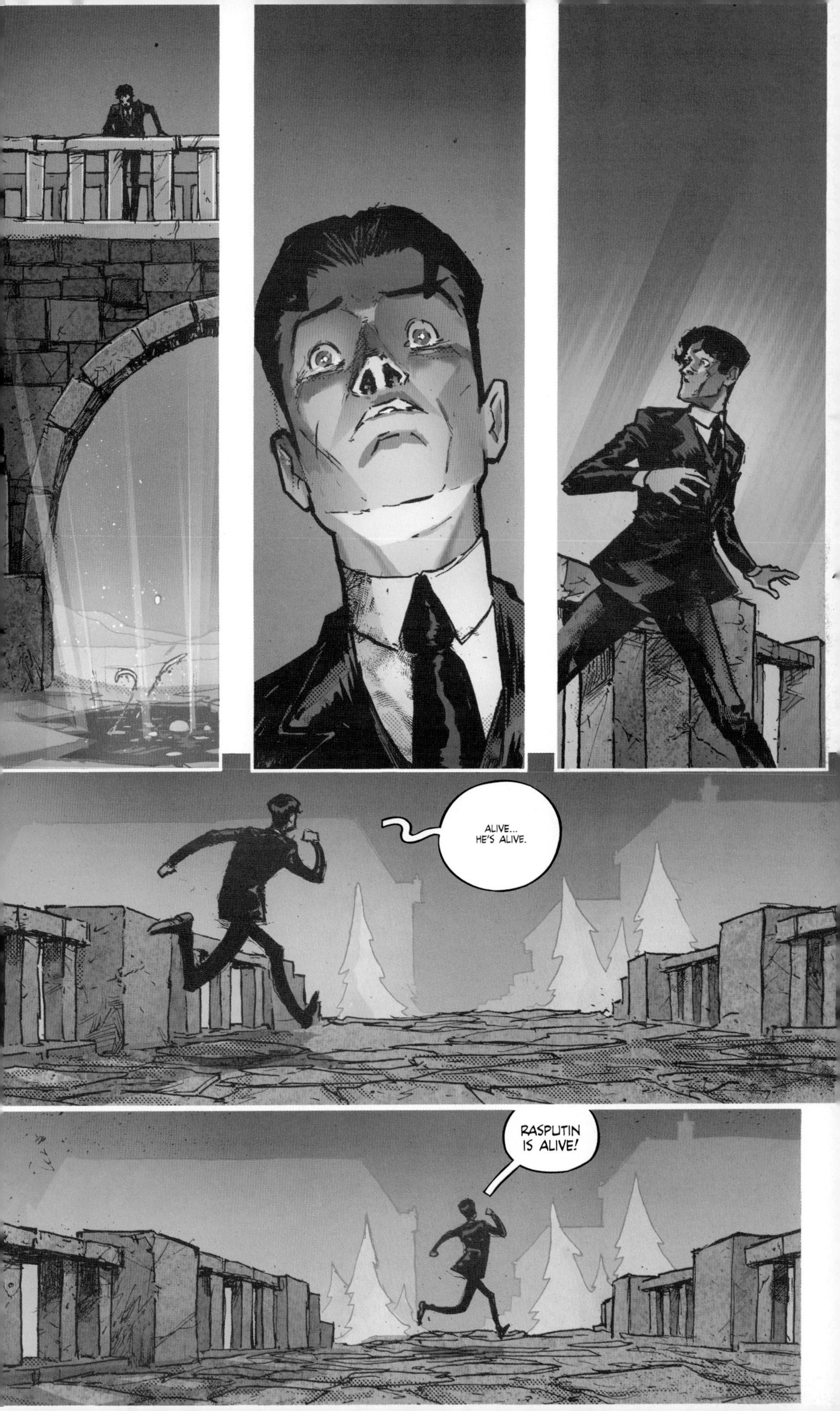

ALIVE... HE'S ALIVE.
RASPUTIN IS ALIVE!

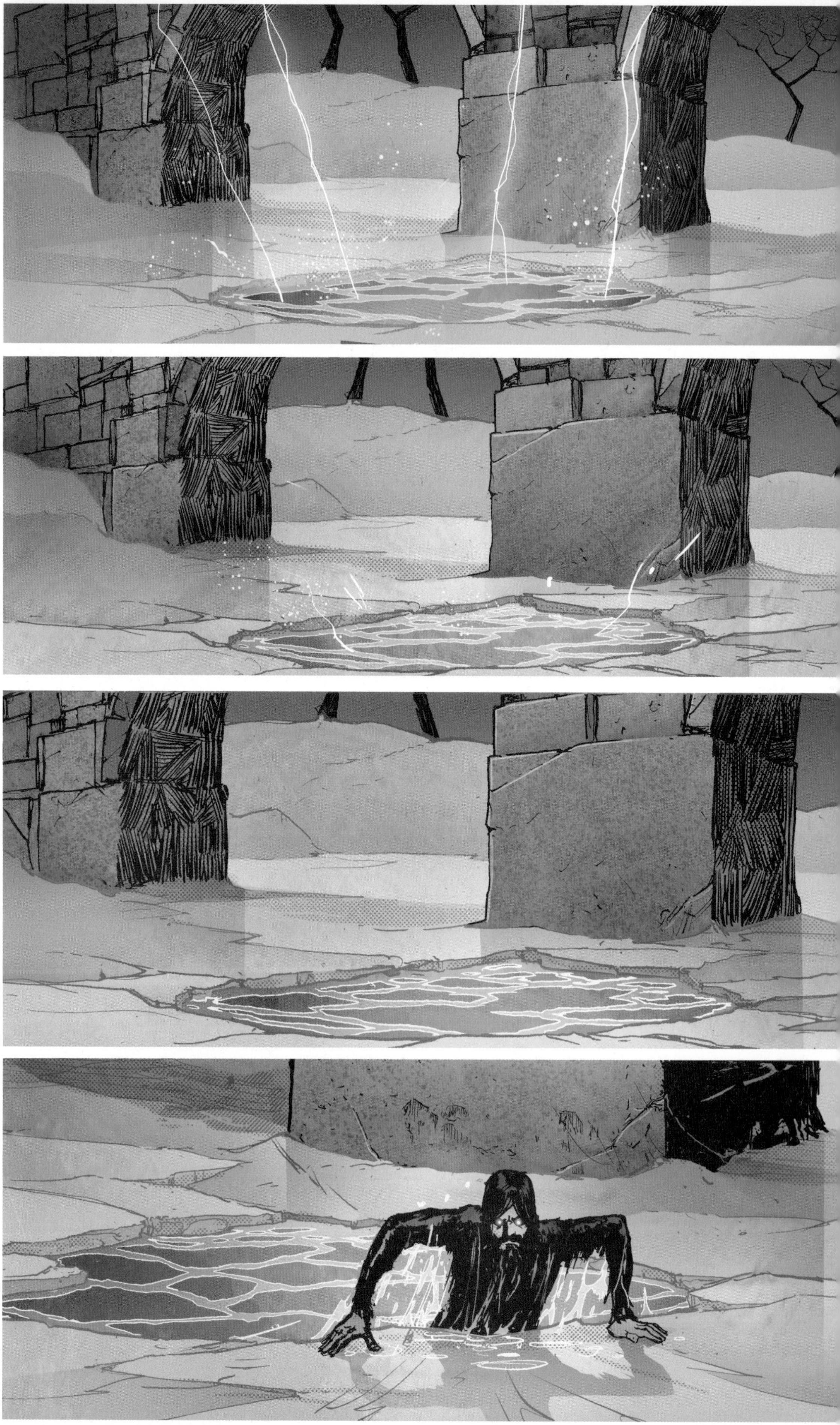

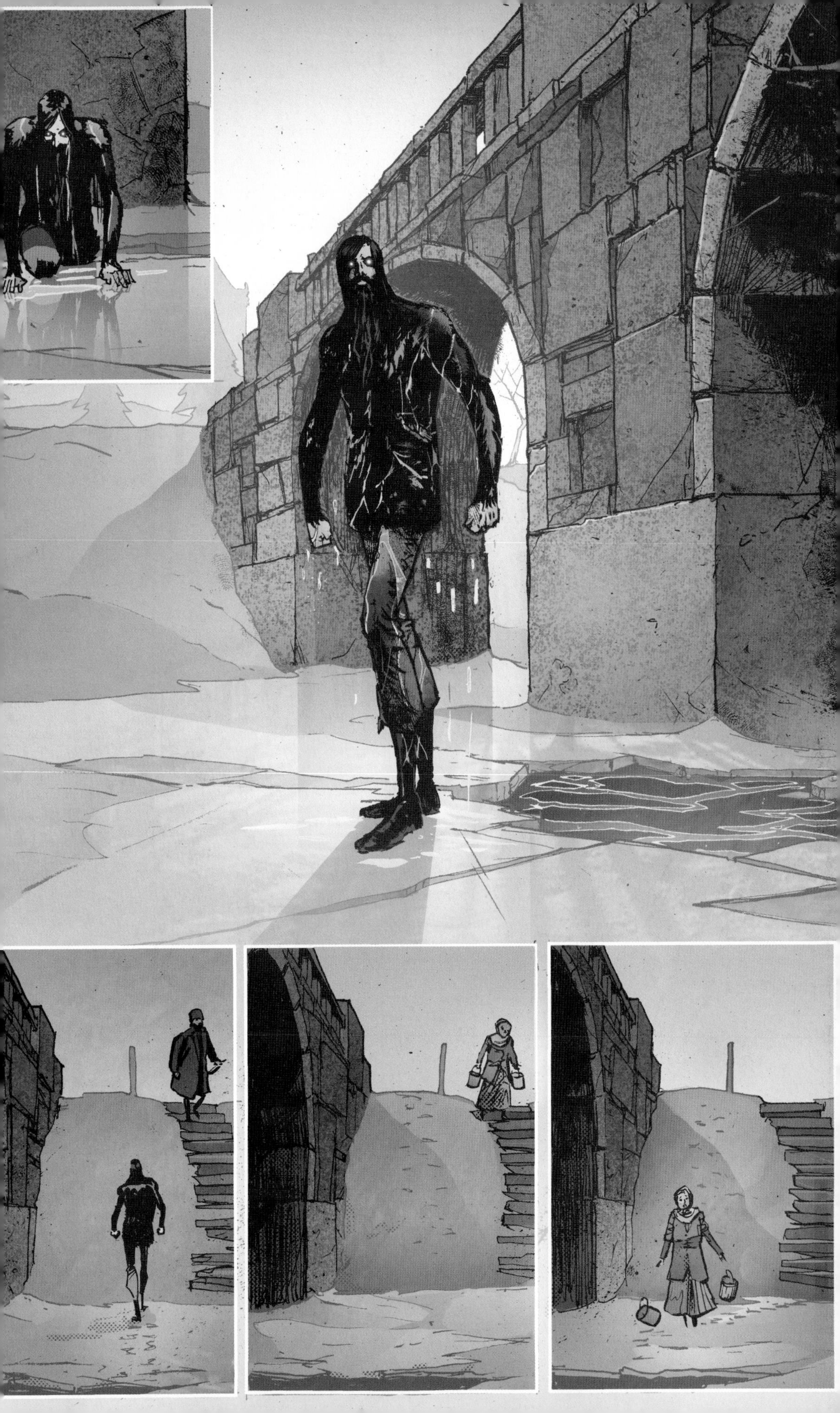

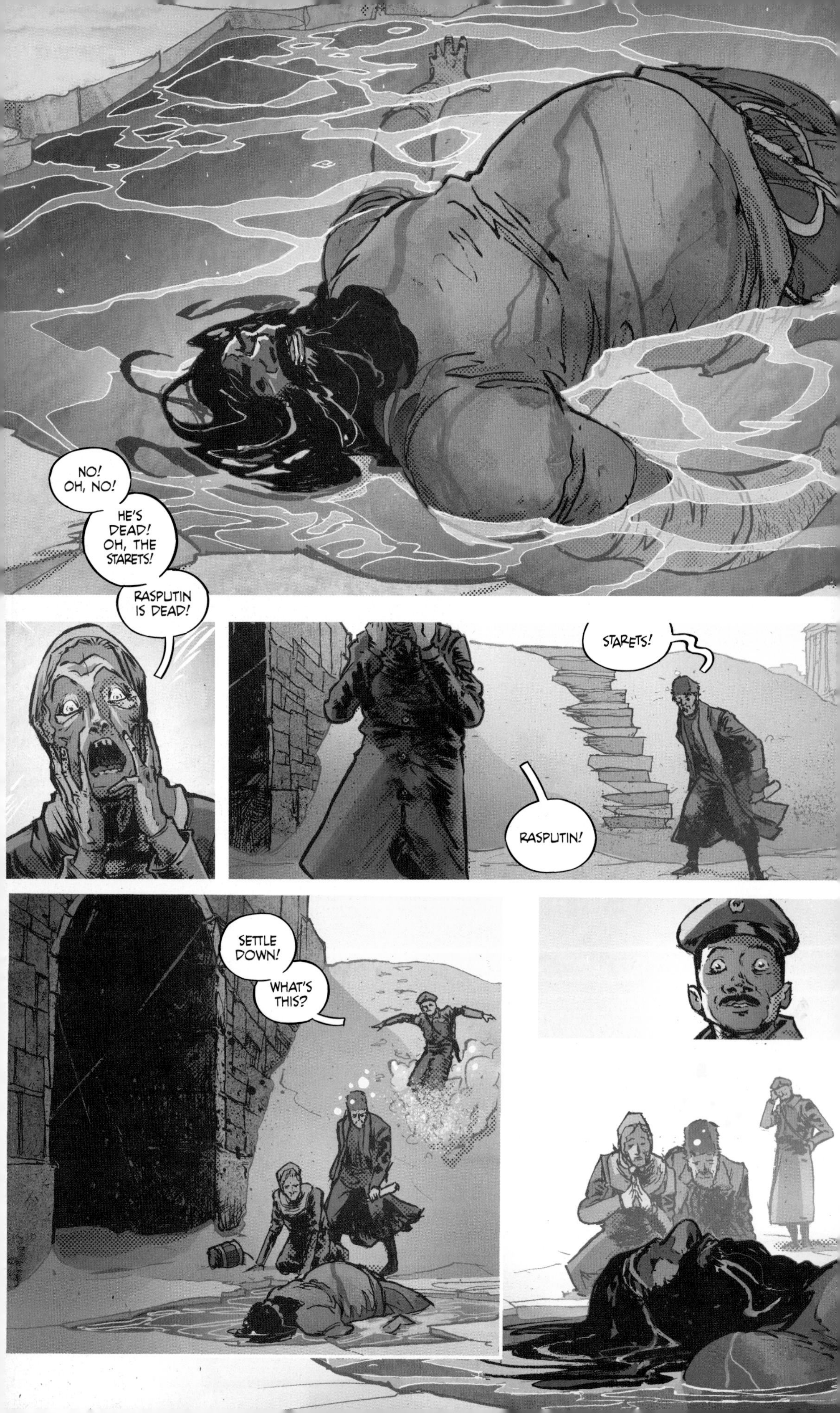
NO! OH, NO!
HE'S DEAD! OH, THE STARETS!
RASPUTIN IS DEAD!
STARETS!
RASPUTIN!
SETTLE DOWN!
WHAT'S THIS?

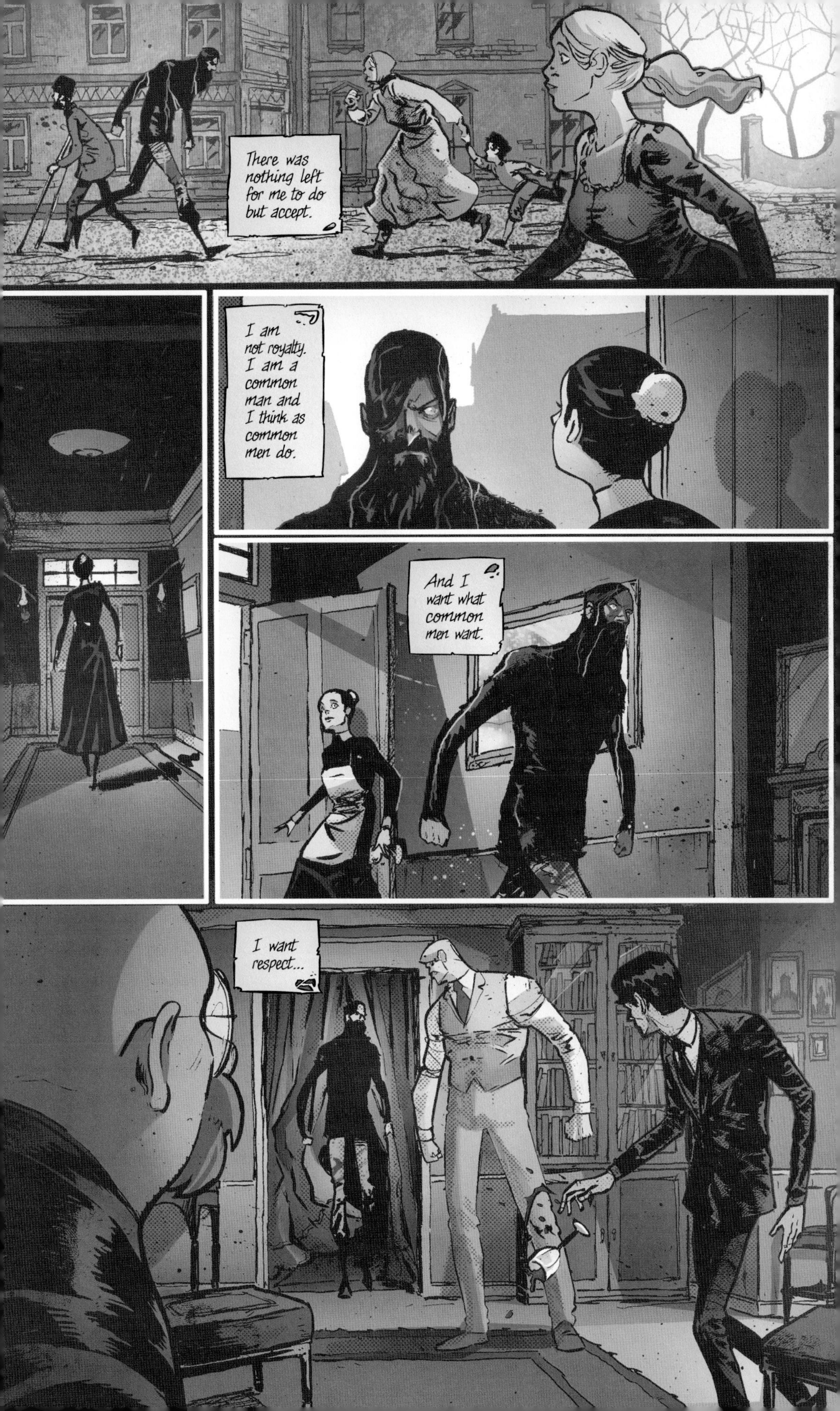
There was nothing left for me to do but accept.
I am not royalty. I am a common man and I think as common men do.
And I want what common men want.
I want respect...

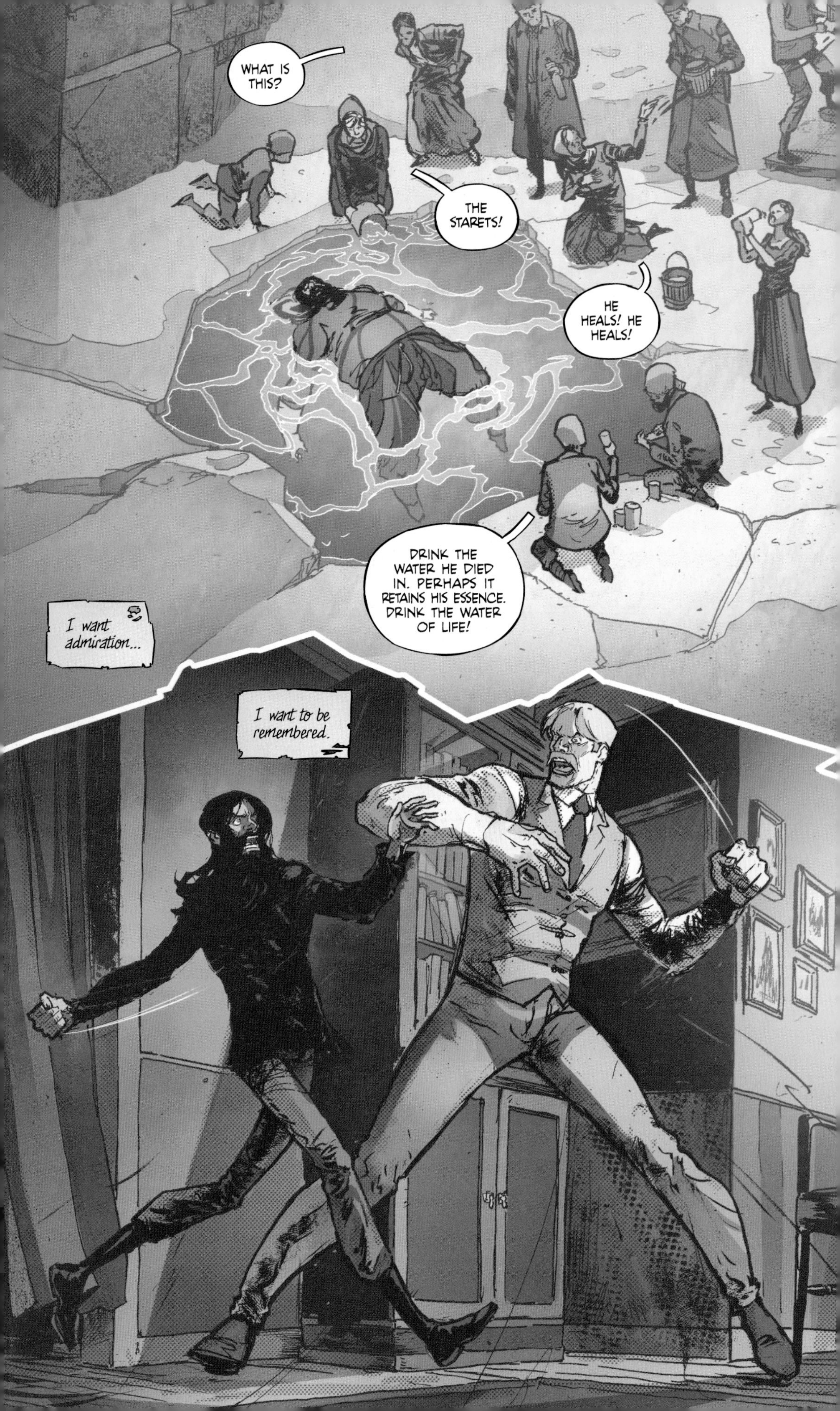
WHAT IS THIS?
THE STARETS!
HE HEALS! HE HEALS!
DRINK THE WATER HE DIED IN. PERHAPS IT RETAINS HIS ESSENCE. DRINK THE WATER OF LIFE!
I want admiration...
I want to be remembered.

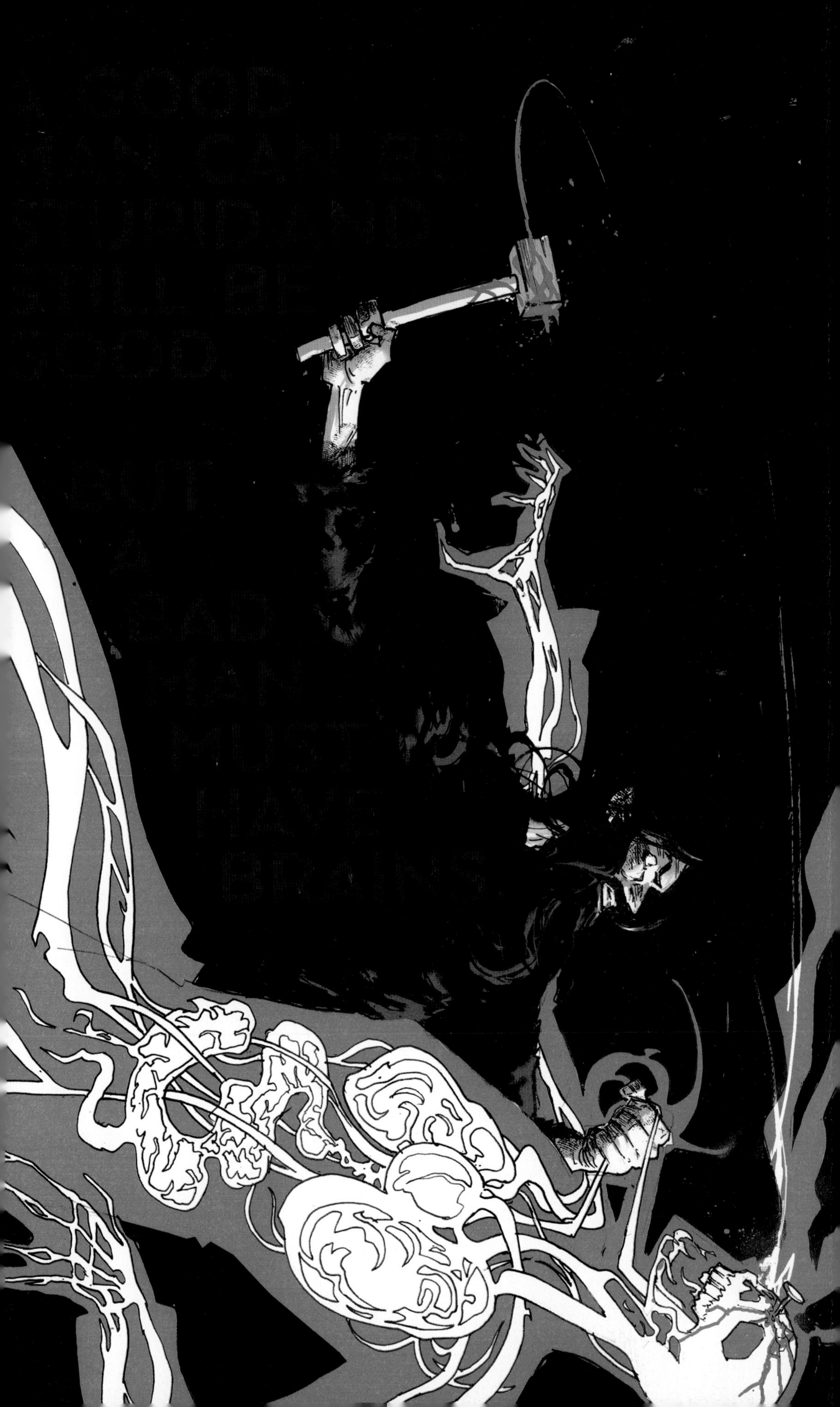
A GOOD MAN CAN BE STUPID AND STILL BE GOOD.
BUT A BAD MAN MUST HAVE BRAINS.

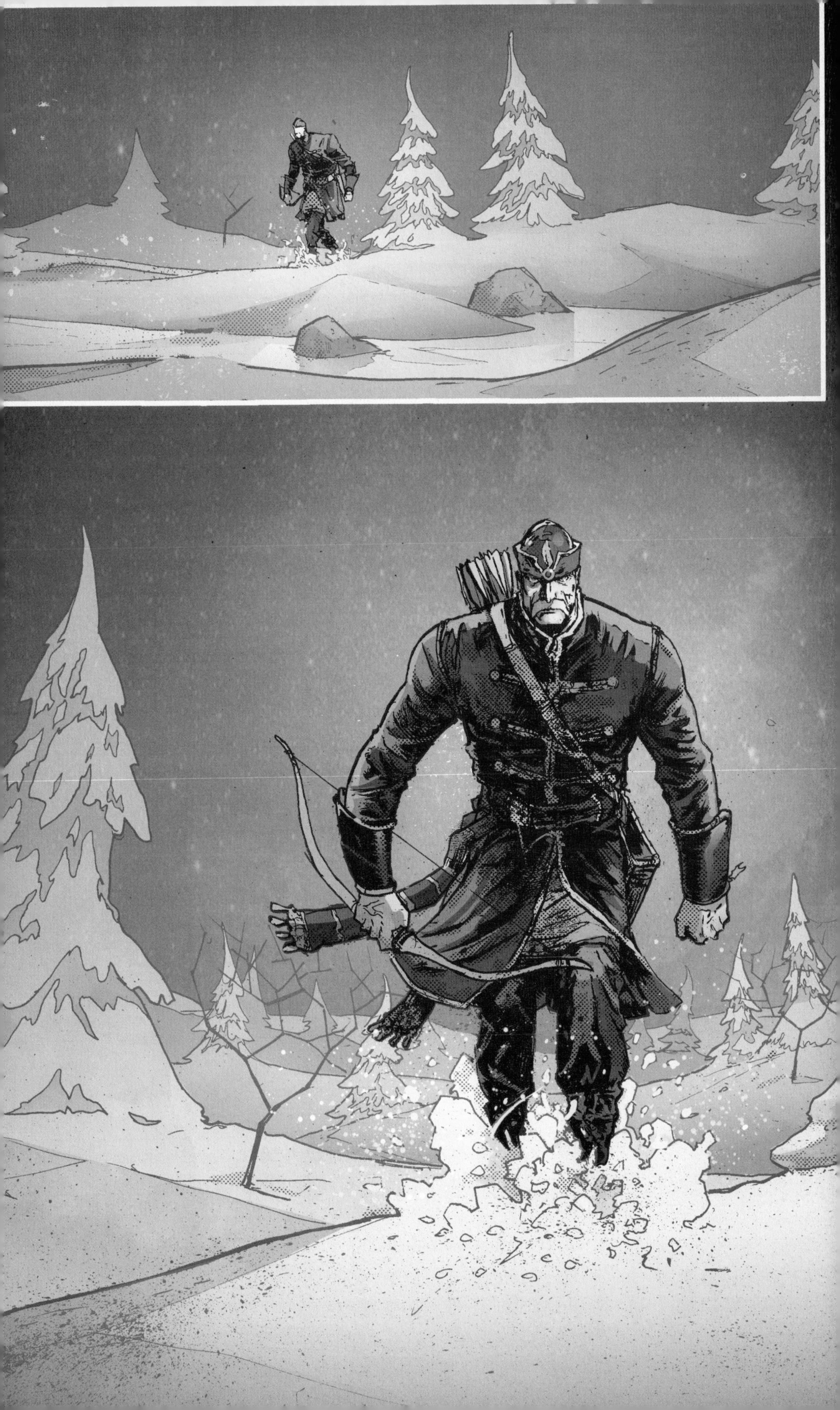

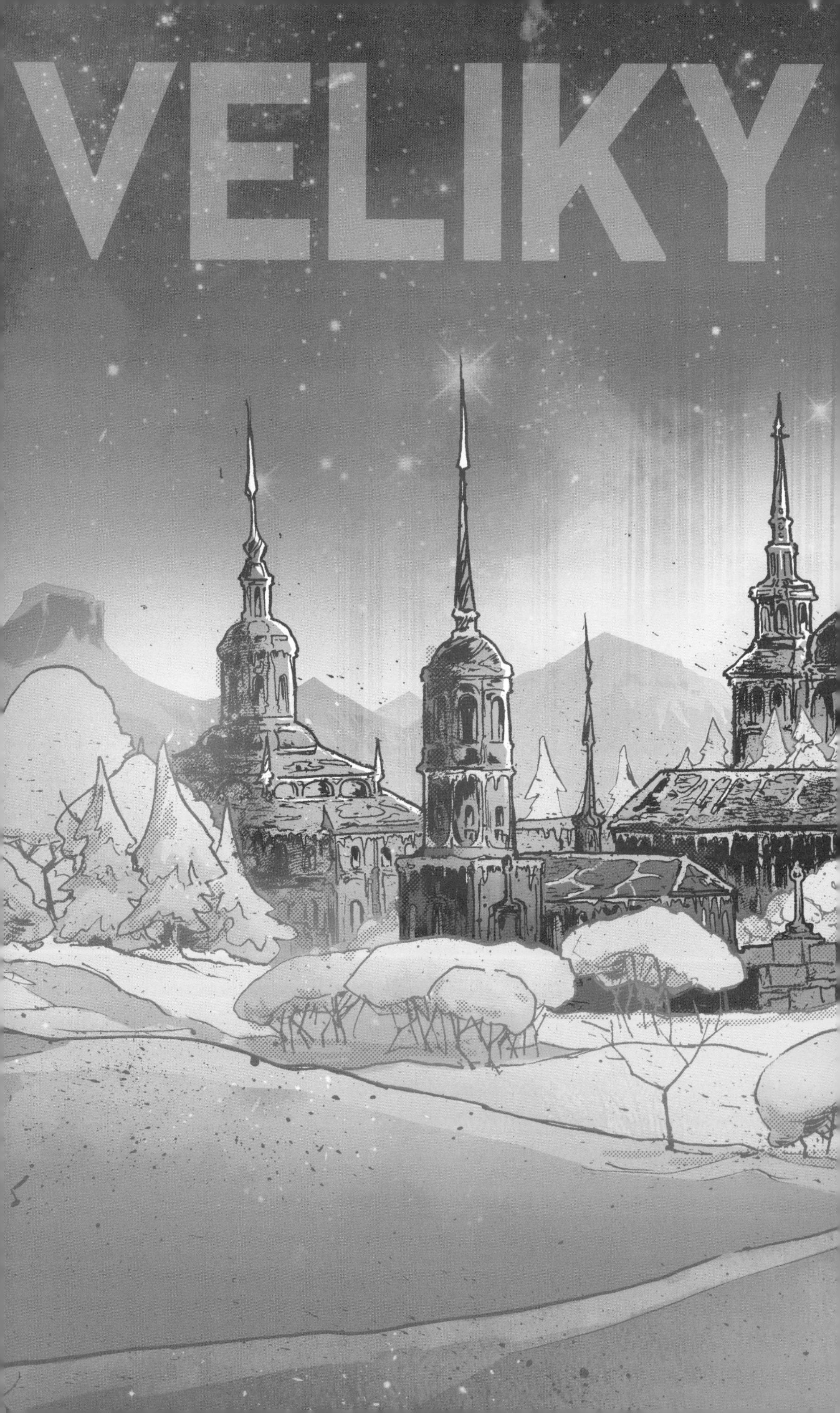
VELIKY

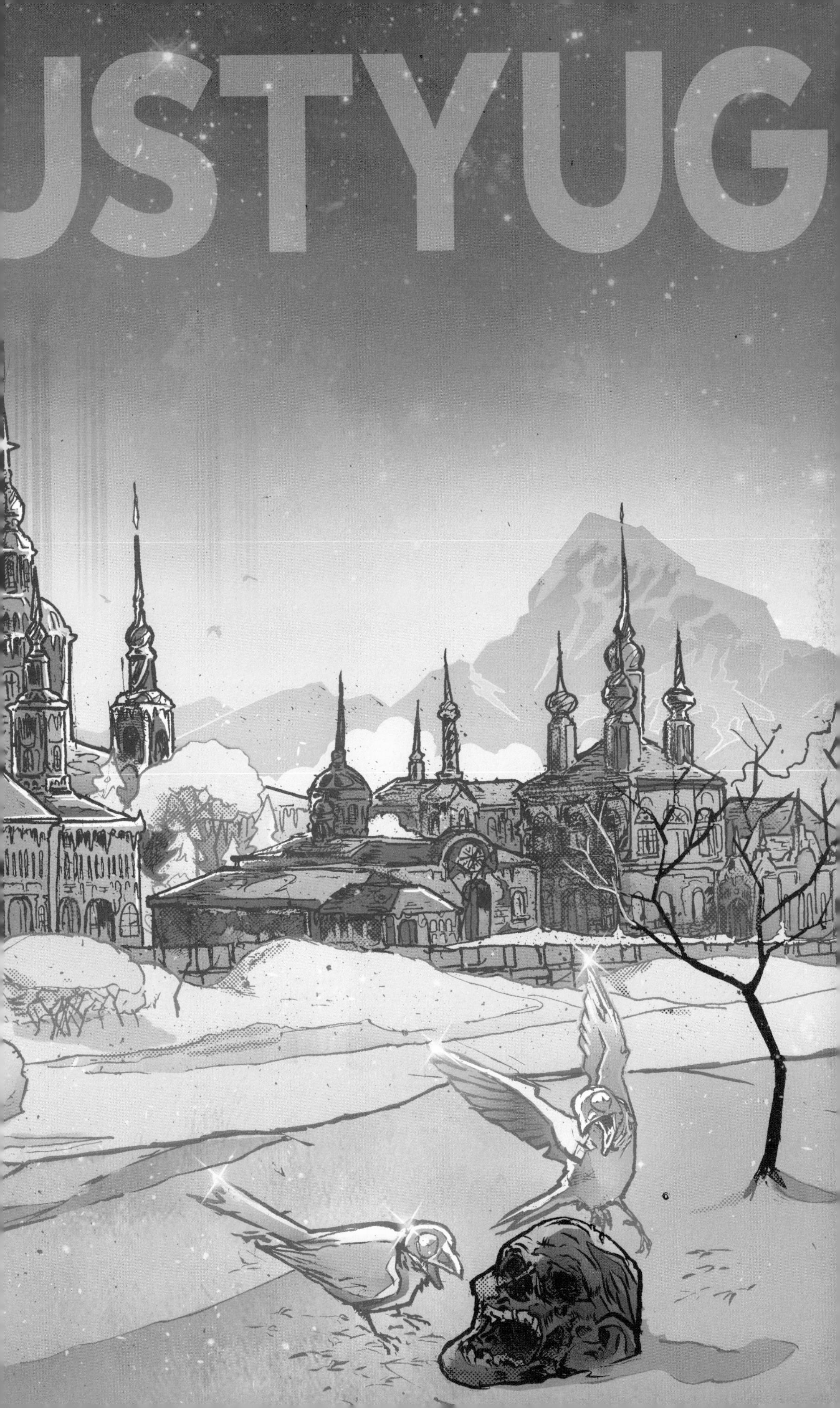
USTYUG

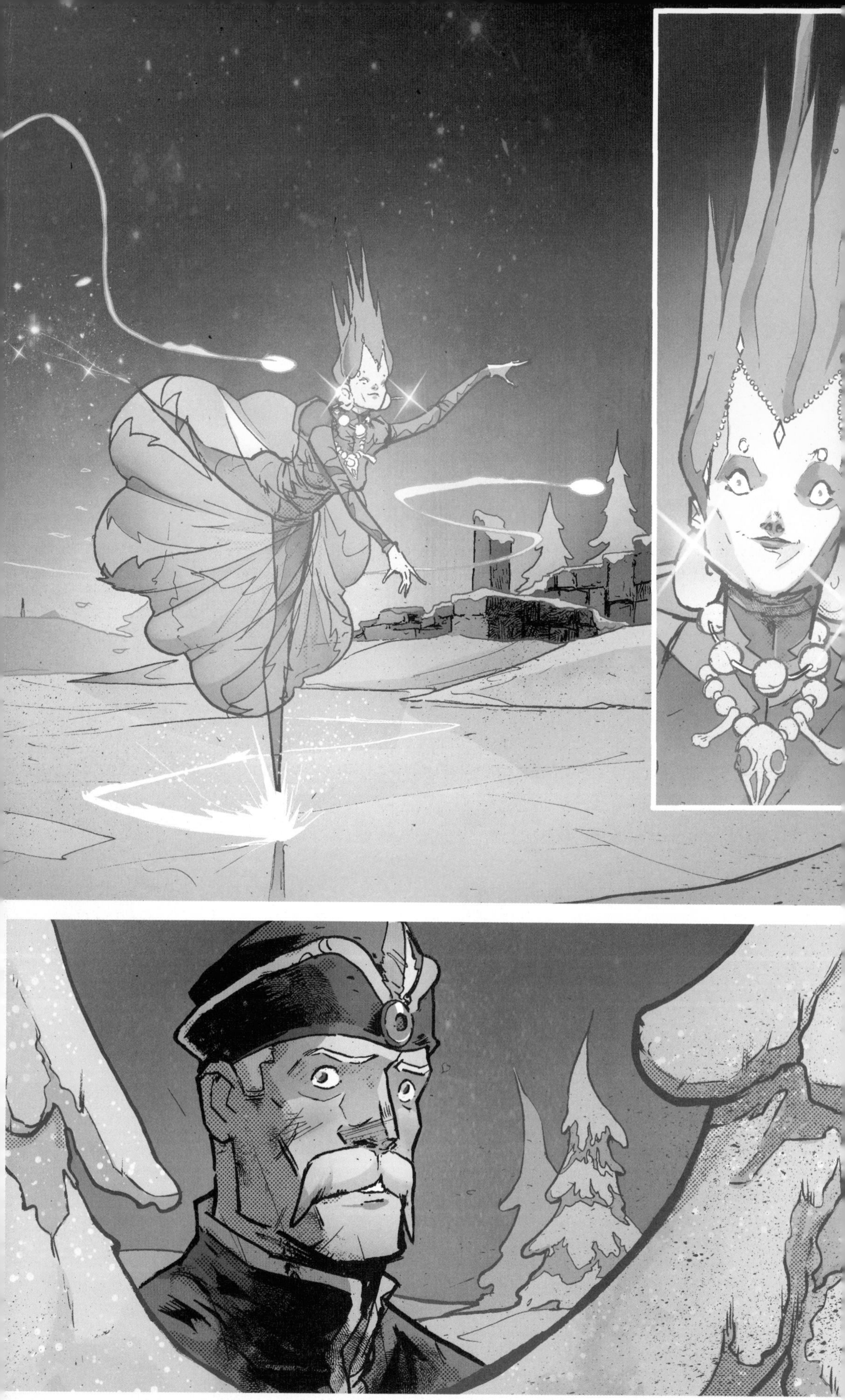

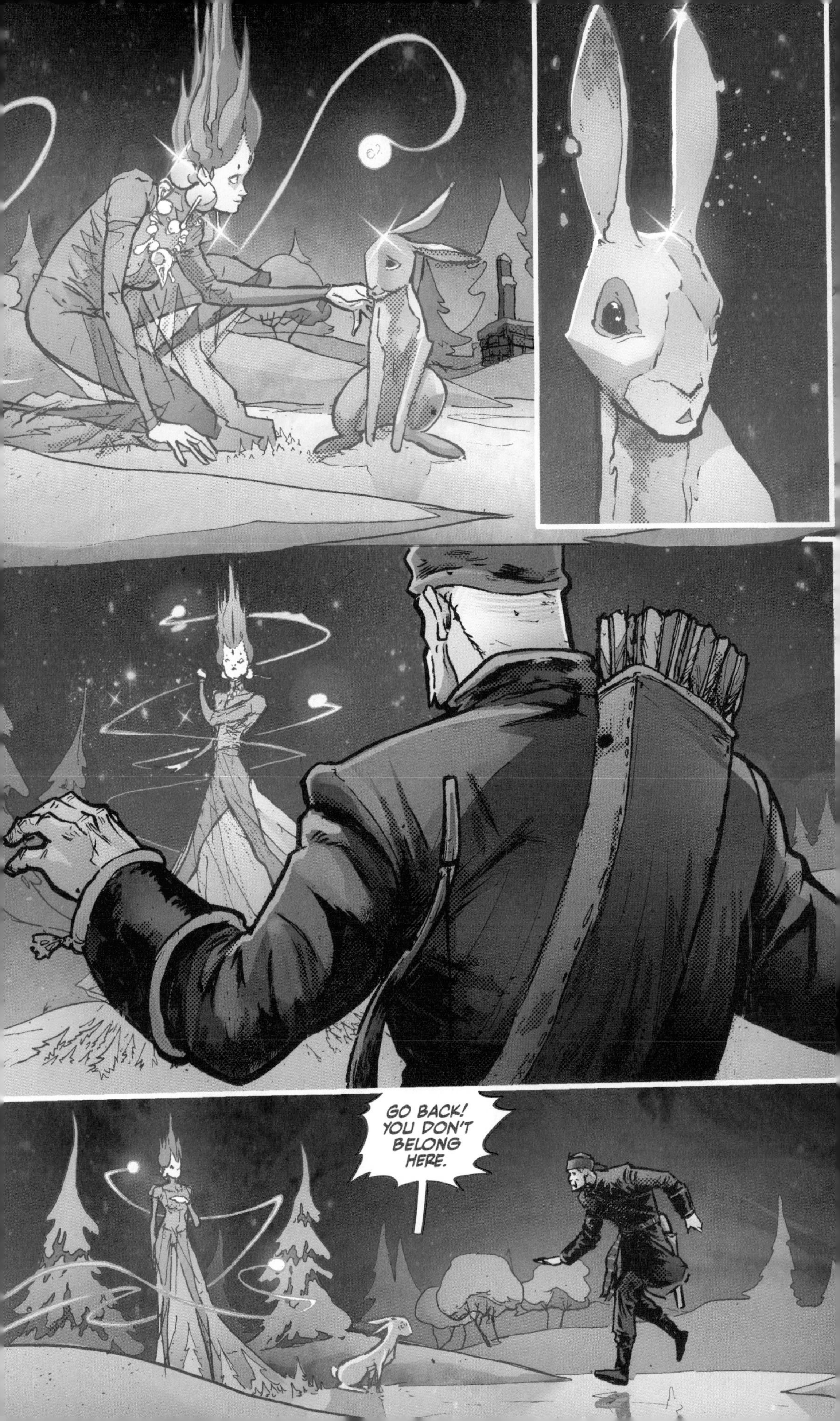
GO BACK! YOU DON'T BELONG HERE.

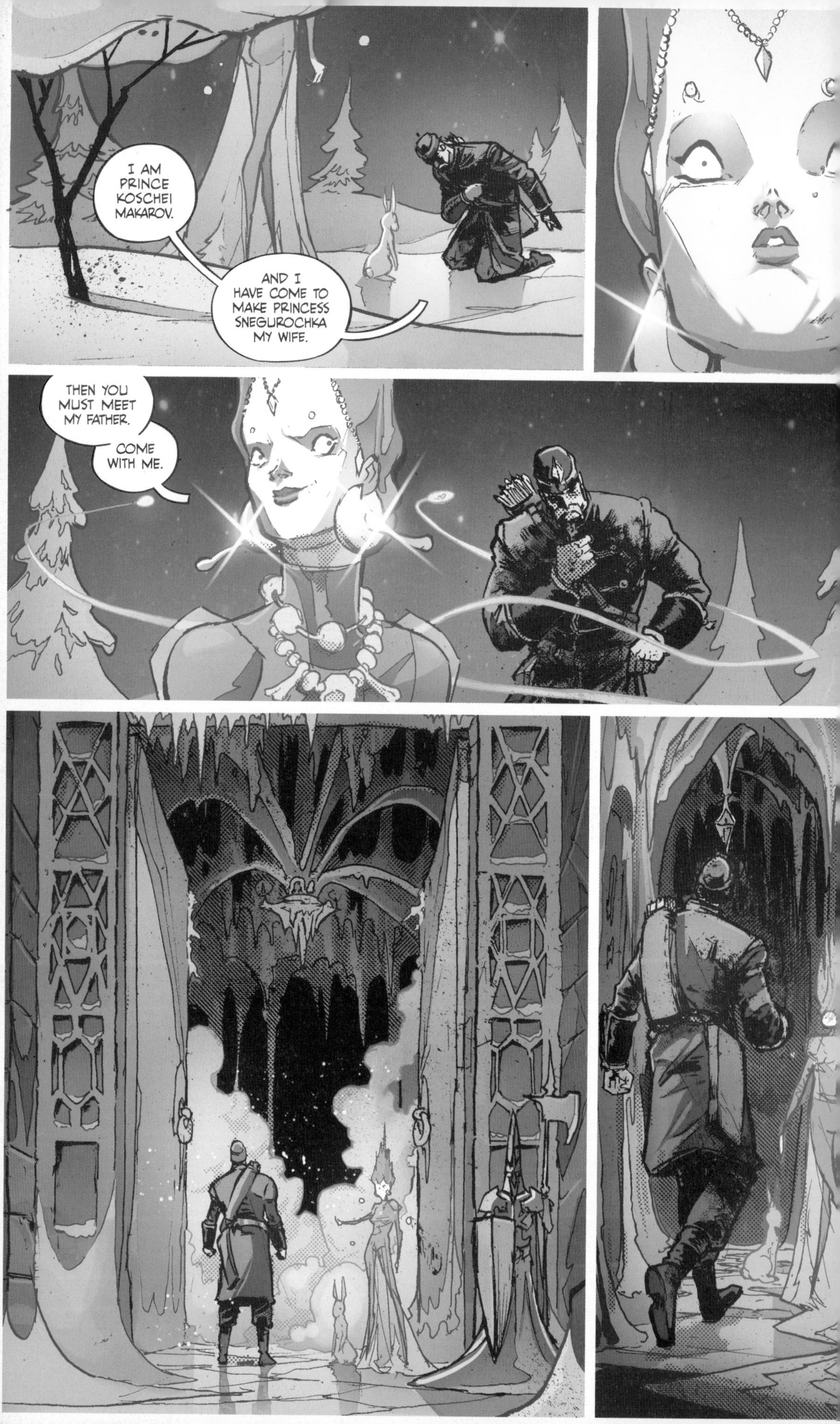
I AM PRINCE KOSCHEI MAKAROV.
AND I HAVE COME TO MAKE PRINCESS SNEGUROCHKA MY WIFE.
THEN YOU MUST MEET MY FATHER.
COME WITH ME.

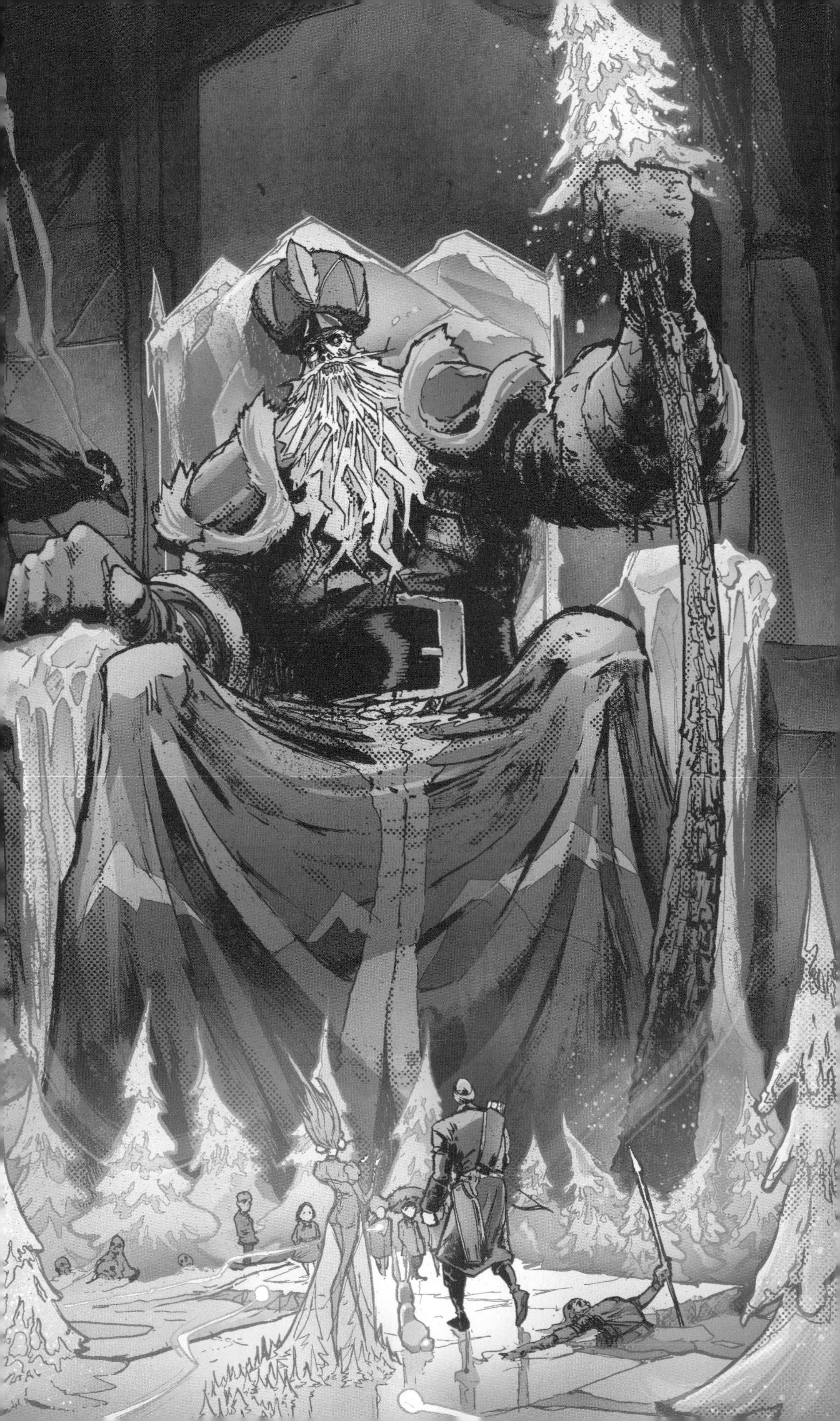

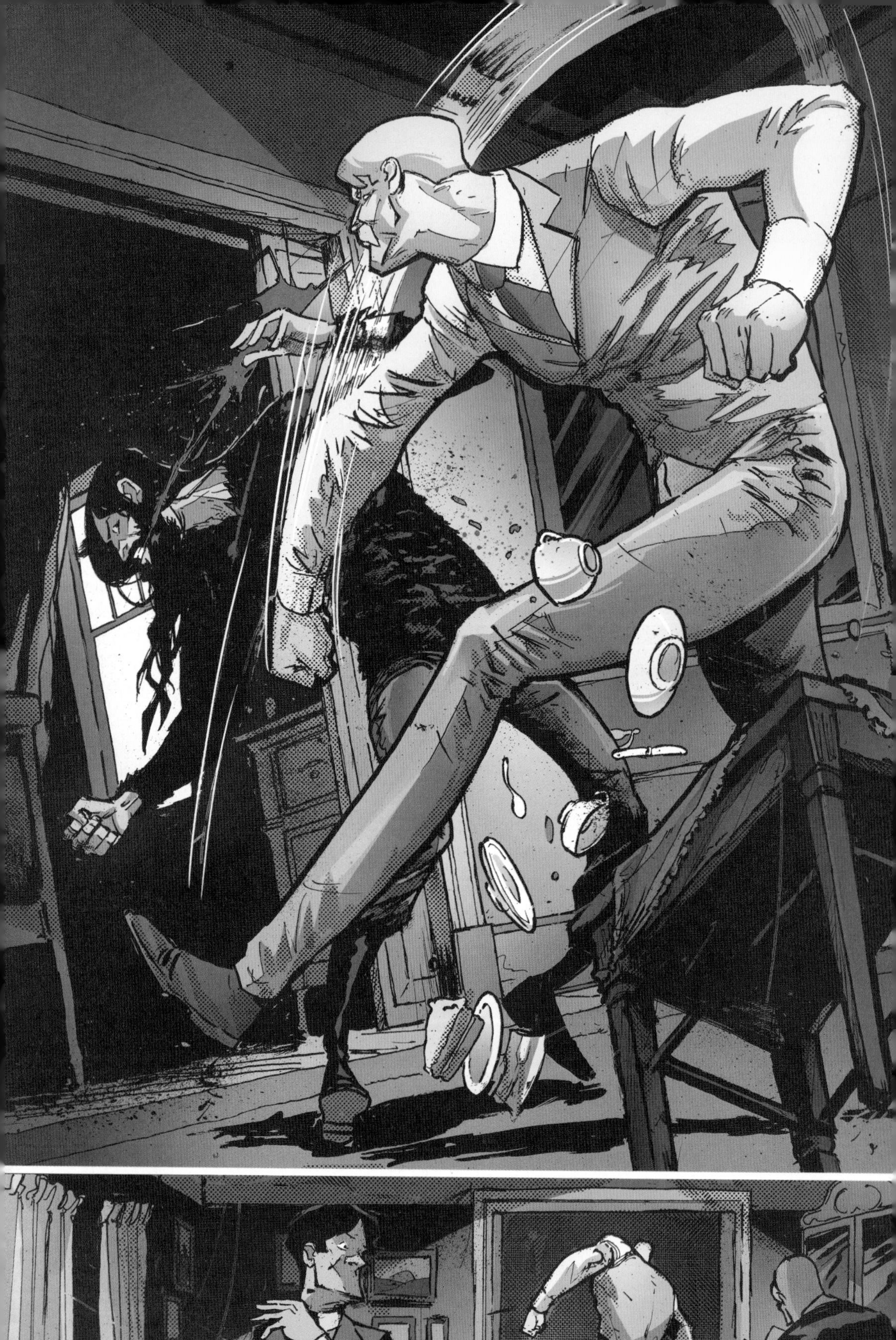
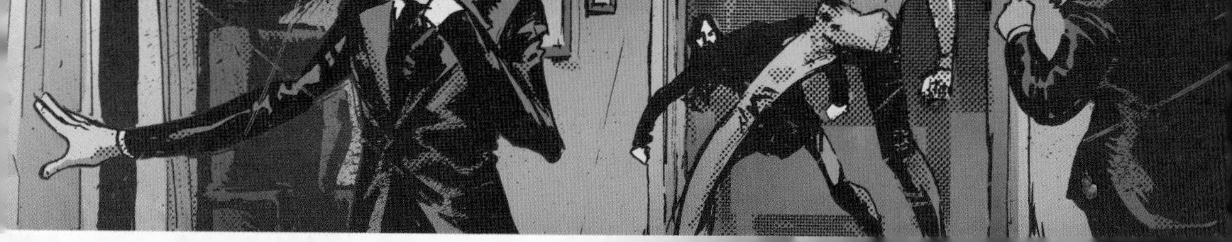

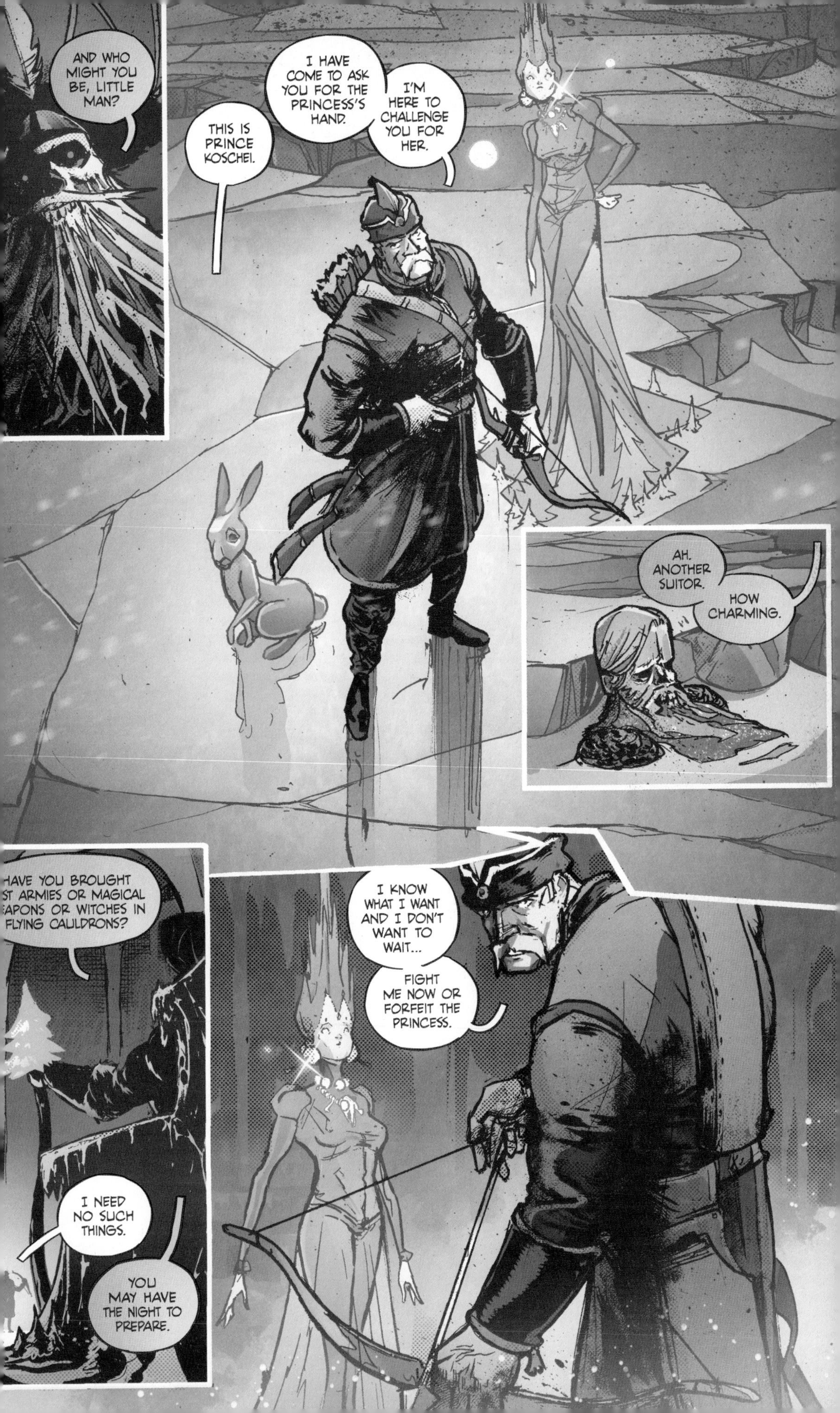
AND WHO MIGHT YOU BE, LITTLE MAN?
THIS IS PRINCE KOSCHEI.
I HAVE COME TO ASK YOU FOR THE PRINCESS'S HAND.
I'M HERE TO CHALLENGE YOU FOR HER.
AH. ANOTHER SUITOR.
HOW CHARMING.
HAVE YOU BROUGHT ST ARMIES OR MAGICAL EAPONS OR WITCHES IN FLYING CAULDRONS?
I NEED NO SUCH THINGS.
YOU MAY HAVE THE NIGHT TO PREPARE.
I KNOW WHAT I WANT AND I DON'T WANT TO WAIT...
FIGHT ME NOW OR FORFEIT THE PRINCESS.

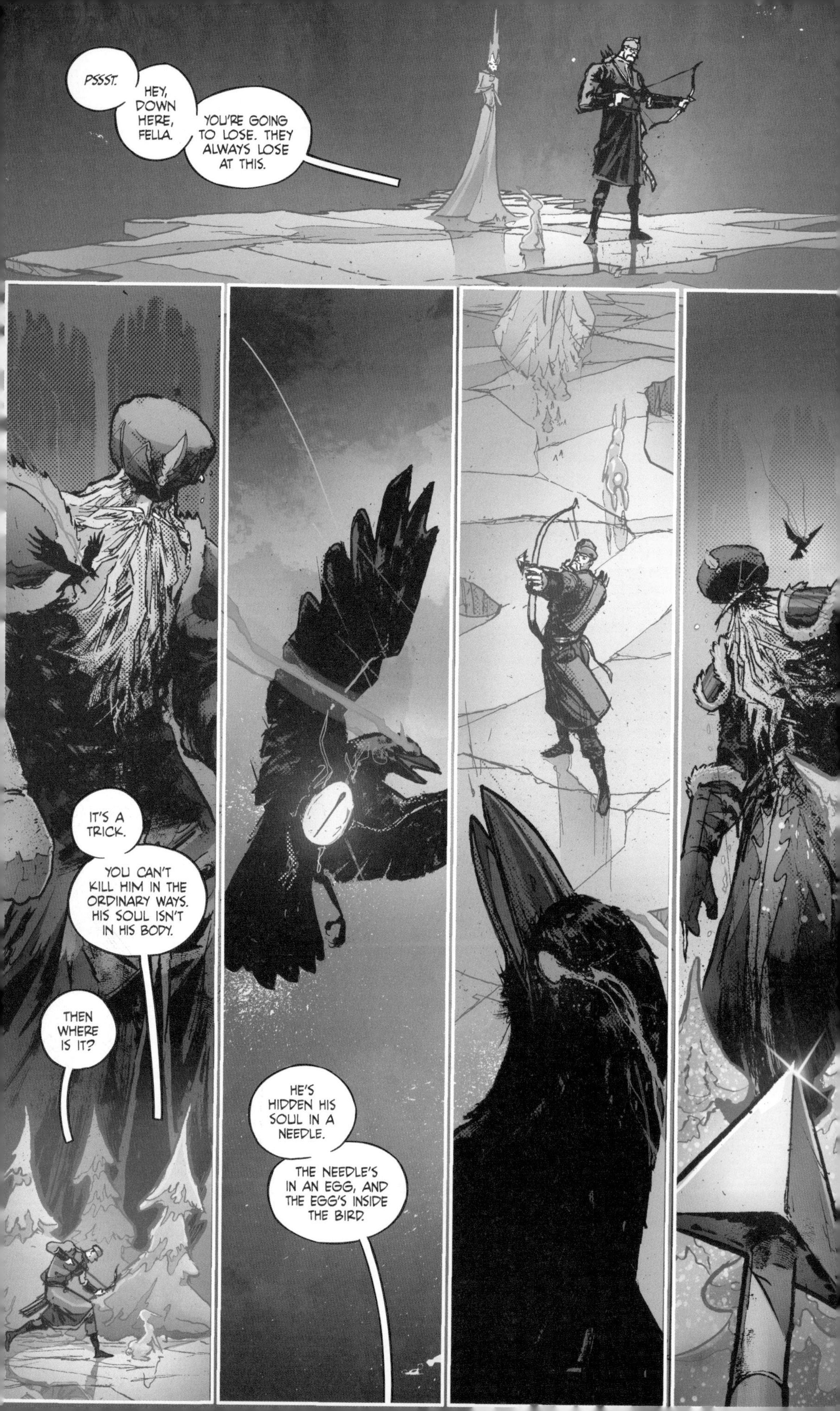
PSSST.
HEY, DOWN HERE, FELLA.
YOU'RE GOING TO LOSE. THEY ALWAYS LOSE AT THIS.
IT'S A TRICK.
YOU CAN'T KILL HIM IN THE ORDINARY WAYS. HIS SOUL ISN'T IN HIS BODY.
THEN WHERE IS IT?
HE'S HIDDEN HIS SOUL IN A NEEDLE.
THE NEEDLE'S IN AN EGG, AND THE EGG'S INSIDE THE BIRD.

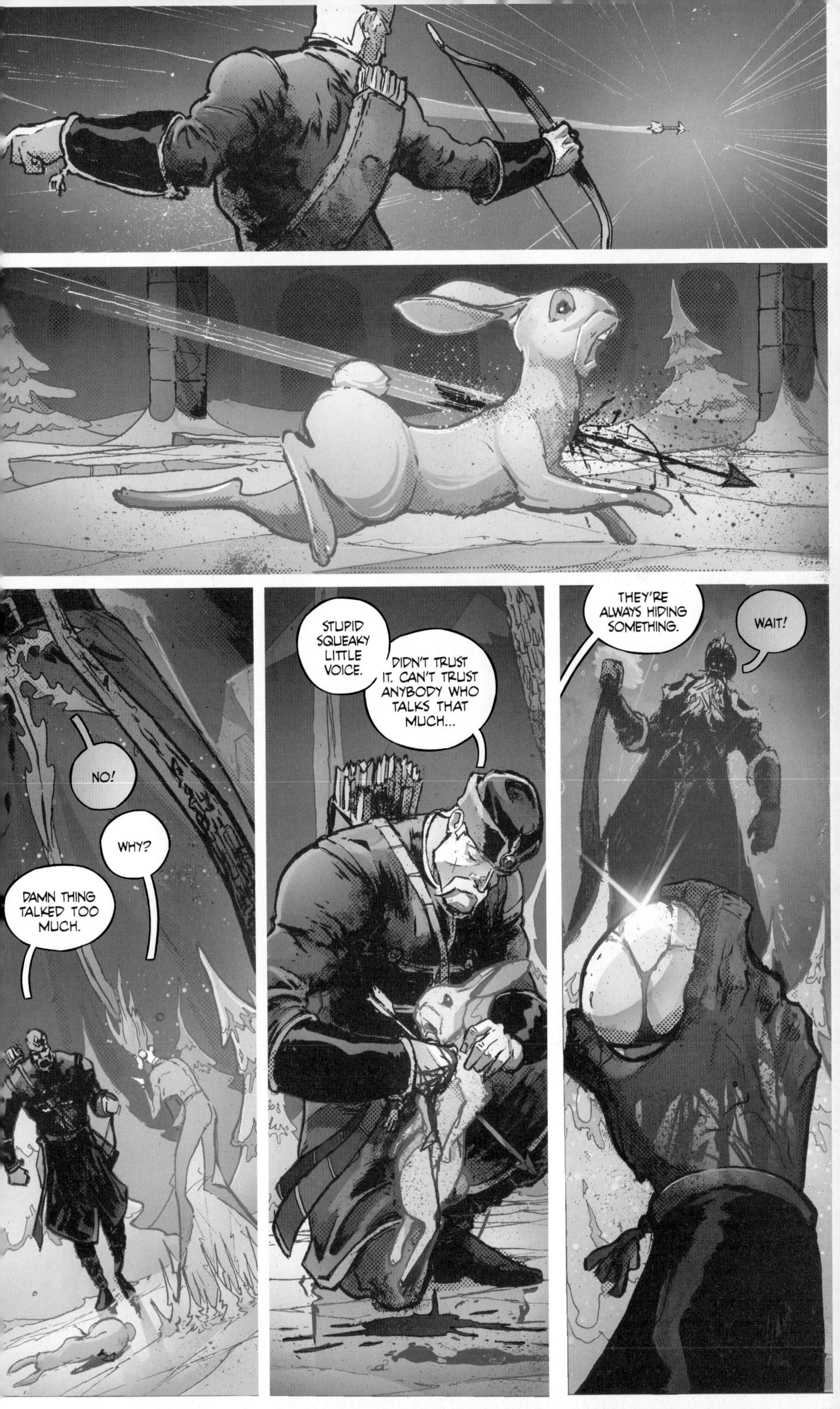
NO!
WHY?
DAMN THING TALKED TOO MUCH.
STUPID SQUEAKY LITTLE VOICE.
DIDN'T TRUST IT. CAN'T TRUST ANYBODY WHO TALKS THAT MUCH...
THEY'RE ALWAYS HIDING SOMETHING.
WAIT!

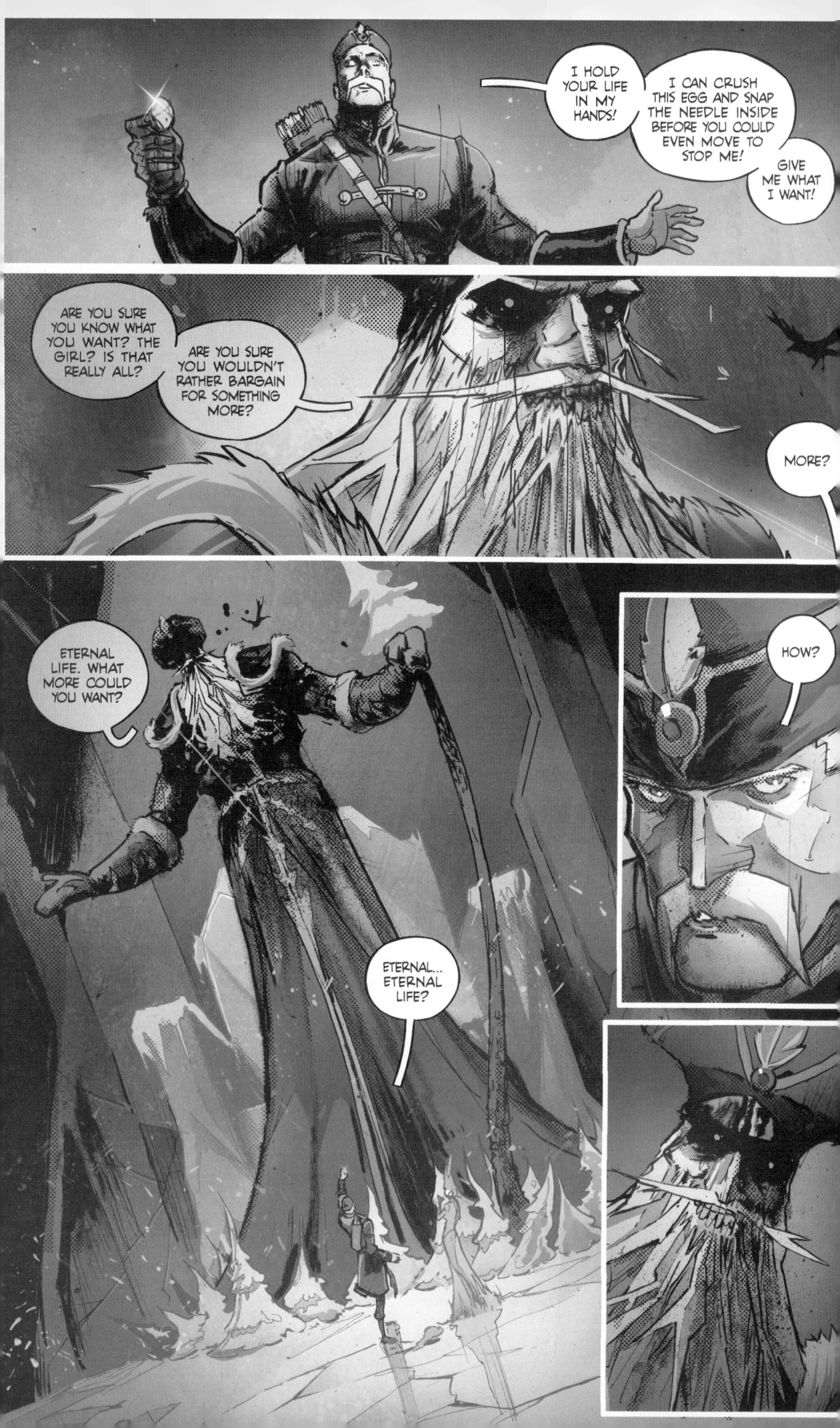

I HOLD YOUR LIFE IN MY HANDS!
I CAN CRUSH THIS EGG AND SNAP THE NEEDLE INSIDE BEFORE YOU COULD EVEN MOVE TO STOP ME!
GIVE ME WHAT I WANT!
ARE YOU SURE YOU KNOW WHAT YOU WANT? THE GIRL? IS THAT REALLY ALL?
ARE YOU SURE YOU WOULDN'T RATHER BARGAIN FOR SOMETHING MORE?
MORE?
ETERNAL LIFE. WHAT MORE COULD YOU WANT?
ETERNAL... ETERNAL LIFE?
HOW?

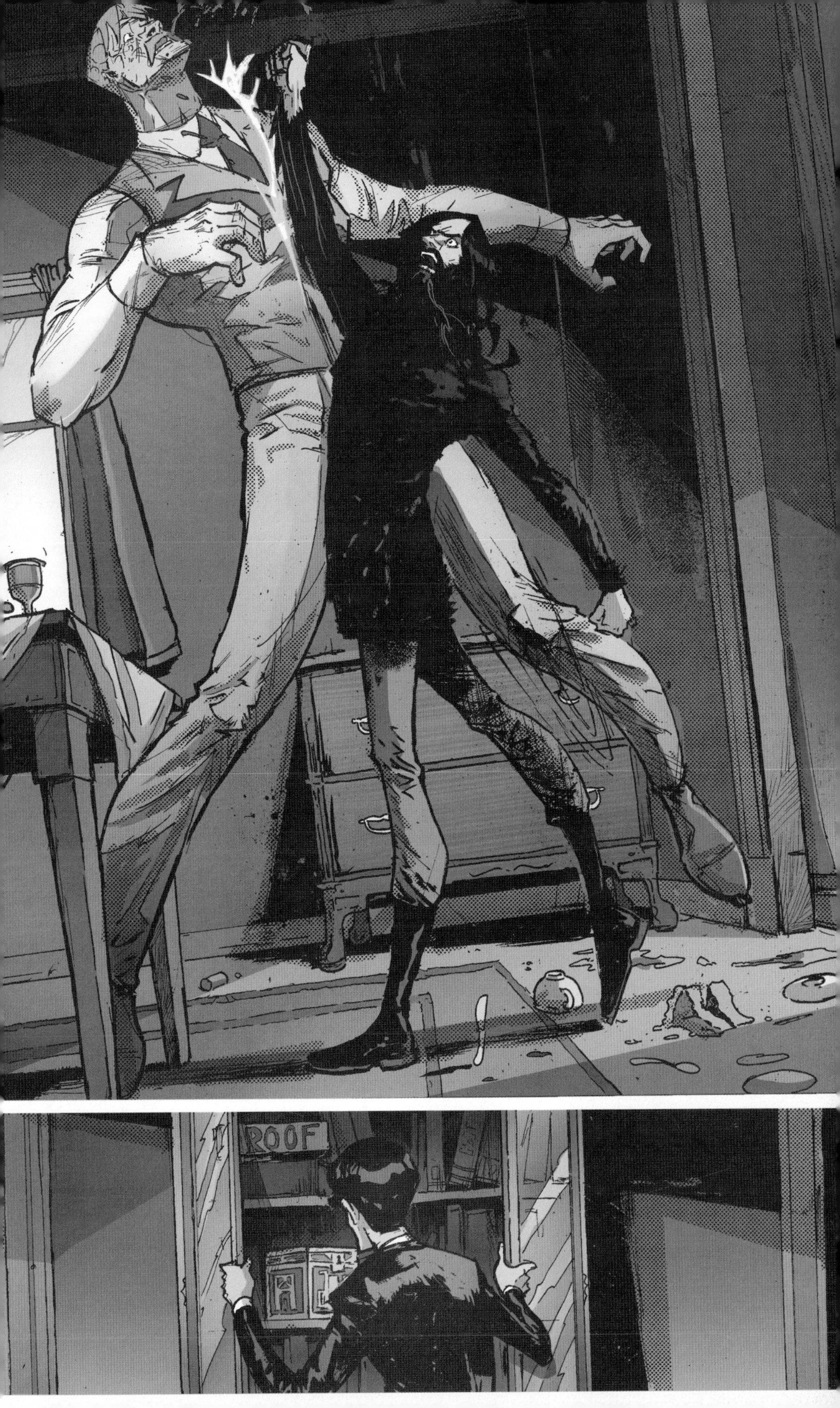
ROOF

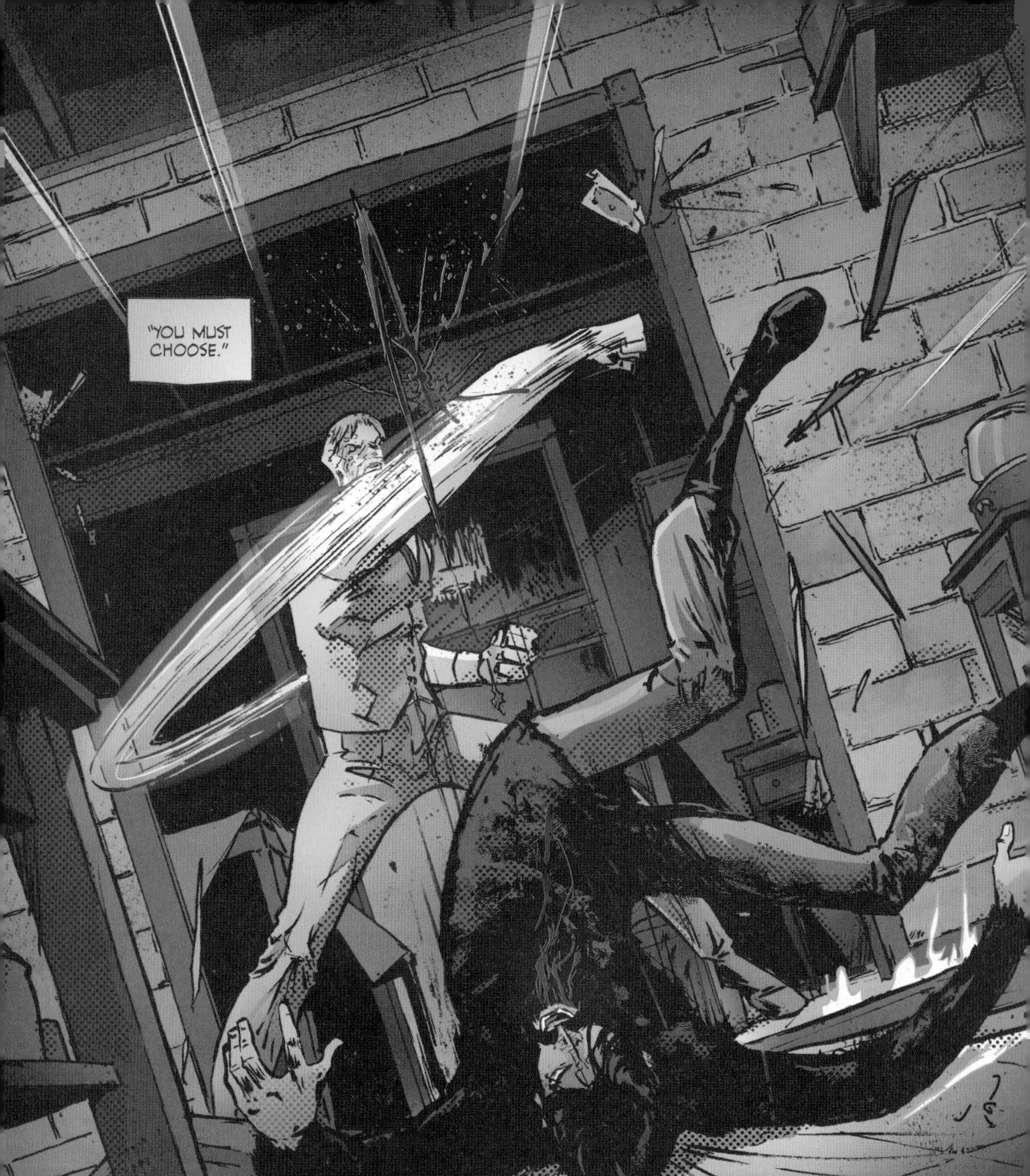
"YOU MUST CHOOSE."

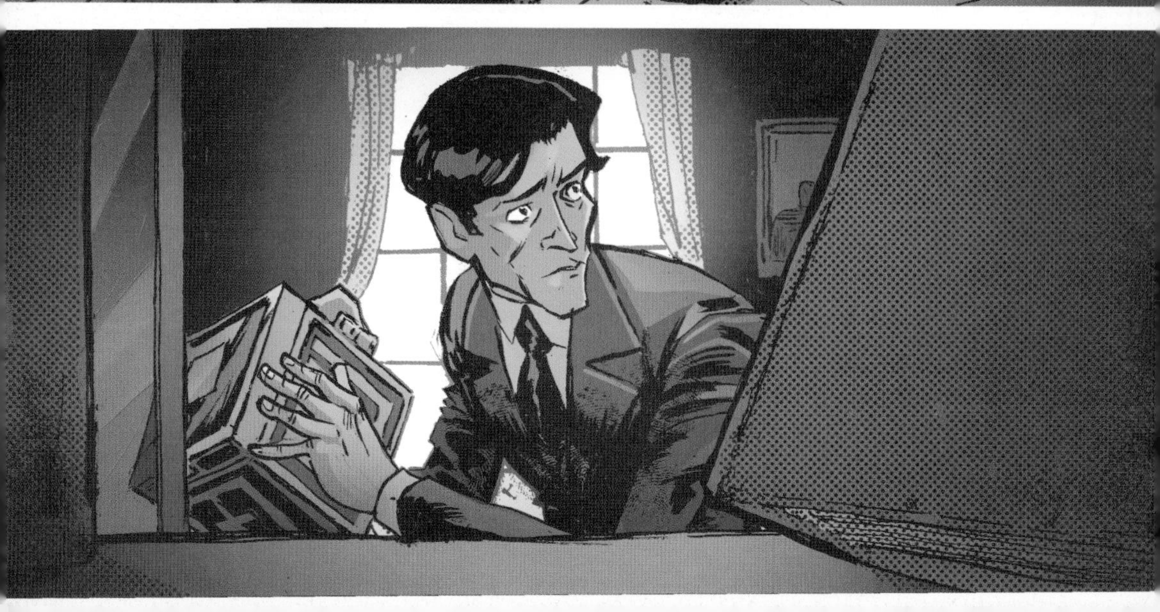

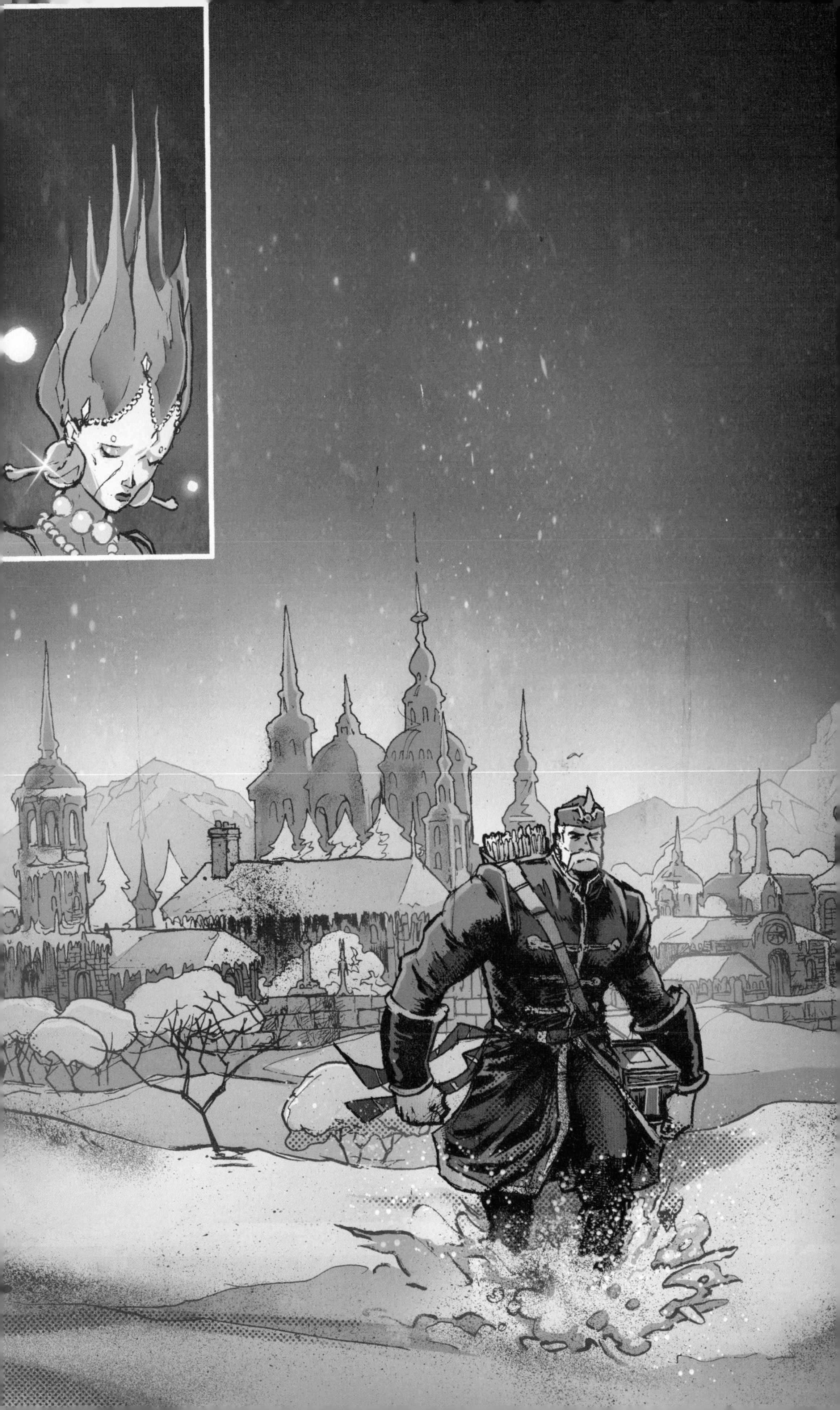

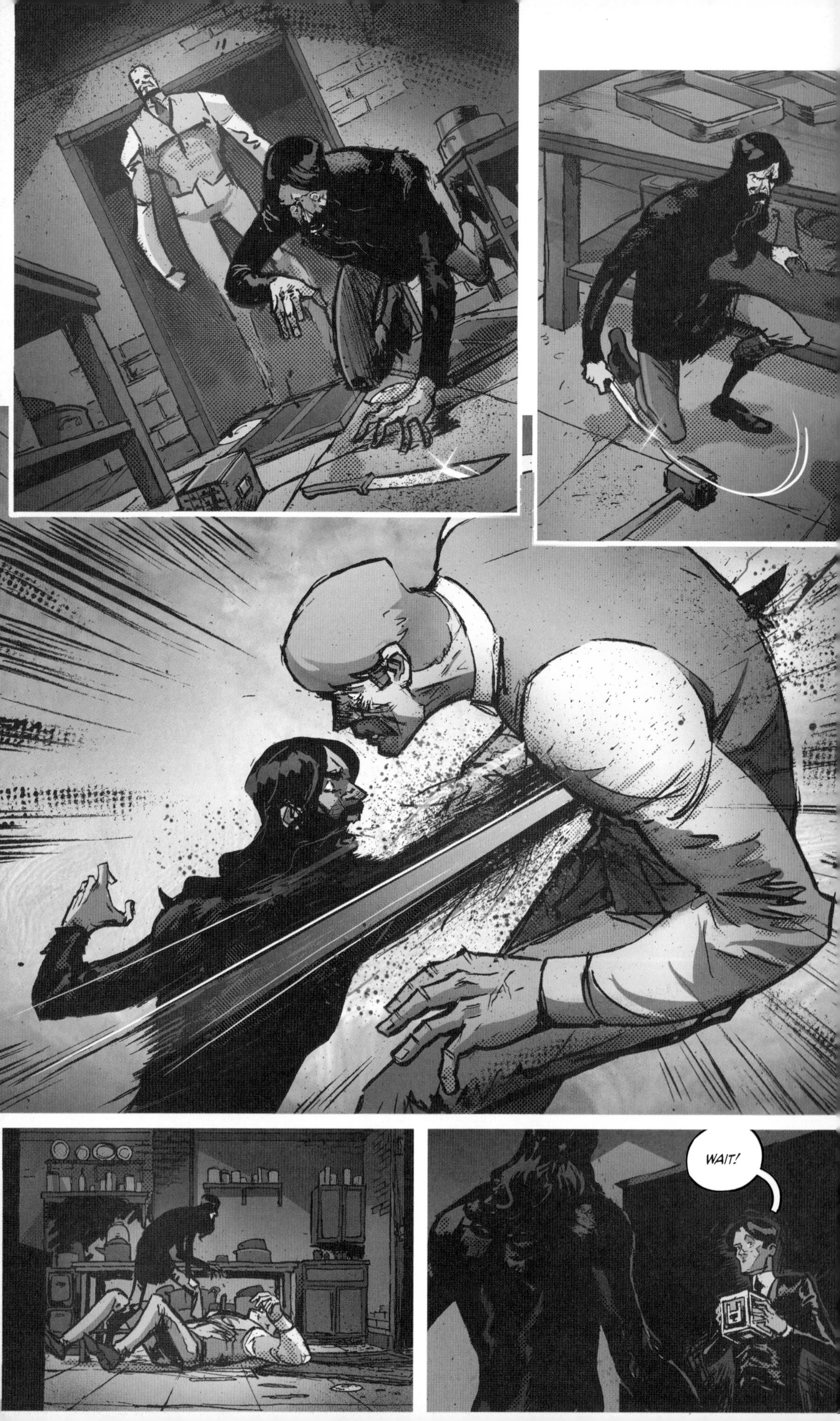
WAIT!

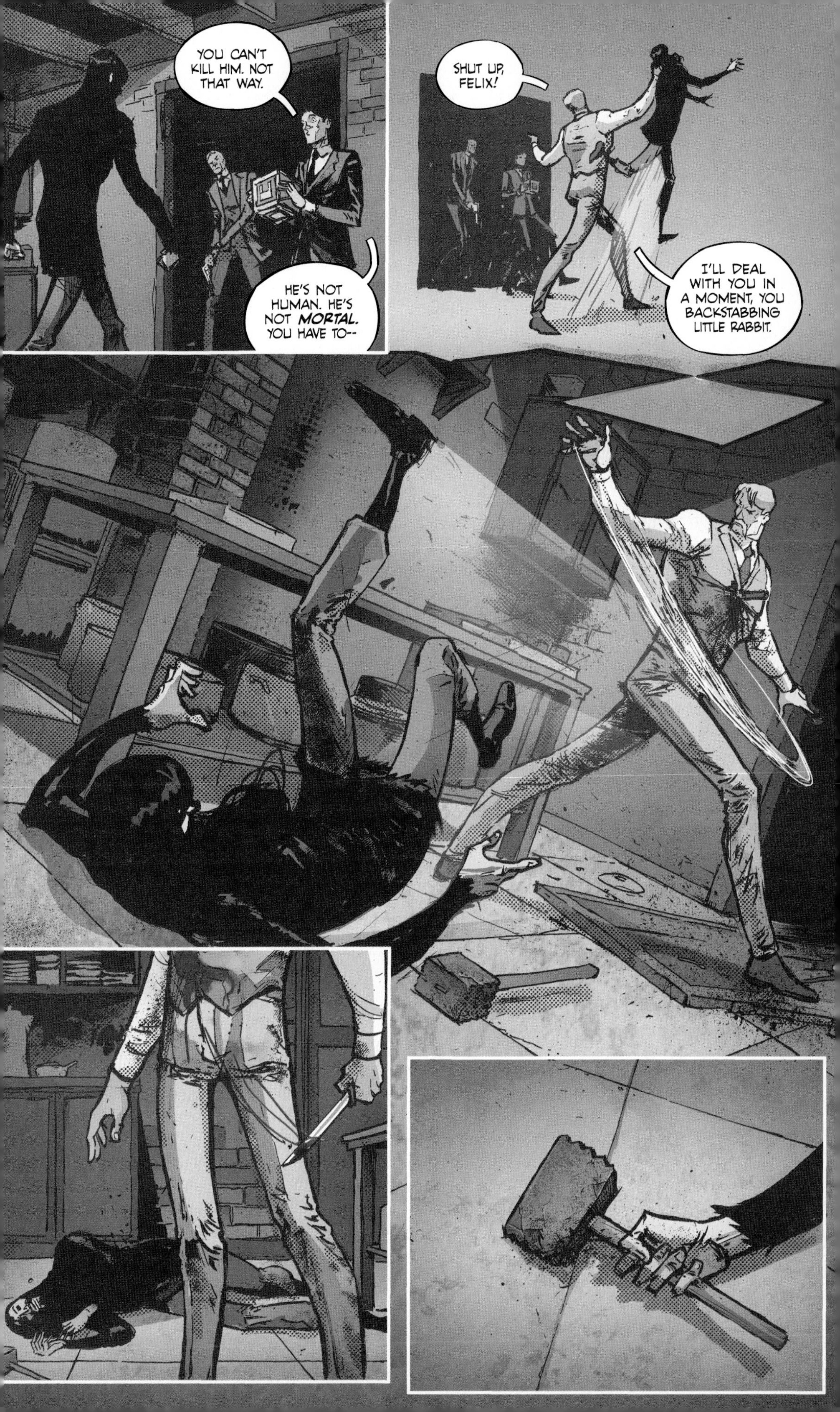
YOU CAN'T KILL HIM. NOT THAT WAY.
HE'S NOT HUMAN. HE'S NOT **MORTAL.** YOU HAVE TO--
SHUT UP, FELIX!
I'LL DEAL WITH YOU IN A MOMENT, YOU BACKSTABBING LITTLE RABBIT.

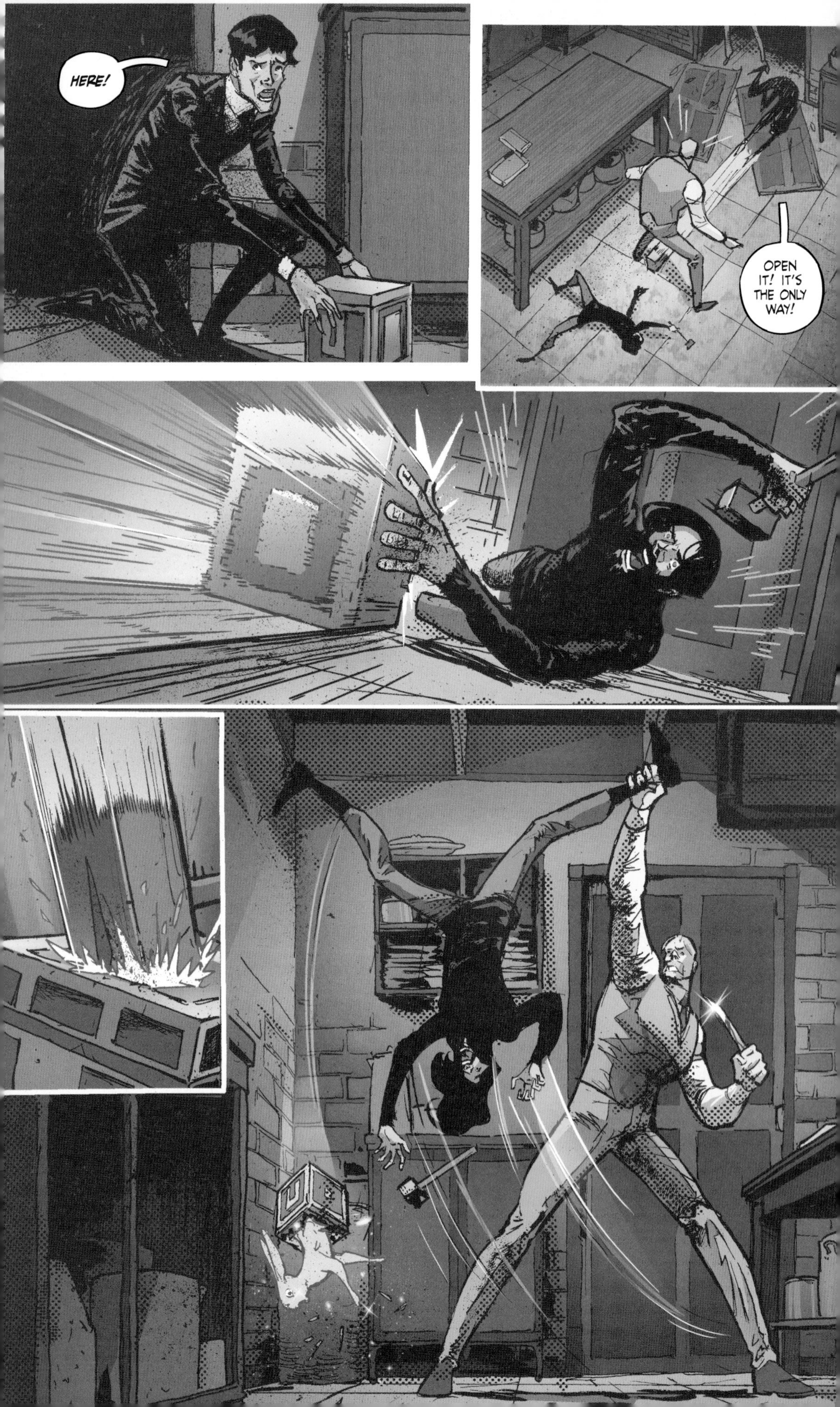
HERE!
OPEN IT! IT'S THE ONLY WAY!

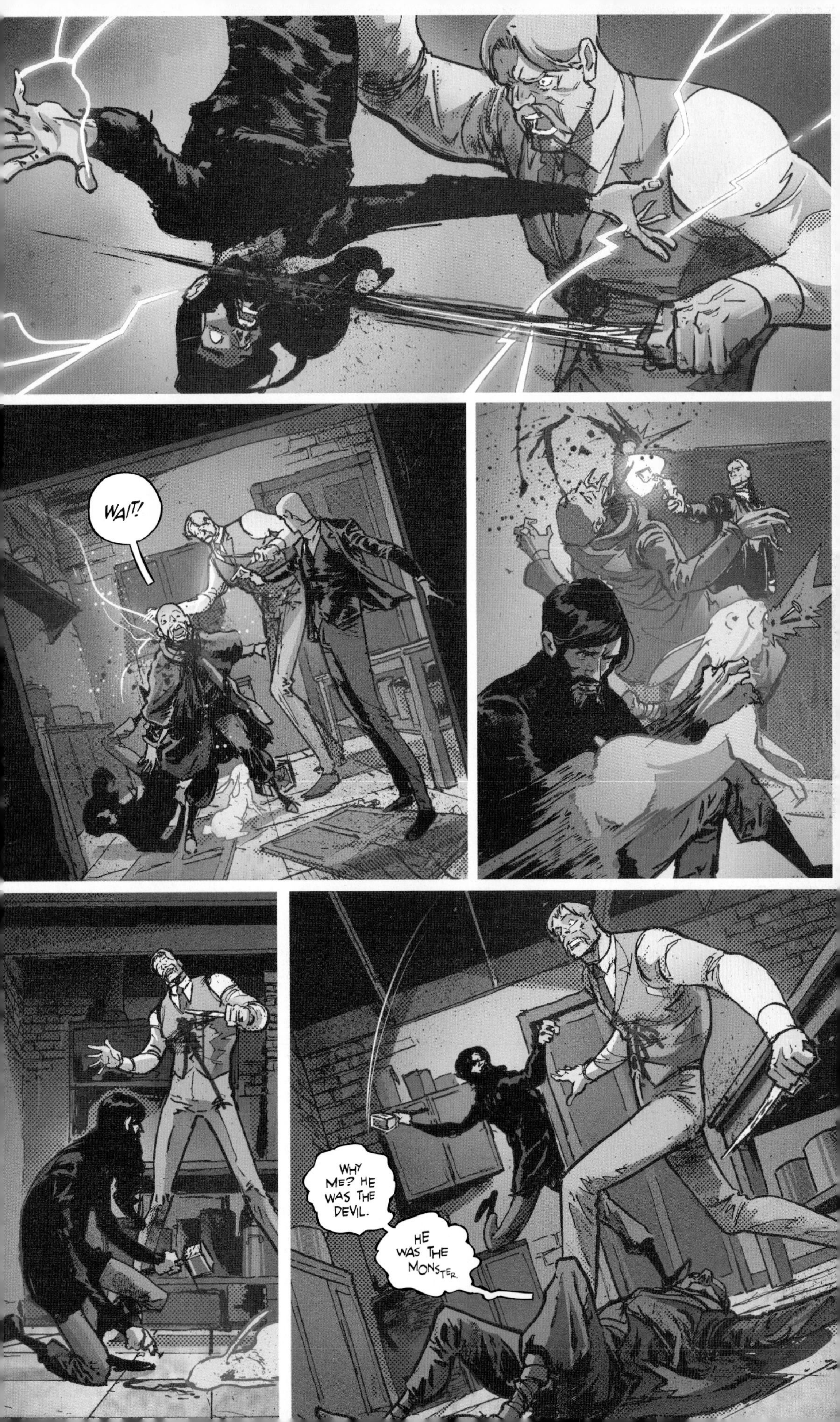
WAIT!
WHY ME? HE WAS THE DEVIL.
HE WAS THE MONSTER.

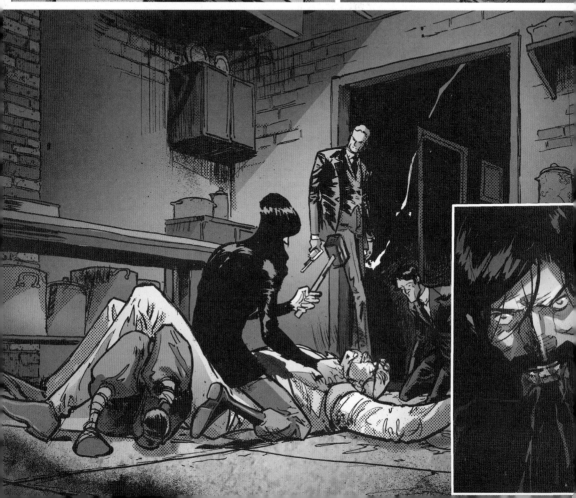

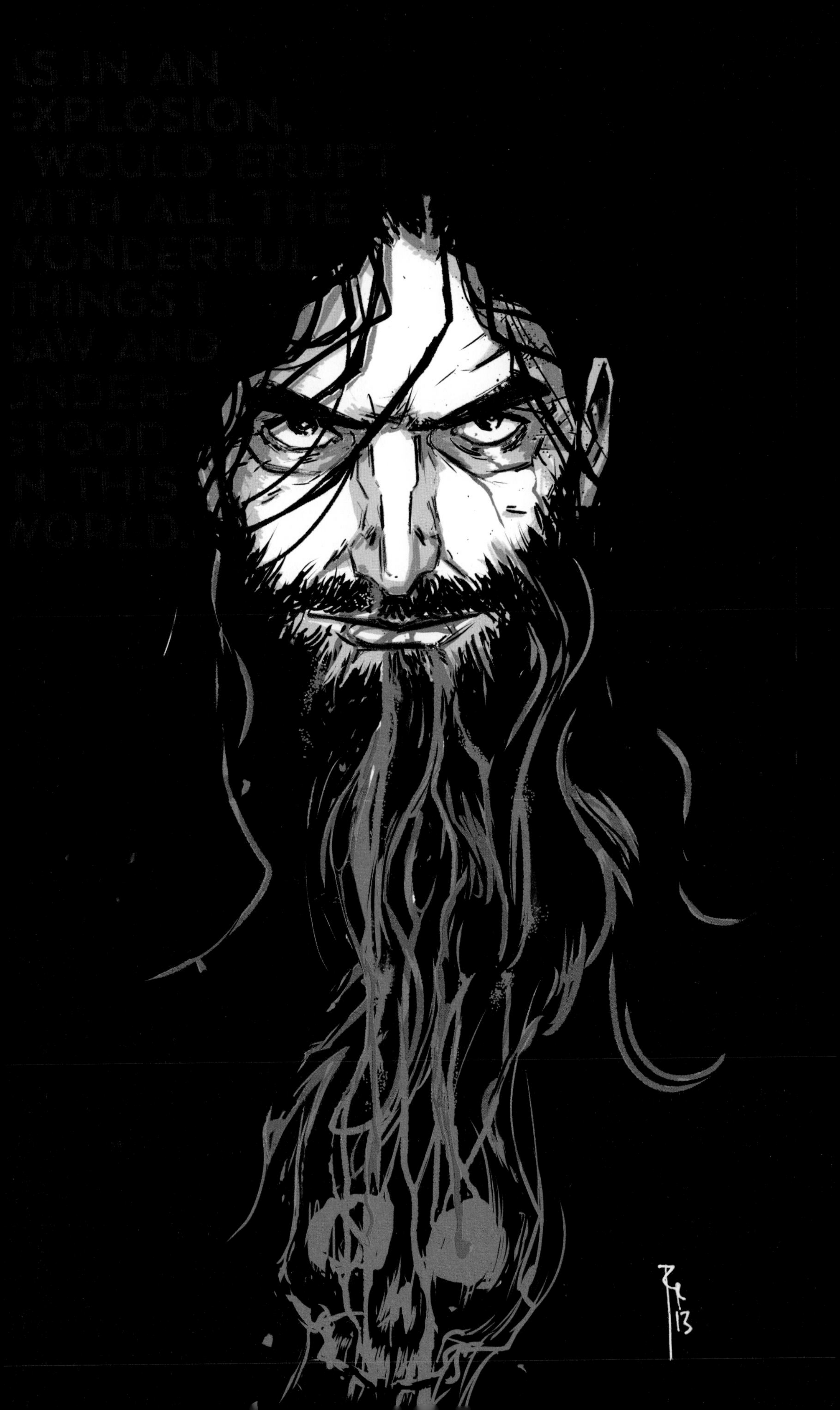
S IN AN
XPLOSION,
WOULD ERUPT
VITH ALL THE
VONDERFUL
THINGS I
SAW AND
JNDER-
STOOD
N THIS
WORLD.

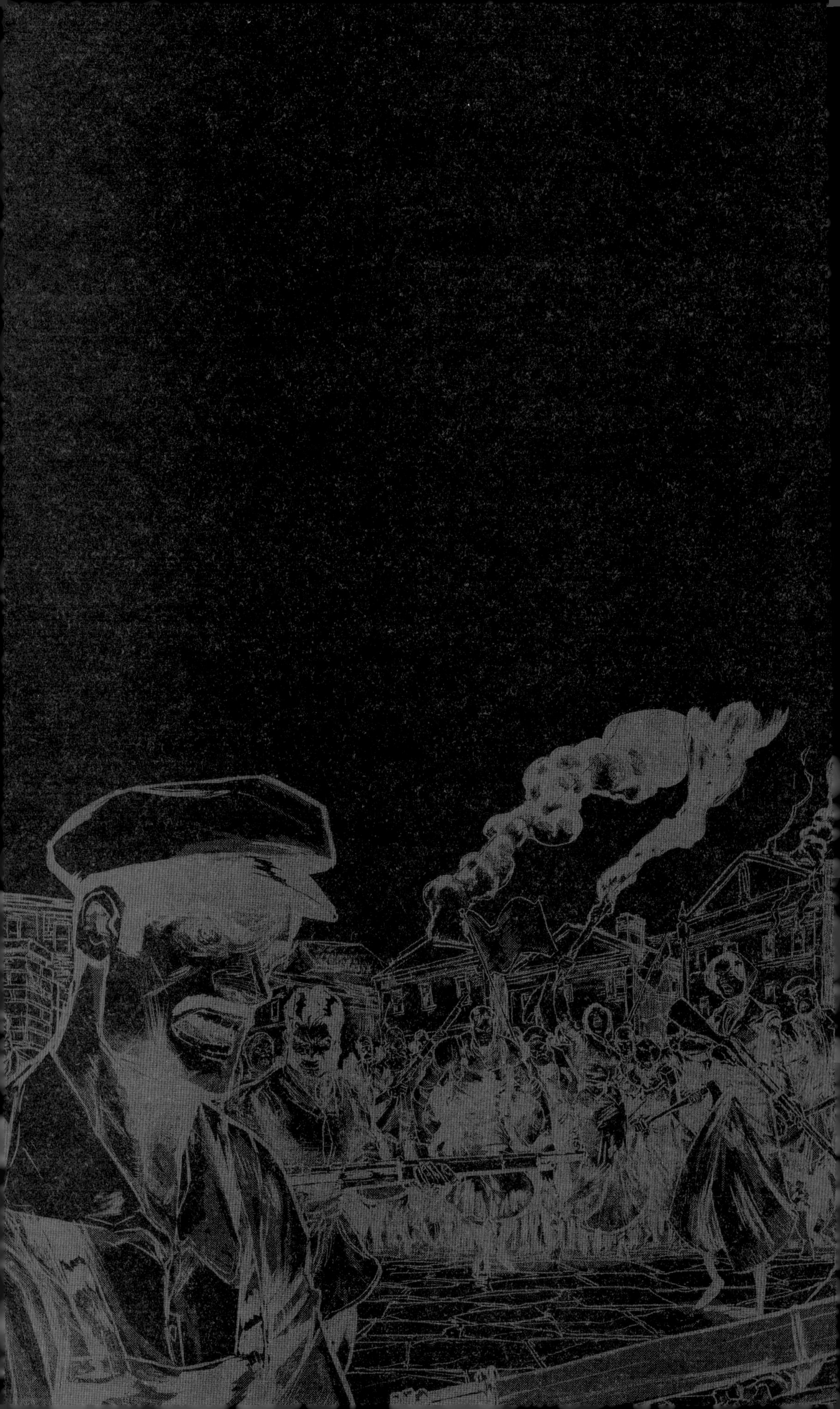

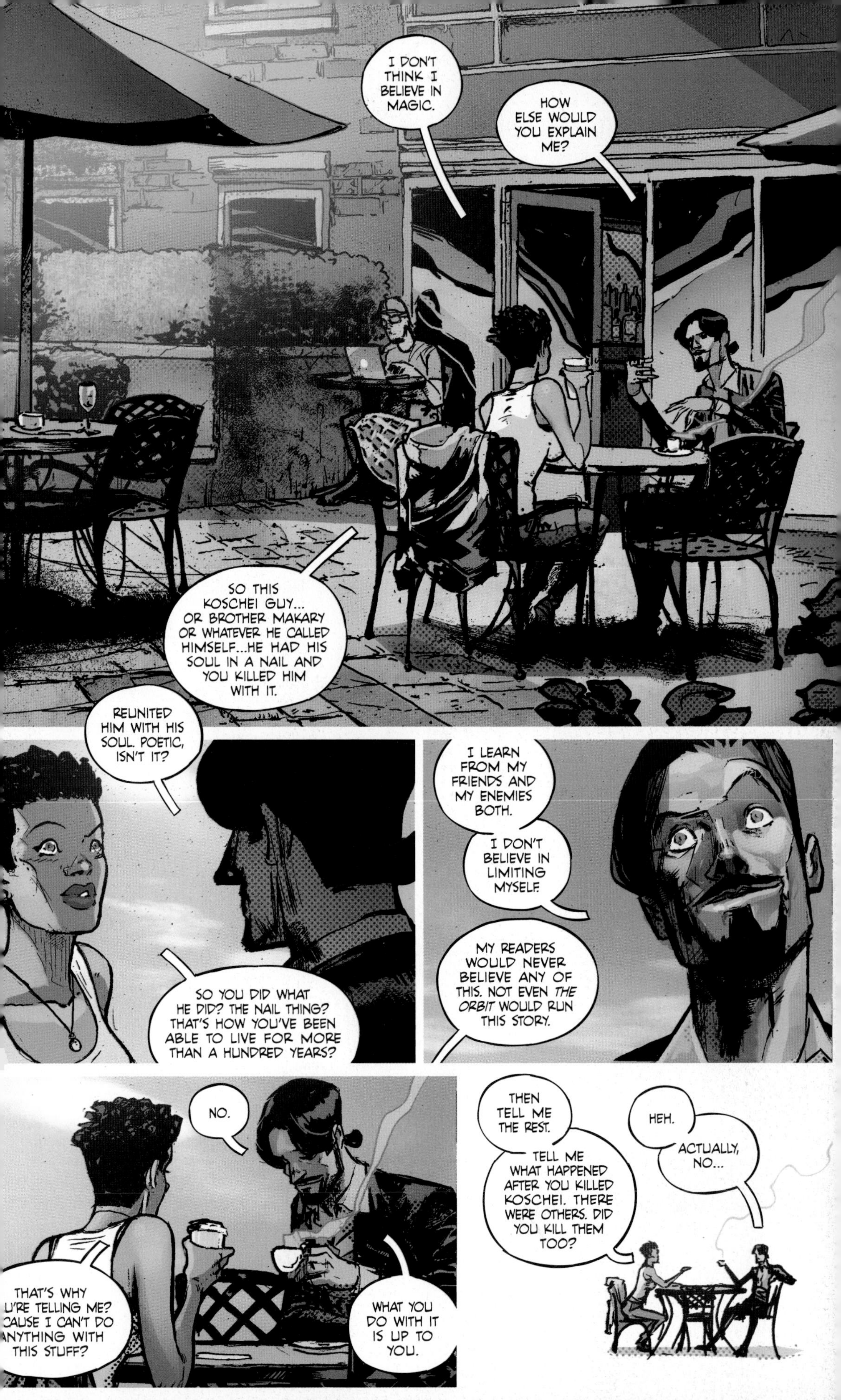
I DON'T THINK I BELIEVE IN MAGIC.
HOW ELSE WOULD YOU EXPLAIN ME?
SO THIS KOSCHEI GUY... OR BROTHER MAKARY OR WHATEVER HE CALLED HIMSELF...HE HAD HIS SOUL IN A NAIL AND YOU KILLED HIM WITH IT.
REUNITED HIM WITH HIS SOUL. POETIC, ISN'T IT?
SO YOU DID WHAT HE DID? THE NAIL THING? THAT'S HOW YOU'VE BEEN ABLE TO LIVE FOR MORE THAN A HUNDRED YEARS?
I LEARN FROM MY FRIENDS AND MY ENEMIES BOTH.
I DON'T BELIEVE IN LIMITING MYSELF.
MY READERS WOULD NEVER BELIEVE ANY OF THIS. NOT EVEN *THE ORBIT* WOULD RUN THIS STORY.
NO.
THAT'S WHY U'RE TELLING ME? CAUSE I CAN'T DO NYTHING WITH THIS STUFF?
WHAT YOU DO WITH IT IS UP TO YOU.
THEN TELL ME THE REST.
TELL ME WHAT HAPPENED AFTER YOU KILLED KOSCHEI. THERE WERE OTHERS. DID YOU KILL THEM TOO?
HEH.
ACTUALLY, NO...

"MY FATHER'S INFLUENCE OVER ME WAS NOT STRONG."

"TO MY GREAT RELIEF I HAVE NEVER BEEN TEMPTED TO KILL AGAIN."

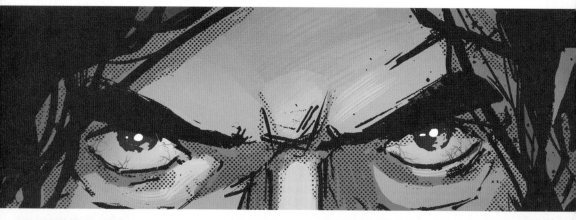

LISTEN. DO YOU HEAR THAT?

ARE YOU GOING TO SHOOT ME AGAIN?

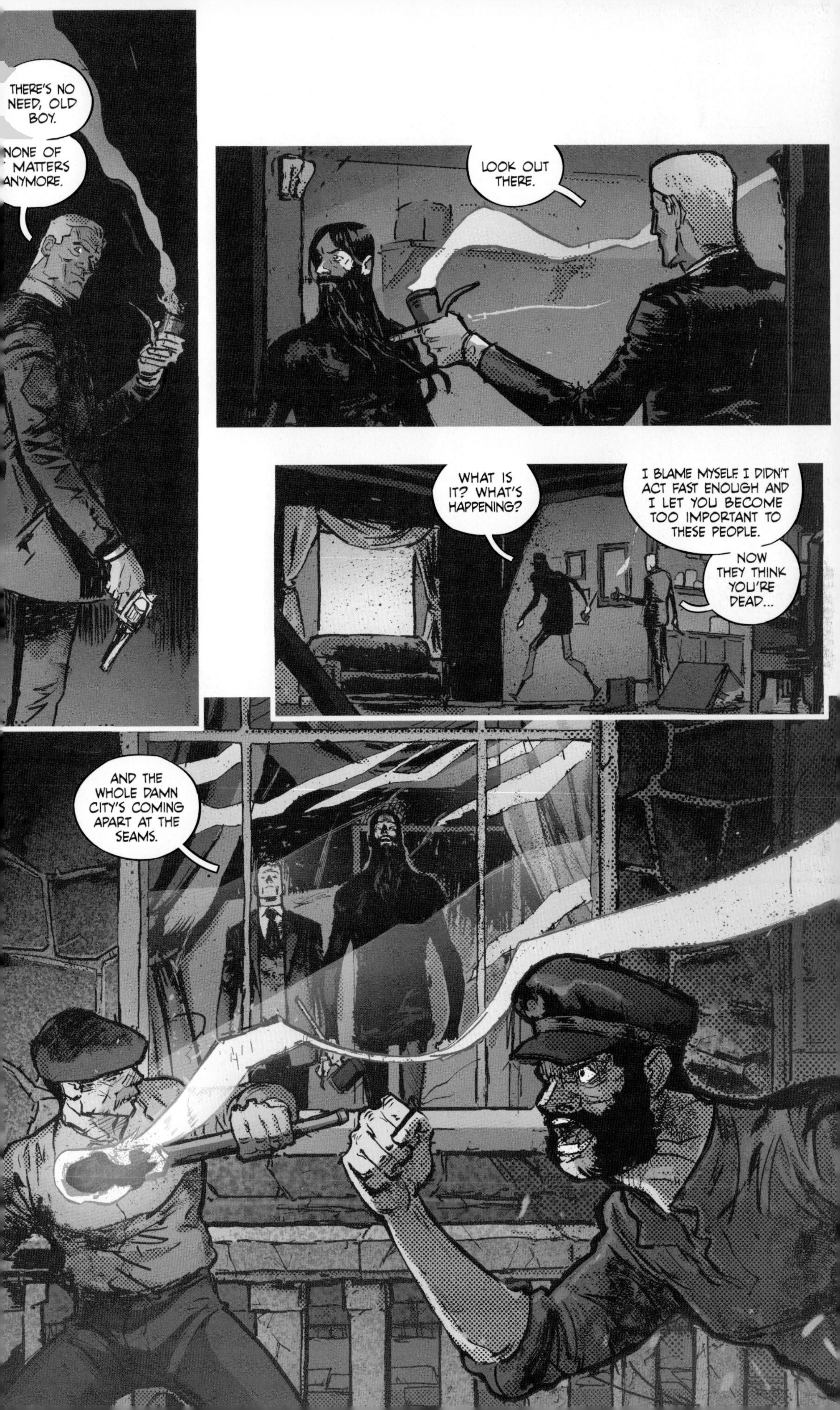
THERE'S NO NEED, OLD BOY.
NONE OF MATTERS ANYMORE.
LOOK OUT THERE.
WHAT IS IT? WHAT'S HAPPENING?
I BLAME MYSELF. I DIDN'T ACT FAST ENOUGH AND I LET YOU BECOME TOO IMPORTANT TO THESE PEOPLE.
NOW THEY THINK YOU'RE DEAD...
AND THE WHOLE DAMN CITY'S COMING APART AT THE SEAMS.

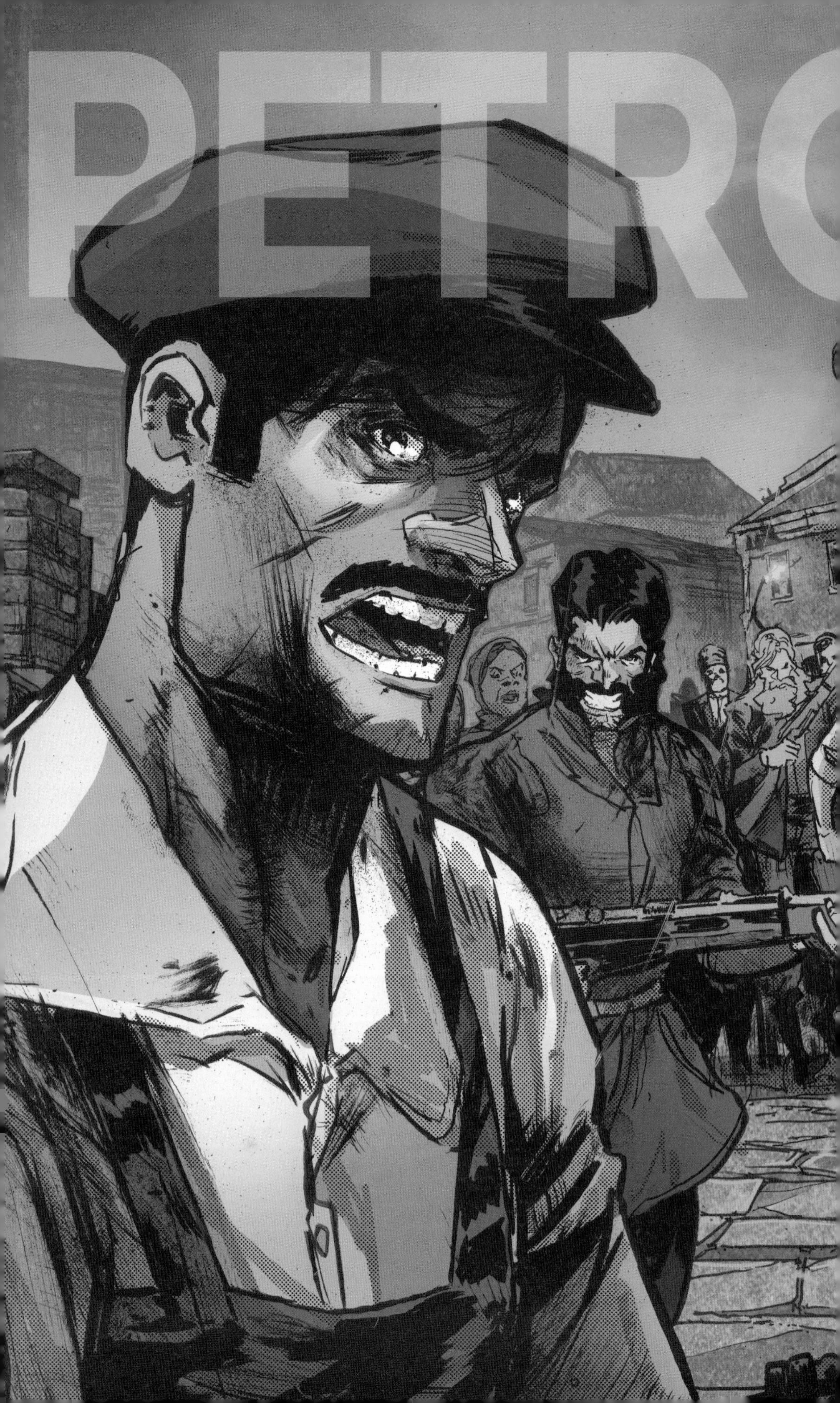
PETRO

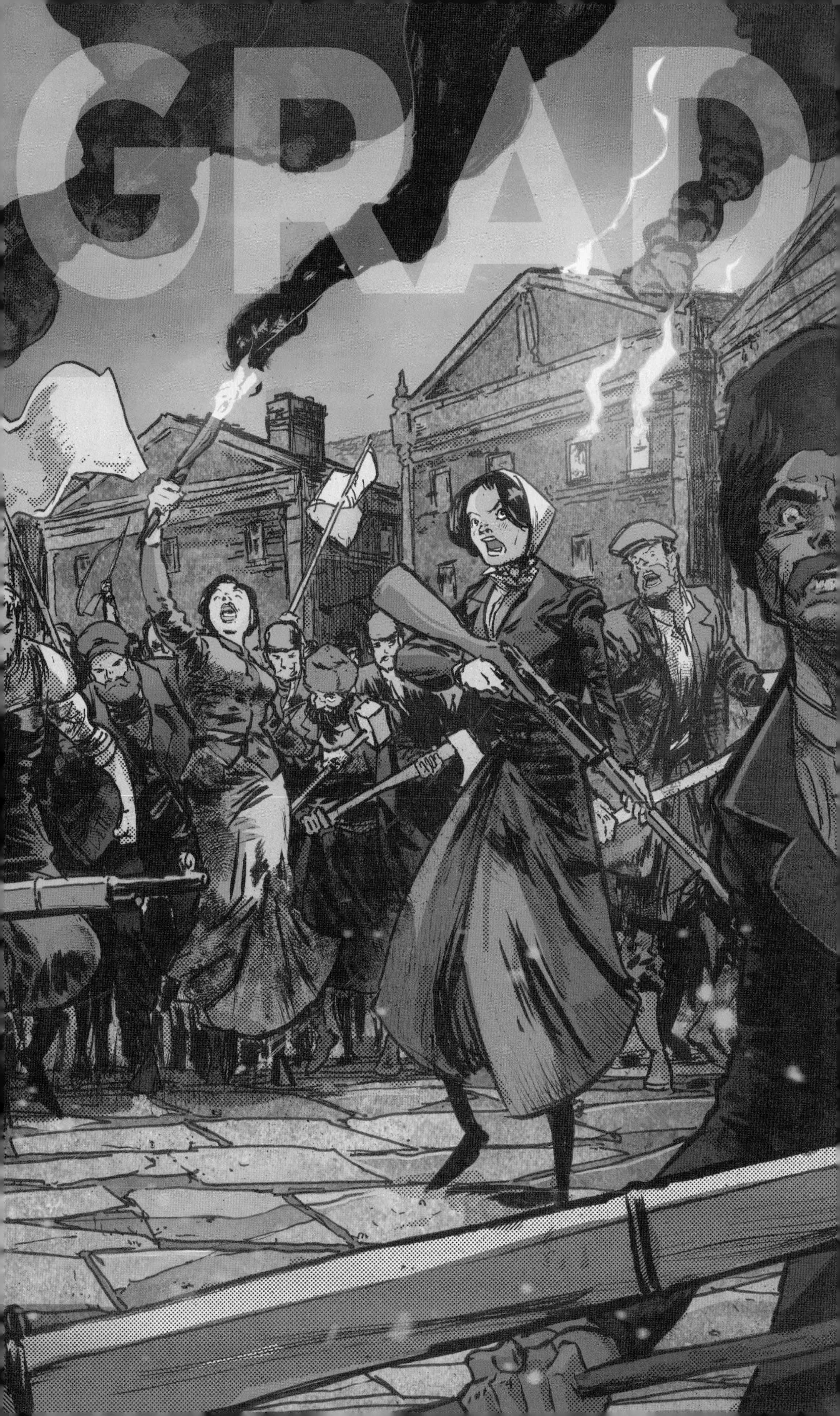
GRAD

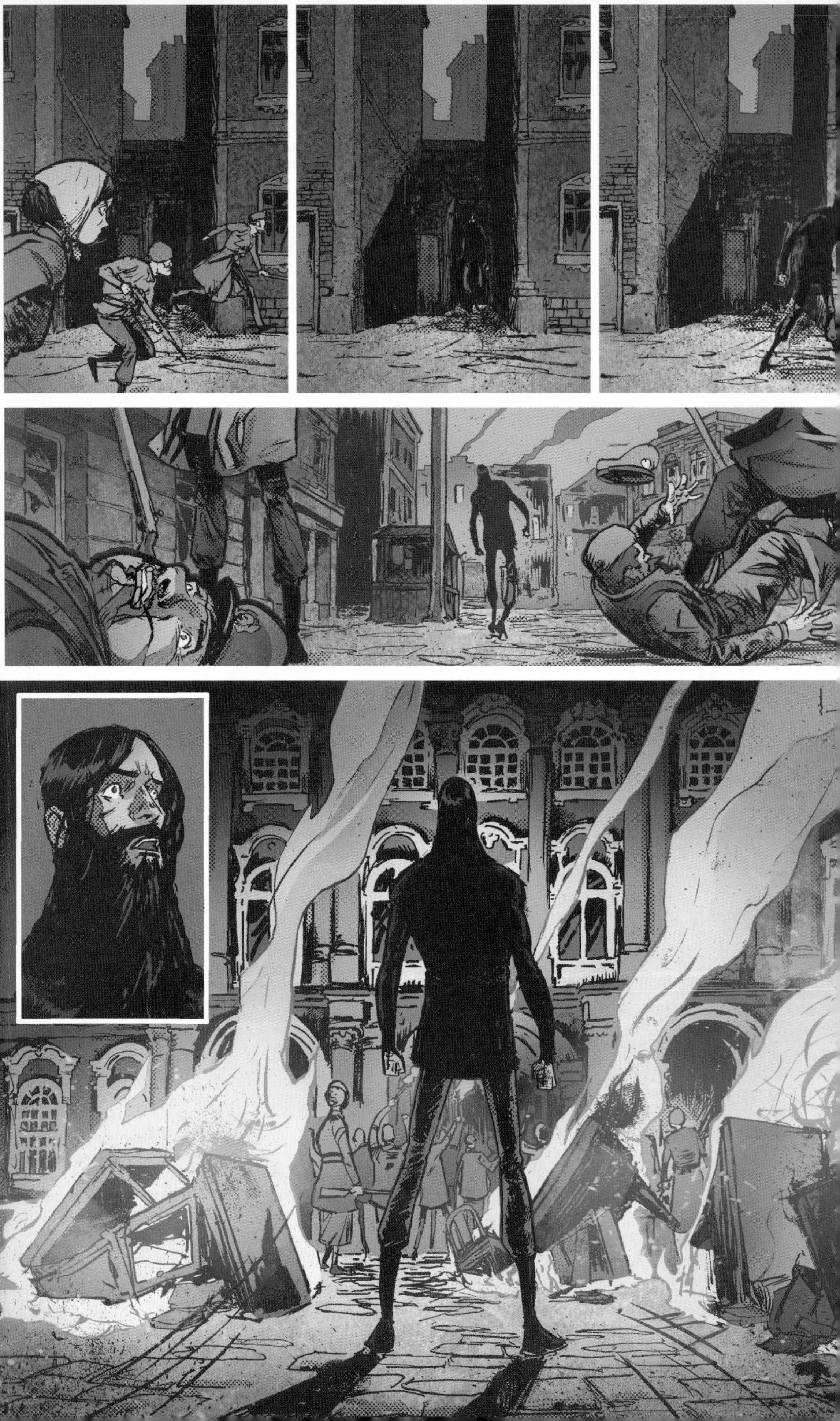

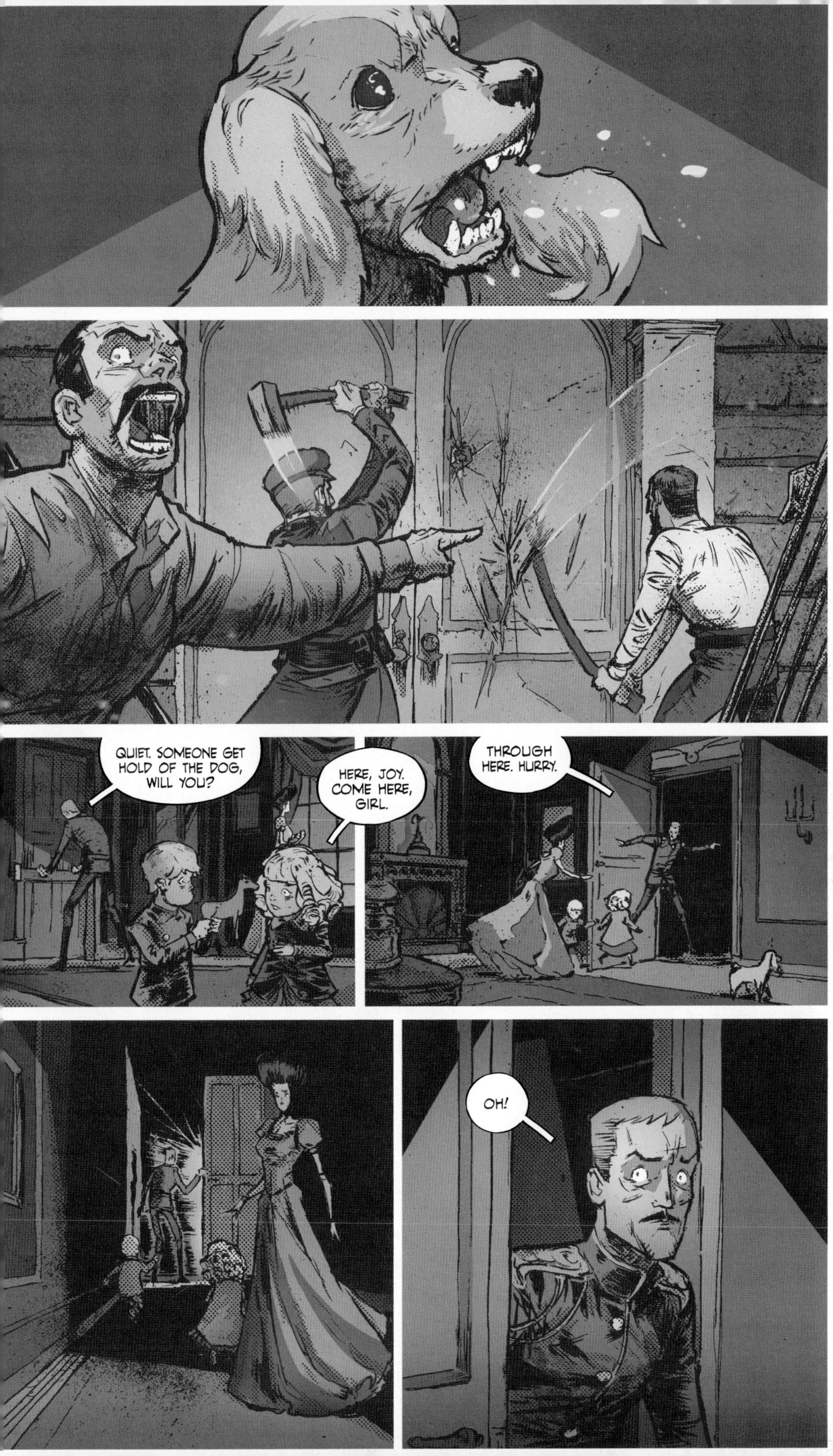
QUIET. SOMEONE GET HOLD OF THE DOG, WILL YOU?
HERE, JOY. COME HERE, GIRL.
THROUGH HERE. HURRY.
OH!

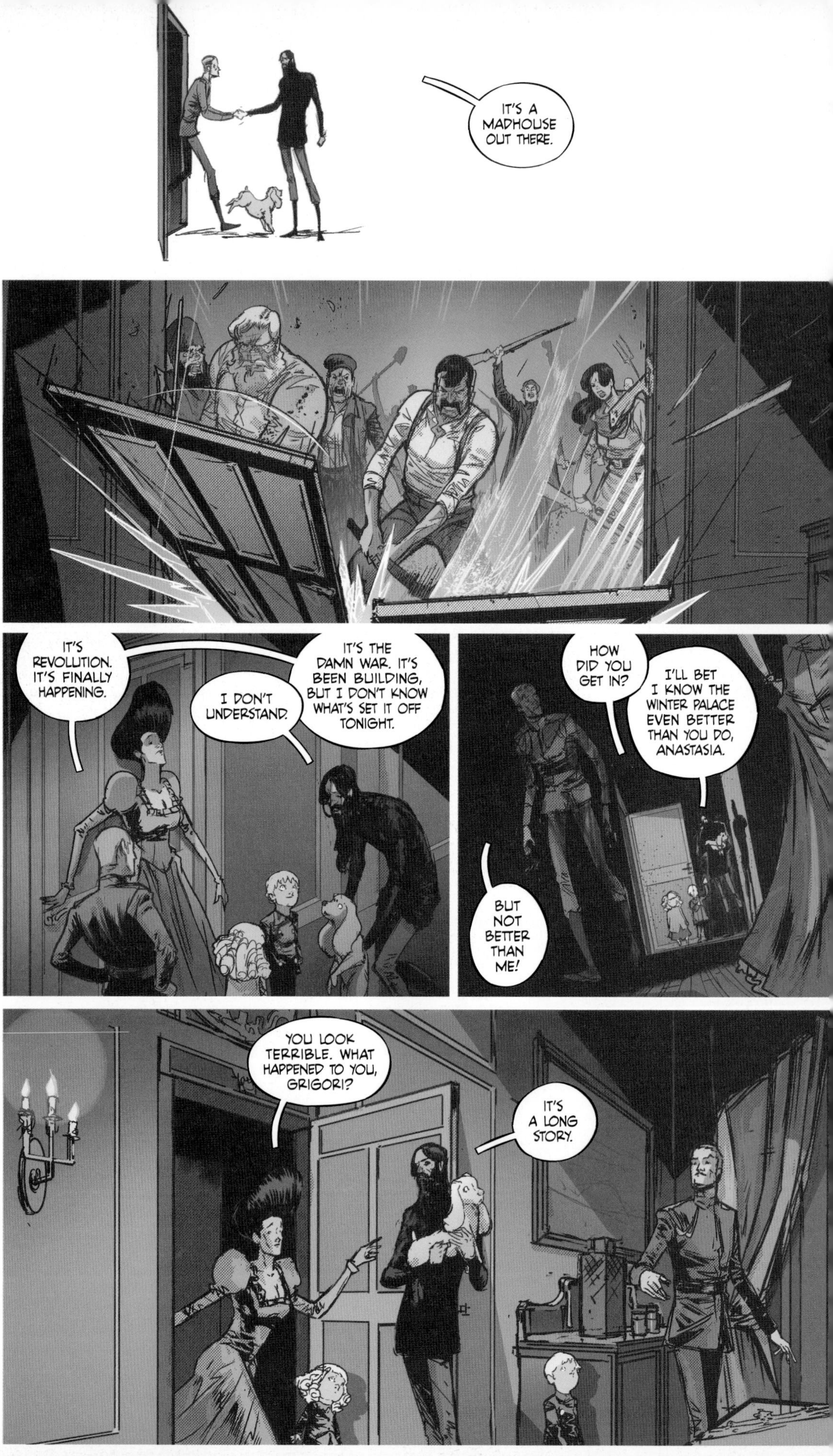
IT'S A MADHOUSE OUT THERE.
IT'S REVOLUTION. IT'S FINALLY HAPPENING.
I DON'T UNDERSTAND.
IT'S THE DAMN WAR. IT'S BEEN BUILDING, BUT I DON'T KNOW WHAT'S SET IT OFF TONIGHT.
HOW DID YOU GET IN?
I'LL BET I KNOW THE WINTER PALACE EVEN BETTER THAN YOU DO, ANASTASIA.
BUT NOT BETTER THAN ME!
YOU LOOK TERRIBLE. WHAT HAPPENED TO YOU, GRIGORI?
IT'S A LONG STORY.

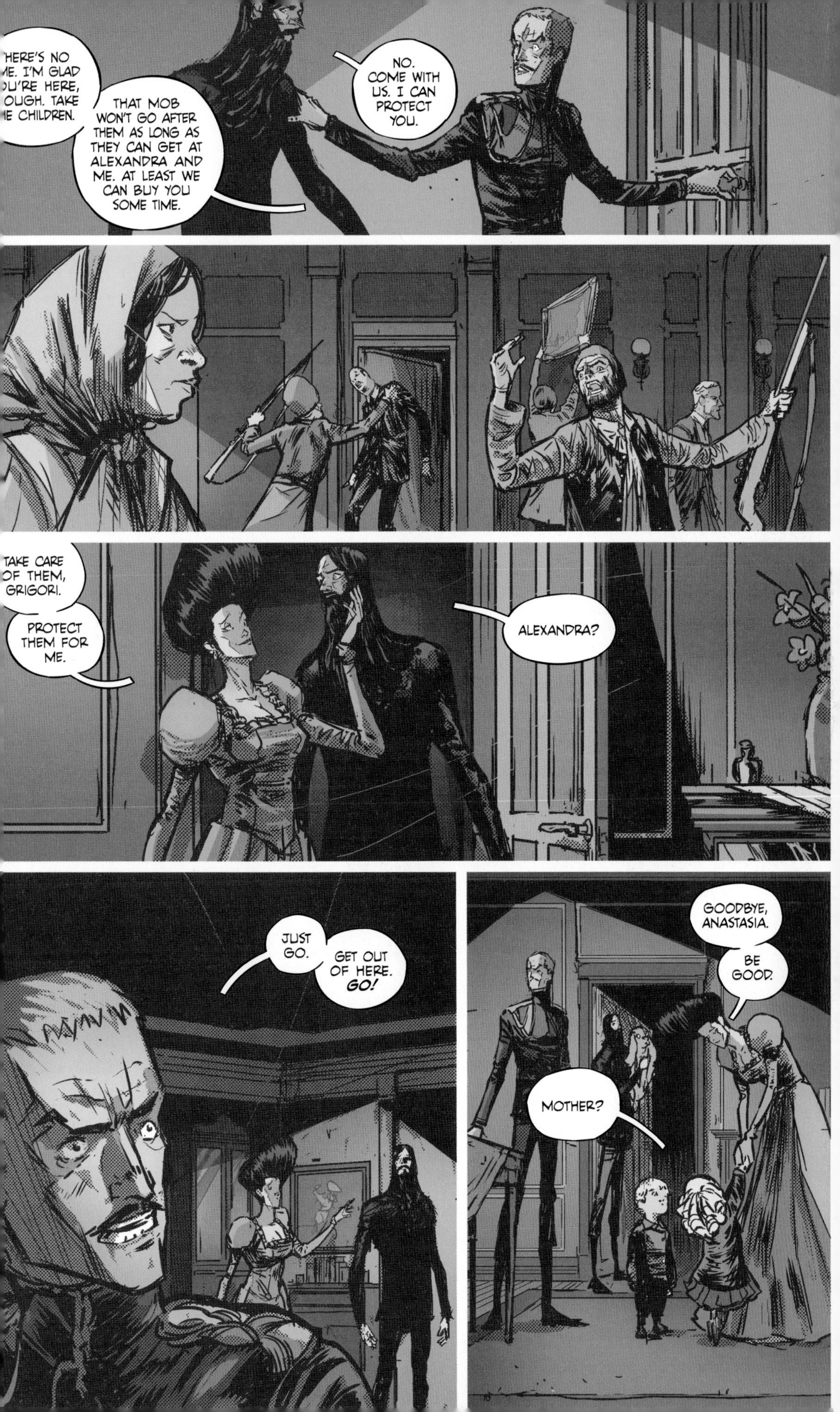
HERE'S NO ME. I'M GLAD OU'RE HERE, OUGH. TAKE E CHILDREN.
THAT MOB WON'T GO AFTER THEM AS LONG AS THEY CAN GET AT ALEXANDRA AND ME. AT LEAST WE CAN BUY YOU SOME TIME.
NO. COME WITH US. I CAN PROTECT YOU.
TAKE CARE OF THEM, GRIGORI.
PROTECT THEM FOR ME.
ALEXANDRA?
JUST GO.
GET OUT OF HERE. *GO!*
GOODBYE, ANASTASIA.
BE GOOD.
MOTHER?

NICHOLAS?
DON'T.
DON'T SAY ANYTHING. YOU'LL ONLY MAKE IT WORSE.

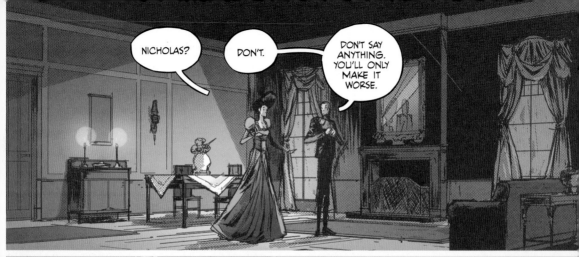

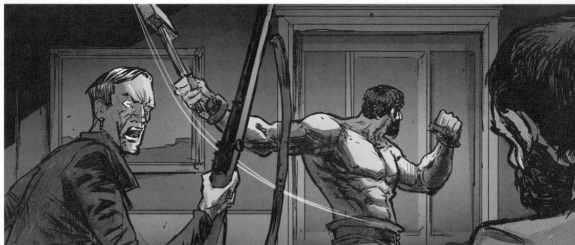

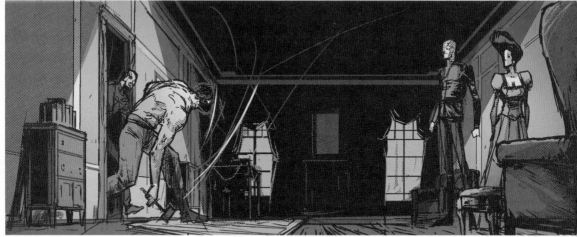

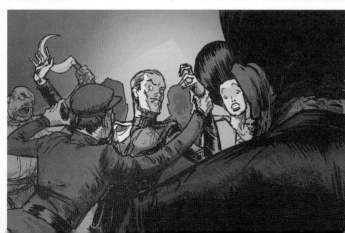

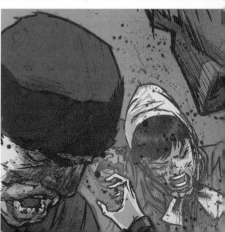

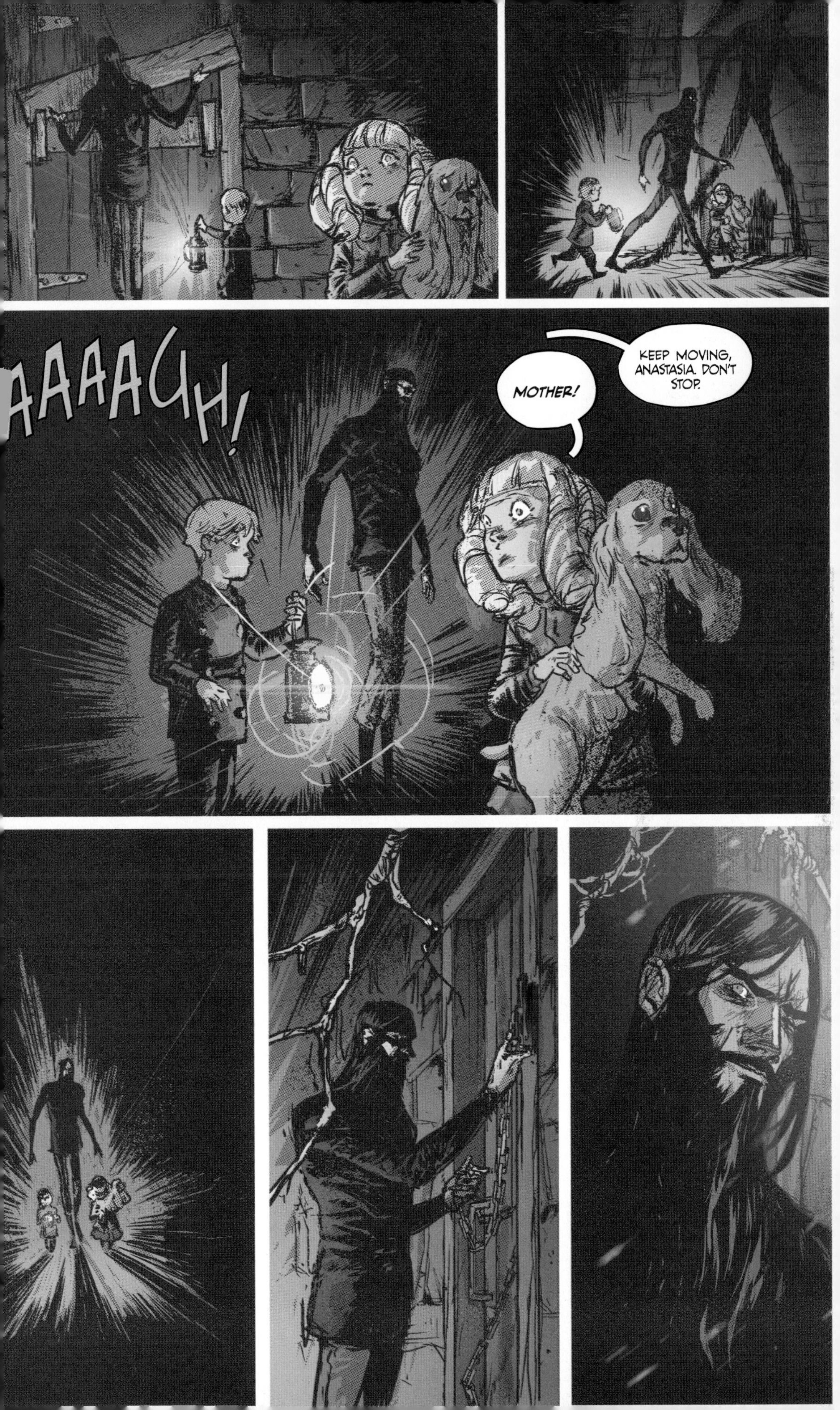
AAAAUGH!
MOTHER!
KEEP MOVING, ANASTASIA. DON'T STOP.

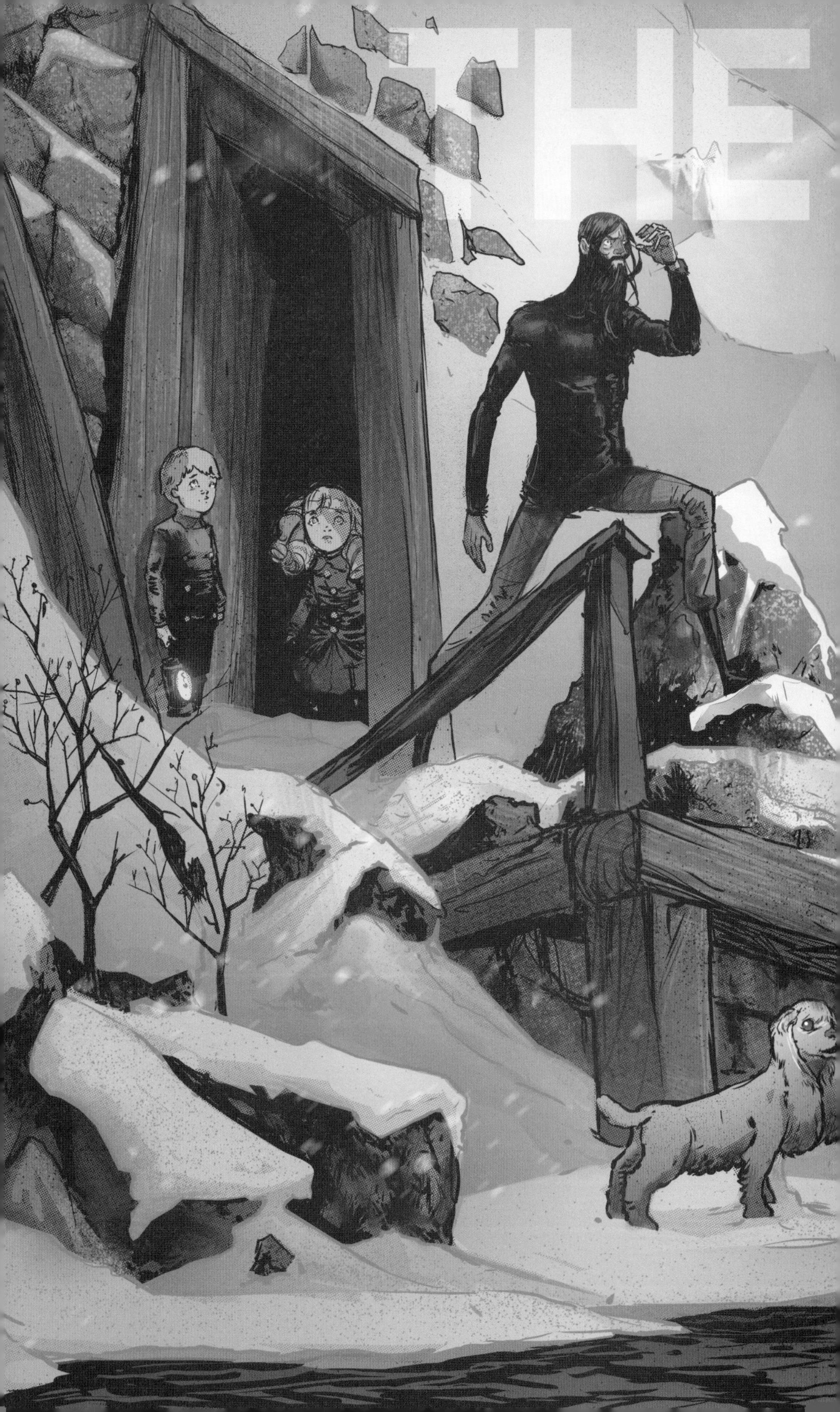
THE

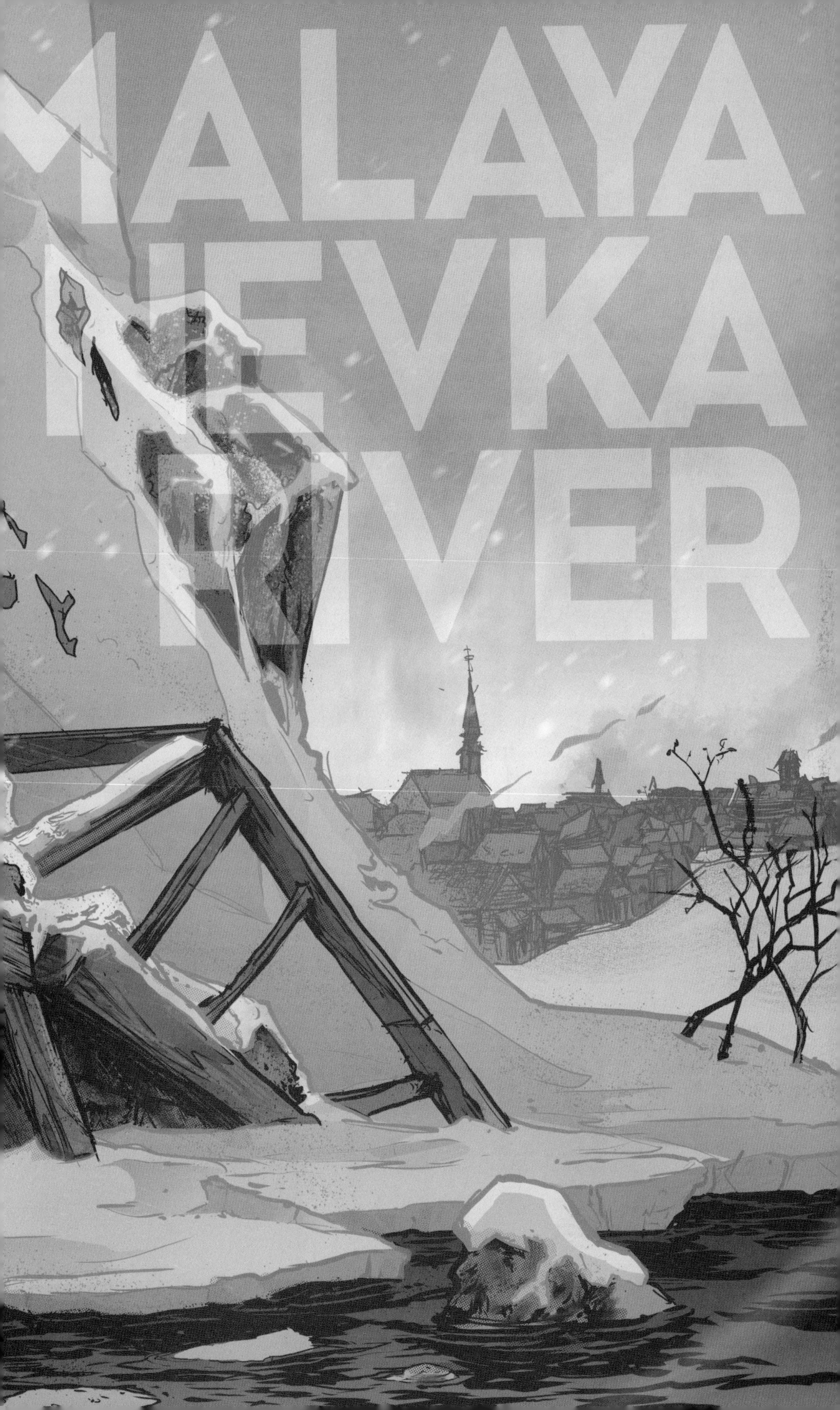
MALAYA
NEVKA
RIVER

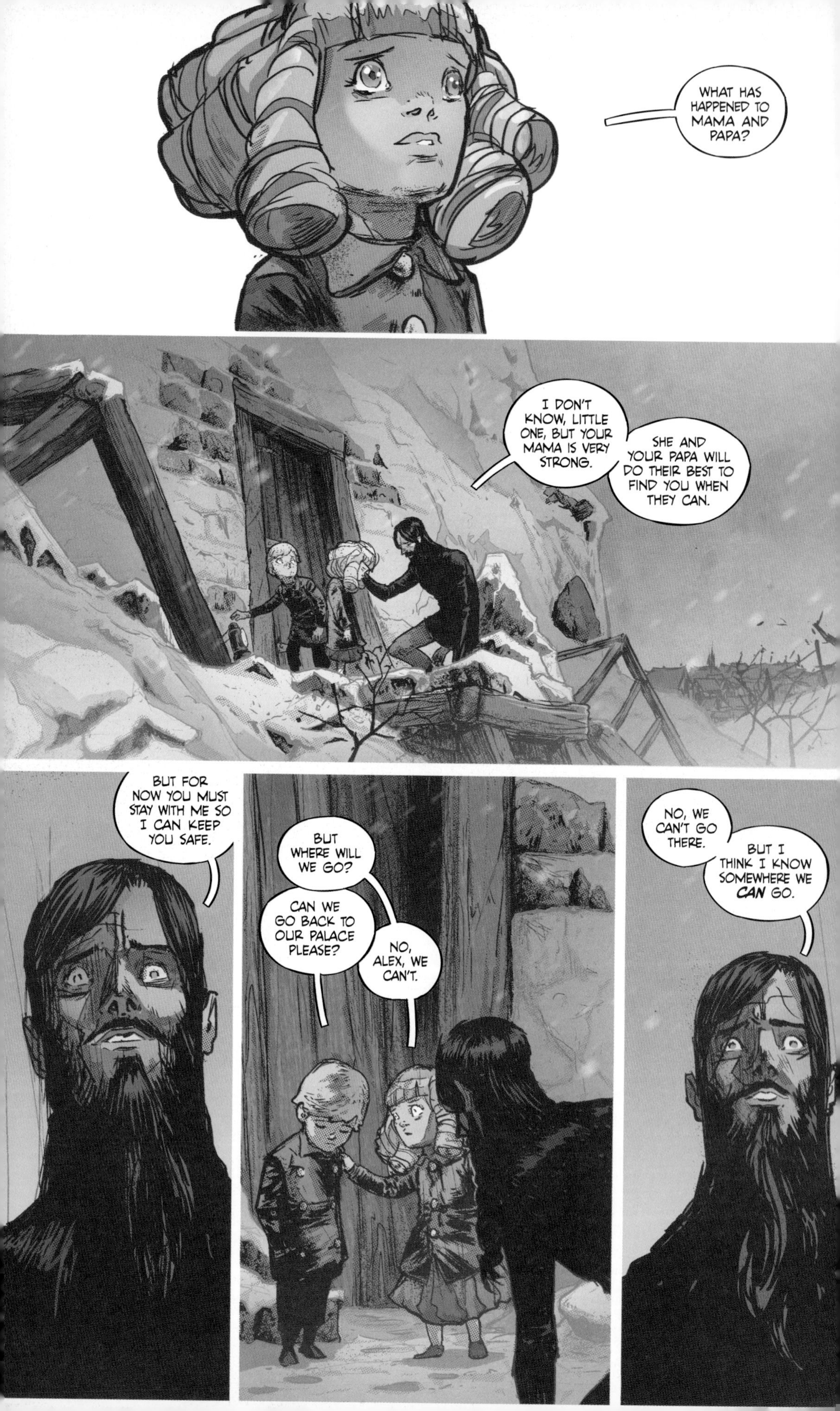
WHAT HAS HAPPENED TO MAMA AND PAPA?
I DON'T KNOW, LITTLE ONE, BUT YOUR MAMA IS VERY STRONG.
SHE AND YOUR PAPA WILL DO THEIR BEST TO FIND YOU WHEN THEY CAN.
BUT FOR NOW YOU MUST STAY WITH ME SO I CAN KEEP YOU SAFE.
BUT WHERE WILL WE GO?
CAN WE GO BACK TO OUR PALACE PLEASE?
NO, ALEX, WE CAN'T.
NO, WE CAN'T GO THERE.
BUT I THINK I KNOW SOMEWHERE WE *CAN* GO.

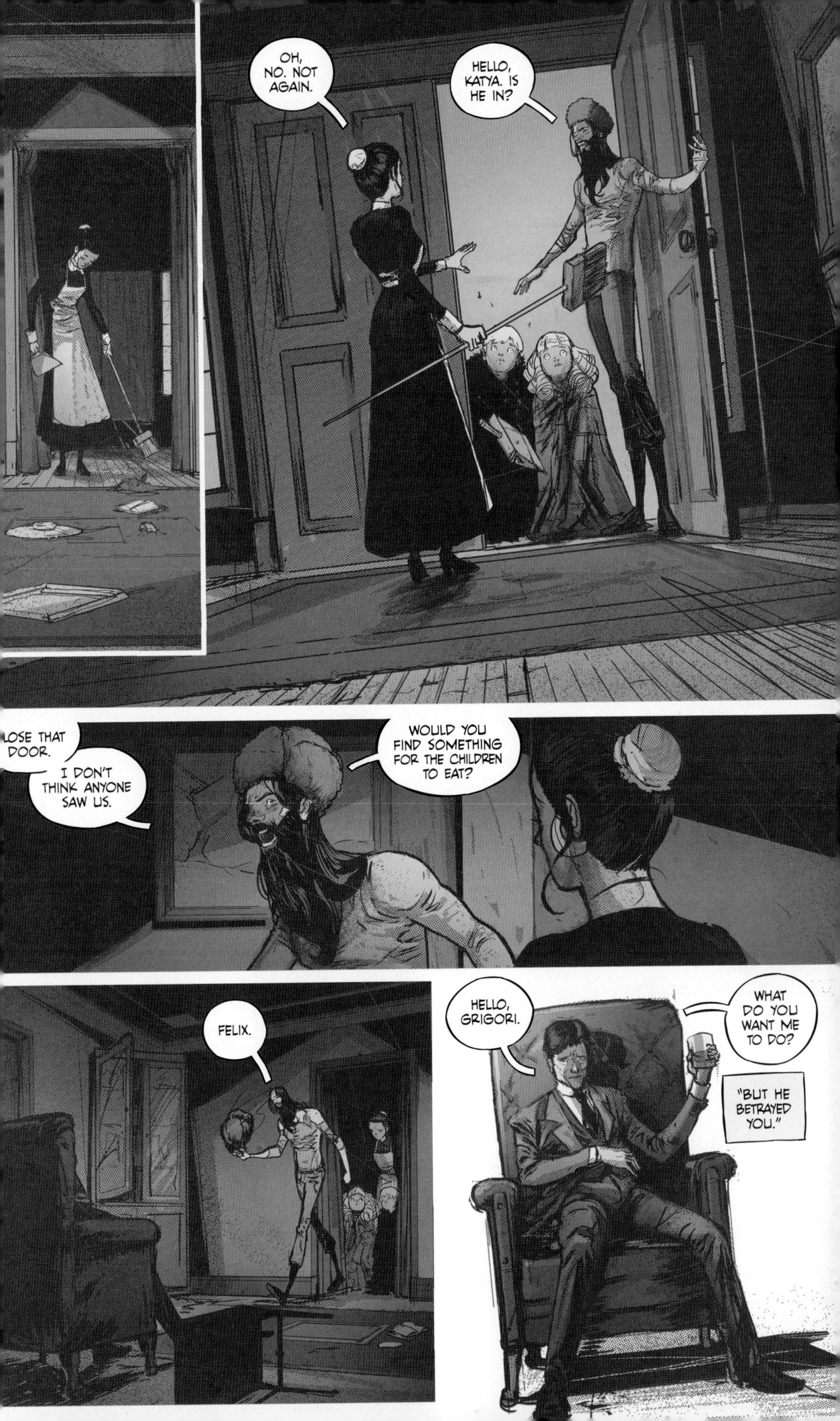
OH, NO. NOT AGAIN.
HELLO, KATYA. IS HE IN?
LOSE THAT DOOR.
I DON'T THINK ANYONE SAW US.
WOULD YOU FIND SOMETHING FOR THE CHILDREN TO EAT?
FELIX.
HELLO, GRIGORI.
WHAT DO YOU WANT ME TO DO?
"BUT HE BETRAYED YOU."

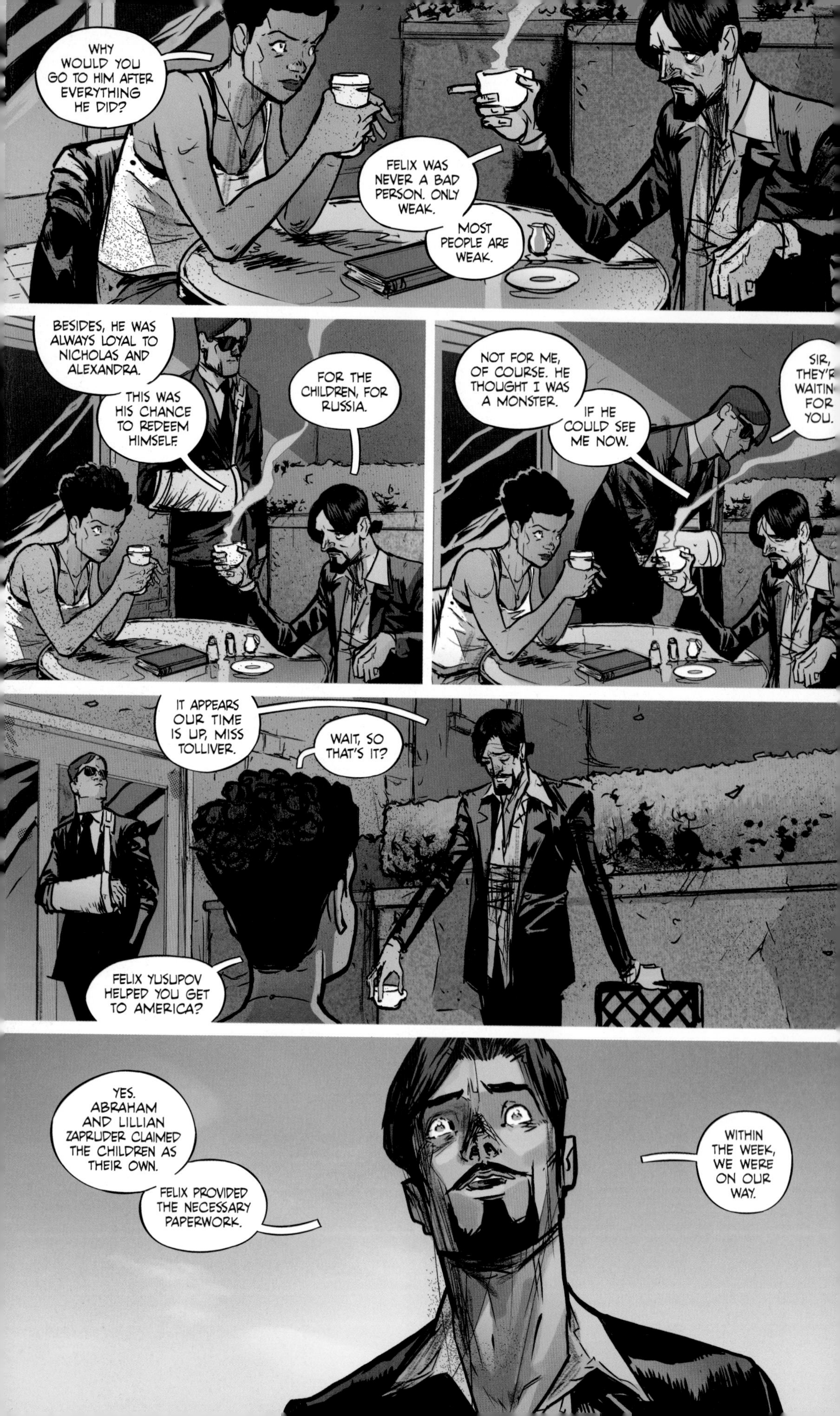
WHY WOULD YOU GO TO HIM AFTER EVERYTHING HE DID?
FELIX WAS NEVER A BAD PERSON. ONLY WEAK.
MOST PEOPLE ARE WEAK.
BESIDES, HE WAS ALWAYS LOYAL TO NICHOLAS AND ALEXANDRA.
THIS WAS HIS CHANCE TO REDEEM HIMSELF.
FOR THE CHILDREN, FOR RUSSIA.
NOT FOR ME, OF COURSE. HE THOUGHT I WAS A MONSTER.
IF HE COULD SEE ME NOW.
SIR, THEY'R WAITIN FOR YOU.
IT APPEARS OUR TIME IS UP, MISS TOLLIVER.
WAIT, SO THAT'S IT?
FELIX YUSUPOV HELPED YOU GET TO AMERICA?
YES. ABRAHAM AND LILLIAN ZAPRUDER CLAIMED THE CHILDREN AS THEIR OWN.
FELIX PROVIDED THE NECESSARY PAPERWORK.
WITHIN THE WEEK, WE WERE ON OUR WAY.

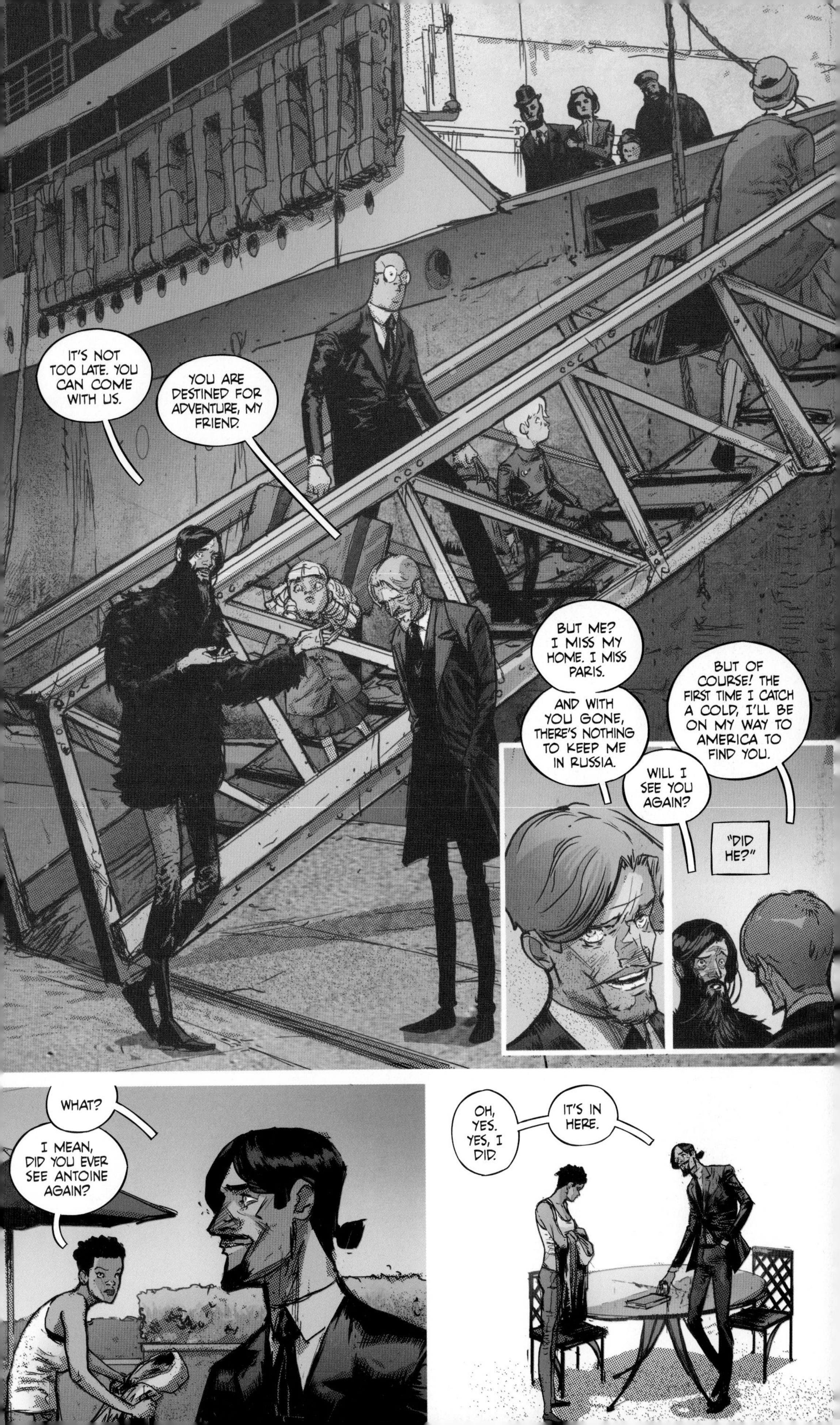
IT'S NOT TOO LATE. YOU CAN COME WITH US.
YOU ARE DESTINED FOR ADVENTURE, MY FRIEND.
BUT ME? I MISS MY HOME. I MISS PARIS.
AND WITH YOU GONE, THERE'S NOTHING TO KEEP ME IN RUSSIA.
WILL I SEE YOU AGAIN?
BUT OF COURSE! THE FIRST TIME I CATCH A COLD, I'LL BE ON MY WAY TO AMERICA TO FIND YOU.
"DID HE?"
WHAT?
I MEAN, DID YOU EVER SEE ANTOINE AGAIN?
OH, YES. YES, I DID.
IT'S IN HERE.

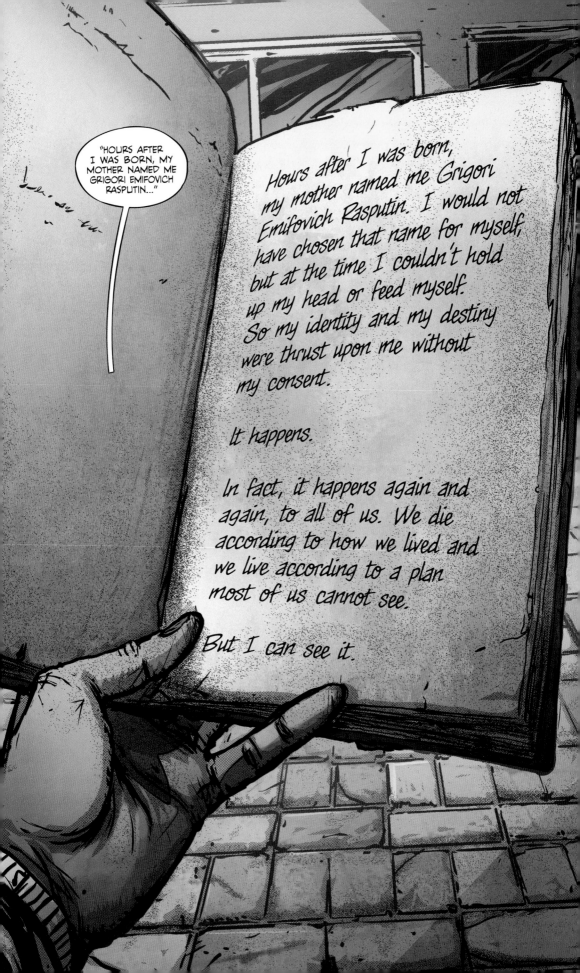

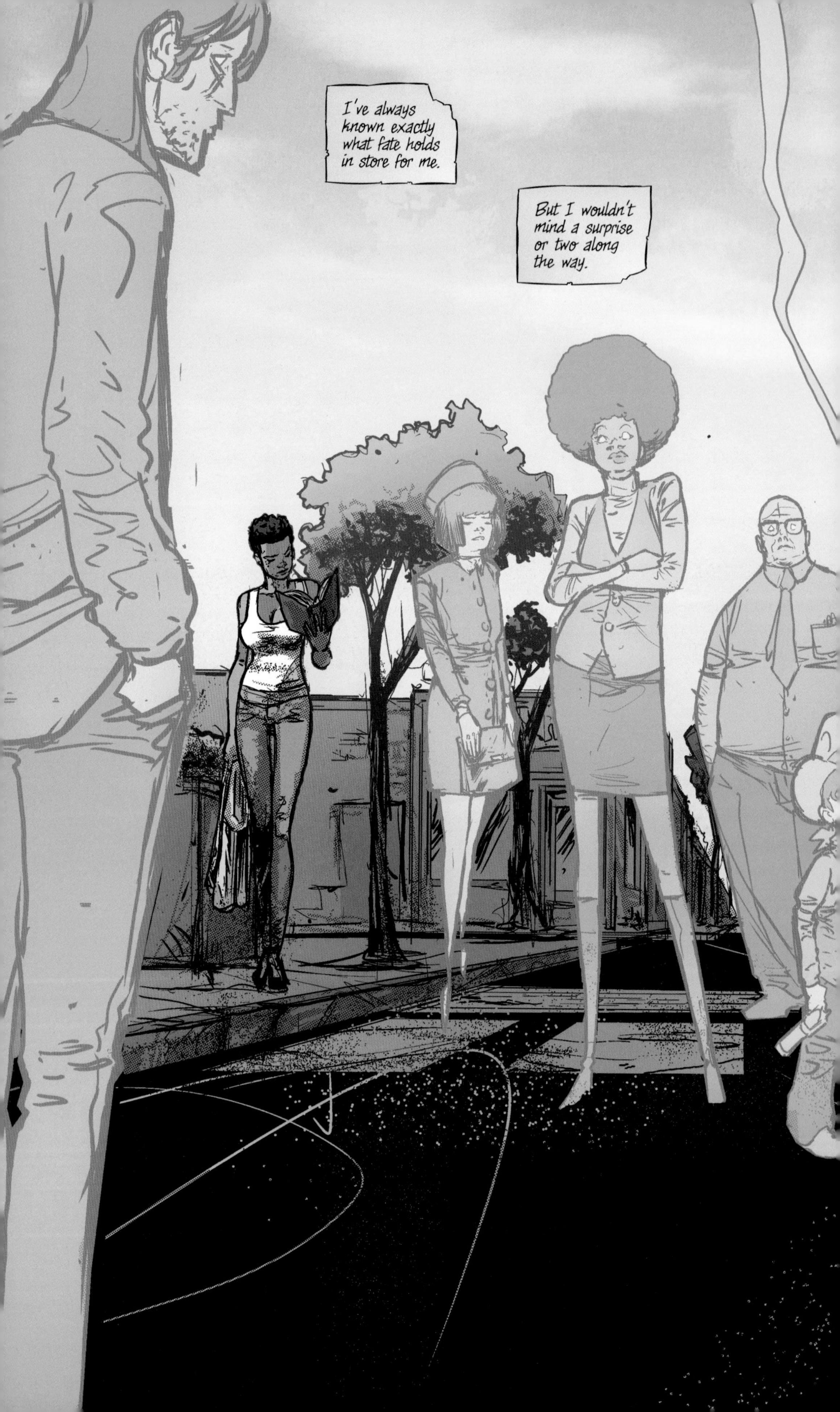
I've always known exactly what fate holds in store for me.
But I wouldn't mind a surprise or two along the way.

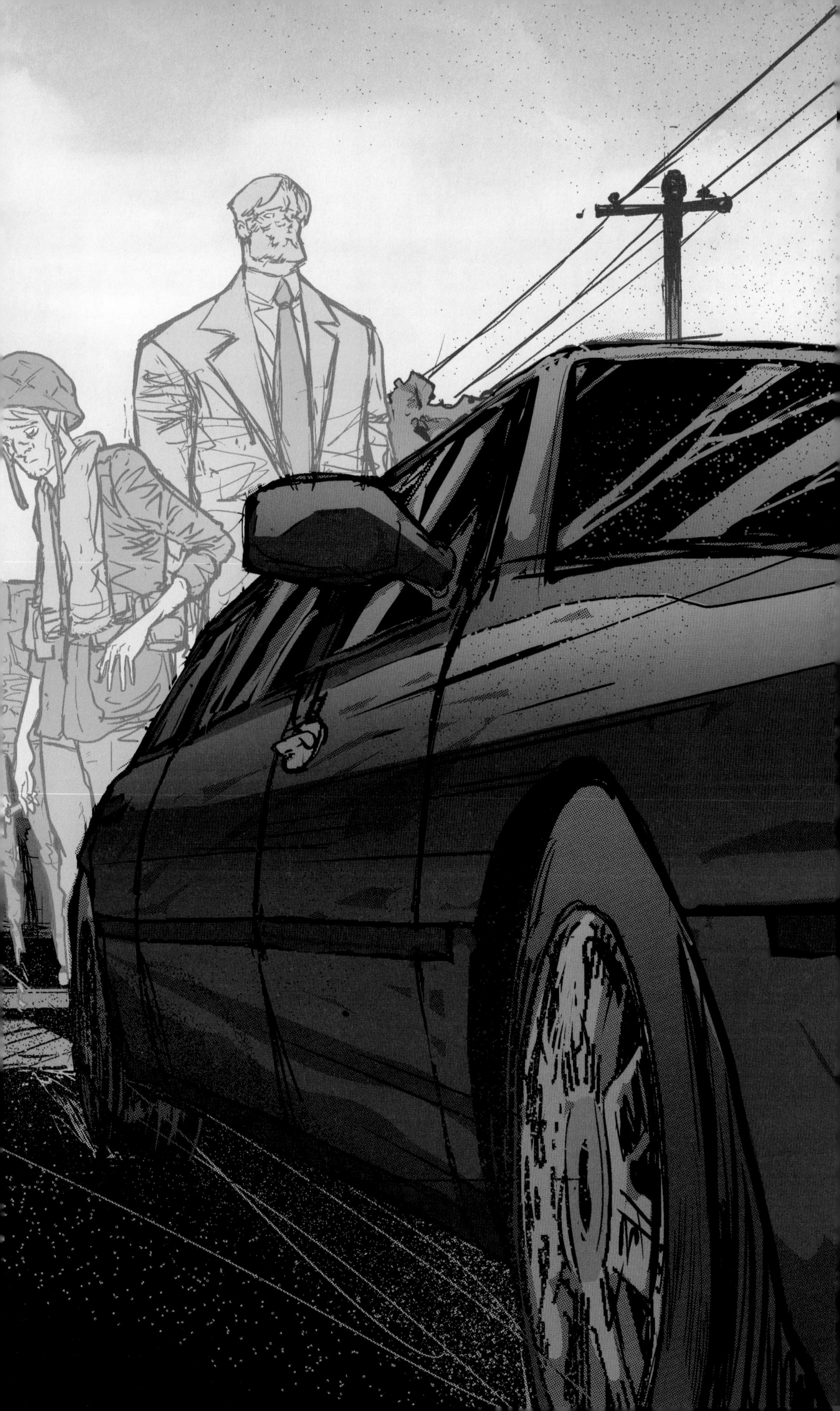

BEHIND THE SCENES
WITH THE STARETS

RASPUTIN #10
By Alex Grecian for Riley Rossmo,
Ivan Plascencia, and Thomas Mauer

PAGE 1 (5 panels)

P1: Shanae and Rasputin are sitting across from each other at an outdoor cafe in Dallas, having coffee. It's a bright sunshiny day. We don't have to be super accurate with the background here because this is not the same as our own Dallas. We've established now that we're in an alternate history, a different America. Raz has a book, a leather-bound journal, sitting on the table beside him.

> SHANAE
> I don't think I believe in magic.

> RAZ
> How else would you explain me?

P2: Tight on Shanae, watching Raz over the rim of her cup.

> SHANAE
> So this Koschei guy… Or Brother Makary or whatever he called himself… He had his soul in a nail and you killed him with it.

> RAZ
> Reunited him with his soul. Poetic, isn't it?

> SHANAE (cont'd)
> So you did what he did? The nail thing? That's how you've been able to live for more than a hundred years?

P3: Reverse on Raz. He's relaxed, smiling.

> RAZ
> I learn from my friends and my enemies both.

> RAZ (cont'd)
> I don't believe in limiting myself.

> SHANAE
> My readers would never believe any of this. Not even the Orbit would run this story.

P4: Same. Raz is taking a sip of coffee.

> RAZ
> No.

> SHANAE
> That's why you're telling me? Because I can't do anything with this stuff?

> RAZ (cont'd)
> What you do with it is up to you.

P5: Reverse again. Shane's setting her cup down and leaning forward.

> SHANAE
> Then tell me the rest.

> SHANAE (cont'd)
> Tell me what happened after you killed Koschei. There were others. Did you kill them too?

> RAZ
> Heh.

> RAZ (cont'd)
> Actually, no…

PAGE 2 (5 panels)

P1: Koschei lies dead on the floor. This can be as gruesome as you like, since it's out transition. He's got a nail in his head, his eyes wide and staring, and there's no doubt that he's gone. Raz is

still straddling him
or sprawled atop him,
depending on how you
laid out the end of #9's
fight scene. But the
focus is on Makary so we
understand he's gone and
not coming back to life.

CAPTION *(Raz)*
"My father's influence
over me was not
strong.

P2: Pull back. Rayner
is holding his gun up,
loosely pointed at Raz.

CAPTION
"To my great relief
I have never been
tempted to kill again."

P3: Felix is cowering in a corner
of the room behind Rayner,
petting the rabbit that came out
of Makary's box last issue.

P4: Tight on Raz. He's rising
with the meat mallet in his hand.
Blood's dripping off it. He's kind
of a scary mess.

P5: Raz is approaching Rayner,
ready to smash him with that
mallet. Rayner's holding the gun,
but he's not aiming it.

    RAYNER
    Listen.

    RAYNER *(cont'd)*
    Do you hear that?

    RAZ
    Are you going to shoot me
    again?

PAGE 3 *(4 panels)*

P1: Rayner lowers the gun to his
side.

    RAYNER
    There's no need, Old Boy.

    RAYNER *(cont'd)*
    None of it matters anymore.

P2: Rayner's gone to the front
window and parted the curtain,
but he's not looking outside.
He's gesturing for Raz to come
take a look.

    RAYNER
    Look out there

P3: Raz goes
to the window
and holds the
curtain aside.
He's looking ou
now, but we're
behind him and
can't see what
he sees outside
He and Rayner
and the curtain
are all in our
way.

    RAZ
    What is
    it? What's
    happening?

    RAYNER
    I blame myself. I didn't act
    fast enough and I let you
    become too important to these
    people.

    RAYNER *(cont'd)*
    Now they think you're dead…

P4: Big panel. Reverse and we're
looking in from outside at Raz,
at his face behind the glass. We
still can't see what he's looking
at, except for maybe a hint of a
person or two running by Felix's
house. Mostly we just see how
astonished (and bloody) Raz
looks.

    RAYNER *(Caption)*
    "And the whole damn city's
    coming apart at the seams."

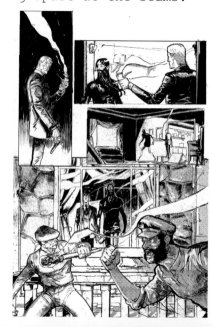

PAGES 4&5 *(1 panel)*

Double-splash! Pull way
out from the last panel
of the previous page
and maybe we can see
Raz's face on the other
side of that window, but
it's across the street
from us. Between us and
that window are Russian
peasants rioting in the
street. Some of them may
actually be carrying
torches. Some have guns.
Most of them are running
in one direction (toward
the Winter Palace, which
we can't see here), but
a few might be going the
wrong way, trying to get to their families and homes. A carriage has
been overturned and set on fire, maybe a horse is running wild down
the street. Utter chaos everywhere.

CAPTION *(Translucent)*
PETROGRAD

PAGE 6 *(5 panels)*

A three-tier page. The first three
panels run across the top of the
page and use the same background.
The only thing changing is Raz.

P1: A trio of rioters runs down
the street from right to left.
Behind them, in the background of
this panel, is the dark mouth of
an alley.

P2: Same. Raz emerges from the
shadows of the alley. He hasn't
cleaned up, still covered with
blood, his body canted a bit to
one side because he's limping on
the leg that Makary lifted him
by.

P3: Same. Raz hurries away in
the opposite direction from the
rioters. He's going to our right,
propelling the story forward.

P4: Long panel across the middle
of the page. We're looking down
a street as Raz runs away from
us. Other people are engaged in
dramatic actions at the sides
of the panel: looting a shop,
beating up a policeman, etc.

The bottom tier is two panels,
one significantly smaller.

P5: Tight on Raz, looking beyond

us at something. He's filled with
fear and anger.

P6: Big panel. Reverse the angle
so we see what Raz was looking
at: The Winter Palace. But there
are people all around it with
torches and guns. We're behind
them. They're trying to figure out
how to get in and kill the Tsar.
So we're behind Raz. In front of
him are the revolutionaries and
in front of them is the palace.
If possible, maybe use the exact
same angle as our first view of
this place, back in issue 4.

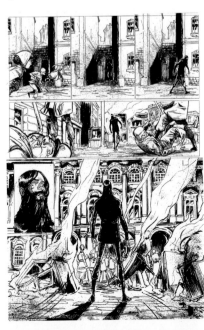

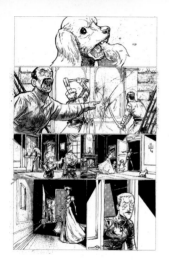

PAGE 7
(6 panels)

Panel two on each of the next few pages should be similar in size, shape and placement in order to establish mounting secondary action taking place. Ivan, is it possible to do something with the scheme or values to make the second panel stand out from the others without indicating any kind of time change?

P1: Tight on Alexei's dog Joy, who's jumping and yapping.

P2: Inset panel of the mob attacking the front doors of the palace.

P3: Pull back and the Tsar is bolting a door. One of those big bars that set into brackets on either side of the door. The Tsarina is holding hands with Alexei and Anastasia. Joy's jumping around Nicholas's feet, barking at the door.

> NICHOLAS
> Quiet. Someone get hold of the dog, will you?
>
> ANASTASIA
> Here, Joy. Come here, girl.

P4: Nicholas is opening another door at the back of the room, ushering his family through. The dog's happily following along.

> NICHOLAS
> Through here. Hurry.

P5: They're hurrying down a dark narrow hallway. There's another door at the far end.

P6: Nicholas is opening that door, but reacting to something we can't see on the other side of it, pulling back.

> NICHOLAS
> Oh!

PAGE 8 *(5 panels)*

P1: It was Raz! He's standing there on the other side of the door and the dog is running to him, excited to see him.

> RAZ
> It's a madhouse out there.

P2: Inset panel of the mob breaking down the front door of the palace.

P3: Reverse and we're behind Raz as he stoops to pick up the dog. Nicholas is waving his wife and kids through the door, past Raz as they speak.

> NICHOLAS
> It's revolution. It's finally happening.
>
> RAZ
> I don't understand.
>
> NICHOLAS *(cont'd)*
> It's the damn war. It's been building, but I don't know what's set it off tonight.

P4: Raz is following the family along another passage, carrying Joy now.

> ANASTASIA
> How did you get in?
>
> RAZ
> I'll bet I know the Winter Palace even better than you do, Anastasia.
>
> ALEXEI
> But not better than me!

P5: Another big room with another door at the back of it. There are a couple of chairs and a table there, but not much else.

> THE TSARINA
> You look terrible. What happened to you, Grigori?
>
> RAZ
> It's a long story.

PAGE 9
(5 panels)

P1: Nicholas
has this
next door
open and is
grabbing Raz
by arm.

NICHOLAS
There's
no time.
I'm glad
you're here,
though.
Take the
children.

NICHOLAS (cont'd)
That mob won't go after them
as long as they can get at
Alexandra and me. At least we
can buy you some time.

RAZ
No. Come with us. I can
protect you.

P2: Inset panel of the mob
running through the halls,
pulling tapestries down and
assaulting a servant.

P3: Tight on the Tsarina as she
caresses Raz's cheek.

TSARINA
Take care of them, Grigori.

TSARINA (cont'd)
Protect them for me.

RAZ
Alexandra?

P4: Pull back and Nicholas is
watching them. He's angry, just
now catching on that there was
something going on between his
wife and Raz.

NICHOLAS
Just go.

NICHOLAS (cont'd)
Get out of here. Go!

P5: Raz has the dog in one arm
and is holding Alexei's hand
while Anastasia follows them into
the darkness beyond that door.
Anastasia is looking back at her

parents. She's crying. Raz is
looking back too, regretfully.

ANASTASIA
Mother?

TSARINA
Goodbye, Anastasia.

TSARINA (cont'd)
Be good.

PAGE 10 (5 panels)

P1: Raz and the kids are gone.
Nicholas and Alexandra are
standing together in the middle
of this room.

TSARINA
Nicholas?

NICHOLAS
Don't.

NICHOLAS (cont'd)
Don't say anything. You'll
only make it worse.

P2: Inset panel as the mob pounds
on the door to this very room.

P3: And here the two actions
merge as the door comes down and
we're looking past the mob at the
royal couple, who look scared but
stoic.

P4: The mob rushes at them and
Nicholas takes Alexandra in his
arms.

P5: And now they're lost from
view behind the murderous mob.

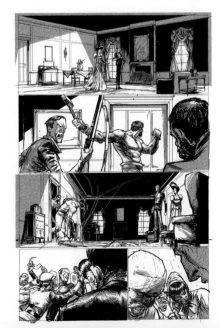

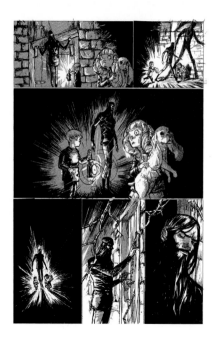

PAGE 11 (6 panels)

P1: Raz and the children are in a dark tunnel. Raz has put Joy down and is boltin the door on this side sorta the way Nicholas bolted that other door back on page seven.

P2: They're walking down the tunnel in the dark. Anastasia is sticking close to Raz, almost clinging to him. Raz

P3: Anastasia and Alexei are reacting to a sound behind them. Maybe Joy is here, too, barking.

> TSARINA *(off-panel)*
> Aaaagh!
>
> ANASTASIA
> Mother!
>
> RAZ
> Keep moving, Anastasia. Don't stop.

P4: They're completely isolated now, walking in the dark. Maybe drop in some small panels focusing on their feet and/or Raz and Alexei's hands together, Joy trotting along with them, the three of them and the dog very small in the distance surrounded by black, etc. Just to show that they're walking for a long time.

P5: Raz is throwing a bolt on a door.

P6: Tight on Raz. He's squinting at a sudden light, but we can't see what he sees yet.

PAGE 12 & 13 *(1 panel)*

P1: Another double spread. Our last one! We're at the edge of a river, looking across the river at Raz and the two kids in the background. They're standing at a cave-like entrance hole to that tunnel. Raz has just opened the door and they're dramatically posed against that blackness behind them. The partially iced-over river is right in front of them. Above them, on a sort of cliff-like bank, are bare trees, some of the roots poking out through the dirt.

Raz is holding both children's hands and Joy is running ahead of them to the river bank.

> CAPTION *(Translucent)*
> THE MALAYA NEVKA RIVER

AGE 14 *(5 panels)*

1: Tight on little Anastasia,
no is looking expectantly up at
az. She's on the verge of tears.

ANASTASIA
What has happened to mama and
papa?

2: Raz kneels down in the snow
eside her. He's got Alexei there
oo and has a hand on each of
neir shoulders as he talks to
nem.

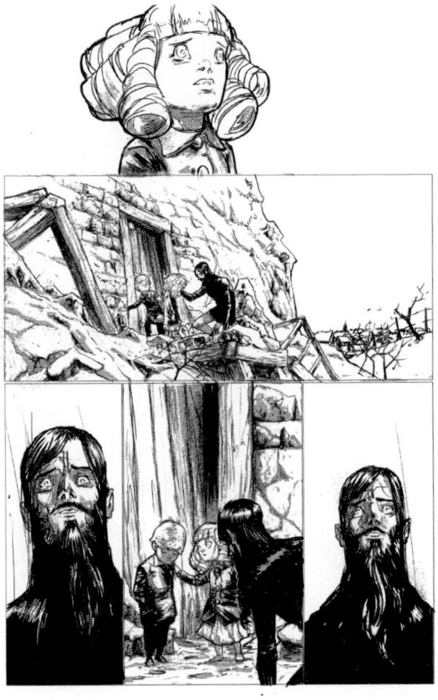

RAZ
I don't know, little one, but
your mama is very strong.

RAZ *(cont'd)*
She and your papa will do
their best to find you when
they can.

3: Tight on Raz.

RAZ
But for now you must stay with
me so I can keep you safe.

4: Reverse on Anastasia. She's
colding her brother.

ANASTASIA
But where will we go?

ALEXEI
Can we go back to our palace
please?

ANASTASIA *(cont'd)*
No, Alex, we can't.

P5: Same as P3.

RAZ
No, we can't go there.

RAZ *(cont'd)*
But I think I know somewhere
we can go.

PAGE 15 *(5 panels)*

P1: Back to Felix Yusupov's house. Katya, the maid from issue one, is navigating through the damage done during the fight between Raz and Makary in the previous issue. Furniture is toppled, broken glass covers the floor, it's a mess. She's headed to the front door.

P2: We're behind her as she opens it, and there's Raz with the kids and the dog. He's covered Anastasia with a blanket so her dress will be less distinctive and little Alexei is wearing Raz's fuzzy black coat. Raz himself is wearing a distracting hat: http://s87.photobucket.com/user/Maxx_1953/media/Mink_Full_Fur_Russian_Hat_302_zps722e06b4.jpg.html These disguises aren't much, but they're clearly the best he could do.

KATYA
Oh, no. Not again.

RAZ
Hello, Katya. Is he in?

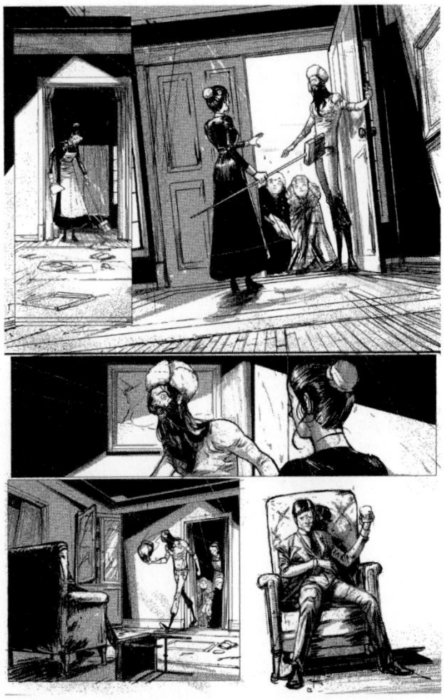

P3: Raz pushes past her, bringing the children along. He's talking to Katya over his shoulder.

RAZ
Close that door.

RAZ *(cont'd)*
I don't think anyone saw us.

RAZ *(cont'd)*
Would you find something for the children to eat?

P4: Raz (now without the children) is entering a dark room, Felix's study. We're behind a chair looking at Raz framed in the doorway as he enters. Felix is slumped in the chair with a drink in his hand, but we can't see that yet.

RAZ
Felix.

P5: Reverse and Felix is speaking. He looks like shit, not smiling, holding his drink, surrounded by the remains of his study. The chair is the only upright piece of furniture in the room.

FELIX
Hello, Grigori.

FELIX *(cont'd)*
What do you want me to do?

CAPTION
(Shanae, off-panel)
"But he betrayed you."

PAGE 16
(5 panels)

P1: Back to the coffee shop, with Raz and Shanae. Raz is smiling ruefully.

SHANAE
Why would you go to him after everything he did?

RAZ
Felix was never a bad person. Only weak.

RAZ *(cont'd)*
Most people are weak.

P2: Same. A Secret Service agent with his arm in a sling has approached the table. This is Ralph, from issue six.

RAZ
Besides, he was always loyal to Nicholas and Alexandra.

RAZ *(cont'd)*
This was his chance to redeem himself.

RAZ *(cont'd)*
For the children, for Russia.

P3: Same. Ralph is bending down to talk to Raz.

RAZ
Not for me, of course. He thought I was a monster.

RAZ *(cont'd)*
If he could see me now.

RALPH
Sir, they're waiting for you.

P4: Raz is pushing back to stand up.

RAZ
It appears our time is up, Ms Tolliver.

SHANAE
Wait, so that's it?

SHANAE *(cont'd)*
Felix Yusupov helped you get to America?

P5: Raz is tightening his tie.

RAZ
Yes. Abraham and Lillian Zapruder claimed the children as their own.

RAZ *(cont'd)*
Felix provided the necessary paperwork.

RAZ *(cont'd)*
Within the week, we were on our way.

1: Big panel. Raz is standing beside a ship's gangplank with
Antoine. The Zapruders are ushering the two children up the ramp.
There's a couple good pics of that sorta thing here: https://www.
pinterest.com/gem8/set-now-is-the-hour/

> RAZ
> It's not too late. You can come
> with us.
>
> ANTOINE
> You are destined for adventure,
> my friend.

2: Push in on Antoine a bit.

> ANTOINE
> But me? I miss my home. I miss
> Paris.
>
> ANTOINE *(cont'd)*
> And with you gone, there's
> nothing to keep me in Russia.

3: Reverse on Raz.

> RAZ
> Will I see you again?
>
> ANTOINE
> But of course! The first time I
> catch a cold, I'll be on my way
> to America to find you.
>
> CAPTION
> *(Shanae, off-panel)*
> "Did he?"

Make these last two panels the bottom tier of the page.

4: And we're back for good to Shanae and modern America. Tight on
Raz, who is shaking away the cobwebs of the past. He's leaving our
framing device, too, so he should have a faraway look on his face
(and I wouldn't write that direction for any other artist).

> RAZ
> What?
>
> SHANAE
> I mean, did you ever see Antoine again?

5: Raz is smiling now, tapping that journal that's still laying
on the table.

> RAZ
> Oh, yes. Yes, I did.
>
> RAZ *(cont'd)*
> It's in here.

PAGE 18 *(5 panels)*

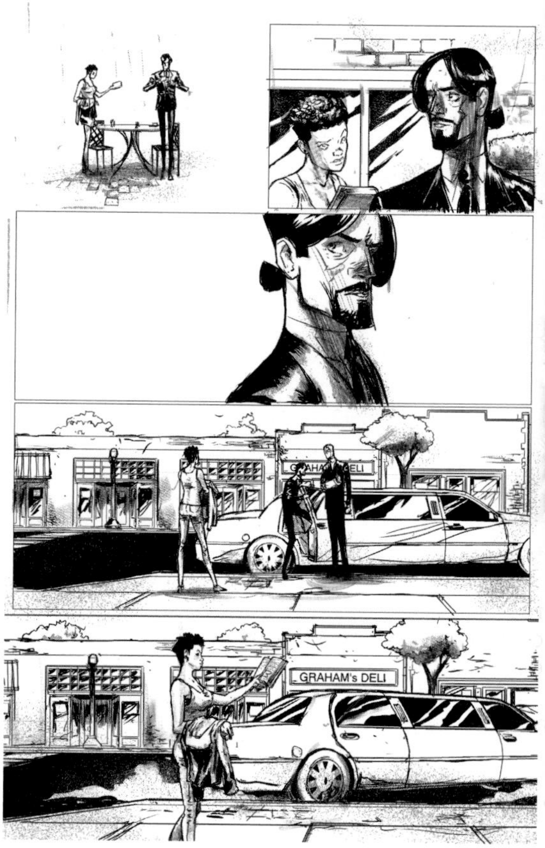
GRAHAM's DELI

P1: Shanae is picking up the book.

SHANAE
What is this?

RAZ
My memoir.

RAZ *(cont'd)*
I've been working on it since you appeared at my door.

P2: Shanae looks a little shy.

SHANAE
You'd let me read this?

RAZ
I wrote it for you.

P3: Raz is straightening his jacket and turning, but looking back at Shanae. He's got a big speech here, so leave plenty of room for Tom.

RAZ
Once upon a time everyone thought they knew everything about me. Everyone wanted a piece of me.

RAZ *(cont'd)*
I was not born to power, was never meant to be a tsar or a president. What power I had, I took.

RAZ *(cont'd)*
But I've spent a century being a secret and I have to admit there's a little part of me that wants to be known again.

P4: Now he's not even looking at her, walking away toward a limo that we now see idling at the curb. Ralph is holding the door for him. Shanae's not so far from him that he should seem to have to shout.

RAZ
I leave it to you. You decide my fate. You decide what my story should be.

RAZ *(cont'd)*
I look forward to hearing from you.

FROM INSIDE THE LIMO
Father, we're late!

P5: We can see the limo driving away from the curb, but Shanae is the focus here. She's opening the book.

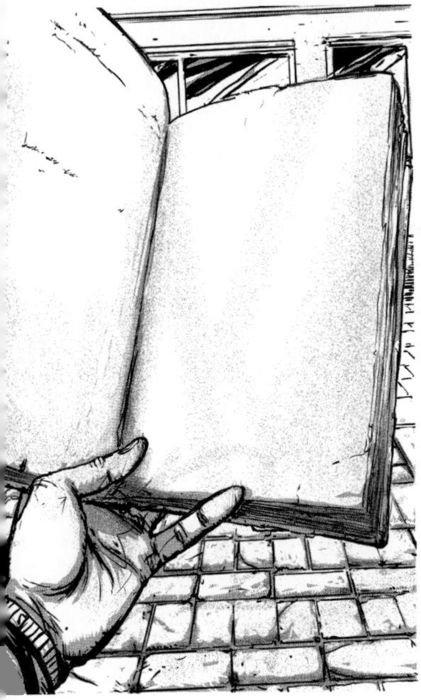

PAGE 19 *(1 panel)*

P1: Full page. We're looking over her shoulder as Shanae reads from the book. We can see the print on the page(Tom, we don't need everything here, so feel free to crop it off at the sides and the bottom however you need to. This is repeated from the first issue.)

SHANAE (reading out loud)
"Hours after I was born, my mother named me Grigori Emifovich Rasputin…"

ON THE PAGE
Hours after I was born, my mother named me Grigori Emifovich Rasputin. I would not have chosen that name for myself, but at the time I couldn't hold up my head or feed myself. So my identity and my destiny were thrust upon me without my consent.

t happens.

n fact, it happens again and again, to all of us. We die according o how we lived and we live according to a plan most of us cannot ee.

ut I can see it.

'AGES 20&21 *(1 panel)*

'1: Final double-spread. Our only one without a big translucent lace-marker. We're leaving Shanae behind and we're out in front f the limo. It's heading toward us and we can see Shanae reading utside the coffee shop in the background. But between the limo and hanae is a mob of ghosts. Young people, old, white, black, men, omen, dressed in period clothing from the last century of American ashion. (I'll help find reference.) They're all following along in az's wake as he rides away into an uncertain future. We're ending his on a big ambiguous note.

CAPTION *(RAZ)*
I've always known exactly what fate holds in store for me.

CAPTION *(RAZ cont'd)*
But I wouldn't mind a surprise or two along the way.

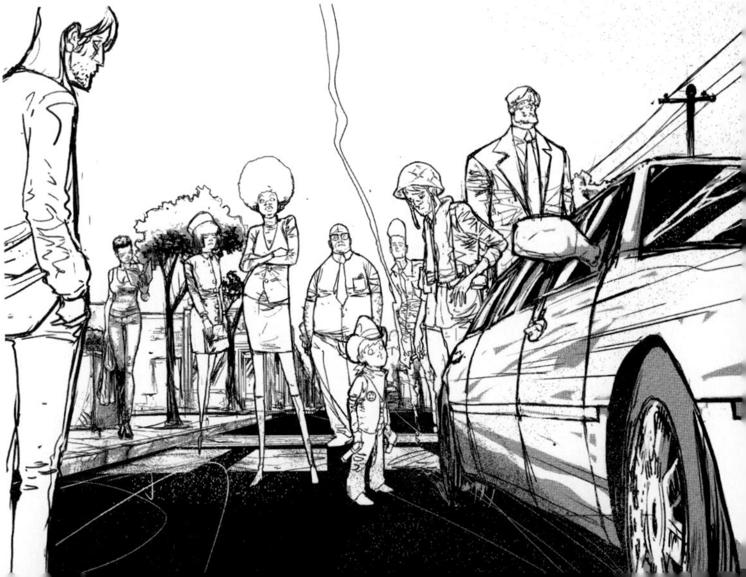

INSIDE BACK COVER

Tom, for the inside back cover, I'm gonna provide you with a list of the quotes we've used throughout the series and their attributions, so we can credit everybody. Don't let me forget.

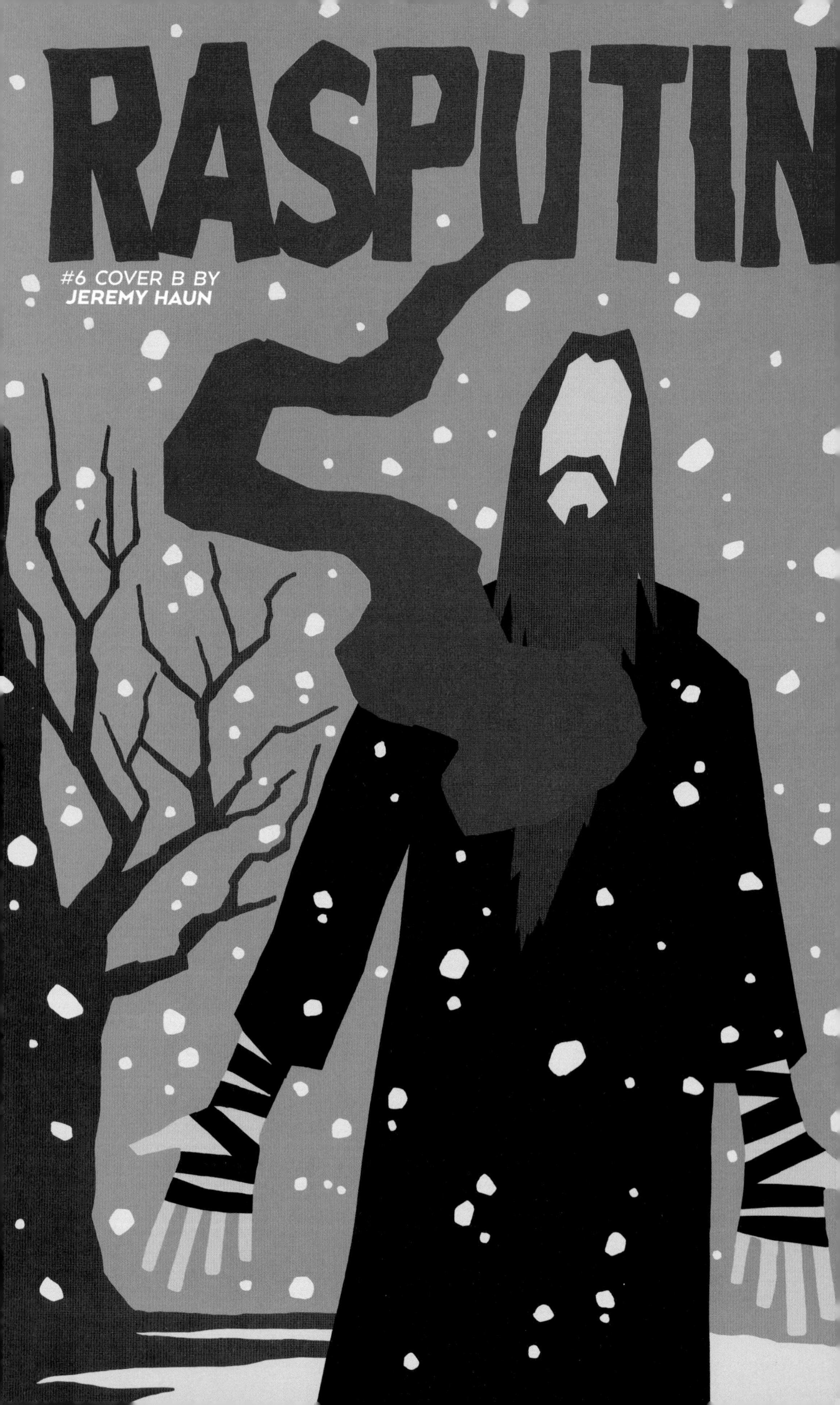
RASPUTIN
#6 COVER B BY
JEREMY HAUN

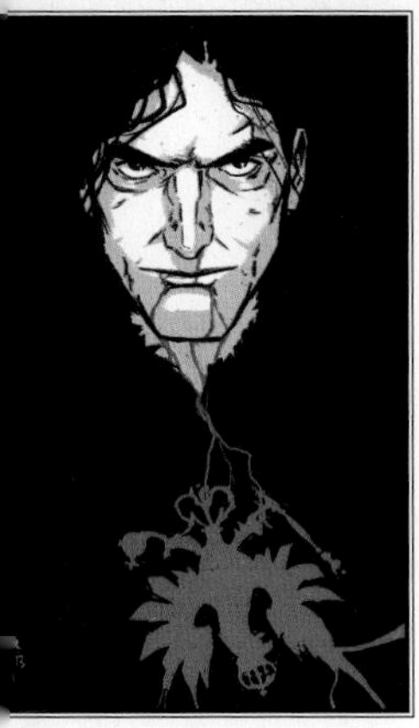

/hen the legend
comes fact, print
e legend."
—Dorothy M. Johnson

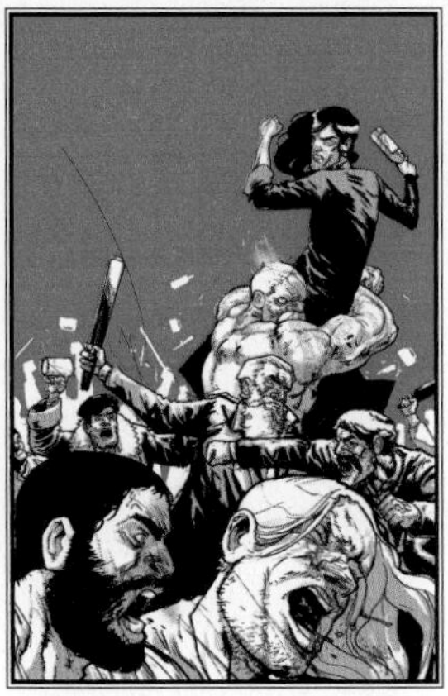

"If he didn't complicate his life so needlessly, he would die of boredom."
—Boris Pasternak

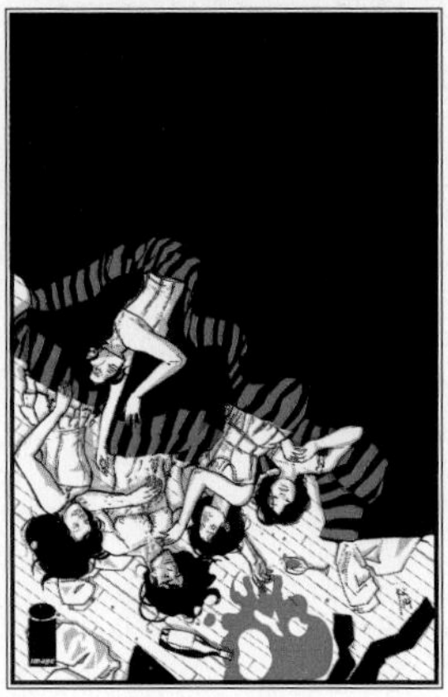

"Civilization is like a thin layer of ice upon a deep ocean of chaos and darkness."
—Werner Herzog

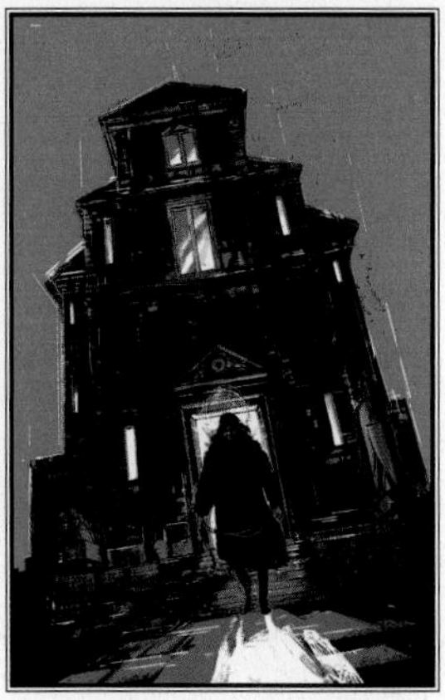

"Not everything has a name. Some things lead us into a realm beyond words."
—Aleksandr Solzhenitsyn

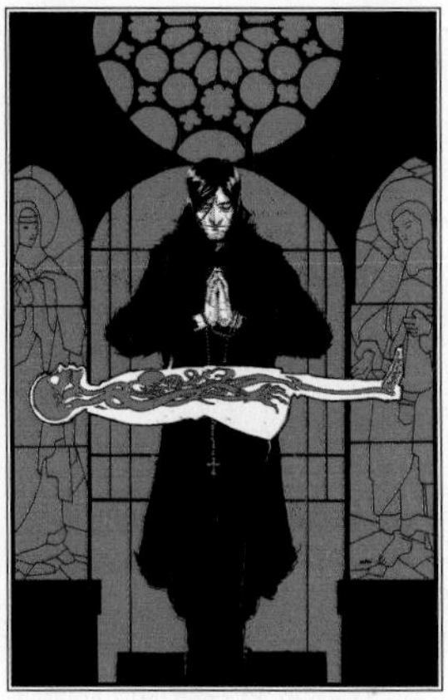

"Without knowing what I am and why I am here, life is impossible."
—Leo Tolstoy

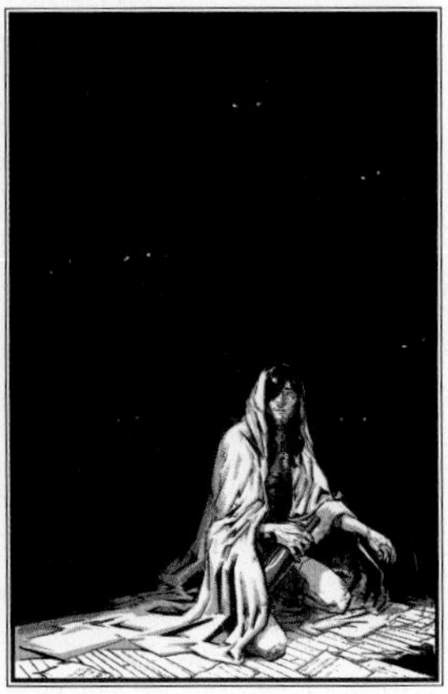

"You must pay for everything in this world, one way and another."
—Charles Portis

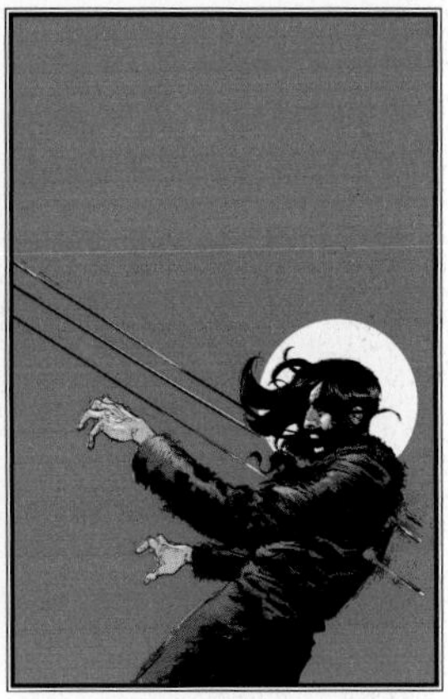

"A man must be sacrificed now and again to provide for the next generation of men."
—Amy Lowell

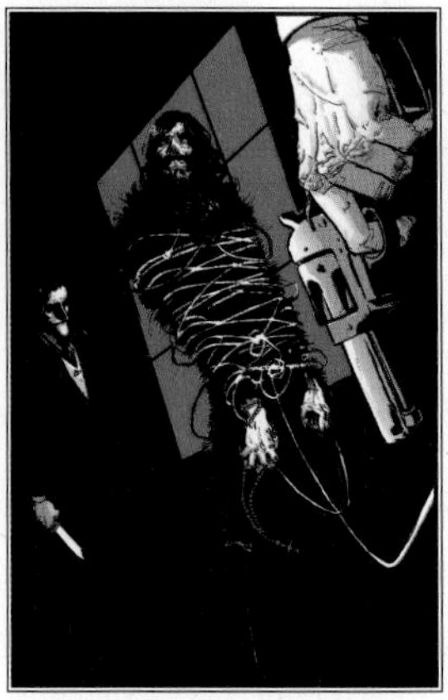

"As human beings, our greatness lies not so much in being able to remake the world—that is the myth of the atomic age—as in being able to remake ourselves."
—Mahatma Gandhi

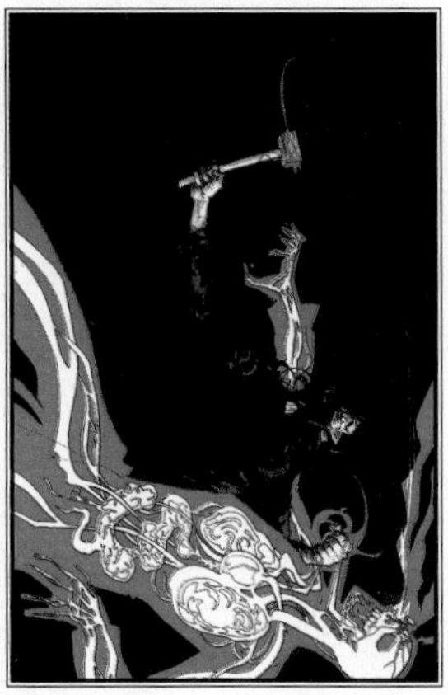

"A good man can be stupid and still be good. But a bad man must have brains."
—Maxim Gorky

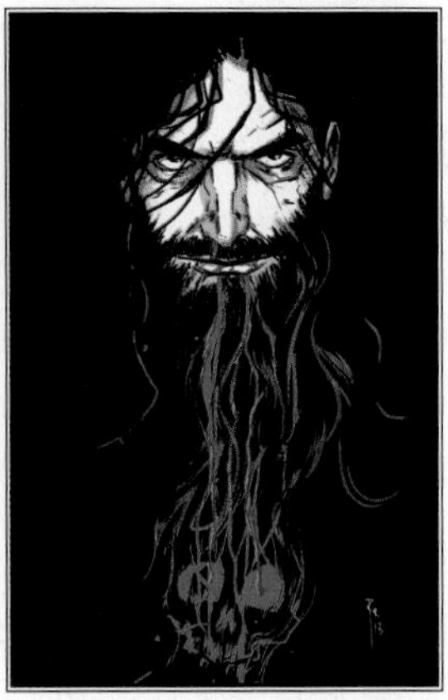

"As in an explosion, I would erupt with all the wonderful things I saw and understood in this world."
—Boris Pasternak

ALEX GRECIAN is the national bestselling author of *THE BLACK COUNTRY, THE DEVIL*
WORKSHOP, THE HARVEST MAN, and *THE YARD*, the debut novel of Scotland Yard's Murd
Squad. He co-created (with Riley Rossmo) the long-running and critically acclaimed graphic nov
series *PROOF*, which NPR named one of the best books of 2009. He lives in the Midwest with h
wife and son. Visit his website at alexgrecian.com.

Prolific artist RILEY ROSSMO is responsible for creating or co-creating many critically-acclaim
comic book series including *PROOF* (with Alex Grecian), *BEDLAM, GREEN WAKE, COWBO*
NINJA VIKING, and *DRUMHELLAR*. He has worked for Image, Marvel, Valiant, and DC, for whi
he draws *HELLBLAZER*. He lives on the Great Canadian Plains with his wife. Visit his website
rileyrossmo.com.

IVAN PLASCENCIA (IVANPLX) has been a professional comic book colorist and graphic design
since 2009. His first work as a color artist was on *THE ASTOUNDING WOLF-MAN* for Skybour
He has worked for Todd McFarlane Productions, Top Cow, Valiant, Red 5 Comics, and Zenescop
among others. He lives in Mexico City. View his work at ivanplascencia.deviantart.com.

Letterer and designer THOMAS MAUER has worked on a number of Harvey and Eisner Awa
nominated and winning titles, including the *POPGUN* anthology series and the webcomic *TH*
GUNS OF SHADOW VALLEY. Among his most recent works are Image Comics' *BANG!TANG*
COPPERHEAD, and *FOUR EYES*, as well as Black Mask Studios' *THE DISCIPLES*. H
lives in Magdeburg, Germany with his wife and sons. Visit his website at thomasmauer.co

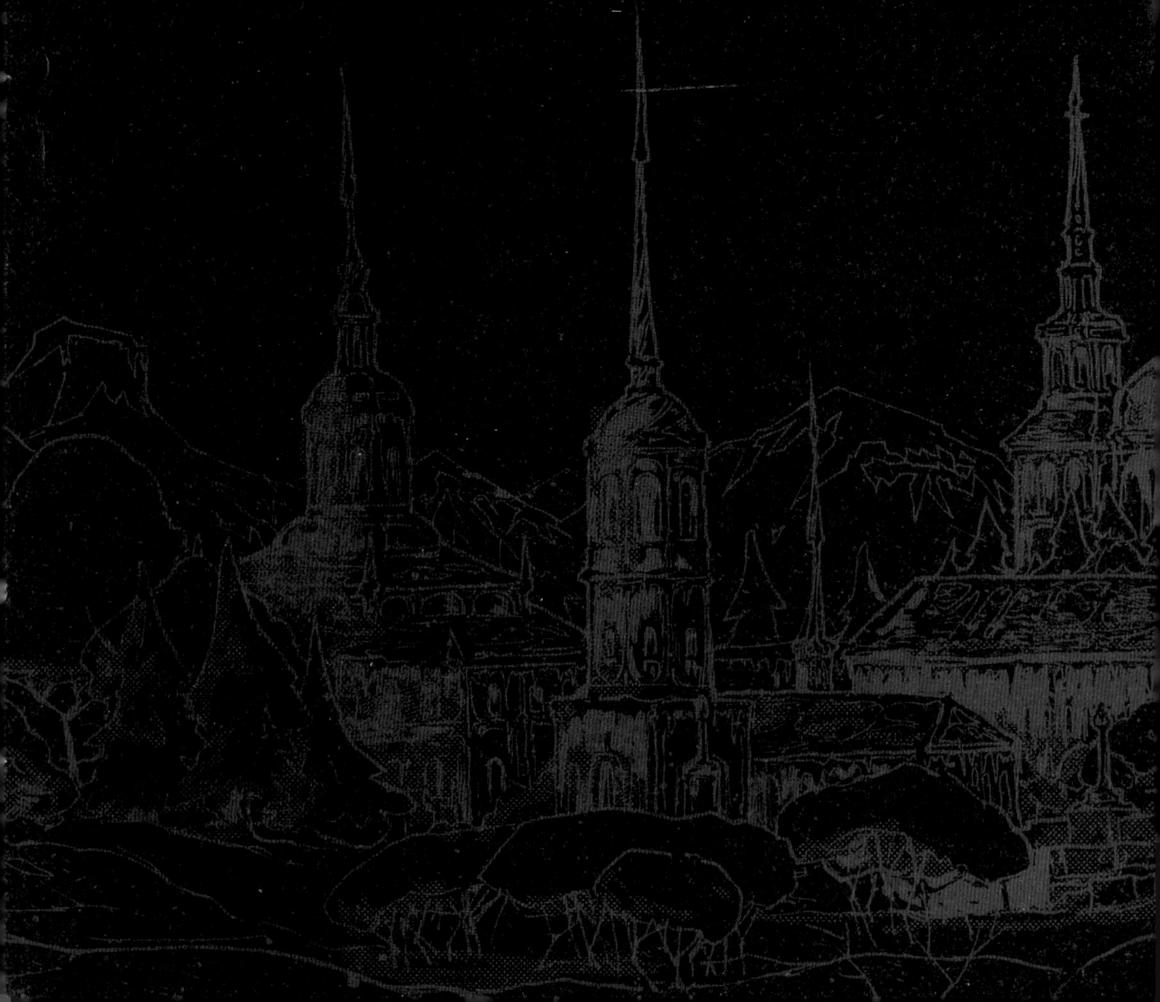